<u>**Writing As: J. Risk**</u>

REALMS BOOKS:

THE ALTEREALM SERIES
1 *The Huntress*
2 *The Seer*
3 *The Empath*
4 *The Witch*
5 *The Chronos*
6 *The Warrior*
7 *The Telepath*
8 *The Healer*
9 *The Kinetic*

THE SOLRELM SERIES
Coming soon:

Concealed

GEMINI LEAGUE
Coming soon

Dark Moon

Konner nodded, "is Terah over with Rae?"

Lucus smirked and shook his head slowly, "no." He pointed to the doors that lead to the common house, "she's in there with Lillee and Kisa, they're baking cookies to thank Shaelan for helping her when she was found."

Konner looked at the door. "Who's helping?"

Lucus jammed his hands in his pockets. "Pax is manning the fire extinguisher in case the smoke alarm goes off again." He closed the door to his room, "I had to get changed. I was covered in batter." He grinned, "using the beaters is more complicated..."

Konner darted for the door and ran down the short hall to the dining area. He stopped so suddenly, he swayed for a second. The entire island and floor, and possibly the wall too were covered in flour. It looked like someone had set off a bomb inside the flour canister. Nakisa sat on the counter, holding the cooking timer, and staring at it. Lillee was waving a towel in the direction of the oven. Terah, who looked like she'd been rolled in the flour stood holding a tray and frowning at it. Her hair was pulled up into an unsuccessful bun on the top of her head, hair sprung out of it all over her head giving her a mad scientist look. He looked over to see Paxton sprawled in one of the chairs, the fire extinguisher sitting on the table in front of him. He gave him a hard look, to which the teen shrugged as if to say 'what else could I do'.

"You're back." Nakisa hopped off the counter and came running over to him. She hugged him, with flour-covered clothes and all. Pulling back, she smiled up at him, "we're making cookies." She grinned, "it's a lot harder than it looks."

"So I see." He stepped carefully on the flour-dusted floor and went over to stand on the other side of the island.

Terah had her head down and was scraping charred cookies off the tray, her forehead was covered in flour, along with her cheek and most of her top. She gave him a quick look, "we're making thank you cookies for Shaelan," her forehead creased, "it's not going well."

Konner cleared his throat and didn't know how to approach the situation. An armed enemy, he could handle, with the expectant faces of the three females that had destroyed the kitchen, he had no idea what to do.

ANIMAL SENSES
1 *Heart*
2 *Scent*
3 *Passion*
4 *Courage*
5 *Solace*
6 *Faith*
7 *Spirit*
Coming soon:

8 Fury
9 Pride
10 Torment

MAGIC SEASONS ROMANCE
1 *Beltane Magic*
2 *Solstice Heat*
3 *Harvest Dreams*
4 *Autumn Dance*
5 *Winter Mist*

Dreams
Three steamy stories that started with a dream

Curses
Two tales of curses.

After the Silence

SINGLE TITLES
Solitary Witchling
Salvation
Café Serenity

Coming soon:
Outcasts

SPIRIT

Animal Senses Series Book 7

Jacqueline Paige

Published by Exordium Books (FRP)
Copyright © 2022 Roxane Kerr

Excerpts from *Fury Book 8* in the *Animal Senses Series* by Jacqueline Paige copyright ©2022 Roxane Kerr

ISBN: 978-1-990763-15-1

From the author:

I am absolutely thrilled by the response to my shifter world. What started out as a solo novel, turned into a trilogy to expand into where we are today is amazing. The response from readers fills my heart with so much joy, that I can't even express it.

The main question I keep getting asked is, 'are there more?', the answer is YES. This is number seven and right now I know there are at least five more—but I'm sure there are many I'm not even aware of yet.

For my readers, beta readers, proofreaders, and everyone else that's helped me create this world (clearly) thank you.

xox

Jacqueline

Chapter One

Konner stepped outside and inhaled slowly. The air was cool and damp, he'd take that over the dry air in the house. The planning part always got on his nerves. He understood the need for it, but once he left the safety of the Sanctuary, he liked the action. Idling, and just biding time never sat well with him. One of the main reasons he was part of the incursion team was for the action. Too much of his daily routine was standing around waiting—and running things. He liked that once he was called out for the team he wasn't in charge, didn't have to run anything or figure out the plan—the possibility of violence was a nice bonus as well, he had a lot of frustration to burn off.

Glancing back at the house, that three mated couples were in, he blew out a slow breath and walked over and sat down on the steps of the gazebo. That was going to be uncomfortable, being around all the side-looks and secret smiles. At least they weren't here long enough that he'd have to walk around in there with his breath held so he wasn't breathing in the staunch odor of sex. He didn't begrudge them to find their mates, he wasn't that much of an asshole. Repopulating his almost extinct clan was heartbreaking and it left him a little jaded too often.

Thirteen. There were thirteen of his people left. *So far*, he reminded himself like a mother would a child. He wasn't giving up until he'd searched every single body of water on the planet.

Popping open the buttons on his shirt, he pulled the material apart so the shirt he wore underneath was exposed to the damp air. Looking down at it, he rubbed his hand over it and was satisfied to feel it wasn't dried out. Thousands of dollars had been spent to design this piece of material that was the exact opposite of a wetsuit. Instead of repelling moisture, it soaked it up like a sponge. It wouldn't sustain him by any means, but it did delay the need for finding water.

He'd watched carefully when Deacon had driven them to this location, hoping to catch sight of a lake or even a pond that would suffice if needed. The operations started at dusk tonight, two of them back-to-back, so with a little luck, he wouldn't need to go for a swim before they were back on the road heading to the next step in bringing an end to Aiden Tomas' empire.

He tracked his new partner, Asher, as he came out of the house and went to where he'd parked the van under the tree in the backyard. He'd never worked with him personally, but a few of the others on his team had and all accounts retold said he was a silent, focused man. Konner could relate to that and be thankful there would be no awkward cordial conversations with him.

Opening the pocket on his pants, he pulled out his phone, the one that was not part of the Alliance's gear. Tapping the screen, he checked for messages and was happy there were only two. The first one was from his great aunt, Alviva, the Alpha of his clan, he smirked wondering who she'd gotten to type it for her. Modern technology was not something she got on well with. She had a feeling that this was going to be a good trip for him, and she looked forward to meeting who he would bring home with him. Rubbing his hand across his forehead, a little harder than necessary, he closed it without a reply. He wasn't going to call her 'intuition' bad, but it had been nine years since he'd found one of theirs and he was a little more skeptical than she was.

The second message was from Auburn, reporting that two of the construction contracts were fulfilled and he had two more for Konner to approve before he sat down and roughed out plans for them. He read the names and didn't recognize them, but he'd do his checking when he had a few moments. Turning off the screen he leaned on his knees, at least their construction business was thriving. Clans from all over North America were building. Konner's clan didn't need the money, not really, they had more than they could ever spend.

The ache in his chest started, the one he got when he thought about the thousands of his kind that were gone. At one point there had been so many of them, they'd split up across the map into smaller groups to live near small lakes so they could stay off the radar of one-forms. There wasn't a day that went by that he didn't regret his predecessor's decision to do that. That had been their downfall. Without modern communication, help hadn't been easily gotten when they were hunted.

Ten years ago, he'd visited the last location and collected up the hidden records and clan accounts and taken them home to add to the others. He used the accumulated money of the lost to look after the remaining members and search the globe for more.

The sound of a door had him look up. Calum Dante was walking toward him. He'd never met the man personally, but he knew his reputation. He smirked, during Alliance council meetings, his name was mentioned more than the word 'funding', so his being here on these operations, almost insured the success of the objectives. He was a big man and there was no question in Konner's mind that he was a cat predator in his other form, the way he moved was silent sure and he was aware of every nuance around him.

He sat straighter as he reached him. Calum's inquisitive look landed on the phone he held. Konner smiled slow, "it's secure and approved." He motioned to the house, "one of the tech team members, Fallan, set it up for me last year, to keep in touch with my Alpha and business dealings." He left out the part where the searches on his computers at home would alert him to any possible headlines in the news he should know about.

Calum leaned against the side of the gazebo and nodded his head. "Construction, isn't it?"

"Mainly," Konner didn't feel the need to share that he had his hands in many profitable pies. Many of which helped the Alliance as well as his clan's portfolio.

Calum rubbed his hand along the back of his neck. "I have a few jobs to add to your list."

"Oh?" Konner was good with discussing business. It kept his mind off other things he didn't need weighing him down right before the operation.

"You probably already have the one for Blair's clan. The Eldon-Sorum clan."

Konner lifted the phone, "I just read that we have a work order for them."

Calum motioned to the house, "that's Blair and Kobie."

"They're expanding?" This would save him researching the clan if they were right here.

"Long story short, Tomas got all but nine of her clan, we recovered several from him on the last run. Blair became Alpha when he mated Kobie, so he's young and freaking out," Calum grinned, "and he needs more housing."

"Wait, Blair, he's the one that took out his own brother..."

"That's him."

"Wynter gave me the rundown. Nox explained it in *great* detail to her, which," he smirked, "thrilled her, to say the least." Konner nodded, "I'll let Auburn know to get on the plans for that right away." He meant it too, his own kind were scarce, but any clan that had found their lost loved ones and brought them home deserved top priority in his mind. "What's the other one?"

"The other one is a little more complicated." Calum looked amused.

"Complicated how?" Konner tucked the phone back into the pocket and gave Calum his undivided attention.

"Well, Deacon," he motioned to the house again, "has just become an Alpha of a newly registered clan under the Alliance."

Deacon was an Alpha now? Konner tried to remember what he was in his other form but couldn't recall ever seeing him shift. "I'm a little surprised we have so many new Alpha's on this operation, shouldn't they be at home looking after things?"

"Blair and Kobie are meant to do this." He motioned around them, "Deacon, he has no others in his clan as of yet."

Konner's chest tightened; he knew the pains of that all too well. "What happened to them?" He liked Deacon, they worked well together. They hadn't mentioned a thing about any of this on the drive.

"We don't know yet. Gia wants to search and has no real idea where to start," Calum gave him a calculated look, "his kind originate from South America."

Now he had his attention. "South America?"

Calum nodded, "I talked to Shep to get the ball rolling with communications," he looked down at him, "but as you know it's a shitshow right now with everything else going on." He cleared his throat, "we don't know who to trust down there now and who not to." He rolled his neck, in the first sign of tension since he started talking, "Ambassadors are on the suspect list until proven otherwise." He gave him a pointed look, "maybe you could share contacts with Gia."

Konner sucked in a quick breath, he knew Calum had more knowledge than probably the Alliance, but he was certain his business was kept between a few only. He also hadn't been informed about how serious things were within the Alliance.

Calum gave him a steady look, "everyone that comes in contact with Devin Addison I know about." His tone was quiet. "You are not the exception."

"They were supposed to be here."

"Yes. Took a lot of loud words to get Devin and Rayne to stay away this time, but after the last one blew up, I wasn't taking chances."

Konner nodded; thankful he didn't have to worry about VIPs right now on top of everything else. He didn't want to share things about his life with a stranger, but if there were other lost clans out there, it would be wrong to not help point them in the right direction. After all, he'd found all the ways not to search. "I can talk to my contacts down there and get them to check around. What clan are we looking for?"

"Maned wolf. We need to know how many came here and if any remain there."

"Maned wolf." Konner blew out a steady breath, "I might have to look that one up."

Calum grinned, "I believe Deacon had to as well."

Konner smiled, "and I thought I was lost at times."

"Deacon was the epitome of lost once upon a time, but now," Calum looked over and watched his mate as she was talking to Kobie outside the door, "with Gia, he's on the right path."

"What's the clan name?"

"Parrish." Calum looked back at him, "I doubt there are any orders for them, but I know his mate wants indoor plumbing and at least one other building put up, just in case others are found."

Konner couldn't help but grin, "I'll get on that indoor plumbing right away."

"She would cherish you if you did."

Calum straightened from where he leaned as his mate started toward him. "I apologize in advance."

Konner looked around, "for?"

"My lovely mate is going to grill you on information about your kind, for medical reasons."

"I've heard she's an apt healer." Konner didn't know why she'd need information on his though, he wasn't intending on getting injured.

Calum chuckled, "apt doesn't describe the speed she absorbs information and data." He held out his hand as she reached them.

"Robbie is doing so much better." Shaelan smiled up at him, "he may be able to try a shift later this week."

Calum lifted their hands and kissed hers, "for which you'll want to be present."

She smiled up at him, "of course."

Shaelan was a lovely woman, peace seemed to ooze from her every pore. Konner had been on the team that was called to her clan to clean up the—*insane* shit that had been happening. He'd heard the stories and still didn't see this woman in front of him taking down the corrupt false Alpha.

He stood up, needing to feel respectful toward her. "How is your mother doing?"

She gave him a surprised look, "she is less frantic now." She smiled, ."the clan is doing great though, seems tv and microwaves made everyone happy."

He couldn't help the smile that formed, "modern technology is a wonder."

"It is." She lifted the tablet in her hand. "A whole library in the palm of my hand." Her smile was big.

Calum sighed, then motioned to the steps Konner had been sitting on, "you might as well get comfortable, she no doubt has endless questions."

Shaelan gave the side-eyed look, "I need to know things in advance to be the most helpful."

"I know." Calum kissed her hand again and released it.

Konner elected to stand for the time being. "I'll try to help."

"The Alliance doesn't have a great deal on your kind, it's Konner, right?" She looked down at the tablet then back to him.

He nodded. "There's a good reason why they don't, by the time they started collecting health information and data on my clan, there wasn't many of us left."

The compassion on her face was clear as day. "I know. I'm sorry."

He could feel the emotion coming from her and it was genuine. He only inclined his head, not wanting to get into that part regarding his clan.

"I just need to know how to better help, so next time when we..."

Konner jerked his head to look at her, "next time?"

"Oh," she looked to her mate, "I thought you knew."

Calum swore softly, "shit has been so out of sorts since they breached the system." He swore again, "I thought Devin had contacted you."

Konner did sit down now before his legs gave out beneath him. They'd found one of his clan? "Where?" He looked from her to Calum.

"The last house we breached before we had to go off the grid for a week."

"She was in very poor health." Shaelan said quietly, "Deacon found her lying in the bathtub..."

Konner looked down at his hands until he could mask his emotions. *She*. They'd found a female.

"Every bone in her body was basically visible, I-I..."

The emotions pouring off her had him snap out of his grief, he looked back up at her. "Bathwater, city water, wouldn't have sustained her." He told her quietly.

"I started an IV drip, trying to rehydrate her, but I'm afraid it didn't do much."

Konner blew out a breath, trying to steady his emotions before he spoke. "A regular saline solution is a mere band-aid, a temporary fix."

Shaelan nodded, the emotion no longer on her face, now she had a clinical expression and one that said she needed more information. "Is there something I need to have on hand to help immediately?" She held the tablet up, her hand hovering.

"The saline, if no freshwater source is close at hand will stall further deterioration, eating a protein bar and other snacks the teams carry won't do much." Reaching into the pocket of his shirt, he pulled out one of the packets he always carried and held it out to her.

She took it and flipped it over, reading the ingredients.

"It's dehydrated kelp and seaweed," he lifted his hand toward it, "and other plants that have the properties we require." He watched her tuck it into the hand that held the tablet and start typing onto it. "Mixing it with distilled water will restore some strength."

Shaelan nodded, "how much can they have at once?"

"As many as needed, it's our form of a protein bar." He shrugged a shoulder, "my clan drinks it as you would water on a daily basis."

She nodded again and kept typing, then paused and looked at the packet again. "Where do I get this?"

Konner held out his hand for the tablet, "may I?"

"Oh, yes," she handed it to him, he looked down at it and didn't bother to read the information she'd typed, he knew the number by heart and typed it onto her screen before holding the tablet out to her again, "call there, tell them it's for Konner Flores and they will ship whatever you need without question."

Shaelan glanced at her mate, and then turned, "oh," she stopped, "cuts, abrasions?" She made a face, "and young ones, are they treated the same?"

"Distilled water poured over it—it needs to be distilled so it's chemical-free, or lake water if it's handy, same for our eyes," he glanced at Calum, "if they're dry." He pointed to the package she clutched in her hand, "a paste with that if it's bad." He was happy she wanted the information but knew the chances of coming across any of his own for her to need it were next to never, especially children. "Our young ones are no different than any other child," he shrugged, "they're able to swim when they're born, but don't go through the change until they're around ten." He motioned to his eye, "the only way to tell is the silver ring around their pupil, it expands underwater to absorb reflections beneath the surface." When she leaned closer, he lowered his head so she could see his eyes. "Was there anything else you needed to know?"

"No. Thank you. I need to call Rayne, we need distilled water," she looked at the packet and started walking, "a case of this Biotrien, all teams need it on hand..." she kept walking, talking to herself.

Calum watched her for a moment and then turned and looked down at him, "she's on a mission now." He cleared his throat. "I'm sorry you weren't informed. Shit went sideways fast." He motioned to his mate that stood outside the door with the phone against her ear now, "Shae went in the chopper to Devin's campground with her..."

Konner inhaled through his nose slowly, "I understand." He did, mostly. "I wasn't reachable for a few days, so it's no one's fault." It still would have been nice to see her, maybe go and make sure her body was put to rest in the way of his people. On the floor of the water to feed the environment so new life could grow. He couldn't think about that now. "Where are they in finding out how the Alliance system was breached?"

"They're weeding through the trail slowly, I'm told." He paused as Konner stood up, "You were out looking when you picked up to come here."

It wasn't a question. He couldn't hide the surprise on his face.

Calum shrugged, "I noticed the coordinates weren't anywhere near your very fortified sanctuary."

If Konner learned something with certainty today it was that all the hype about this man in front of him was well earned and correct. "I was. I track news headlines and any oddities near water, I go search it."

Calum nodded, "I'll keep that in mind and give you a heads up if I hear of anything."

"I appreciate that."

"How many have you found?"

Konner eyed him for a moment, having help from a man like Calum Dante could never be a bad thing. "Not as many as I hope for. The last one was nine years ago, and two years before that."

Calum held his look, no emotion on his face at all. Without further talk, he nodded, "here's hoping we find more on these operations." He glanced at the house, "I'm going to see if they sorted out the lack of a flyer on team two."

Konner watched him walk away. He touched the phone through the material, debating for a moment if he should inform his Auntie that one had been found and lost. Sighing, he gave his head a shake. He'd do that in person after he was back home.

He was almost to the house when Deacon came out the back door, his fiery little mate right on his heels. He still couldn't believe he'd found a mate and become an Alpha since the last time they'd been out together.

Deacon stopped and spun around to look at her. "What the hell do I know about meetings and," he waved a hand around rapidly, "councils?"

Konner smirked, seeing Deacon seated at one of the dry council meetings was more than a little entertaining. He didn't relish them, himself, but his aged-set-in-her-ways great aunt refused to go. She outright refused to leave the Sanctuary in the past five years.

"I can help with that." Giana Marin stepped right up to him and rubbed her hand over his chest.

Konner could see the tension settling in the big man immediately. He sighed and walked toward them before his heart started aching from the demonstration of what a mate's union could bring to a chaotic world. "Sorry to intrude," he offered a polite grin, "I overheard." He motioned to where

11

he'd been walking, "I *may* be able to help."

Deacon gave him a quick look, "you have a way out of this council *stuff*?"

Konner smirked, "not necessarily." He stopped a respectable distance from the man's mate. "I go to them for my Alpha, she doesn't care for the modern society much."

Gia smiled up at her man, "see," she held out her hand toward Konner, "he can give me the run down and I'll represent for us."

Deacon blew out a breath, reaching and clasping his hand over hers still where it rested on his chest. "I don't do politics." He said in a gruff tone.

"I know." She smiled at him, "I *know* how it works though and we need the Alliance to help us find your family and others like you."

Konner paused to wonder what clan this little mate was if she wasn't the same kind as Deacon. Shaking his head, he got back to the task at hand. "Calum and I were just discussing my contacts in South America," both turned to him, their focused gaze zeroing in on him like he was to be dinner, "I have no problems getting them to check around for you while they're doing the same for me."

Gia smiled at him, "that would be awesome. Thank you."

Konner inclined his head, noting that Deacon didn't seem nearly as enthused as his mate, in fact, he looked a little green like he might want to throw up. "It's no problem, I understand the pains that go with searching for surviving members."

Her expression changed to compassion, "I'm sorry to hear that, but thank you for helping us."

He nodded, then cleared his throat, he couldn't deal with much more female compassion today. "I was also told you want indoor plumbing and another building erected?"

Deacon nodded now. "The indoor plumbing ASAP before the ground freezes I guess."

"I'll get that started." He paused as he reached for the phone in his pocket, "oh, it's my clan construction company that," he motioned to the house, "is why Calum was talking to me about it."

Gia bobbed her head, "that's handy, that you're here with us."

He inclined his head; no words were necessary. "It might be a week before I can get someone there, but I'll get Auburn to contact you for details." He pulled the phone out, "what sort of building are you wanting?"

"Oh," Gia looked up at Deacon for a moment, "I think a small functional two-bedroom for now?" She watched her mate as she spoke, "just in case." She smiled up at him, then turned to Konner, "I think it would be a little too cozy to share the no-bedroom cabin."

Deacon rolled his shoulders, and turned to look at him, "I have ideas for the cabin too," he pointed to the house, "maybe after we do this, we can talk about it."

Konner nodded, "I'll just put some of Auburn's time on hold then and get the details to him later."

"We'll have to talk about financing…"

Konner shook his head as he typed a message to his clanmate, telling him to expedite Blairs and more rushed things were on the way. "Don't worry about the financing right now, the Alliance is helping with clan expansions since we've had to rearrange our lives for safety purposes." Sending the message, he looked back up at them, "We'll worry about all the finer details at a later date but getting the plumbing in before winter is a *now* thing." He offered a polite smile.

"Yes." Gia gave him a big grin. "Definitely a *now* thing."

"Guys."

They all turned to see Jesse standing at the door.

"I guess we better get back." Gia took Deacon's hand. "Thank you, Konner."

Deacon gave him an appreciative look before following her back.

Konner looked over to see his riding partner coming back from the van. He hadn't lied, entirely about the Alliance funding, he just left out the part that it was his foundation that initiated it.

"Ready to kick some ass?" Asher asked him as he walked by. "I am more than ready."

Konner put the phone away and followed the tall lanky shifter into the house. He could only hope there were asses to be kicked at this point, he needed to burn off the anger of another lost member of the water clan.

Chapter Two

"Testing, testing. I need to run a check before everyone is barking things at me." Illias voice came over the radio. "Our lovely Princess and Prince will be designating the who goes where and all that, so I need to make sure they have it set up on their end."

"Talk less, test more." A female voice said over the radio.

Konner looked to see Asher smirking, so it had to be one on his team.

"I couldn't have said it better." If he wasn't mistaken it was Devin Addison's voice now. "Is this heard by both teams?"

"That's a yes to team one." Konner recognized York's even tone.

"Team two as well," Jesse replied.

"Check individual now," Illias said in a clipped way. "Team one check."

"Received," York replied.

There were a few moments of silence. Konner was glad they were making sure all the last-minute shuffling hadn't postponed things. Jesse and his mate had gone to help team two at the last minute, he'd caught a part of the conversation between Calum and Jesse, and both had agreed, it would be best if she wasn't present at their location. Bear and Noah had also gone to help team two.

"Okay boys and girls, the comm system is tip-top." Illias announced, "I told you I could do the work of two."

"Before I leave to be overwatch, just remember to monitor the anti-tracking screen."

"I've got it, Torin, you go be a bird, I've got this." Illias laughed.

Torin was part of the tech team and was to work with team two, but his being a flyer was deemed necessary so he could check the area around the house they were hitting. This left the cocky Illias running both team's comm systems, and the prince monitoring from their undisclosed location. Konner agreed overwatch was a valuable thing but could do with less chatter.

"Talk, talk, talk." Asher looked over at him for a moment before moving his gaze back to the road. "If you need me to grab anything or meet you to help when you're coming out just give me a shout."

Konner nodded, without looking back at him. "Will do."

"I like working with you, much more than Nox." He made a sound of annoyance, "I think he wanted me to bow down and kiss his feet."

Konner did grin to that. "Nox is," he gave him a brief side glance, "better on a mission than he is as company."

"That's a polite way to put it." Asher nodded and then turned his attention back to the road.

"Do you know why Jesse pulled his mate from team one?" If there was something he needed to know going in, he preferred some warning.

"I know bits of it." He cleared his throat, "Evanna, who is also Leah sometimes has some sort of personality disorder," Asher looked over and shrugged, "I didn't get into the details with that." He checked the mirrors and then turned the corner without signaling, "Leah was taken when she was really young, but got away when she was sixteen." Asher paused to look at him to see if he was listening. "Her family is at this first house, but with her disorder, it could," he waved a hand around, "be debilitating, I think Jesse said, for her to see them in these circumstances." He motioned toward the windshield, "that's all I know."

Konner took a moment to digest all that. "I'm glad he made the call to help the other team. Things can get messy enough without something like that."

"I agree."

"I've worked with Jesse a few times, he's good at what he does."

"No one better." Asher nodded but didn't look at him.

"Creed and Torin are in the air," Illias announced. "From this point on the comms will be separated so the teams can focus on those members they were directly working with."

That ended their odd version of small talk. Konner put his earpiece in and clipped the sides of his vest together. He hated wearing it, it made him hot, and the heat was not a friend to his kind, but it was necessary.

Asher pulled the van over in the designated spot.

They both sat in the silence looking up in the sky, even though they'd never see Creed in the dark from this distance.

"All clear." There was no mistaking Calum's deep voice over the comms.

Asher had the van moving before Konner could look at him. He appreciated that he did his part without hesitation.

When they went around the corner, he leaned to see a very large, out-of-place eagle sitting on the roof of the house. He tapped the dash, "here is good." He motioned to the shrubbed fence line on the other side of the house, "pull up there, leave room for the rest to be close by."

Asher nodded and stopped the van without comment.

Konner was out the door and running across the lawn to the tree with the low-hanging branches. When he reached it, he squatted down, his back to the tree so he could see the rest of the team as they reached the house.

Deacon and Calum moved silently toward him. Their steps

in synch like a silent dance. Konner motioned to the side of the house and knew he wouldn't have to spell it out as they went past him to be unseen below the window line of the house.

York came from the other direction and signaled that two were coming in from the back. He kept going until he was right beside the front door of the house.

"At the back door." A whispered male voice announced in his ear. A quick headcount told Konner that it was Blair and Kobie at the back of the house.

"In place at the front," York said.

"We have the side, waiting on a go." Deacon's level tone spoke through his earpiece.

Konner looked to see Webb coming along the sidewalk. He'd keep watch in the driveway until they were coming back out. He gave him a quick nod and moved over to the other side of the front door. "Breach in three." He wasn't much for long-drawn-out entries.

York moved to the door and waited for Konner to touch his shoulder, so he knew he was in place.

"Two." He said quietly. York stood up and prepared to breach the door lock. "One. Breach."

York kicked the door, and it gave way.

Konner moved to step into it and crouched down, so York would have a clear view. The process was more intense with them using dart guns instead of bullets. No one told the enemy that they were using non-lethal force, so the chances of being shot with a dart instead of something more permanent was always a risk.

"Through the back," Blair announced. "Porch to the kitchen."

"Side door breached." Deacon announced, "taking the lower stairs."

"Taking the upper ones." Calum's quiet voice told him.

Konner was constructing a diagram of the layout in his head as his teammates called out where they were. He was still in the front door, covering the stairs off the entrance as York checked the rooms to the left. When he came back out and nodded, Konner stood up and motioned to the upstairs, "heading upstairs."

"Back of house is clear." Blair appeared at the end of the hallway, "checking the first floor." He gave York a nod.

Konner went up the stairs first. This was so quiet, where were the guards or security in this house. The shoes by the door told him there were people here somewhere.

"Locked doors in the basement." Deacon's tone was somber, cutting the locks now.

Konner paused and glanced back at York, he nodded and motioned up. Giving Konner the clear to go down and back up Deacon. As he moved by him, Blair appeared at the bottom of the stairs.

"First floor clear." He said as Konner moved quickly past him.

Reaching the stairs to the basement, he was met on the landing by Calum, who held a man by the collar on his neck. Konner moved out of the way so Calum could take him outside.

"Bringing one out for the refuge center. He's fully mobile." Calum informed those waiting in the van. "No tranq will be necessary, completely co-operative."

Konner couldn't dwell on the state of those helping Tomas, whether forced or not. As he reached the basement the scent of urine and blood hit his nostrils and he had to bite back the curse before he said it over the comms.

Deacon turned to see him coming down the narrow hall. The expression on his face matched the feeling of anger inside Konner. They locked them in this dank basement. He watched Deacon cut the lock and turned the next door to his right.

"Upstairs is clear," York announced.

"Locked cabinets on the main floor," Blair said into the comms, so Devin could communicate to the cleanup crew that whatever was in it they needed.

Konner grabbed the lock on the door and gave it a quick jerk. One of the few advantages his kind had on land is they retained their incredible strength. The entire hardware assembly came off the door with the lock. He stepped back and opened the door slowly, raising the dart gun as he did. In the back corner, a woman was huddled, scared, and shaking. "It's all right, I'm here to get you out." He lowered the gun and held up his other hand, "I'll be right back."

He stepped out of the room and back into the hall. Deacon was opening the second door on his side. Konner made fast work of the lock on the last room and inside found a young woman with a small girl. He went into the room, "are you both all right?" She nodded and clutched the child to her as she stood up. "We're here to get you home."

As they stepped out into the light, he looked to see Deacon helping a frail woman out of the second room. He looked down at the woman in front of him, she was older and malnourished, but there was no mistaking the resemblance to Jesse's mate.

"My mother?" She hugged the little girl to her.

"I'm here, Ashtyn." The woman from the first room came out into the hallway.

Deacon was helping one of the women walk down the hall, the other one followed with an expression of confusion on her face.

"We work for the Alliance, we're here to get you out."

Konner could do this job for thirty years and he would never tire of the look those they freed got when they realized they had been rescued.

Deacon motioned to the stairs while holding the woman's elbow.

Konner turned around and squatted down in front of the little girl, she was probably no older than four. "What's your name?"

She glanced at her mother for approval before speaking. "Gemma." She whispered.

"Okay, Gemma, how about you come with me, and we'll go outside and get you some juice." He glanced up at her mother, she nodded, her eyes glassy with tears.

Picking her up, he motioned to the stairs.

Deacon paused at the bottom, "what's your name and clan?" He waited for the woman behind him to answer.

"Isla Stone, Burke clan"

"I'm Mila Knight, from the same clan." The unsteady woman told him.

Gemma's grandmother touched his arm. "I'm Lyvia Cardenas. Are we really going home?"

Konner nodded, "you're free." He didn't know where they were going, according to Wynter, Jesse's mate had been the last one at the clan's home and they weren't going back there. It wasn't his place to tell them the Burke clan was no more.

"Coming out with Isla Stone, Mila Knight," Deacon glanced back to him.

Konner pressed the mic button on his comms, "Lyvia, Ashtyn, and Gemma," he smiled at the girl in his arms, "Cardenas from the Burke clan."

He stood at the bottom with the little girl and let the others go up the stairs first. When they reached the landing Blair and Calum were there to help. Konner knew that York and Webb would be outside keeping watch.

"Are they in good health?" It was Jesse, he must have gone through Illias to patch the comms through.

"All are mobile and in acceptable health considering the circumstance," Calum answered. "Shae will check them all over and let you know."

"Thank you." That wasn't Jesse that answered. It had to be Evanna answering, "tell them Leah will see them soon."

Calum relayed the message in a hushed tone.

The grandmother to the girl he had stopped in the driveway and looked up at Calum. "She made it home?"

Konner didn't want to draw attention to the two women crying, now clinging to each other, he moved by them with long strides. "What kind of juice would you like?" He turned to see Gemma watching him with huge dark eyes.

"I like apple." She said quietly.

"Apple it is." He moved quickly toward the van that Shaelan stood beside. Gemma wrapped her arms around his neck and squeezed tight. This makes all of it worth it. He thought, he didn't care she wasn't his clan or if she was an Oompa-Loompa, he smirked, this little girl in his arms was why he did what he did.

"Calla is on route to pick up the members of the Burke clan to take them to the Dyer clan." Illias paused, "she'll meet you on route to the next location."

"Copy." York nodded to him as he reached the van.

"Gemma likes apple juice," Konner told his teammate in a serious tone.

"Good thing I have some of that here." York nodded and motioned to Shaelan, "I think I have some cookies too. I'll get those while you let this nice lady check you over, okay?" He leaned down on his knees, so he was face level with her.

She nodded and released the hold on Konner's neck and let him set her in the van.

"Team two recovered two from Lois White's clan, a mother and daughter and three collared men." Illias shared. "Alliance security is waiting at drop-off points. Team two moving onto the next location now."

Konner nodded to Asher as he reached the van. "Let's go." He got in and closed the door.

Asher didn't ask any questions, just put the van into gear and pulled away.

Chapter Three

Konner rounded the corner and met up with York, who jerked his chin toward the last room at the end of the hall. They both moved toward it.

The collared security had really been stepped up at this location. It had taken a few scuffles to subdue them and make them realize they were here to help, not punish them. The scars on them pissed Konner off and made him want to beat someone until the air left their body for the last time.

Konner made a quick assessment of each of the men's eyes, hoping to find a tell-tale silver ring, but had found none. As they'd handed off the fifth one to Blair, he'd pointed them in the direction the captives were being held. If he hadn't, the team may not have found it.

"There's a hidden room, a door behind a wall panel." Konner told Illias, "have the cleanup crew check for shit like that at the last two locations and give team two a heads up."

"That's a new move. I'll relay." Illias answered.

York was still running his hand along the wall. Konner looked at the floor and where the trim met the floorboards. He pointed when York glanced at him, there was a section that had been cut.

York went over and pushed on the wall, a quiet click and the wall moved. "This is some spy shit now." He mumbled as he pulled it open.

Konner wasn't going to argue with him. It was hard enough to find the locations where they were holding their kind of people, now if they were going to start hiding them at those spots, it was going to mean a longer operation time. Being somewhere longer increased the chances of being caught.

Ducking down, he turned to fit through the narrow space and was surprised to see it was a room on the other side. York stood with the door open.

Konner moved past him and went into the room. The odor of stale air and unwashed bodies hit him immediately. Blankets strewn on the floor were abandoned. Standing as far from the door possible were six boys, most he figured in their mid-teens. He lowered the dart gun, "We're here to take you home."

The smallest of the boys started to step forward and one of the older ones stopped him. "Wait, Talbot." He narrowed his eyes and looked at York and then back to Konner, "who are you?"

"The Alliance sent us, son," York said before Konner could speak.

"For real?" The smallest one asked.

Konner grinned, "for real. We have others waiting outside to get you home."

"Team one, we've found two males, they've been beaten pretty bad and are refusing to leave."

Konner and York exchanged a quick glance. "Come on boys." He watched them move slowly toward the opening. The last one, probably eighteen, nineteen held his arm over his abdomen, the way he was hunched told him there was a problem. He held up his hand for him to stop, and motioned to his waist, "let me take a look."

"You're going to have to handle this, Blair, they're refusing to leave," Jesse stated.

"Names?" Blair asked abruptly.

Konner lifted the boy's shirt and sucked in a breath. His abdomen was dark purple and swollen. He hit the comm button, "I may have broken ribs here, Shaelan" He forewarned Shaelan, then let the boy go by him.

"Rydge Molina and Auden Cohen," Jesse said replying to Blair.

The reply came quickly, "tell them we found their families and they are safe." Blair said brusquely.

"That worked." Jesse said over the radio, "we're going to need medical assistance for these two."

"As soon as Shae has checked the boys over, we'll head to you." Calum's tone didn't waver, as he spotted the boys coming down the stairs toward him.

Konner leaned down and checked the boy's eyes as they went by him. None had silver in them, but that was okay, these were some clan's children and now they could go home.

"Pryce Neal, Talbot Brewer, Bowen Harrell," Calum said in a quiet voice, "and Carver Vargas from Sorum clan."

"I'm going to need more buildings *fast,*" Blair said as he jogged up the driveway with Kobie right beside him.

Konner grinned; his clan was growing fast today. It made his chest ache, in a good way, that they've found so many from that clan.

"Luca Burns from the Burke clan," York announced.

Konner turned to look at the boy standing beside York, he had to be at least eighteen, which meant he would have been just a small boy when he was taken.

The one he was walking with stopped, his breathing ragged, it must be hurting him to move. "Need you here, Shaelan." He used the mic to be sure she heard.

"On my way."

He stopped and touched the boy's arm as they neared the vans. "Just rest for a sec." He leaned down so he could see the boy's face. "Lift your chin, and inhale slowly through your nose." The boy listened and then froze.

"Uncle Ash?" He croaked with a dry throat.

Asher spun from watching Shaelan come toward them and looked at the boy. He went over confusion on his face. Konner watched his eyes widen and then recognition appear in his eyes. "Galen?" He rushed over and started to grab him, then stopped and placed his hands on his shoulders. "It is you." He cleared his throat and hit his mic button, "Galen Hayes from the Cain clan." His voice shook with emotion.

"Hi." Shaelan was beside them now, "I just want to lift your shirt and take a look," Asher moved to lift it for her. Konner watched a guarded look move over her face, "have you had your first shift, Galen?"

He nodded, just barely.

"Okay," she smiled, "that's good, we don't need your animal making an appearance right now." She motioned to the van, "let's get you perched in the door."

Asher moved to help him.

Konner looked down at Shaelan, "broken ribs?"

She nodded, "moving too much could puncture an organ, if it hasn't already." She motioned to the van, "can you grab the big box for me?"

Konner holstered his dart gun and ran to the back of the van. Opening the door, he popped it open and pulled out the large case of medical supplies.

"The best I can do right now is give him something to dull the pain and wrap them, but I need an ultrasound, x-rays, to check more." She looked at Asher, "we'll have to get him in the front seat, reclined to get there."

Asher was nodding and helping Galen take his shirt off.

The youngest of the found boys came running over. "Is he going to be okay?"

Shaelan's serious expression changed to a pleasant smile, "he'll be fine."

The boy nodded, "they beat him because he wouldn't let them take me."

Konner watched Asher's jaw clench. "Calum, we need you here." He used the mic, rather than yell it down the street.

Asher leaned down and put his hands on the other boy's shoulder, "who did?" He asked in a low tone.

"The men that come every few days to check us out." He looked scared.

"Did they leave, they weren't in the house?" Asher's tone was softer now, but the expression on his face was anything but the look in his eyes was pure revenge.

Calum came over, Konner motioned to the boy. "Can you take," what had the other boy called him? "Talbot, to see who we brought out before them?"

"I can," Calum said slowly, then glanced to Asher and his nephew. "Did one of them do that?" He watched his mate slowly wrapping large gauze around them.

"To be determined," Konner answered as Asher held his nephew upright.

Calum nodded, and held out his hand to Talbot, "let's go take a look, then you can ride with my friend Deacon and his mate, Gia."

Talbot took his hand, "Kobie said I get to go home."

"That's right, you do."

"Konner, you're to drive the two from the White clan to the campground," Illias said quickly.

Konner glanced at Asher, then pressed the mic, "with Asher?"

"Negative. Just you. Quinn is already on route to the next location to fill in for the last two stops tomorrow."

Konner and Asher exchanged another look.

"Calla is swinging back and going to call you to pick up the rest of the Sorum clan."

Shaking his head, having no idea, Konner hit the mic button again, "where am I meeting up with a vehicle?"

"I'll text you the location in two," Illias sounded distracted, "Asher, you'll meet Quinn at the same location."

Asher looked over at him again and then turned to see Shaelan still wrapping Galen's ribs.

She glanced over at him, "he'll have to be transported to the clinic at the Alliance headquarters."

Konner kept quiet, he had no idea such a clinic existed, and he was one of the few with inside information into the Alliance.

"Help me get him into the seat and then you can take the other van and Cal and I will get him where he needs to be."

Asher pondered that for a moment, then he nodded. "At least I know he'll be safe on route."

Calum came up behind him, "of course, he would." He put his hands on his hips and shook his head, "the guards, or whatever they're used for weren't responsible for this," he motioned to Galen. He leaned over and looked down at the boy, who was bravely trying to breathe through the pain, "my mate will get you fixed up in no time."

Galen just nodded and winced as she taped the wrap off.

Calum pointed to the van behind this one. "You two can take that one and meet up with Quinn."

Konner went around to the other side and opened the other door, leaning in, he pulled his bag out from under the seat and then stretched over to grab his run pack and other gear. Inclining his head to Calum, then Shaelan, he walked back to the driver's side. As he climbed in, it occurred that maybe Devin Addison was calling him to the campground because he knew about his clan's death ritual.

Chapter Four

Konner glanced in the mirror at his two traveling companions. Niema and Baylee, a mother and daughter that had been held by Tomas for the past ten months. He'd learned a few things from them that had caused his blood to chill in his veins. They'd been held all this time while Tomas looked for a male of their kind. There was only one reason he would want a male from the polar bear clan, and it sickened him. They'd been sleeping for most of the trip, and he didn't blame them, they probably hadn't slept much during their captivity. The few stops he'd made were to get food for them, real food, not protein bars and jerky.

He rolled his shoulders, fatigue was starting to set in, he'd have to find water soon and stop for a break. Hopefully, the one he marked on his map had plenty of fish because he was almost out of water to mix the Biotrien with, and to be honest he needed something more to sustain him.

A sound behind him had him glance over his shoulder. Baylee was waking up. "I'm going to stop in a bit for a break and go for a swim." He watched her in the mirror.

"I'd love to go for a swim." She smiled a sleepy smile.

"Only if it's safe." Her mother said in a quiet voice.

"It's pretty secluded," he wasn't sure if they were talking about shifting and swimming, but no matter where they were two white bears were going to stand out.

"You can swim, no shifting though." Her mother settled that issue right now.

"I can do without shifting ever again."

Something in her tone stabbed him through the heart. Had they been forced to shift during their captivity? "Where we're going, to the prince's campground is very remote and very protected," he was assuming the last part, "so you can shift any time you want while you're there." His Alliance-issued phone rang. He glanced at it, forgetting it wasn't going to reveal any number on the screen. Grabbing it, he answered. "Hello."

"Konner."

It was Wynter, there was no mistaking her gruff voice with anyone on the planet.

"Boss." He smirked, he enjoyed calling someone else that.

"I'm finding out shit after it happens and it's pissing me off."

Konner watched the road, he didn't know of anything that didn't aggravate his team leader, except maybe strong drinks and loud country music.

"I just found out they yanked you from the team at the prince's bidding. What the hell happened?"

He glanced to see his passengers were foraging in the snacks. "I'm not sure, but I am currently transporting two of your kind, from the White clan to the prince's campground until we can get them home."

"What? Who? Two of mine were found on your raids?"

He nodded, "Yes, Niema Brycan and her daughter, Baylee."

"Shit on a stick. Why the hell wasn't I told this? I'm going to," she stopped abruptly, "how are they?"

"Would you like me to put you on speaker and you can ask yourself?"

"Yes, do that." She sounded more impatient than normal.

He put the phone back into the holder and glanced at

Niema, "my boss wants to say hello." He tapped the speaker button.

"Niema?"

Konner watched in the mirror to see the reaction. When the woman's eyes widened, he knew she recognized the voice.

"Wynter?" Niema looked relieved.

"I just found out, god damned red tape bullshit, I should have been told sooner. Are you okay?"

Konner noted there was genuine concern in his harsh leader's voice.

"We're unharmed, tired though and I don't think I'll ever leave the house again."

"Listen, my man, Konner is one of my best. You can relax and know he's going to get you where you're going safely." She yelled something away from the phone, "I'm going to get a hold of Lois as soon as I hang up and make sure they're on the way to get you." she made that grunting sound she always did, "even if I have to come and get you myself."

"I told mama you'd find us, Wynter," Baylee said, and it was the first time Konner had heard her speak louder than a whisper.

"Doesn't matter who got you out, Baylee, what matters is you are, and you can be sure that those responsible for taking you will be—" she cleared her throat, "handled."

Baylee relaxed against her mother's shoulder, looking relieved for the first time since he'd picked them up.

"How far out are you, Konner?"

Konner glanced down at the map sitting on the passenger's seat, "About four hours, maybe five, this part of the drive is redundant."

"Middle of nowhere always is." Wynter said something again away from the speaker, "have you been driving this whole time?"

Konner inhaled a deep breath, "mostly. I'm stopping in about twenty for a quick recharge and then I'll push on until we're there."

"Right, good. Head on a swivel, that's precious cargo you're carrying there."

To his surprise, her tone had softened briefly. "I'll protect them at all costs, Boss, you know that."

"I do. I'm going to call Lois right now. You tell our prince he'll be hearing from me."

"Will do, boss." The line went quiet.

"You work with Wynter?" Baylee asked.

Konner nodded, "I do, I'm part of her team."

"She's great, so much fun."

He glanced to see the young woman smiling. He'd known Wynter Carr for eight years now and fun had never been a word he'd use in relation to her. Not knowing what to say, he just smiled at her in the mirror and then turned his attention back to the road. "It will be close to dusk when I stop, so make sure you stick close to the van," he motioned to the trees along the road, "it's too easy to get turned around in there."

"We'll be careful." Her mother told him.

Konner put his absorbent vest back on and brushed off the water on the outside of it. He'd have to wait a few minutes until the outer part dried before putting his shirt back on, but he felt ten times better than he had before stopping. There was something about water that was unaffected by man that appeased his very soul. He smirked, he might have a slight boggy odor for a few hours, but he didn't care.

He looked over to see Baylee wrapped in a blanket as her mother guided her to trees to get dressed again. Seeing her splash around made him feel like a hero. It was confirmation to her that she was actually free now.

Reaching the van, he opened the door and checked his phones, Niema had told him to leave them she'd keep a listen for them. A few messages on the one, nothing he needed to deal with right now and the other one had no calls listed. When the assigned one rang in his hand, he jumped like a frightened child.

Shaking his head, he answered it, "hello."

"Konner, it's Calum."

His spine stiffened, he didn't know the man well, but he was pretty sure Calum Dante didn't call people up just to chat. "What's going on?"

"We just packed it in here and are heading back to Blair's."

"Everything go well?" He still felt ripped off that he hadn't been able to stay to complete the last two raids on more of Tomas' stash houses.

"It was very lucrative," Calum told him in a serious tone. "Add ten more to the count, and a few what we're figuring are top of the food chain in the whole of things."

That had Konner's attention. "I'm intrigued."

"They're on route right now with the special ops boys." He sounded amused, "so with luck we'll have more news soon."

Konner had never worked with that team, but if there was a ranking for how aggressive the Alliance teams were, they were at the top. He'd heard some of the things they'd done, and it chilled him to the bone, despite how necessary it was at times. "I look forward to hearing more."

"We also liberated a lot of paperwork and records."

"Records?" He watched Baylee come out of the trees, fully clothed again, she was smiling, the first real smile he'd seen on her face.

"Yeah." Calum had a growl to his voice now, "they're fucking selling them to the highest bidder. All over..." He stopped abruptly, realizing they were still talking over airwaves, regardless of how secure.

"How detailed are these records?" He scowled at the ground, hating that his earlier thoughts had been right. They were matching the clans and breeding them.

"I can't be sure, I only got a quick look at them, the S.O. have them now on their way back to Shep, Devin will have copies."

Konner nodded, he had to see those for himself. "I suspected, well, no not that I didn't, but my passengers shared with me that they were treated fairly while they looked for a male to go with them."

"It's sickening and the shit is going to be ended."

Closing his eyes, he blew out a breath, trying to keep focus. "How is that boy, Galen doing?"

"He's going to be okay. Shae was just talking to the doctors looking after him."

That eased some of the pain in his chest. "And the two men of Blair's the other team found?"

"We're heading there now for Shae to patch them up, they refused any other stops until they saw their families."

Konner didn't blame them at all for their obstinance, he would likely be the same way. "We'll be at the camp early morning." He lifted his hand toward the lake, "I just had to stop and refresh a bit."

"Enjoy your downtime, things are going to get fast and lethal from here on out."

Konner smirked, "I look forward to it." As he was sure every shifter on the teams did. Ending the Tomas empire had been on a lot of to-do lists for the last twenty years.

"I'll let you go."

"Thank you, for calling and letting me know." He cleared the lump out of his throat, "it almost gives me hope." That was something he hadn't felt in nine years, not since he'd found Olanna living in a tiny lake in the middle of no mans' land.

"If there any of yours out there, we'll find them."

To have a man like Calum say that, made the weight on Konner's shoulders lighten. Calum Dante didn't do anything half-hearted. "Yes, we will."

Calum chuckled, "I have to go, the young Alpha is doing the math in his head and the longer he thinks the more glazed his eyes become."

Konner grinned, "tell him to feel blessed because he is."

"Will do. I'll call if I find out more."

Konner nodded but didn't get a chance to reply when Calum hung up.

"Good news?"

He looked to see Niema and her daughter standing beside the van. He looked at the phone and then nodded his head slowly, "I think for the most part it was." Motioning to the van, he smiled, "shall we?"

Chapter Five

Konner was impressed, if not a little intimidated to see the armed security at the gate entering the campground. He knew how remote this land was, he'd searched the lakes here years earlier before the prince had taken refuge here. If they had the entrances covered and the area along the roadway it would have been an almost impossible task to get on the land any other way. All of this was a good thing, considering the rescued that had no clan or weren't able to face life out of captivity were here. Feeling safe was likely on the top of their list of needs.

He slowed and pulled the van up the drive outside a large building. Stopping, he looked around, this was where they'd directed him. There was an armed man standing at the door, this had to be where the prince and princess were. "Looks like this is the place." He said as he opened the door.

A tall woman with short brown hair came out of the building, she stopped and looked him up and down. She didn't fit the description of the princess.

"Mister Flores, I'm Doctor Collins, I'm going to escort your passengers down to my colleague at the clinic for a quick checkup."

Konner opened the side door on the van so Niema and Baylee would get out.

"The prince is waiting to speak to you." The doctor told him as she came over. He turned to see her motioning to the door of the building she came out of.

Nodding, he reached in and grabbed both phones and his run pack. He put it over his shoulder, it wasn't really a run pack like all others in his world had, it was more of a waterproof swim pack. Tucking the phones into opposite pockets of his pants, he closed the door.

"Thank you." Baylee launched herself at him and hugged him tightly.

He gave her a quick hug and decided polars were a strong lot and he'd have to remember not to upset his boss, not that he would, she just plain scared him. The females in his clan were the aggressive ones, but Wynter Carr——she was the epitome of aggression. That thought brought him full circle. The reason he was here, was to lay to rest a female of his own kind. Blowing out a breath, he gave Niema a polite nod and went over to the door.

When he stepped inside, he had to force his nerves to settle. He'd never met the prince but had heard many things about him. He was said to be blunt and straight to the point, which in Konner's opinion wasn't entirely a bad thing. Word around the council said his seconds were fiercely protective of him. He didn't know one of them but had recently met the other, Calum, and his opinion on where the Alliance was heading once the king stepped back was going to be in a good direction.

"Konner. Oh good, you made it."

He turned to see a woman with long blonde hair walking toward him. She was almost ethereal, and that was saying something considering the females of his clan all held that otherworldly shimmering glow. He inclined his head to her and kept it down.

"We don't have time for that posturing crap."

Konner lifted his head to see a tall man coming toward him. He resembled the king in many ways. A little scruffier looking than he'd pictured the prince, but the way he carried himself was just the attitude Konner could appreciate. That don't fuck me vibe was what the Alliance and the whole shifter world needed to take them forward. The king had it in spades, but at times, in his opinion was too forgiving. "Sir," he inclined his head briefly this time.

"Devin will do," he put his arm around his princess, "and Rayne."

Konner nodded. "It is my pleasure to meet you."

"I'd meet a lot more that work on the Alliance teams if I wasn't sequestered away here most of the time." He sounded annoyed.

"It's what is best for now," Konner shrugged, "I hope the future brings better things for all our kind."

"If it kills me," Devin growled.

Rayne motioned to a doorway, "let's move into the office." She smiled at him, "would you like some coffee or something?"

"I actually can't drink coffee. It's dehydrating and that doesn't quite work out well for my kind."

She tilted her head, "I didn't know that. Is there something you'd like instead?"

Konner cleared his throat, "any herbal tea would be welcome."

Devin chuckled, "oh herbal teas we have, *all* of them."

Rayne gave him a look, "shush, Shaelan uses them for so many things when she's here, and I'm enjoying them too."

Devin motioned to the door and started walking, he grinned as Rayne went the other way, "I still think you add coffee to them."

She laughed and kept going.

He didn't know what he'd expected from this royal pairing, but so far, he was a little more than shocked. "Calum called me and told me they'd recovered sales records from the last place they breached."

Devin walked around to the other side of the large wooden desk and stood there. "They did, I was just trying to figure out what some of the short forms they used could be for."

Konner glanced around to see the room had tables lined up along one wall with stacks of files and papers on them.

Devin hissed out a breath, "I'm trying to play catch up with all things Alliance." He held out a folder.

Konner took and raised an eyebrow, "I wish you luck with that."

Devin nodded, then motioned to the chair so he'd sit down. "If Tomas would just die it would make things easier."

Konner opened the folder and then looked up at him, "we've definitely put a dent in his empire this year."

Devin put his hands on his hips and nodded, "yeah, but I still want to see him roasted on an open spit."

"There's a lovely image," Rayne walked in carrying a tray with her, "or I think it is, I'm not one hundred percent sure what a spit is." She set the tray down on the desk, "is that the thing over the fire turning in the flames?"

Devin smirked.

"Well seeing Aiden like that might even make me feel the warm fuzzies."

Aiden? She used his first name. "You know of Aiden Tomas?"

Rayne motioned to the tray, "sadly, seems like a lifetime ago now though." She smiled, "please help yourself, I brought a few different kinds." She picked up a cup and held it out to her mate. "Where are we?"

Konner leaned forward and picked up the first tea bag he came to a dropped it in the cup.

Devin sipped whatever she handed him, "we were just going to look at those records Beck found at the last house."

Beck had found them. He'd have to call him and get more details. Konner opened the folder and looked at the top page in it, it was an account record. Aside from the dates and dollar amounts, he wasn't sure what it said. He looked up at Devin, "can I get a copy of these?"

Devin smirked, "that is your copy, Calum told me to have one for you."

Closing the folder, he clutched it in one hand. "Thank you." He watched the princess pour hot water into the cup he'd dropped the bag into and then she sat down and clasped her hands in her lap. The mood was suddenly more somber. He knew it had been coming but had hoped to never have to do it just the same.

Devin sat down. "I've been catching up on a lot," he sighed, "I blew off my responsibilities for a long time." He motioned to the table of piles, "I have access to everything, and I will confess I was shocked when I read through your files, the searches, and such." His brows were knit together, pain on his face.

Konner inhaled slowly through his nose. "It's been hard."

"Where have you searched for your people? It wasn't in the files, that part, maybe I could..."

Konner offered a polite smile, "I have enough looking, you need to keep your focus on the whole of the Alliance, not just my clan." He picked up the cup and blew on it, not even sure what he'd put in it, just knew he needed a moment to compose, and taking a drink was the best stall tactic ever. Swallowing the hot liquid, he detected mint and green tea, not a bad choice. "I've checked every area there was a settlement of my kind in, some twice over the years. Being as the sheer number of waters out there, in the last few years I've limited searches to completely remote areas or any that have had odd news sent out about them."

"Odd news?" Rayne asked hesitantly.

He set the cup down again and turned to her, "yes, stories of people see people swimming in the middle of a storm or thinking they saw a mermaid," he shrugged.

"Ah, I see. Have you found many that way?"

Konner nodded, "a few. An adult male nine years ago and a female a few years before that."

Rayne was now giving him an odd look, a slight smirk on her face. "Did you start searching as a boy? Because if you tell me you're older than you look, I'm going to have to ask what skin regimen you use."

Konner grinned at her unique way of asking his age. He leaned closer and whispered, "if my kind always has access to fresh water and the proper food, we hardly age at all."

Her eyes went wide, "really?" she looked him up and down, "so you're..."

"A few decades away from a century of life."

"Are you serious?" That was Devin now, as he stood up and came around the desk and looked at him. "Shit, I thought wolves lived long."

Konner sat back and shrugged, "my Alpha is my great aunt, and she might be slow on land, but she can still give me a run for my money in the water."

Rayne had both hands over her mouth now, looking at him. "I'm jealous. You look like you're thirty-five at most." She dropped her hands, "so you say no coffee or anything that dehydrates?"

Devin rubbed his hand over his forehead, "I don't see you without caffeine—ever."

Rayne moaned, "sad thing, neither do I."

Devin went back around the desk and picked up another folder, he didn't offer it, just continued to stand there and hold it. "Calum blasted me because I hadn't called you."

Now that he'd met him and seen what he was attempting to do, Konner didn't feel as harsh toward the royal son. "I was unreachable for a few days, so you may not have even if you tried." Setting the folder on his lap, he picked up the cup to keep his hands busy, "I was underwater for most of it, so you would have gotten voice mail at best."

Devin nodded, even though his expression led Konner to believe he knew he was stretching the truth. "You will be called first, going forward." He held out the folder, then lifted it away again, "these are going to be hard to look at, you understand?"

Konner put the cup down and put out his hand. "I can assure you I've likely seen worse."

Devin held his look for a moment, something close to a kinship going through his eyes. He gave him the folder.

"I spent as much time with Terah as possible when she was brought here," Rayne said softly.

Terah. Nodding, he looked down at the folder as he opened it. His vision blurred for a moment as the image registered. When it cleared, all he could see were ocean blue eyes looking at the camera as the picture was taken. "Her clan must have been from one of the groups closer to the oceans than the inlands," He cleared the lump out of his throat, and briefly looked up at Rayne, "my clan's eyes are more green hues as we settled in the North with the colder climates." He looked back down at the folder.

"I didn't even realize that," Rayne said so softly it hardly registered she'd spoken.

The woman, Terah, in the photos was so thin, Konner could see her skeletal structure. "They starved her," he said, his emotions getting the better of him, causing him to pause. "It would have been the only way to keep her as their prisoner." He couldn't look away from those eyes but continued talking despite what the sight of them was doing to his heart, "at full strength, nothing could have kept her there, our females are twice as strong as we are."

"She was born there," Rayne whispered from beside him.

Konner looked away from the photo to Rayne, he had to blink to bring her into focus, "I'm sorry?"

"She was born there, Konner, never exposed to clan life or the outside before Deacon carried her out of there."

He scowled, "that's—how is that possible? Our kind can only become pregnant in the water, in our true form." He shook his head, "in natural water, not some tank somewhere."

Rayne looked at Devin and then back to him, "her mother was pregnant with her when she was taken."

Konner clenched his fist and put the back of his hand over his mouth. He closed his eyes and had to concentrate on breathing through the anger he felt. Dropping his hand, he looked back to Rayne, "she told you this?"

Rayne nodded. "She was a showpiece," she looked down at her hands in her lap, "in some tank…"

Konner stood up and paced to the other side of the room. He couldn't sit there and hear this. He'd failed. He held up the folder he gripped tight in his hand and looked at those eyes again. He'd failed this beautiful creature by not finding her mother, finding her. Inhaling a deep breath, he blew it out slowly, attempting to find some composure in front of the royalty behind him. "I'm sorry." He cleared his throat which was tight with emotion.

"If you need to break something, I understand." Devin said, "I certainly did when I learned that."

"Just please, go outside if you must." Rayne said, "I can't keep having people fix walls and things in here."

Konner closed his eyes and dropped his chin. Turning, he looked at the prince and then his lovely mate, her face was filled with so much concern it caused a hitch in his breath. "I'll be fine, I assure you this is not the first heartbreak I've faced with my clan." He cleared his throat, "I'm sure it won't be the last." He lifted the folders now bent from his grip and straightened them to hold them correctly. "Where is she?" It would be like stabbing himself in the heart, but he needed to see her if they hadn't buried her. If they had, he would be digging her up and taking her to rest at the bottom of the lake.

"With so many around the main area of the camp, we took her to the small shelter on the other end of the lake." Devin came around the desk.

Konner felt relief, he'd be able to take her to the bottom of the lake to put her to rest.

"I have to be honest here, Konner," Devin leaned back and crossed his arms over his chest, a serious look on his face, "the fish population isn't going to survive, you really need to take her under wing and guide her."

Rayne nodded, "the small animals on land aren't faring well either, everything scares her, and then she kills it. She can't help it really, it's a gut reflex, that's what the doctor called it. We moved her so she didn't get startled by anyone out for a run…"

Konner stood there, looking from one to the other, his mind felt like a skipping disk. He opened his mouth and then closed it again, replaying their words in his head one more time. "She's alive?" His voice sounded hoarse.

Rayne looked startled and turned to her mate.

Devin frowned, "yes." His eyes widened, "you thought she'd died." He rubbed his hand across his brow, "I thought— we didn't call sooner because she was in bad shape, and we didn't want to get your hopes up."

Konner sat down in the chair before his legs gave out completely. "I thought I was coming to lay her to rest in the lake." He said more to himself than the two people standing there with their mouths gaping open.

"We are completely failing at this leader of the people thing." Rayne looked at Devin. She turned back to him, "she's amazing with the children, pulls them around and lets them ride in the boat…" she sighed, "we should have led with that."

Devin pulled her against his side and hugged her. "Dad better live forever."

Konner knew they were talking but couldn't focus through the static in his head. Terah was alive. He wouldn't be laying her to rest, he would be taking her back to the rest of the clan. He felt faint and placed his hand against his chest as he took careful breaths to settle his heart that was thudding so loud, he was sure his hand was jumping from the impact.

"Konner? Are you all right?"

At the mention of his name, he looked up at her. "Uh, it's just—been so long since I found the last one," he shook his head, still not sure this was really happening. "She's healthy enough to travel?" He slumped back in the chair, not caring about composure for the moment. "I'm at a loss."

Rayne smiled down at him. "That's understandable." She turned to Devin. "Did you want to take him over to meet her?"

Devin nodded. The phone sitting on the desk rang loud. "As soon as I deal with whatever this is about."

Konner got to his feet, suddenly remembering he was standing in the prince's office. He motioned to the door, "I'm going to go get some air for a moment."

Devin picked up the phone and put his hand over the mouthpiece. "I'll come to find you when I'm done."

Konner nodded, and bowed his head down for a few seconds, showing respect to both, and then turned on his heel and walked out the open door. He kept going until he was standing outside the door beside the guard. He turned and looked at him for a second and then gave him a nod before looking back to the driveway.

Konner went over to the van opened the door and dropped the folders on the seat. He leaned his forehead against the cool metal frame and stayed like that. "She's alive." Holding his hand up, he opened it and then nodded when he saw it shaking. "Okay." He straightened away from the door and then closed it and opened the side door. Reaching into the cooler, he grabbed the last bottle of his water reached into his pocket and pulled out one of the packets. He needed to get it together. He couldn't go meet her when he was standing here shaking like a scared child.

Pouring the powder into the bottle, he put the cap back on and gave it a vigorous shake. He closed the van walked over to the edge of the drive and looked down at the lake. It was a lovely lake. He debated for a moment getting the binoculars out of the van and trying to see if her could see her but didn't want to look like some kind of creep to anyone standing there.

His mind was buzzing. So much to take in at once. Tomas was breeding shifters and selling them. He scowled at the ground; had he figured out how to do that with the water clan? Nodding to the dirt beneath his feet, he turned and pulled out his phone. Scrolling through the contacts, he brought up one that had been detrimental in him achieving the safety of his kind. What did he want her to actually do though? He needed to figure that out before calling and sounding like a rambling idiot.

He looked over at the guard, "can you tell the prince I'm just going for a walk down to the water when he comes out?" The man barely moved his head to acknowledge he'd spoken. Konner debated for a moment whether to just go down the embankment, then decided a long walk would help him get his head together.

Starting back down the worn narrow road he'd driven to get to the house, he tried to force his muscles to relax. Lifting the phone, he stared at the screen, would she still use this number? She worked for the Alliance and after the changes the past few weeks many weren't using their regular phones now. Shaking his head, he smirked at the phone, she'd secured this very phone, so the chances her own was that way were high. He hit send and lifted it to his ear. She answered on the third ring. "Fallan, it's Konner Flores."

"Konner, it's been a while."

He turned to take the path to his left. "It has. I know you're busy, so I'll get right to it."

"I'm very good at multi-tasking." She chuckled.

"I'm sure you are." He watched two young boys, probably no older than seven dart out of the trees and run along the path for a few feet before racing back in. "I need you to do some digging for me."

"If you're calling me, it must be something you want to be kept quiet."

He smiled, "it is." He could smell the water now, even with everything between here and the beach.

"Our you scratch my back, I scratch yours relationship has been fruitful up to now, so how can I help?" He could hear her typing on a keyboard while she talked. "I don't know if you've been brought into the loop, but the last raid the teams did—" he paused and thought about the folder he'd left in the van, would Reeves be able to help decipher the information, "but they found records of sales—"

"Oh, I'm *privy* to that sick shit."

He inclined his head, "how would they go about something like that? They can't exactly advertise by conventional methods."

"Your timing is top-notch, Konner, the big man just issued a request that my team works with some of the others to see if we can decipher it." She snorted, "while we're still tracking down the breach."

"How is that going?"

"Whoever is on the other end of the keyboard for Mister Tomas has some mad skills, but we're getting closer."

He nodded and then stopped to look at several small new buildings that lined the one side of the dirt path. They weren't from his company, but he had been consulted on the fastest way to construct them. He recalled something about it giving some of the refugees something to do. "So obviously Tomas has some high-tech friends."

"Yeah, but the thing is, the system we set up," she mumbled something, and he heard more keystrokes, "there's no way it was done completely from the outside."

He looked at the bottle in his other hand and moved it to watch the liquid swirl inside it. "I'm sure your team will ferret out the traitor."

"Oh, for sure." She chuckled, "the dark web."

He frowned and started walking again.

"They have to be using some board on the dark web, highly encrypted, hard to get into if you're not looking for it—to sell our kind to the highest bidder."

He didn't know what that was but felt some hope that she

did. "Can you find this *dark web*?"

She laughed, "of course, I can, all of us on the team can, with our skills there's nothing on the planet we can't get into."

Konner stopped at the end of the trail and looked in the two directions it branched off into. If he reached the water too soon, it would be too tempting to swim to the other side and find Terah on his own. He turned in the other direction. "Is there any way to find out details of previous sales?"

"That's," she blew out a loud breath into the phone, "going to be a challenge, but I might find some trails to follow if I dig deep enough."

A woman with a small child froze on the edge of the path and watched him with fear in their eyes. Konner slowed his stride and smiled at her, not wanting to alarm her. She turned with her child and went back in the direction they had come from. This entire camp would be filled with scared, unsure members of their community. He waited until they were out of sight before walking again. "I know you're looking for the Alliance as well, but if you come across any information that I'd be particularly interested in, it would be greatly appreciated."

"You know I would anyways, Konner, you don't even have to ask. Your contacts have gotten several of mine out of *that* country to the safety of here, I'll always owe you for that."

He paused to look at a large building, a newly painted sign that said showers stood out against the old structure. A woman came out of the door and then stopped and looked at him. She clutched the items in her hands tighter against his chest. He gave her a nod and smile, hoping to put her at ease. When she scurried off in the other direction, he looked down at what he was wearing and realized the last time they'd probably seen someone in gear like he was wearing would have been when they were rescued from hell. He hadn't even considered it earlier and should have been more sensitive to the injured souls seeking safety and refuge here. "I'm just glad to help, any from our world."

"I got," she stopped abruptly, then it sounded like she was walking somewhere, he heard a door, "I got wind of something earlier," her voice echoed now like she was standing in an empty room, "and I think it will matter to you."

He turned off the marked path, afraid to alarm any more survivors by strolling past them, and walked through the trees. "Like what?"

"Dane was contacted by the princess a few days ago and was asked to look into locations in all of North America that had large tanks installed or where they were purchased. Like big fish tanks." She clarified. "That's got to be for your kind, right? I mean why else would the princess want to know something like that."

Konner turned and looked back in the direction of the house. Rayne was looking for more of his kind. He closed his eyes and settled his thoughts before replying. "Yes. New information has been discovered regarding that."

"Yeah, that's what I thought. I asked Dane to share if he found any."

Looking around, he continued moving through the trees. "Thank you."

"Look, you know the Alliance will do anything to help, all of us, well, except sneaking clans across the ocean, so if there's any of yours out there, we're going to find them." He heard the door again and heels on the hard surface.

"I know, it's just—hard."

"I hear that." The echoing stopped telling him she'd gone back to where she had been before. "I better go, Illias is messaging for me to stop doing my nails and pick up the pace." She laughed.

"Yes, I'll let you get back to it and hopefully I'll hear from you soon."

"You know it." The sound of keys was moving fast now. "Later."

Konner hung up and looked at the phone. He was still shocked the princess had them looking for tanks installed across the country. He knew it would lead to a lot of dead ends, but if there was a chance that even one of them found a member of the water clan, he'd exhaust himself traveling to every location. He stepped out of the trees to find he was looking at the lake. His gut tightened again.

Walking slowly toward the water's edge, his heart felt lighter to see several children running along the shore chasing a ball. Two women stood off to the side, tracking their every move. Other than guards, he hadn't seen any males since arriving. He supposed he shouldn't find that surprising, really, considering their captors used men of their own kind to keep them in line.

Turning, he walked to the opposite side of the beach area, giving the woman a wide berth so his presence wouldn't startle them. There were old wooden beach chairs sitting off to the one side, so he headed toward them.

Sitting on one, he opened the bottle and took a long drink. He shouldn't need to put anything in his system after the fish he'd eaten on that stop, but his nerves were shaking, and he was sure his body was burning through them fast.

Capping the bottle, he tapped the screen on his phone and brought up his office number. Reeves hardly slept, so chances of him being there already were high. He hit dial.

"Tell me you're on your way home." That is how he answered the phone.

Konner grinned, "in the next day or so, why, what's going on?"

"Lucus and Paxton pissed off Nolyn again and this time she might actually string them both up."

Konner rubbed his hand over his brow. This wasn't a new or occasional crisis. Lucus and Paxton were two young teens in their clan. "What did they do this time?" He looked over and watched the children running. It had been years since the boys were that size. Before he'd moved the clan to the land they were on now, both of their parents had disappeared. Lucus had been an infant and Paxton was two. Now at fourteen and sixteen, they kept life interesting.

"They painted her door *pink*." Reeves groaned, "I don't even know where they got pink paint from or how they made pink paint."

Konner cringed. Nolyn was in her early twenties and a child from his original clan group. Her mother had died after childbirth and her father had gone to mourn and never returned. She was a brilliant young woman and taught all the children, so upsetting her wasn't going to end well. She was also very goth, and a pink door would definitely upset her. Konner smirked and blew out a breath, "okay, *after* they repaint her door black, you can tell them the docks need scrubbing."

"Which docks?"

Konner grinned. "All of them." Not only did they have docks at three locations around the large lake, but they had an inland fishery that was surrounded by a complex dock and gate system to transfer fish to the lake to keep it well stocked. "Even the fishery."

"Oh, yeah that's going to chaff some knees." Reeves laughed. "I remember doing that when I was about eighteen and thought I didn't have to listen to you."

Nodding, Konner turned to see the Prince and Princess walking along the open trail from the house. "Yes, you had a few years of rebellion after I found you."

"And look at me now. Running the office and taking care of business while you're away."

"You have come a long way." He cleared his throat, "Listen, I haven't called Auntie yet—I'll wait until she's awake later, but we're going to be adding another member to our clan."

"What?" There was a clatter that sounded like a broken cup. "Shit, oh that burns. Hang on."

Konner turned to see the children running toward Devin and Rayne, both smiled as they approached them. The prince and princess were doing a lot for the shifter world.

"Okay, sorry. You found someone?"

"Yes, well my team did a few weeks ago." He looked out

across the lake, "she was in rough shape so it's going to…"

"But she's okay, right?"

"I am just about to go and meet her, but as far as I know she's physically recovering."

"Jesus. Holy shit. Where did they find her?"

Konner stood up as the royal couple got closer. "She was born in captivity, Aiden Tomas had her." He frowned; he didn't even know if she had a last name. "I don't have details yet, but her mother was pregnant when she was taken…"

"Oh my god."

"Get the records out of the case in my office, carefully, and have them ready, once I have more information, I'll text it to you and we can see if we can narrow down who's group her mother was part of."

"Right. I'll uh, set them out on the table in your office," he made a sound of annoyance, "because spilling shit on them out here would be bad."

Konner nodded, "very bad." He cleared his throat and smiled back at Rayne. "I have to go. Keep this to yourself until I call Auntie."

"Jesus, don't wait too long, I might have a meltdown trying to keep this quiet."

Konner laughed, "I have every confidence in you and Reeves?"

"Yeah?"

"Tell the boys I am *not* impressed."

"Oh, I will definitely relay that message."

"I'll talk to you later."

"Wait, Konner?"

He watched Devin squat down and talk to one of the children. They weren't afraid of him, which made sense they saw him all the time. "Yes."

"What's her name? I mean, I just, does she have a name?" He could picture Reeves pacing around the office, as he did often when he got excited.

"Terah." Konner looked out over the water again.

"Terah. Yeah, it gives me hope, you know, that there's more of us out there still."

Konner straightened his spine; he couldn't get all emotional again. "There is and we'll find them. I need to go now; the prince is taking me to meet her."

"Holy shit. The prince. Yeah, okay. Go." The line went quiet.

"Everything good?" Devin stopped a few feet from him.

Konner nodded, "yes, just a few of the boys in my clan are up to no good, again."

"Teenagers?" He tucked his hands in his pockets and glanced over to where Rayne was sitting on the ground talking to a few of the young girls.

"Yes, fourteen and sixteen."

Devin chuckled, "Oh I remember how Calum, Gage, and I were at that age." He looked at him, "I'm surprised our parents didn't kill us and try for something better behaved."

Konner laughed, "they're probably glad for it now." He didn't know Gage. "Calum is a very important cog in the Alliance's wheel."

Devin laughed, "Calum is like some kind of superstar in our world, half the time I don't know whether to be impressed or annoyed."

"I've only experienced the impressed part, myself."

Devin nodded, "yeah, wait until you know him a few years, he gets his digs in when you least expect it." He turned away from his mate, "Rayne's going to stay here," he motioned to the boat sitting out of the water at the other end of the beach. "I know you could probably swim there, but I don't think I could keep up with you."

Konner grinned, "I could pull the boat over."

Devin shook his head, "as fun as that sounds, it's kind of a kiddy ride since Terah got here and I don't think it would portray adult prince all that well."

Konner tucked his phone into his swim pack and did it back up. "I enjoy being over the water almost as much as in it." He gave him a serious look, "and it would be bad to meet up with her *in* the water if she's as aggressive as you say."

Devin's eyes went wide, "I didn't think of that." He shrugged, "makes sense though, I wouldn't run up on wolves that I didn't know."

Chapter Six

As Devin rowed them across the lake, Konner couldn't help thinking back to eleven years ago when he'd found Olanna. He hadn't been joking when he'd said it was better to not meet up with Terah the first time in the water. Olanna had tried to kill him, more than once when he'd found her. It had taken three days of him trying to get close enough to her, while out of the water so her could tell her he was there to help and not hurt her.

He leaned down and let his hand drag through the water. It was so clean and cool, he really wanted to go for a swim. He thought of Olanna now, a mother of two children and Auburn's mate. Her daughter Nakisa would be ten soon, if he remembered right. Soon she'd go through her first shift. It was a special time with his small clan when that happened. It renewed hope and that was in short supply lately. Each birth and age of the change also brought other emotions into play. Would they be the mate to one of those living with them now or would they be without that special companionship for many long years?

Lifting his hand, he rubbed it over his face and closed his eyes, just letting the slight breeze move over him. Would Terah be a mate to one of those already found? There were only two adults, three if he included himself that were unmated. Reeves and Nolyn. With each change, everyone would take turns swimming with them to see if that fated connection was there. To outsiders, it would seem archaic to find your mate was only ten years old, but it was the only way to not give up completely. Knowing you had a mate was better than being left wondering for decades.

If one of the members of the group were her mate, it would mean they were not allowed, as in forbidden, to swim with her until she was of age and agreed, of course, that was always a factor since their clan joined the Alliance almost a century ago. The females always gave consent prior to mating.

Konner glanced back at Devin and wondered if his mating with the Princess had been a smooth one. He looked down at the water, not all were. He recalled Raelyn and Malachi. That had been anything but smooth. He knew shortly after Konner had found him, but she outright refused until she knew more of him. He grinned, and now with their second child on the way, they were inseparable.

His gut tightened and he was sure if it was because he knew his Auntie was going to insist he swim with Nakisa after her change, or if it was because the shore was getting closer. Probably a bit of both. His gaze locked on the small shelter, he decided he'd worry about Nakisa later, he just needed to get through this moment and meet Terah.

As if she knew he was anxious to see her, she came out of the shelter and dove into the water. He followed the ripple of the water, trying to decide which direction she'd gone. He hadn't even really gotten to look at her, she moved so fast. The clean water here would do her good though, help to replenish her and heal her.

Devin turned the canoe to move away from the shelter, probably worried he'd hit her if she popped up in front of them. Konner wasn't about to tell him that she could flip this canoe without much effort if she swam under it.

"Will she know we're up here?"

He glanced back to see Devin looking at the water. "She will." Konner watched the water beside them and saw a brief flash go by. She already knew, she was down there deciding if she wanted to be seen or not right now.

"I'm going to take us over to the post off to the left side."

Konner nodded and dragged his gaze from the water so he could reach out for the post as they coasted closer to it. His stomach was doing flips like he was a giddy teen, anxious for something. It was completely ridiculous to be his age and feel this. His heart was pounding hard inside his chest. Grabbing the post, he pulled the canoe closer and used his strength to turn the back of it toward the shore. When the back hit the ground. He wrapped the rope around it and tied it off. Turning, he looked at Devin who sat there with one eyebrow raised and a smirk on his face.

"That's one way to do it." He put the paddle down and looked at the shelter. "Do I leave you here or make introductions?"

Before Konner could open his mouth to decide the water splashed right in front of him. He looked down to see just her face out of the water, she was watching him. The blue of the eyes from the picture was almost completely covered with silver right now. Her skin was shimmering as his kind did when in the water. Blinking, he realized he was sitting there with his mouth gaping open, he smiled down at her.

She went back under the water and then was gone from his sight.

As he leaned over to look into the water, there was a splash in front of the shelter, and then she launched herself from the water up onto the small dock out front of it. Her hands slapped against the old boards as she lifted the rest of her body out and sat there with her feet dangling into the water.

Konner sucked in a breath. She was completely naked, which wasn't unusual for his kind, but she was not the frail woman in the photos now. Devin's fish had gone to a restoring some flesh on her bones and judging by how well she looked now, he owed the prince a large shipment of fish.

Turning, she reached for a wrap sitting beside her and put her arms in it, covering herself up. "I did not know you would be here, or I would have put on that suit Rayne gave me." She said in a rasping voice while looking at Devin.

"It's fine, Terah." He cleared his throat, "I brought someone for you to meet."

"I'm trying to follow the rules." She said as she stood up and hugged the robe to her body.

"You're doing fine."

Konner felt the canoe rock as the prince got out of it, but he was unable to move or speak. She was lovely. Long wavy black hair that hung down past her waist, her cheekbones were high and prominent, no longer bones surrounded by indents. Her long black eyelashes framed her eyes, making the blue of them stand out more.

When he realized both were standing there looking at him now, he stood up slowly and stepped out of the boat. As he moved over to the stand in front of her, he fought a part of himself that want to pick her up and hug her to him. Perhaps it was all the years that he'd searched without finding but the idea that this gorgeous creature in front of him was alive and well was causing a whirlwind of emotions inside him. "I'm sorry, I know I'm staring, but," he lifted a hand and motioned to her, "you've recovered a great deal since the picture was taken when you arrived."

"Pictures?" She turned to Devin.

"The photos." He supplied.

"I see, yes." She looked down, "I feel much better now." She looked him over slowly, and then her gaze landed on his face again. "You are one of them. That freed me."

Konner looked down at his cargo pants again and regretted

not changing. "I work with them, yes, I wasn't there when they found you." He was afraid to step closer, "I have many questions though."

Terah glanced at Devin, then back to him. "You are here to talk to me?"

Konner looked at the lake, trying to decide how to explain who he was and why he was here.

"Actually," Devin spoke quietly, "Rayne wanted the doctor to check you over again, just to make sure everything is all right."

"I feel good." She offered him a proud smile, "I slept out of the water last night without pain."

Konner straightened, he'd forgotten what it was like, the pains of being out of the water for short periods of time. He'd have to plan a route back that allowed for frequent stops so she could be in the water.

"Did you want to gather up your things?" Devin motioned to the shelter, "you can stay on the other side..."

"With the children?" She looked excited.

He nodded, "yes, they've been asking about boat rides."

"I will get them." She went back into the shelter.

Devin turned and looked at Konner, a questioning look on his face.

"How long is she comfortable out of the water?" He kept his voice quiet.

"Not long." The prince gave him a look telling him he knew that was going to make the trip harder.

Konner nodded and rubbed his hand across his forehead. "It will take me some time to plan a route back, to my chopper..."

"You have a chopper?"

Nodding, Konner jammed his hands into his pockets. "Our location is hard to get to on land, not impossible, but flying in is much easier."

"And you just leave it somewhere waiting?"

Konner grinned, he made it sound like he'd left the

helicopter parked on a street corner. "I have a few secure locations around the province."

"You fly it yourself?" The prince seemed genuinely interested.

"Yes, I got my license about five years ago, it's much easier to just go and not arrange a pilot."

"I need to do…"

Terah came out of the shelter; she was wearing a dark blue bikini. She smiled at Devin and handed him a small bundle of things wrapped in the robe she'd had on. "I will see you over there." Without delay, she turned and dove into the water.

Both stood there and looked at the water where she'd disappeared.

"You know, I have to admit I was a bit surprised that your kind didn't," Devin motioned to his feet.

"Grow a huge fin and have our legs meld together magically?" Konner smirked at him.

"Yes." Devin smiled at him.

"That's mostly legend," he waved his hand around, "the story is passed down from the elders."

Devin nodded his head slowly, "so how do you swim so fast then without it?"

"Webbed hands and feet," he lifted his arm, "fins along our arms and lower leg," he shrugged, "and sheer strength."

"Speaking of strength, we better get going or she'll be there before we're in the canoe again." He moved around him to get back in it.

Konner looked at the water and wanted to swim over. He wanted to see her move in the water and just look at her. She was alive.

Chapter Seven

Konner leaned against the tree, his eyes never straying far from the building that Terah was in with the doctor. Pulling his phone out, he dialed his aunt's number. Hopefully, she answered without hanging up on him this time. Modern technology and Alviva Flores did not go well together.

"Konner?"

He grinned, "yes."

"Did you find some? I had one of my feelings."

He could barely hear her, "Auntie, hold the phone closer to your face."

"Is this better?"

He winced, now she was screaming in his ear. "Much."

"Did you find some?"

"One, Auntie, she was in very poor health…"

"A female. That's marvelous. Have you been in the water with her yet?"

Konner sighed softly, so she wouldn't hear him, "no, Auntie, I've just met her. My team recovered her a few weeks ago."

"Recovered?"

The door opened, making him pause and watch. A young boy came out. Leaning back again, he debated on telling her everything right away or waiting until he was there with her. "Yes, from Aiden Tomas."

"Someone needs to burn that cur at the stake."

He smirked, if his aunt had her way many would be burned while staked to the ground. "She was born in captivity, Auntie, her mother was taken when she was pregnant."

"I know of two that disappeared while carrying young, Konner, was she one from our clan?"

It pained him to hear the anguish in her voice. "I don't know yet, Auntie, I'll speak with her after the doctor is done checking her." He cleared his throat, "it's going to be a slow trip back, she needs the water often."

"You do whatever you need to bring her home, nephew, she needs to be with her people."

He nodded, "she's going to need time to adjust, she knows nothing of clan life, or even life outside a tank, Auntie."

"We'll embrace her and help her, you know that."

The door opened again; this time Terah came out. She stopped outside the door and raised her face to the sunlight and his breath got caught in his throat. She still had the swimsuit top on but was now wearing a long flowing blue skirt. "I need to go." He said softly, "I will call when we are on our way back."

"*Kenna friðr,* Nephew." She hung up before he could tell her to also feel peace.

Sighing, he tucked the phone in his pocket and went over toward Terah, who still stood there in the sun. It was fall here, the air was chilled, snow would soon be covering the ground, freezing the lake, but she'd never had the simplest thing like sunlight before. If she wanted to stand there all day and feel the sunlight and fresh air on her face, then he had no problem standing beside her.

She gave him a quick once over and then looked up at him.

"Everything go well with the doctor?"

She smiled slowly, "yes, she says it is a miracle."

Konner grinned back at her. She had no idea how much of a miracle she was—to him, to his clan. He motioned to the path, "I need to go up and move my van to the cabin, would you care to walk with me?"

She nodded, "yes, then you can talk to me," she paused, her nose wrinkled in as she thought, "that is why you are here?"

Konner nodded, "you are the only reason I'm here." He smiled at her and watched the tension in her face ease.

"Yes. Let's walk and talk." She looked at the slip-on shoes in her hand. "I have trouble walking in these."

Konner glanced at the path, "we can take a different route, that won't hurt your feet if you like."

He was rewarded with a bright smile. "Okay."

At this point, he would have walked the entire area to make sure she was comfortable. The walk was slow as she stopped to look at things and touch them. He was fascinated watching her touch a plant and then put her finger to her tongue to taste what she'd hand her hand against. It was common for their kind to rely on taste rather than scent. Once in the water, their nostrils didn't have the same ability as they did out of it. In the water, taste, sight, and the vibrations of the atmosphere around them replaced the simple ability to smell.

He watched her do it again with a weed, then make a face from the taste of it. Going over, he plucked the weed from the ground held it up to his nose, and inhaled slowly, showing her.

With a focused, cautious look, she leaned toward it as he held it in front of her nose. She sniffed briefly and then stopped and slowly took the scent into her system. Her nose wrinkled and she hissed from the smell of it. "I do not like that one." She swatted it away from her face.

Konner chuckled, "above water, the scents of things can be very offensive at times."

"There is so much." She said looking around. "I don't know what any of it is."

"You will learn."

Clasping her hands around the shoes she carried, she glanced at him from under her lashes, "I won't go back in a tank ever."

"No, you won't." He cleared his throat, "I will make certain of it."

She studied him for a moment and then nodded. "Okay." She started walking again.

"Did you think that was why I was here?"

Shaking her head, she didn't look back at him. "No. Rayne told me someone was coming here soon that would take me somewhere that the fish don't run out."

Konner grinned, "that's true, but there are other things to eat than just fish."

Stopping, she turned and gave him a startled look. "I like fish."

"They are good." He agreed and started walking again.

"You like fish too?" She slowed to walk beside him.

It occurred to him that she hadn't realized yet that he was like her. He had assumed she would know by his scent or his eyes. Cursing inside his head, he put his hand in front of her, so she'd stop.

"Do you hear that?" She whispered and looked into the trees.

Konner stilled and listened. It sounded like someone crying.

Terah dropped her shoes on the ground and went into the thicker growth of the tall weeds.

Konner jolted and followed her. She shouldn't be wandering in that without something covering her feet.

She squatted down in the growth and was talking softly.

He caught up to see a small child curled up and crying.

"Hello." Terah leaned right down, her face almost on the earth. "I'm Terah, what's your name?"

The little girl stilled and looked at her. "Kavi." She sniffled and wiped her eyes. "I don't have a mom and daddy now."

Terah scooped her onto her lap and brushed the blonde curls back from her face. "Mine is gone now too."

"Really?" The tear-filled brown eyes looked up at Terah. "Does it make you sad?"

Terah nodded and wiped her cheeks off with the material from her skirt. "Yes." She hugged her to her chest. "Would you like to walk with us?"

The child nodded.

Terah stood up, holding her in her arms, and started walking back to the path.

Konner followed and picked up her shoes.

"It's all right." Terah's rasping voice whispered to the girl.

He was just about to ask where she was supposed to be when Terah began humming to her. It wasn't the type of humming that one-forms made, it was the song of his people. It was a magical melodic sound that he hadn't heard, out of water since he was a child. It was a calming peaceful song, and it settled the little girl in her arms. She rested her face against Terah's chest and took sighed in a ragged way.

Konner was stunned, could barely form a complete thought. His kind had different vocal cords, ones that allowed them to communicate underwater, mostly with various vibrations in a range of pitches, but no one, except his Auntie, hummed out of the water now. He wasn't even sure if the others knew how to do it out of the water. He frowned; he wasn't sure even *he* could.

He continued up the path toward the house, not speaking. He didn't want the melody to end. Had her mother taught her how to do this? He needed to know who her mother was, and where her family was from.

As they rounded the corner to the path leading up to the main house, a woman came running toward them. "You found her." She gasped to catch her breath, "I've been searching everywhere."

Terah looked down at the little girl. "She was mourning in the trees." She gave her a small smile, "she is much better now."

The woman held out her arms, "thank you."

Terah placed Kavi in them. She brushed the curls back from her face again and then stepped back.

The woman turned and looked over at the guard, "tell them we found her." He nodded and opened the door. She turned back to look at Terah and then Konner, "thank you again. She just wanders off in stealth mode on me." She turned and walked down the path.

Konner didn't watch her go; he was too busy looking at Terah. "Where did you learn how to sing like that?" He knew the emotions he felt inside were bleeding out in his voice, but he couldn't help it.

"My mother. She would do that when I afraid." She smiled, a faraway look on her face for a moment, then she blinked and saw he was carrying her shoes. "Thank you." She held her hand out for them.

Konner handed them to her.

"Oh good, you're done with the doctor."

They turned to see Rayne standing at the door.

"Devin and I were wondering if you'd like to have lunch with us." She smiled at Terah, "it's a tuna salad."

Terah looked up at Konner and then back to the princess. "I would like to try that."

Rayne smiled and motioned to the door, "perfect."

Konner came back, the maps in his hand. He paused at the door to the office and listened to hear Rayne and Terah both laughing. Her laugh sounded so much like her song, melodic and touching.

Devin stood by the desk watching him when he went in. "They're trying on clothes."

Konner didn't care what they were doing, as long as she was happy, that's all that mattered. Motioning to the table, he waited for Devin's nod before he went over and opened the map on it. "The first part of the trip will be easy enough," he tapped his finger on the map, "there's water available in every direction you look."

"Where's your chopper?" Devin came over and stood beside him.

Showing him on the map, he leaned on the table and looked down at it.

"Your map shows the water more than the roads." The prince grinned, "I guess driving is not your priority."

"It's a secondary thing for us."

"How long can you go without the water?" Devin tucked his hands into his jeans.

"Three days," Konner tapped his chest, "four if I'm wearing this and have to push it." He undid a few buttons to show him the material underneath it. "It holds water and moisture against my skin."

"I don't suppose you carry extras with you."

Konner rebuttoned his shirt. "No. With the design, they have to stay wet, so I'd have to carry them around immersed in water."

"If it's money..."

Konner smirked, "it's not money." He shrugged, "with the team, I'm in and out, we're never gone long." He rubbed his hand across his forehead, "the new protocol of riding with transports though," he blew out a breath, "I'm going to have to rethink things." He looked back to the map. Before he could concentrate on it, his phone rang.

Pulling it out, he looked at it and hoped he wasn't about to get Fallan into trouble with the Alliance, but she wouldn't call unless it was important. "Excuse me." He answered it and stepped away from the prince. Shifter hearing was exceptional. "Fallan."

"Turns out tracking large fish tanks wasn't all that hard."

Devin watched him with mere curiosity on his face and from what Konner could tell, he wasn't judging.

"That's good news?"

"Yes and no. There's a lot of them."

Konner looked at the floor, "is there a way to weed out those actually used for fish?"

"Not really, but I'm calling to see if it's okay with you if I take it to some of the higher-ups and get permission to go through them, maybe get a little help."

Konner looked over at Devin again, "I may be able to help with that. I'm with the prince right now, hold on I'm going to put you on speaker." Lowering the phone, he tapped the screen and walked back over to Devin, "earlier I asked Fallan, from the tech team to see if there was a way to find out about large tank sales across the continent. After what your mate said about Terah being a showpiece." Devin raised an eyebrow.

"I take it the information has been found." He looked at the phone.

"She's found a lot, but with everything going on, she's going to need help weeding through them."

"Fallan?"

"Yes, sir?"

Devin nodded his head slowly, "what do you need to do this?"

She made a hissing sound, "well first I need Nate to not be pissed I did this. He doesn't like us branching out without backup from the team."

"That shouldn't be an issue, taking such an initiative," he looked at Konner, "on your *own*, should be rewarded." He gave Konner a questioning look.

"Right. It was exactly that."

"Explain what you've found." Devin leaned back against the table and crossed his arms over his chest. Konner didn't know him well enough to know if this was good or bad.

"Konner mentioned sales and large tanks, so I did some digging and found manufacturers—there's not as many as I thought there would be, that specialize in them large enough to hold," she paused, "people-sized bodies," she mumbled that sounded like she was cursing, "but the list of purchased ones is long."

Devin nodded, "and there's no way to know if they are just zealous people with pet fish or not?"

"Right. So, narrowing it down will take a lot of digging, checking addresses of sales, the registrations on who or what is there..."

"Okay." He rubbed the back of his neck and then walked quickly to his desk. He opened a binder and started flipping through pages in it. Konner went closer to the desk so he wouldn't have to yell. "Just give me a second." He glanced at Konner, "I'm just looking at the list of teams that have been cleared to bring into things."

"Cleared, like we can trust they're not traitorous bastards?" Fallan asked.

Devin grinned at her wording. "Yeah. That."

"I have that list here."

He gave the phone a surprised look. "That saves time. What team is best to hunt down this for you?"

"I don't know what the research group does really, I mean that sounds like it fits, doesn't it?"

Devin looked down at the list. "And they've all been cleared to do things?"

"Yeah. All of their computers are being monitored now as well, along with anything else in this building or taken out of this building."

"Okay, you have my permission to get them on this, and if there are any locations that need eyes on, work with the surveillance team. They can set something up."

"That works. This will save me a lot of hours, thank you. I have a long list of things to be doing."

Devin straightened from the desk and crossed his arms again. "Let's keep this between us, for now, call me when you find anything."

"Ah, will do, sir." She cleared her throat, "Konner, that other thing, I'm still working on it."

Konner watched the amused look on Devin's face. "Thanks, Fallan. I owe you."

"Nah, you and I bounce back and forth, it's all good. I better go. Later." The line went quiet.

Konner tucked the phone back into his pocket.

Devin looked at him for a moment and then flipped back a few pages in the binder. He ran his finger down the page. "Fallan Norris, tech team." He glanced up at him, "you've worked with her before? Off the record?"

Konner nodded, "yes, she set up the security for the Sanctuary and my network," he tapped the pocket he'd just put the phone in, "my phone, so it's secure."

"And you do what in return?" He stood up and moved around the desk.

He debated briefly on lying, but so far, he felt the prince wasn't all about following protocols. He hoped he was right. "Help smuggle hers across oceans and borders."

"Hers?"

"Her clan. Most of hers are still on other continents and it's not a safe place for them to be."

"Does the Alliance know this? My father?"

Konner went back over to the map and looked down at it. "Some. But it's breaking treaties and agreements with ambassadors to take them out of their zones, so," he shrugged and looked over his shoulder at him, "I help. I have contacts keeping an eye out for mine as well, so it's no different passing other information down the line." Devin stood beside him now. "Calum asked me to help Deacon look for any of his as well."

"You're a handy person to know."

Konner smirked, "none of it goes against the Alliance." He sobered, "some of the ambassadors are not representatives because they are in it for the good of our kind."

"Does my father know this?"

Konner nodded, "he does, but dealing with it is hard to do with everything else he has to deal with."

"Yeah." Devin inhaled a deep breath and nodded before releasing it, "I've been trying to come up with something that makes," he motioned to his desk, "all that easier—it's out of control, so many branches all over the world and it's," he sighed, "a mess."

Konner gave him a quick look, "I have enough trouble looking after mine, I don't know how your family does it."

"Not very well apparently." He gave him a steady look, "I don't have a problem with Fallan helping you out, sounds like it's doing good." He cocked his head to the side, "what's the other thing she's working on?"

Konner held his look, "figuring out those transactions they found."

Devin nodded, "again it would only help, so okay, as long as she's not falling behind on whatever it is she's supposed to be doing, I guess it's all good."

Konner grinned, "she can use three keyboards and watch five screens at the same time, I don't think her getting behind in her work will be an issue."

Devin gave him a wide-eyed look, "I can barely handle typing on my phone." Shaking his head, he motioned to the maps, "let's get a route planned so we can get you and Terah on the road."

Chapter Eight

"I have to leave?"

Konner spun around to see Terah and Rayne standing in the doorway. She was wearing a long floral print dress. The top of it was fit close to her form, then it flowed out from her waist. She looked amazing in it. To any other woman, it would be too light to wear during this cooler season, but one of his wouldn't be bothered with the temperatures. He noticed the panicked look on her face and realized he hadn't answered her. "I'm taking you back to the Sanctuary."

Terah looked at Rayne, then jerked her head back to look at him. "I can't. I can't go. I can't do it again, be without water." She clutched her waist as if she were remembering the pains that were a result of being out of the water too long.

"I'm going to plan a route so there are..."

She sucked in a breath and shook her head. Spinning around she ran out of the room.

Konner went after her. If she went outside and managed to get down to the water, he'd be chasing her around for days. He caught up to her just as she reached the door. Reaching over her head, he placed his hand on it so she couldn't open it.

"Please let me go." The panic in her voice broke his heart.

"Terah, I will not make you go without water." He touched her shoulder and felt her trembling beneath his hand.

She turned and shrunk back from him until her back was pressed up against the door. "Please. I can't do it again. You do not understand..."

Leaning down, right in front of her face, he made sure she had no choice, but to look right at him. "Calm down." The terror in her eyes only enhanced his need to find Aiden Tomas and stick a knife through his heart. "Terah, stop." He allowed his voice to vibrate, in a way that resembled communication under the water. It was painful to do, and he'd likely need to drink an entire bottle of water after doing it, but it did settle her enough to look right at him. "Take a deep breath, through your nose," lifting his chin, he leaned closer so she would be sure to pick up his scent as she did it.

She sucked in a breath, her blue eyes rounded, and were staring at him when he looked at her again. "You are like me." Her voice was filled with amazement. "I thought I was the only one that remained."

As he went to step away from her, she grabbed him around the waist and clung to him. He could feel her shaking and smell her tears. Wrapping his arms around her, he cradled her against his chest. "You are not the only one." She sobbed and he thought his heart was going to shatter inside his chest. To live as she had and think she was the last one of her kind, he couldn't imagine it. No matter how dire things had felt in the decades of searching, he'd always had his great aunt with him, he'd never been completely alone.

Terah pulled back and looked up at him, her cheeks shimmering where the tears had fallen, "are there more?" She was unlike any other woman he knew, not even bothering to wipe them away.

He brushed the hair back from her face and nodded. "Yes, so far there are thirteen more of us at the Sanctuary."

"What is the Sanctuary?"

"It's our home. It's private, safe, and secure with a huge lake and rivers running through it."

"And fish? It has fish?"

Konner laughed, "it has a never-ending supply of fish." He wasn't lying, they had their own fishery.

Terah made a noise that was close to a squeal and spun around.

Devin and Rayne stood there. Rayne wiped the tears off her cheeks.

"Endless fish," Terah said and went quickly back to Rayne. She stopped in front of her. "I will send you some." She told her in a serious tone.

Devin looked over their heads at him, an amused expression on his face.

Konner lifted one shoulder as if to say they could probably do that.

Terah spun again, the material spiraling out from her body, she stopped and looked down at it, smoothing her hand over it. "Rayne gave me this *dress*." She smiled at him.

"It's lovely." He motioned to her bare feet. "We're going to have to find you some shoes to go with it." The happiness left her face, he smirked, she really didn't like footwear.

"Are we going now?" She looked from him to Rayne and then back again.

Konner began walking back to the office. "I need to plan a route with a lot of lakes and water on along the way, but we can leave in the morning."

"Okay. Yes. A lot of water." She nodded and followed him into the office.

He leaned on the table and looked down at the map. Terah stood beside him looking at it as well, he was doubtful that she had any idea what she was looking at.

"We need a name for here?" Rayne said quietly as she came into the room with her mate.

"The house?" Devin came over to the table.

"Not here, here." Rayne nudged him with her elbow, "*here,*

the campground."

Devin frowned and looked from the map back to her. "It's the campground."

"What was it called before when it was used for actual campers?"

Konner wanted to ask if he could borrow a pen, but with the intent look the princess was giving Devin, he didn't want to interrupt.

He shrugged, "Pine River campground."

"Because of all the trees?"

Devin shook his head, glanced at Konner for a second before answering Rayne. "No, because the Pine River runs along the edge of the land."

"Well, that's boring." Rayne crossed her arms over her chest and looked at the floor. "It needs to be something, peaceful," she shrugged, "so many are here to heal and recover."

"Is this something we need to discuss now?" Devin gave Konner an apologetic look.

A line appeared between Rayne's brows as she looked at him. "I think so yes. I hear 'we're going to the campground' or 'at the campground' and many others twenty times a day. If we're living here and people are here, it should have a name." She glanced to Terah, "don't you think so?"

Terah looked at her and nodded. "Everywhere should have a name." She smiled at Konner, "like the Sanctuary."

Devin inhaled a breath so deep that Konner watched his shoulders rise and fall when he exhaled. "What name would you like?"

Tilting her head to the side, a focused look on her face. "What projects peace?" When her mate didn't speak, she frowned hard, "what about Tranquility?"

Devin jolted like she'd just smacked him. "I don't think I can call out over the radio 'send them to Tranquility." He shook his head.

Rayne surveyed him silently for a moment, then the

expression on her face eased. "Serenity." She nodded.

Devin shook his head, "big no to that one too."

Blowing out a long sigh, Rayne put her hand over her mouth, her gaze moving randomly around the room. "Arcadia." She nodded. "That one works."

"Arcadia campground?" Devin asked cautiously.

"No." She smirked, "just Arcadia. Let's go home to Arcadia." She nodded looking quite pleased.

Devin glanced over at Konner for a moment, a look of acceptance slowly coming over his face. He turned back to her, "Arcadia it is." He cleared his throat, "isn't there somewhere else with that name?"

"Not in our world, our kind will know it as here." She smiled at him. "I'm going to call your mother and tell her." She leaned over and kissed his cheek and then walked from the room.

Devin rubbed his hand over his chest and turned back to him. "I guess I live in Arcadia now."

Konner smirked, "as opposed to Tranquility?"

"Right. Arcadia is good."

Chapter Nine

Terah broke the water's surface and then just floated there, only from her eyes up out of the water. She looked along the shore to see who was there. Not many were at this time of the morning. The sun was barely sitting in the sky. She watched Konner as he came down to the water with a bag. He bent down and took off his boots and then pulled the legs of his clothes up. She thought maybe he was going to come for a swim with her, and she felt a flutter inside her chest. There had been no one to swim with her since she was a child. No one like her at least.

He walked out and then reached into the bag and took out a bottle. He was filling bottles with water from the lake. She smiled; this was good. That other water in the plastic bottles tasted strange.

Pushing back with her arms, she closed her eyes to feel the water sliding over her body. It felt nothing like the small tank or water from the pool. It soothed and gave her energy. She had never felt as strong as being in this lake made her feel. Her mother used to tell her stories about lakes and deep rivers, but this was the first one she had ever felt for herself.

She was never going back. Ever. She would rather die than go back to that pain and isolation. For more years than she could count, she'd been completely alone. In that small space with barely a tub big enough to fit her whole body in. The only others she saw in that time were the men with thick collars around their necks and one woman. Most of them didn't speak to her.

A few of them did, but it was usually with voices that were filled with a pang of sadness, and she didn't know if it was for her or themselves. The woman did not have a collar on, and she did not feel sadness, she was cold. Terah wasn't sure, but she thought now that she may have been a doctor. She glanced at the shore again, not like the doctor here. The man and lady doctor that was here had such kindness and very caring.

Terah dropped beneath the surface and looked at her arm. She ran a webbed hand along the part from her elbow to her shoulder. How many needles had that cold woman put in her arm? She didn't know, could not count that high. She didn't know what was in the needles, only that it made her care less about everything after it. Rayne and the one doctor here were talking about it when Terah had been resting. They thought it was to keep her quiet and happier.

Turning, she swam with all the strength she had. Their needles had failed. She had never felt happiness since her mother had died. Breaking the surface again, she rose far above the water and then opened her arms to splash back in. The first time in all these years she'd felt anything close to happiness was when she'd swam in this water. Turning, she looked to see Konner standing on the shore, his hands on his hips, looking in her direction. When she'd found out he was her kind. That had been joy and relief. Relief that she wasn't alone anymore.

When the men without collars had moved her to the houses, the women there had talked to her. No one in those places was happy, but the company was nice. She loved the children, and could forget about her pain when she was with them. Rayne told her that the children that were at the last house were also saved. All of the children needed to be saved from that life.

Diving down, she went all the way to the bottom and swam fast for a moment, she couldn't think about all of that right now. Not when she was in this lovely lake and swimming free, it was not the time for sad thoughts. Turning, she shot upward to the surface again and then paused to watch Konner once more.

She swam toward him, keeping her eyes on him. He was taking her to where he lived, where more of her kind were. Her heartbeat was so fast every time she thought of being with people like her.

When the water was shallow enough, she could stand, she wobbled and put her hands out to steady herself. Walking like this was hard to do. Her feet, when like this were not meant to move in this manner.

"We're going to go in a half-hour," Konner said loud enough she could hear.

Looking up from the water, she nodded at him, then watched him pick up the bag and walk away. She didn't know how long a half-hour was. She couldn't tell time. Willing her body to change back, she decided she better hurry, so she didn't delay leaving.

The first few steps were always hard for her, she wasn't used to walking at all. A few steps down a hallway had been the most she'd really gone before, or from a building to a car to a house, but nothing like this. The sand felt strange on her feet, but she could feel the moisture in it and that made her smile. Looking up, she saw Konner had stopped and was watching her, she smiled at him and tried to walk faster. The smile on his face was real, she knew that. There was nothing better than a real smile from someone. It made her think of hopes and dreams and things better than the life she had lived so far.

Chapter Ten

Konner watched her swallow the Biotrien mix and then just sit there for a moment.

"It tastes like plants in the water." She said quietly.

He grinned, "yes it does, but it's also full of things that are good for you."

"Okay." she lifted the bottle and looked at it. "Can we put fish in a bottle?"

Turning his attention back to the road, he shook his head, "I don't think they'd keep well in a bottle."

"That's too bad." She said quietly and watched out the window.

"Were you in a car before we found you?"

She nodded her head slowly, "yes. There were no trees there only buildings. I went from the house to the other place where I could swim in the big glass box."

"A tank."

He could feel her eyes on him. "A tank." She repeated.

In the past day, he'd come to realize how limited her vocabulary was and it dawned on him she couldn't read. That was something he planned to correct once they were home.

The questions he had for her just kept growing and he'd been trying to think of ways to ask her without bringing back the memories of her life before. There was no way to go about it that wasn't going to take her back to that, but it was going to be a long drive to get to the helicopter, so he may as well try to find out some things along the way. He'd finally read the folder that contained her picture. There was very little information in it. Her medical stats and last name. Matthews. The name didn't mean a great deal to him, although with all the names of those lost in his head, there was no way to check that until they were back at the sanctuary. "In your time there, where all the buildings are, did you ever see anyone else like us?"

She nodded and then took another small sip from the bottle. "Yes." She said quietly.

Konner held his breath hoping she'd continue, but she didn't. "When you were little or-or lately?"

"I remember many when I was little." She tugged on the seatbelt and tried to turn in the seat, "there was a really big tank," he glanced over at her, "but not of glass—"

"A pool."

"A pool. I remember going to the side of it was bad, it hurt."

He frowned at the road; they'd used something to keep them in the pool. An electric perimeter?

"There was an old one with us and she would watch me when my mother wasn't there. I liked her."

"Do you know what her name was?" For the old one to even look old, she must have been quite the age.

Terah was silent for a moment. "No. I don't."

"That's okay. How many were there?" He didn't even know if she could count.

"There was Mother and the old one," her tone said she was thinking about it, "two boys, they were fun to swim with." He looked over to see her smiling, "three girls, big like Mother, and two men, big like you."

"So there were ten of you?"

"Is that ten? I can count to five, a little girl at the house helped me learn that."

Glancing over, he saw she was puzzling it out on her hand. "We'll teach you how to count and read."

"Books?" Her voice was breathless. "The little girl would read me books."

Konner nodded, "yes, we have a lot of books and one of ours teaches the children..."

"There are children?"

"Yes. There are five, but only one of them is still small. He's six, Kole." Turning his attention back to the road, he steered around the large potholes. "One of our women is pregnant, though, so we'll have a baby soon."

"They wanted me to have a baby." She stated it without emotion. "I tried to have one, then I wouldn't be alone, but no baby."

Konner gripped the steering wheel harder. "Who," he inhaled, to relax his throat, "who did you try with?"

"Malik and Rafferty." She looked out the window, "I think Malik was one of the boys from the pool, but I didn't see him for a long time so I'm not sure."

Rage was chocking Konner. He leaned forward picked up his bottle of water and took a drink, to try to settle down before he attempted speaking. Both of the men's names were names associated with water in some way. They'd been named by clans as was tradition. "Where was he all that time?"

"I don't know. They got mad if we tried to talk." Her voice was clipped.

"Did you," he looked over at her, "this will seem like a strange question," she was giving him her full attention, "did you try to make a baby in the water?" He had to know if Tomas knew.

She shook her head. "No. In a room."

He heaved a sigh of relief.

"Was that the wrong way to do it?"

Squeezing his eyes shut for a second, he glared at the road. It was all wrong. Every single part of it was wrong. Vile. He puffed out his cheeks and blew out a short breath. "We can only make babies in the water." He didn't go into any other details. Terah would not be having a baby anytime soon. Their women could only conceive and carry a child when they were in top health and Terah had never been that way her whole life.

"Oh." She looked back out the window. "I don't think they know that." She said without looking away from the trees. "Is it bad that I'm happy they don't know that?"

He shook his head, "no it isn't. What they're doing is wrong, Terah." He cleared his throat. "The men, Malik and Rafferty, did you see them more? Do you know where they were kept?"

She shook her head, "I didn't see them after being in the room with them."

Konner's hopes died inside him.

"I heard them say they were being sold and they would have new ones soon." She turned to look at them. "I could hear through the glass. They didn't know that."

Konner grinned, even though it wasn't a happy moment. "That was very clever of you."

She shrugged her shoulder, "they thought I was stupid, nothing more than an animal."

"When you're ready, we can talk about some of the things you heard them say."

"Will it help?" She leaned forward in the seat and looked out the windshield at some birds flying over them, "help find more of our kind?"

Konner glanced at the birds and realized she'd probably never seen them before. "Yes, it may help a lot." He motioned to the sky, "those are birds."

"Birds." She repeated slowly, "are they good to eat?"

Konner smirked, "once the feathers are removed and they're cooked, they're pretty tasty."

"Tasty." She tried the word, "I want to try birds."

He nodded, "you will get to. We hunt larger ones at the Sanctuary." He didn't add that guns were required, because he wasn't sure if she'd been exposed to guns or not. He looked at the area they were in and tried to remember how much further he had to drive on this unkept road before reaching the main one. He wanted to get home fast and that wasn't a possibility on this surface. He understood why Devin kept it this way and didn't repair it, driving along this would deter anyone out wandering the area.

Terah settled back in her seat, now that the birds were out of sight. "Do you know what happened to the others? That you were in the pool with?"

"The old one was sick. She said it was from the salt." She looked at him. "My mother got sick too from it."

Konner kept his eyes on the road, he couldn't look at her right now. "They kept you and the boys out of the salt?" He hoped, no prayed he was wrong in where his mind was going with that information.

"We were too little they said."

He closed his eyes briefly, before looking back to the road. They'd had them swimming in saltwater. Saltwater would have dehydrated them slowly, aging them rapidly and eventually killing them. He rubbed his hand over his face, to stave off tears of anger that he felt just under the surface. It would have been the most painful way to die for those like him.

"Are you okay?"

Her concern for him almost put him over the edge. Giving his head a quick shake, he slowed and then stopped the van. Slamming it into park, he turned to see her ocean blue eyes filled with so much concern. He shook his head again, "I am *not* okay." He cleared the emotion from his throat, "swimming in saltwater kills our kind, slowly, painfully."

She nodded, her eyes brimming with tears. "I know. So do they, now."

He reached over and grasped her hand, "you have my word, my oath that I will find those that held you, your mother," he nodded, "and I will bring them to justice and stop them from ever taking one of ours again."

A single tear rolled down her cheek, leaving a shimmering

rainbow trail in its wake. "Okay." She nodded.

He gave her hand a squeeze and then released it. "Keep drinking that, it will help you to heal inside."

She looked at the bottle. "Inside?"

Konner put the van back into drive. "Yes, years of being kept from freshwater, will have done damage on the inside, so that will help."

"On the inside." She placed her hand over her stomach. "Okay." She lifted the bottle and took the cap off.

Konner started driving again. "I need to call a friend, I'll have to put the phone on speaker because of this bloody road, I need both hands on the steering wheel, so just try to stay quiet while I do that." He glanced at her, "the fewer that know you exist and are with me, the better."

She leaned forward and looked out the windshield. "There is no blood on the road."

Konner grinned, "it's an expression, I know there's no blood." He started driving again, "it's hard to explain why I used that word, but we'll talk about it later."

"Okay." She nodded, giving him a look that said he was strange to have said that. "I will be quiet." She took a small sip and then looked out the window.

Konner watched her for a moment, still amused that she'd corrected him. Tapping the screen of his personal phone, he brought up his contact list. He hadn't spoken to Raymond in a few months, but as head of the Alliance Security team, his life a little hectic lately.

The phone rang three times before he answered it.

"Hardy."

"Raymond, it's Konner."

"Konner, let me guess you've purchased a tropical island and need me to come to spend a week there and tell them everything they're doing wrong securing it?"

Konner grinned. Ray knew full well that anything in the tropics would be pure hell for him. "No island, an iceberg in the North Pole."

"Pass." He sounded amused. "What's going on?" He could hear his boots hitting the floor as he walked. "You only call if it's important, which I appreciate that you don't waste my time."

"Things busy right now?" He already knew the answer.

"Damn straight they are and it's about time."

"I'm sure you're up to date on recent events..."

"If it's Alliance related, you know I am."

Konner nodded, then grit his teeth when he hit a bump hard. "I have a huge ask."

"Spill it." Raymond Hardy always got to the point and Konner could appreciate that.

"I need for you to re-question some brought in these past few weeks."

"Okay, what am I asking?"

"If they have any information about water shifters. Anything at all."

"Yeah, I heard one of yours was recovered. How is she?"

He glanced to see Terah looking at his phone intently. "Recovering."

"Glad to hear it." There was a pause. "It will take some time, they're at different locations, but I can do that."

"I'd appreciate it, anything about sales, transfers, newly acquired..."

"You think there's more around?"

Konner slowed for the obstacle course of potholes in the road. "I have reason to believe there is, yes."

"All right then, I'll get that out to my boys and see if we can find you a few leads."

Konner felt relief flood over him. "Anything you find out, run past the prince, he's going to be helping out with this." He didn't want to do anything behind Devin's back now that he knew he.

"I can do that. I like him, he pulls no punches."

"I agree." Konner almost sighed when he saw the end of this god-awful road coming up. "I won't keep you any longer.

I have precious cargo to get home." He looked to see Terah look at him, he couldn't read the expression on her face.

"Travel with care, my friend." The link went silent.

Konner stopped at the faded stop sign and turned to Terah. "If anyone can find out information, it will be Ray."

"What is the precious cargo?"

Smiling at her, he tilted his head. "You are. You are very special and important."

She mulled over what he said for a moment and then she smiled slowly. "I like that." She nodded.

"Okay, now that we're off that horrid road, we can travel much faster."

"I am excited to see your Sanctuary and the endless fish." She smiled again.

"Me too." He turned and pulled out onto the paved road.

Chapter Eleven

Konner grinned when Terah hit the fourth button on the radio, trying to find more music. "We're pretty remote here, probably won't pick up anything else for a while."

She hit the first button again and looked at it.

It dawned on him that even the simplest things like a radio, that everyone took for granted would be a novelty for her. He looked forward to showing her all the many wonders in this modern world.

Glancing in the mirror, he was surprised to see a vehicle behind them. This early in the morning in such a remote area surprised him. He'd been so distracted by her; he wasn't sure how long they'd been there. When they got closer but made no move to pass, his gut told him this wasn't some local out early for work.

He turned off the radio. "Make sure your seat belt is tight and keep your head down."

Terah listened before she spoke. "Are they going to take me?"

The fear in her voice made him angry, that she would think that first. "No one is taking you." He took his foot off the gas, hoping he was wrong, and they were going to go around him. They sped up, coming dangerously close to the back bumper. He wasn't about to drive endless miles like this—if they wanted to try and overtake the van, he was going to make it seem easy for them and then beat them at their own game.

The truck pulled out and sped up, coming level with the back corner of the van. Konner braced for the hit he knew was coming. The van handled like a cement block, making it hard to counteract the force of the impact.

Terah leaned forward and put her arms around her head, protecting it. Smart girl, he thought just before the next hit. The sound of rubber sliding over the pavement echoed through the van.

He looked to see the ditch drop down along the road. Not liking the odds, he accelerated and jerked the wheel to the left, giving him more room to maneuver and keep away from the embankment. If he could toy with them long enough, they should be coming up on the part of the road that had been blasted to go through the rock formation.

"Take off your seatbelt and get in the back, so they don't see you."

She moved quickly without comment.

"Hang onto the bottom of the seat." He quickly glanced to see she was listening and then slowed just enough to make them think they had a chance of hitting the van again.

He could see the tall rocks ahead of them. "Okay assholes, catch up, I don't have all day." He pulled out further into the middle of the road, silently thanking the first god name that came to mind that it was a straight stretch and there was no oncoming traffic.

The truck accelerated; Konner watched it in the passenger mirror as it pulled up. "Hang on tight." The sound of metal from the impact against the back corner made him wince. "A few more hits, Terah, hang on." He wanted to at least reassure her that this was part of his plan.

He cursed quietly when he saw the section of rocks wasn't one of the long ones. Pulling back to the middle of the road, he made sure to give them more than enough room to pull alongside him again. To them, it would look like he was trying to move further away from them.

They accelerated, bringing it up almost even with the van. Konner kept it steady, making sure not to crowd them so they wouldn't realize what was coming. They were close enough to the mirror now, he could see there were two in the truck.

"Pleased to meet you," he whispered under his breath and let up on the gas, just slightly.

The window to do this right was small and he'd only get one chance. He counted it down in his head like he was on an operation. Just a little further. He gripped the steering wheel tight and watched as the front of the truck began to move in front of them. Jerking on the wheel, he drove the corner of the van right into the front tire of the truck. He stomped on the gas pedal and both vehicles slid across the pavement.

The sound of metal bending when the truck hit the rocks was loud to his sensitive ears. He was thrown forward against the seatbelt as both vehicles came to an abrupt stop. Slamming it into park, he glanced back at Terah as he reached down beside his seat for the dart gun. "Are you okay?" She nodded, a little dazed. "Stay here."

Getting out, he ducked down in front of the van and moved toward the truck. He had a few seconds to pull this off while they were stunned from the impact. Jumping up on the crumpled hood of the truck, he aimed the dart gun in through the shattered windshield and shot both passengers. When they slumped over, he lowered the gun and exhaled the breath he'd been holding.

That bought him some time. Hopping off the hood, he ran back around to the van and opened the side door. Terah was sitting right where he'd left her. "Are you okay?"

She nodded, an anxious look on her face.

"I knocked them out." Reaching across the floor, he picked

up the bottle she'd dropped. "Drink this, while I go see who our friends are."

She took the bottle. "I don't think they are friends, Konner."

He smirked, "not now they aren't." Leaving the door open, he went behind the van and alongside the truck. He stopped and looked at the van. "Shit." He'd not only taken out the truck but there was no way the van was going anywhere right now. The front tire was embedded in the bent wheel well of the truck. Shaking his head, he climbed into the back of the truck and hopped on the other side of it. Using all his strength he yanked open the door. The passenger was slumped to the side, there was blood running down his face, but he was breathing.

"Louis? Carl? answer me. Did you get them?"

He looked around to see a phone on the floor by the man's feet. Picking it up, he looked to see the call was in progress.

"Louis, answer me. What's your location, I'll send backup."

"We're fine." He growled quietly while holding it away from his face, then he hung up quickly. He grabbed the bag sitting between the men and opened it. Ammo, another phone, and some zip ties. He scowled at the unconscious driver. Jamming the phone in the bag, he slung it over his shoulder and then shifted the passenger so he could check for a wallet. None. Leaning down, he found a run pack on the floor. "That answers the question of who you are." He didn't open it, just started looking for a second pack.

He found it, two handguns and a map. He stuffed them all into the first bag. Climbing back over the truck, he went to the van stood on the road, and looked around. They couldn't stay here in case they sent more to look for them. Going over to the van, he set the bag down and opened it. Removing the chips and batteries from the phones, he tucked them both into one of the run packs and closed the bag.

Terah sat on the seat now, the empty bottle clenched in her hands.

"We can't stay here." He assessed her quickly, looking for

any sign of injury, "they could send more." He pointed to the duffle bag that held their water and other supplies. "Grab that," he glanced at her feet, "put your shoes on. I have to make a quick call."

Grabbing the phone from the holder, he hit redial and jammed the earpiece in his ear as he dropped the phone into his shirt pocket.

"Konner, I haven't even finished my coffee…"

"Someone tried to run Terah and me off the road." He knew Raymond would know exactly who Terah was.

"Where are you?" He could hear him running down the hall.

"Don't even worry about us right now. We just left the campground and they appeared when we hit the main road. They may not know where the camp is, but they're watching traffic. He went across the road and looked in the ditch. There was a culvert there to hide what they couldn't carry. "You need to get your team and S.O. to get the prince and princess out of there. Now."

He jogged back across the road and reached in and grabbed the case with extra supplies in it and jerked it out. While he was heading across the road, he looked to see what was around them. "I totaled the van when I ran them into some rock embankments, so we're going to head off into the bush and keep moving until you get the camp secured." He slid down the ditch. "I'm going to leave the Alliance phone in a culvert on the other side of the road, and have the tech team track it." He stuffed the case into the culvert, "along with anything we can't carry."

"Bring up Konner Flores's phone on the tracking system, now." He heard Raymond bark. "Get the team at the campground on the phone."

"We'll send someone for you…"

"Just get Devin and Rayne out of there, Raymond, we'll keep moving until you find where the hell these guys are." He reached the van and then paused, "they were on a call when it happened, I hung up, so we can't wait around for retrieval."

"Shit." He could hear the commotion in the background, "stay on the line, I need to talk to the prince."

Konner nodded and pulled out another bag from the van. He couldn't run through the bush with Terah, supplies, and his rifle. Cursing in his head, he set it to the side and grabbed another bag, "I need you to open the glove box," he pointed to where it was, "and put anything in it into this bag." He noted she'd put the shoes on. "We can't hang around for someone to come and get us."

Despite her eyes being wide, and panic filling her, she nodded and moved between the seats.

He pulled the med kit to the door and took it and his rifle across the street.

"Chopper is on the way to pick up the prince. Find somewhere to hole up and we'll..."

Konner shook his head as he slid into the ditch again, "we're going to keep moving. They could have camps all over this area for all we know." He wedged the rifle case into the other cases and then jammed the bag he'd taken from the truck in. "All of their identification is in a bag with the gear." He stood up, "Terah needs water sources." Climbing back up, he paused on the shoulder of the road, "we'll stay on a Northwest bearing, make it easier to find us later." He thought of the little girl Terah had picked up when she was scared. "Just get your teams to the camp and make sure nothing happens to those refugees."

"I'm on it." Raymond must have covered the mouthpiece because there were muffled voices for a few seconds, "how the hell are we finding you if you leave the phone we *can* track there?"

Konner jogged over to the van, "I guess you better send a good tracker." He closed the bag Terah had put the items into and looked around to see what was left. "I'll keep in touch, once we're deep in the bush."

"Just don't shoot my guys when they get there."

Konner shrugged, "tell them to walk heavily then." He held out his hand for Terah. "We're going to go; I don't know how long those tranq darts will keep them out."

"They're not dead?"

Terah took his hand and got down out of the van. Konner shook his head, "I thought you might want a word with them."

"Damn straight I do. Sink another one into them before you go." Raymond sounded amused.

Konner shrugged. "Will do." He hit the earpiece and ended the call. Taking it out of his ear, he picked up his swim pack and put it into it, then the phone as well. "Okay," he looked down at Terah, who was still oddly silent and still. "We're going to head into the bush while the Alliance comes and gets these guys." He motioned to the van, "and cleans this up." He held up the backpack with a few of the supplies in it. "I need you to wear this." He held it up and put one strap over her shoulder, it wasn't too heavy, so it shouldn't tire her too quickly. "I'll have to carry the water and my bag."

She nodded and put her other arm through it.

"I'll be right back." He ran around the van and climbed up on the hood of the truck. Pulling the dart gun out, he shot both of them again. "Rest well, boys." When he got down, he frowned at the road. "Shit." he climbed back up again, leaving two red darts sticking out of them would scream all the wrong things if any innocent one-forms got here before the Alliance.

Tossing the darts far into the bush on the other side of the road, he went over and put his swim pack over his head and then the heavy bag on his back. He held out his hand to Terah, "let's go find water." Closing the door, he reached in and pulled the map off the sun visor and then closed the driver's door.

Terah took his hand and looked up at him. "I know I'm safe with you."

He paused and looked down into those scared blue eyes. "I won't let anything happen to you."

Chapter Twelve

Konner checked the compass. He had a good sense of direction, but having Terah with him, he couldn't take a chance straying off course missing the next closest water source.

She turned and looked back at him, stopping because he did.

He pointed in the direction she was to go. He needed to keep an eye on her and check no one was tracking them from behind at the same time. They'd been moving for two hours, roughly, and in that time, they'd heard two helicopters. Konner hadn't been able to see which direction because of the canopy of the trees blocking his view, but he hoped one of them was taking Devin and Rayne away from the campground to somewhere safer.

Terah stumbled a few steps over some roots above the ground. Konner jogged up to her. "Let's stop for a few, I need to look at the map." He didn't really, but he needed to check on her. She hadn't complained once or said more than three words since they'd left the van.

Stopping, she slipped the backpack off and set it to rest against her leg. "It is hard to balance that and run." She motioned to the pack on his back, "you are used to it?"

Konner took the duffle bag off his back. "I'm used to carrying gear." He squatted down and opened it, scanning the area behind him as he did. Pulling out a bottle of lake water, he opened it. "Drink this." He held it up to her. "You have to stay hydrated."

Terah took the bottle.

"How are you doing?"

She took a sip and then looked around, "I like seeing all these trees," her eyes sparkled, "as I run by them."

Konner grinned, "once we get home, you can wander in them as much as you want." He opened his pack and took out one of the pouches of Biotrien and held it out to her, along with another bottle of water. Opening his swim pack, he checked his phone to see if there were any messages. There weren't.

Putting it away, he got a bottle for himself. That left six bottles. They'd have to reach water in the next few hours or Terah would start to weaken.

Tucking the empty bottle back into the pack, he went over and waited for her to empty the second bottle. Her skin still held a sheen, so she wasn't suffering too much. "We'll keep going this way until we find water and then I'll call and see if they know anything."

She swallowed the last of the Biotrien mix and held the two bottles out to him. "Are there more? Like those men on the road?"

He debated on lying to her but knew most of her life had been a lie. "Probably. That's why we're going to keep moving until we know for sure."

Terah searched his face for a few seconds and then nodded and picked up the backpack again. "I will keep going until you say no more."

Terah was sitting with her back to him, watching into the trees. She was taking keeping watch very seriously. Konner stripped his shirt off and then the absorbent vest, noting it was close to drying out. Setting it along the shore, so it would soak up water, he took off his pants. Checking once more, he saw she gripped the dart gun in both hands and held it in the direction she looked. Hopefully, some poor unsuspecting animal didn't wander into her sight.

Moving out to the deeper water, he dove in soundlessly breaking through the water. There was no pain or discomfort as his skin thickened with the thermal layer that was always present, just unseen. Closing his eyes for a second, he knew when he opened them again, he would see with his changed eyes, and he relished that feeling.

As he opened them, he stilled and took in the environment around him, searching for predators hiding beneath the surface. The vibrations in the water brought nothing threatening back to him. There were fish, and for that he was thankful. He needed to replenish and prepare for the long trek that might be ahead of them if the Alliance wasn't able to get to them tonight.

Moving fast, he swam to the farthest side of the lake and then tread close to the surface, so he could rise above the waterline and see what was on this side. He wasn't comfortable with where they had stopped. It was good for a quick break, but with the growth thick in that area, it left far too many possibilities to surprise them.

Floating effortlessly, he scanned along the shore of this side, there was a small clearing that would be an easier defensible location. After he called Raymond, they'd move over here and wait.

Turning soundlessly through the water, he spotted two deer along the shore where the river fed the body of the lake. He smirked, they had better stay in that area. Terah didn't take being startled well, as a few small creatures had found out while they walked. She had lightning-fast reflexes, and he'd only barely made it in time to spare their lives.

Swimming beneath the surface back toward her, he decided

they were going to have to have a long talk about killing off the ecosystem on land when they got back to the sanctuary. It was a delicate balance of natural predator and prey, each having their own roles to play in the thriving of the land that surrounded the large water system on the property. He couldn't have her killing everything that startled her either. Humor filled him when he thought of Lucus and Pax's reaction if they tried to sneak up on her.

Breaking the surface, where the water was shallow enough, he could walk back to the shore, he stood up. His webbed feet were used to standing and moving like man, but his ankles were not as flexible in this form. It may have looked effortless, but it was a precarious task of keeping his balance as he walked.

A shiver moved over his body as he focused to change back to unscaled skin. Even after all these years of shifting from one to the other, he still felt a loss once air moved over his sensitive skin.

Terah still hadn't moved from her perch on the boulder, looking into the bush. He picked up his pants and pulled them on over the water-soaked epidermis of man. He made sure he made enough noise that he wouldn't startle her and end up with a dart sticking out of him.

"That feels better." He said softly, knowing she'd hear.

Terah still looked at the area in front of her. "Something is moving that way." She turned the gun toward it.

Konner walked over, so he could see her face. "There's a few deer down there."

"Deer?" She looked up at him.

"They'll stay clear of us." He didn't have time to explain how deer would go to almost any lengths to avoid contact with man. Holding out his hand, he took the gun from her. "Thanks for keeping watch, I needed that swim."

Standing, she smiled at him. "It is a peaceful lake." She put her hand over her heart, "it felt," she frowned, searching for the word.

"Calm?"

"Yes. Calm." Terah smiled again. "I like feeling that more than the tightness that makes," she patted her bicep, "muscles hard."

Konner nodded, "being alert is good, but yes, it does get tiring after a while." He motioned to the bag with the empty water bottles. "Can you fill the bottles while I call and see where things stand?" He pointed to the other side of the lake. "We're going to move around to wait over there, it's a better location."

Nodding, she went over and picked up the bag. "How is it better?" She opened it and began to take out the bottles, setting them silently on the ground.

"There's a cleared-out spot, that will make it easier to watch if anything or one is coming toward us." He picked up his swim pack and opened it.

"Oh. Yes. That is good." She waved a bottle at the trees. "It is hard to see around those."

Konner sat on the rock, angling his body so he could keep an eye on her and watch for any movement in the trees. The direction the deer was, he kept to his back. They were a good alarm for anyone trying to come from that direction. Their hooves would alert him to anything near them as they bolted for safety.

He was both surprised and thankful that the signal was strong enough on his phone that the call would be clear. Watching Terah roll up her pant legs, he brought up Raymond's number and hit send.

"Flores?"

"Yeah."

"You're well?" He could hear voices in the background.

"We're fine. Just stopped to take a quick swim." Terah walked out past the point she'd rolled the pants up, making him grin that she'd even bothered.

"We got to the van and those two before their own guys, barely." He sounded amused, "you did a real number on the van I'm told."

Konner shrugged one shoulder, "it was the only way to stop them."

"I understand. Two of mine are waiting there to see if anyone shows up."

Konner's spine stiffened, "they still haven't?"

"Not yet, or they have a way of watching and know we were there."

"Any small drones in the area?"

"Only our own."

Konner rubbed his hand through his damp hair. "Have you found where their base is?"

"Not yet."

He remembered speaking into their phone. "It might be my fault." He checked on Terah again. "Why they're not coming. A call was still active, and I spoke, they had to have heard the crash though."

"We'll find them. We have enough bodies moving through that area now that it's only a matter of time."

Time. Konner looked at the other side of the lake. "We're going to move to the other side of this lake for the night." He stood up and looked in the direction they'd travel to get to it. "It will be too hard for Terah to keep moving all night."

"I can send..."

"No. Keep the teams on task, if I don't hear from you by morning, we'll keep going." Terah carried the full bottles to the shore and then picked up the remaining ones. Konner would have to show her they floated another time. "Prince and Princess secure?"

"They are." Raymond chuckled, "the princess had some strong opinions about being whisked away."

Konner thought of the peaceful serene Rayne and wondered what that would have looked like. "Just as long as they are safe and the grounds are secure, that's all that matters."

"Your roadside friends just arrived back here." His tone had a harsh edge to it.

"Good. Find out anything they know."

"I didn't bring them here to have tea."

Konner grinned. "I'll send you the coordinates of where we're stopping for the night." Terah was putting the bottles back into the bag now. "So, your men don't take us to be the enemy if they pick up our trail."

"I'd fear for their safety if they did come across you."

Konner watched her close the bag and then look down at the wet material against her legs. "They shouldn't be this far out; my gut tells me we need to be looking near the campground." He smirked as he thought of the new name for it.

"I'll send someone that way as soon as we can." He could hear the motion in the background. "Did you do that to this one's face or was it the impact."

"I didn't touch them." Konner's voice dropped, "there wasn't time."

"We'll patch him up and then have a chat."

Konner nodded. "We're going to get moving now."

"Stay watchful, my friend."

"Always." Konner hung up and checked the battery on the phone. He only had one spare with him and didn't want to risk not being able to get a call when needed.

Chapter Thirteen

Konner put the Biotrien back into the waterproof pouch. He only had twenty left. Hopefully, that was enough to do them until they got back to the Sanctuary. Setting the bag back with the others, he undid his shirt. He needed Terah at full strength throughout the night, just in case, they had to move in a hurry.

He paused as he was undoing the vest and listened. She was talking quietly. It was more under her breath, than out loud. Cocking his head to the side, he focused to hear only her and not the sounds around the lake as dusk settled before the night began. It sounded like a list of names she was reciting.

Shaking his head, he decided he'd let her continue, despite the fact she should be silent right now. If it was a comfort thing, he didn't want to take that away from her. Pulling the vest off his body, he walked over to where she was leaning back against the dried-out log. "I want you to put this on." He squatted down and held up the absorbent vest. "It will stay wet throughout the night."

She sat up, her gaze moving over it. She held out her hand.

Konner pointed to her jacket. "It needs to be right against

your skin."

"Oh." She got to her knees unzipped the jacket and stripped it off. When her hands went to the bottom of the shirt she had underneath, Konner lowered his eyes to the ground.

She may be used to being on display, but that didn't mean it was going to be that way once they got home. There she'd have the option of doing whatever made her feel comfortable.

"Turn around, I'll adjust it so it's tighter." He didn't look up until he heard the movement and knew her back was to him. Lifting his chin, he froze. Frowning, he reached out, almost in slow motion. There was a jagged scar that ran from the back of her neck down across the one side of her rib cage. He touched it lightly. "How did you get this?" None of his kind had scars. If there was freshwater nearby, anything could be healed. The fact that it marred her body, heated his blood with anger.

"At first, I refused to change and have their eyes on me." Her voice was emotionless. "They hit me with this long stick."

They'd caned her. Konner's hand shook as he held out the vest for her to put her arms through it. "Does it bother you?" She put her arms through it, "when you're in the water?" He leaned around and looped the velcro through the loops so it would overlap and close together.

"It feels different there." She said softly, "the water doesn't move over it the way it does the rest of me."

Konner clenched his jaw. That part of her would not be able to change in the water. Not only had they marred her body, but they had also prevented her from having full protection when in her true form. He pulled the strap along the back so the material would be snug against her skin. He would have to ask his Auntie if that could be corrected. If it wasn't too deep, they could remove the scar tissue and let it heal in the way of his people, under the surface of freshwater. "We may be able to," he cleared his throat that warbled with emotion, "remove this scaring..."

Terah turned and looked at him. "No. I want to keep it."

Her deep blue eyes stood out in the dim light of dusk. "To remember, always that I am no longer there." She nodded. Sucking in a deep breath, she looked down at the vest when as she ran her hands down over it. "What is this? It feels like my body when I'm swimming." She looked back up at him.

Konner leaned back on his heels, so he wouldn't pull her into his arms and vow to her that no one would ever harm her again. "It took a long time for the scientist to create it, so it felt natural." He blew out a breath, trying to move past the scar that was now going to haunt his dreams. "After many failed attempts that chaffed my skin or gave me a rash." He grinned.

"It feels wonderful." She smirked at him, "no wonder you seem to never tire."

"It will help you rest tonight." He stood up, "we'll have to wet it again in the morning."

Terah picked up her jacket and put her arms into it. She balled up the shirt and held onto it. "Thank you, Konner," she sucked in a sharp breath, "for keeping me safe."

He stood there, his heart pounding in his chest as he looked down to see those beautiful eyes drowning in unshed tears. "I always will." He whispered. "Try to get some rest, I'm going to keep watch."

Konner sat a few feet from the water and listened. The sounds of night echoed across the serene surface. He didn't have to strain to watch and hear if there was any movement in the bush. The creatures in their natural environment would alert him to anyone moving around that didn't belong.

Terah had drifted off to sleep finally. She'd recited those names again until there were long pauses between them as her body slowly relaxed. He'd wanted to ask her about them, but also wanted her to rest, so he'd held his tongue and just listened. It sounded like random names, but his gut told him she just wouldn't be saying meaningless names. They repeated over and over. Were they captives she'd met in her years of confinement? Perhaps those that had come to mean something to her? He wasn't sure, but he planned on asking her tomorrow.

In the low light of the waning moon, he ran his finger over the map and followed it along the path he planned to take tomorrow. To make good time, they'd have to avoid too many stops, so the two rivers that intersected along the way were going to have to do for water sources. If he had more Biotrien, they could take their time, but he needed to reach somewhere by tomorrow night, or the following day would be difficult for Terah. He looked up to where she slept, she looked comfortable enough. Her back was covered, but just knowing about the scar on her back made him snarl into the darkness. Nothing was going to interfere with her health—or freedom again.

Tucking the map into his swim pack, he pulled out the phone and checked it again for messages. He had the ringer off, so it wouldn't sound into the night and alert anyone to their being here. There were no messages. Rubbing his forehead briskly, he brought up Reeves's number. He didn't need his aunt sounding the alarm when they weren't there by morning. Opening the message screen, he quickly typed, *Slight delay in our travels. We'll be there sometime in the next two days.*

He didn't expect a reply and blinked when the screen opened to one. *Got it. Thanks for letting me know, Alvie has been looking over my shoulder half the day waiting for word.*

Konner stared at the phone for a moment before typing again. He should have thought of all of this sooner and had it done already, but he'd been so gobsmacked when he found out Terah lived, his thought process had faltered. *Have Olanna clear out the room beside the in-ground pool bed and move the boys to the other end of the house.* He paused, he didn't need Lucus and Paxton in her face all the time. *Terah has a long road of recovery ahead.* He frowned at the phone; he hadn't even thought of clothes either. *She's around Raelyn's normal size,* he smirked, right now being very pregnant, Rae said she was a beluga whale, *see if we can round up some clothes and things for her as well.* He curbed the inclination of mentioning getting in touch with a surgeon about her scar because she wanted to keep it. It was an awful way to remind herself of her freedom, but he'd respect it and later attempt to talk her out of it.

On it. This will keep everyone out of my hair. Lillee and Kisa have already made her about twenty welcome cards.

Konner smirked, picturing the girl's excitement over meeting a new member. He frowned at the phone and blew out a breath. *No one will be able to swim with her for a while. She is very aggressive and unsure of what outside life is.* Did that explain it? Partially, it did. It was true as well. If she'd never swam with any of her own in all these years, her instinct to protect would override anything else and the younger ones would be in danger until she understood what having a clan was about. He looked out over the water. He also didn't want any mating rushed if she were one of the others. Her body needed time to heal, on the inside. Sure, she was strong in spurts right now, but from years of neglect, she couldn't go a full day without water yet, so there would be no rushing a mating and children.

Okay. Look forward to meeting her. Reeves added three happy face emojis to that.

Guilt filled Konner, he remembered what it was like being that age, wanting nothing more than to find the one that would know him better than any other would. He hoped someday Reeves found that. Konner knew better than anyone what it was like to go decades through life alone.

Closing the screen, he put the phone back into the bag and closed it up. The entire clan was going to be watchful, waiting to see if her heartbeat was in time with one of the unmated males. In an absent gesture, he rubbed his hand over his own heart, wondering briefly what that felt like. Two hearts changing rhythm to sync up with one another. Blowing out a breath, he pulled the swim pack over his head and stared over to where she lay sleeping. Something inside him told him that things were going to be rocky for a while until she settled into her new life. Standing up, he moved soundlessly toward the trees, rest was not going to find him tonight, that he knew without a doubt.

Chapter Fourteen

Helping her secure the vest on, he'd avoided looking at the scar this time, because he needed to have a clear mind and not get bogged down with anger and thoughts of vengeance. He could feel rain in the air, so that moisture, even though rain was anything but fresh or pure now, would sustain him for the day.

"Those names you were saying last night, are they people you've met?"

Terah put her jacket on but left it open.

Konner couldn't help looking at the way her skin shimmered along the edge of the vest. Maybe it was because she was so new to freshwater, but it seemed as if her skin sparkled like no others he'd seen in years.

"No. They are who I came from." She went over and picked up the backpack and put it on.

"You know these off by heart?" He went over and picked up the duffle bag and put it over his shoulder. Adjusting the gun on his side, he made sure he could reach it without hindrance. When he looked back at her, she stood there with a strange look on her face.

"My heart doesn't know them, my head does." She stated with a straight face.

Konner smirked, "off by heart is a saying, it's not literal."

"Oh." She watched him for a moment. "Yes, I know them off by my heart." She smiled.

Konner rested his hand on his swim pack. She knew her history. If the names were in the records he had, he could trace her lineage. "Later, would you mind if I recorded them?" He watched her reaction, "I can look them up when we get back and see where your family was from."

"Record?" That was the only thing she said.

He nodded, "on my phone, it will record what you're saying so I can hear it later."

A shocked look appeared on her face. "Like the radio?"

He opened his mouth to explain, then just nodded instead.

"Okay. I will say them later to your phone."

His swim pack vibrated against his side. With quick movements, he got it out and answered it without looking to see who was calling.

"Flores," Raymond said as soon as the line was open.

"Yeah." Terah watched him carefully.

"We found them."

Konner turned and looked around them.

"They had it well hidden, deep in the bush. Used portable generators and signal boosters to communicate."

"How many?" He pulled out his map and knelt, so he could use his knee to open it up.

"Eight. Fresh from Tomas' idiot survival school."

Konner smirked at the amused tone. "Did they have anything on the camp?"

"They were narrowing down where it was. The prince was surprised they didn't know. Seems they had visitors there from Tomas when the princess arrived. I guess they kept their mouths shut, but—we got them just in time, thanks to you."

Terah came over and looked down at the map.

"Always happy to total an Alliance vehicle to further the

cause." He wondered if it would be taboo to ask Rayne about Aiden Tomas.

"Are you still near that lake?"

Konner looked down at the map, "just leaving it." He followed the river they were going to try to reach by noon. "If we keep going toward the river, we should be there by noon, then it's a quick trip in for our ride to get to us."

"Yeah, I see it. I'll send Tripp from S.O. to meet up with you at the river." He heard a radio squawk in the background, "you'll have to share the route to your place from there."

Konner folded the map and put it in his pack. "No need. We just need a lift to my chopper."

Raymond laughed, "someday you might have to share that chunk of oasis, my friend."

Shrugging, he pointed in the direction they were going to be walking. "I will be more than happy to share it when the time comes, you know that, but until then, let me enjoy my peace and quiet."

"I'm going to let you go. I want to prepare our best guest suites for our new visitors that will be here later."

Konner grinned, hoping they were able to get more information from the men that had been sent to get Terah. "Tell your man to announce his arrival when he gets there, surprises could be painful."

Raymond laughed, "I'll be sure to relay the message."

Konner caught up to her after he put his phone away. "We should be at the Sanctuary by morning."

She stopped and looked at him. "I can't wait to see it."

"Tripp will take us to the chopper, and it will be a lot faster getting there."

Frowning, she studied his face. "Chopper?"

"Helicopter," he pointed up, "we'll fly in."

Her brows creased. "I did not like the chopper to the camp."

Konner rubbed his hand over his jaw, "you weren't in very good shape then. This time I will be able to fly over the lake and land and show you."

She seemed to ponder this for a moment. "I want to see the lake."

Konner lifted his hand for her to start walking again. "We should get moving, the rain is going to slow things down."

Terah blinked, her eyes going wide. "Is that the smell in the air?" She looked up, "rain?"

"That's what it is." He didn't say there was a good chance it would turn into snow if the temperatures dropped enough.

"I've never been in the rain."

Chapter Fifteen

Konner watched Terah stop and lift her face to the sky, letting the rain splash against her face. It was something a child would do in a rainstorm, and it caused his chest to tighten with emotion knowing that she'd been denied the simplest things in life. She looked back at him and smiled, a pure genuine one of joy. He had no choice but to smile back at her. It was the first time he'd seen her without that guarded, watchful look in her eyes. He caught up to her quickly, "be careful, the ground is going to get slick with this much rain."

She nodded and turned her attention to where she was walking. "I like the rain." She said quietly, "I watched it before from a window, but I've never felt it on my face." Glancing up, she gave him a small smile. "It smells," she frowned, "fresh," motioning to the ground, "it is giving all life a drink."

Konner smirked, "I've never thought of it that way."

"I've had a lot of time to think." The words were tinged with bitterness. "I would watch and listen and think."

He caught her arm when she slid sideways on the uneven ground. "Listen?"

Moving with caution to check her balance, she only nodded

her head, while keeping her eyes on the ground. "When I was not in the water, listening is hard to do." She waved her hand beside her head, "the pains and uneasy feeling of my body make it hard to stop and just listen," she used a smaller tree to help get her footing up the lift in the ground, "but when I am in the water, in the glass *tank*," she said the word with a venomous tone, "They didn't know I could hear them like that."

Konner looked down to see her shoes were soaked and only going to get worse. The rain was pelting off them with such a force it would sting. She didn't seem to notice or care. "So, they talked freely around you."

Nodding, she paused and looked up at him, "if they knew I could hear, I don't think they would have changed." she shrugged one shoulder, "who would I tell what I heard?" Her eyes no longer held the joy from her first rain, they were now filled with the pain of memories.

He waited until they were on level ground to continue. "What are some of the things you heard?"

"Most of it," she slipped and grabbed onto his arm to right herself, "I didn't understand." She shook her head, "they talked about the strangest things, money and moving things?" She lifted her shoulders and let them drop again, "I only listened to learn words." Stopping, she touched his arm again and he could see the indecision in her eyes as she debated on saying something. "They would call me a mermaid." Her blue eyes searched his face, "is that what we are?"

Konner had this talk with young ones, more often than he cared to admit, especially with the movies that were out there now. The younger ones were often convinced that Raelyn, with her long red hair, proved the movie and mermaids were real. "Perhaps it was how we were referred to a millennium ago." He steadied her as they moved up the slope covered in thick roots no longer in the ground. "Once we were many," he paused thinking his Auntie would be thrilled to hear him tell the story that the elders had been telling for centuries, the stories of their people, "we filled the oceans and waters, across the globe."

Terah looked at him with wonder in her eyes, again reminding him of how much she had missed out on in life.

"As man or one-forms, that's what we call them now."

Turning her head quickly, she gave him a questioning look.

"Those that don't change into another form, we call one-forms."

She considered what he said and then nodded and continued walking.

"As the one-forms, took to the water for travel and hunting the creatures in the water, our kind moved from the salty bodies of water." He was trying to remember how the story went and hoped he didn't screw it up, lest his great aunt would smack him across the back of his head for it. "We moved inland, to the smaller lakes, with many shores." He pictured when he was a child, gathered with the other children of his clan as they listened to the animated tale their elders told them. "Over time, we learned to walk on land, to shed our bodies of the sea and be like man."

She watched him intently, slowing her steps so she wouldn't slip again.

"After a time, all things evolve." He said as he looked behind them and scanned the area. He trusted Raymond to find their base of operation, but that didn't mean there weren't more out there somewhere. "It's said that we once had no legs and only one long tail and fin to move through the depths of the oceans with great speed, but we no longer needed those to swim the lakes around the globe."

She stopped and looked up at him, hope clearly visible on her face, "are we still many?"

He'd hoped she wouldn't want to know that. Shaking his head slowly, he motioned for her to keep moving. "No. With hunting, and pollution, our numbers dropped to mere thousands over the centuries." Catching her elbow, he helped her right her footing before they continued. "Those numbers dropped more still over the years."

She stopped so suddenly, he almost walked into her, she turned to look up at him, "are the ones at your sanctuary the last?"

Konner blew out a breath slowly, he wanted to be honest but didn't want to fill her with the dread that haunted his every moment. "No. I don't believe so." He took her hand, needing to offer her some form of comfort as she digested this information, "with the way the world is now, with fast boats, sonars to look in the water, I believe our kind have learned to hide."

"Even from you?" She made no move to release his hand.

Konner smirked, remembering how hard it was when he found Olanna. "Yes, even from me." He motioned down his body, "we've adapted so well, we blend in and appear like the one-forms that have hunted our kind endlessly." He paused to look at how her skin glowed from the moisture of the rain. Most of his kind didn't do that unless they were completely immersed in the water, was it because she couldn't control the change? He watched her hands as she moved, she still had fingers, no webs. He had to find out her lineage because anything that surprised him, was something he had to look into.

"The man that kept me, he said there was more, he was working on getting them."

Konner felt her grip tighten in his hand. "We'll find them." He vowed quietly."

"If we're not mermaids, what are we, Konner?"

He looked down at her, and debated on letting go of her hand, but found he was enjoying holding it, so he didn't. "Mermaids had many names in many cultures—they're too numerous to list off." She slid sideways and if he hadn't been holding her hand, she would have hit the ground. Without complaint, she righted her footing again and began walking. "Water spirit is probably my favorite of all of them."

"Water spirit," she said slowly like she was tasting how the words felt on her tongue.

"We're referred to as the water clan, or water shifters with the Alliance," he smirked when she looked at him, "it simplifies explanations."

The serious note in the depths of those blue eyes held his own gaze prisoner for a brief moment. "I want to be a water spirit."

He thought of how she was in and out of the water, the glow she had, the fact that she was intact and whole after the life she'd had. "You are probably the purest form of a water spirit that I've seen in decades."

She smiled, fleetingly, "decades?"

They began to move. Konner noted that the compliment he'd just given her went unnoticed, which was probably for the best, he couldn't afford to have attachments to her. She could be someone else's mate and that, he'd learned the hard way was a painful thing. "Ten years is referred to as a decade."

"You have seen a lot of decades?" It wasn't a jab at his age, and he was thankful for it.

"I've seen enough." He didn't know if she understood the most basic of facts about their people. "We can live a long time." He thought of his Auntie, he wasn't even sure how old she was. "With constant exposure to the right water and nutrients," he patted the pocket that held the Biotrien, "we age very slowly."

She stopped and looked up at him. "How many decades am I?"

Konner glanced around them again, just checking to be sure they were still alone. He looked back down at her, "I have no idea."

She frowned.

"I'm hoping we can figure that out once I get home and look at the records." She watched his mouth as he spoke, he knew it was from the habit of doing that in the water, through the glass, but it unnerved him. "We know your mother was carrying you when she was taken, so that should help narrow it down." He left off the part that if it wasn't written down if her clan hadn't kept up the records, they may never know.

"These records will have my mother in them?" She nodded slowly, "I will talk to your phone now." She leaned closer and patted her hand on his chest.

Konner had forgotten all about asking if he could record the names she recited. He watched the rainfall for a moment; he hadn't even realized it had lightened considerably. Licking his lips, he nodded. "Okay." Releasing her hand, he opened his swim pack. "I'll hold it inside my jacket, so it doesn't get wet.

"Your phone doesn't like water?"

He smirked, "most electronics don't."

"That is too bad." She nodded and watched him open the screen on his phone as he brought up the voice recorder.

"Just say them as you normally would." He told her and then hit record.

Terah took a deep breath and then exhaled it. She closed her eyes, and began to talk softly, "I am named Terah Matthews," she licked her lips, "of Markus and Elise," her mouth curved in a relaxed way, "who came from Dayne, Jillian, and Jack, Nora." She blew out a soft breath, "they were of Xavier, Willow, and Percy, Carolyn."

Konner was mesmerized at the tone of her voice, the serene look on her face as she continued. This was her family line, there may be no last names, but mated couples were recorded and as she continued, he realized he would be able to trace it at least four generations back, maybe five if it were recorded by the clans then. Some of the records were only written from elders' memories, so accuracy wasn't a guaranteed thing.

"Did I do it right, Konner?"

At the mention of his name, he blinked to come back to the present. Her voice, her tone like that was almost hypnotic. He stopped the recording and nodded. "You did."

She looked at him, then at the phone, "can I hear what I said?" Her eyes were wide with excitement.

Nodding, he hit play on it and made sure the volume was

up. He watched her face as she listened to herself speaking the name of her ancestors, she was breathtaking. The look of fascination and pure joy stole the air from his lungs for a moment. He stopped it and wiped the phone against the inside of his jacket. "I better get this out of the wet." He put it in the pack and then inhaled the air around them. With a smirk, he looked down at her. "Have you ever seen snow?"

"Out the window." She gave him a curious look.

Konner grinned, "the temperature is dropping, the rain has slowed," he looked around them, "you may get to see snow before we're picked up."

The animated expression on her face, made him smile. "I want to taste the snow." She nodded and started walking again.

Konner watched her for a moment. Seeing everything as she did was making him feel less aged because some of the time, he felt haggard and tired. Wiping the water from his face, he started after her. As soon as they stopped, he was messaging Reeves to look up her parents' names, with luck, he'd know how old she was then and could at least offer her that. He frowned, part of him didn't want to know, how young she really might be.

Chapter Sixteen

Konner forced himself to look at his phone instead of Terah. She sat on the riverbank, trying to catch a snowflake on her tongue. They'd reached the river about an hour ago and both had gone for a quick swim, to eat.

After the rain, the water was rushing and loud. Terah had been thrilled to swim in fast-moving water. Konner had been terrified and stood on the bank like a watchful father making sure she didn't run into trouble against the strong flow. He shouldn't have worried, wouldn't have with any of the other adults of his kind, but his overprotectiveness with her was hard to control. Considering what she'd been through, the very fact that she was still alive, and they had found her was nothing short of a miracle—he was allowed to be cautious.

Grinning at him, she slipped off the rock and went over to the tree to touch the bark the snow was clinging to. It wasn't cold enough for the snow to stay, not yet, but she was still fascinated and elated that she got to see it.

Forcing his attention back to the phone, he re-read Raymond's message. His guy should be here within the next hour. Closing that message, he opened one to Reeves. He wanted him to start looking through the clan books to see if he could find a mated pair, Markus and Elise. If he could find that, he'd have a starting point at least. He could just wait until he was back there later today and look, but he was anxious, excited, and very motivated right now.

After he hit send, he looked to see Terah standing in the cover of the trees, her hands braced around a man's head. One quick move, with her strength, and she could snap his neck. The expression on his face said he was both surprised and slightly annoyed at the predicament he was in. Konner checked out what he was wearing, it was Alliance-issued gear. "He's here to help us, Terah." He said, trying to keep the smirk off his face. She'd gotten the jump on one of the S.O. guys. He couldn't wait to relay that.

Tucking the phone in his pocket, he continued to sit. Terah slowly released the man's head and jumped down from the log she'd been standing on. Now Konner regretted not paying more attention to what was happening around them. How had she managed to get behind him and get him like that?

The man rubbed his hand along his jaw, giving her a cautious look as she moved in Konner's direction. "That will teach me for letting my guard down and approaching strangers." He grinned, "you have a job on our team anytime you want, sweetheart."

Terah came over and stood beside Konner. "Do I need a job?" She looked from the man down to him.

Konner shook his head, "No you don't." He stood up and motioned to the other man, "especially not on the Alliance Security team."

"I'm not one of them," he smirked, "Special ops."

It dawned on Konner they were both lucky he hadn't reacted to being grabbed and hurt her. He inclined his head to him.

"Tripp Carson." He saluted Terah in a casual move.

"I am Terah Matthews," she said, straightening her spine as if she expected him to deny who she was.

"You guys had one hell of a trek to get this far." He pulled the beanie off and squeezed the water out of it. "I felt like I was chasing my tail a few times with the rain."

Terah leaned over and looked behind him. "You don't have a tail." she touched Konner's arm. "I am going for another swim before we *trek* again." Turning, she pulled the shirt over her head and started to take off her pants.

Tripp turned his back to her.

Grinning, Konner went over and stood beside him. "She was born there, so she doesn't understand clichés and sayings at all."

Tripp nodded but kept his gaze at the trees. "I'm glad she's out." He turned his chin and smirked at Konner, "strong little thing."

Konner nodded, "I'm afraid that is at the expense of all the fish in the campground's lake." He gave him an earnest look, "thanks for not hurting her."

Tripp shrugged his shoulder, "I'm thankful she didn't hurt me."

"How far out are we from your ride?"

Tripp turned with him when Konner looked back to keep an eye on Terah. "Forty-five-minute hike to the SUV, I left it in a little town."

Konner nodded, "it's about an hour and a half to my chopper from there."

Tripp smirked, "I hope you fly better than you drive. The van had to be towed."

Konner watched him track Terah with his eyes. "It was the only way to stop them before we landed in the ditch."

"They slept all the way back to the center." He motioned to the water. "She's not even struggling with the fast-moving water."

Konner watched her for a moment, as she smiled and swam against the rushing water. "As I said, she ate a lot of fish." He knew it wasn't just the fish that had helped her, the fish ate the plants and various other things in the water. It had taken a decade of research to figure out it was the plant life and not the aquatic life that sustained them best.

"I'm going to let my team leader know that I found you." He gave him a blank look, "the river wasn't exactly precise coordinates."

Konner nodded and picked up the bag with the bottles of water in it. Terah floated along the top and watched their every move. He questioned whether she used a swim as a way to observe and not be near them. She had spent her entire life being excluded from everything going on around her. Observing probably felt safe to her.

Terah watched as the other man, Tripp, walked back into the trees. Her heart was still beating fast. When she'd watched him approach Konner, her only goal was to protect him. She didn't even know she could move that fast until she was holding his head in her hands. Letting her body go under the surface, she closed her eyes and let the water brush over her. She liked this moving water; it was exciting to be in.

Opening them, she looked up to see the snow touching the water's surface. Snow was strange, it tasted like the rain had, only it vanished when it hit her tongue. If it disappeared, how did it pile up on the ground? For years, she had watched winter from a window and wondered what it would be like to go stand in it. The people would move it with scoops on a handle and she wondered if it was heavy. The most interesting part of it was after winter it turned into water and then the ground drank it like it had an incredible thirst. She needed to see more snow to figure it out.

Breaking the surface again, she moved closer to the water's edge. Konner was putting the bottles back in the bag. That would mean they were going. Kicking against the pull of the water, she went back over to the edge and slowly climbed up the bank.

Konner was right there, holding up his vest. "You should

wear this again." He set it beside her clothes and then stepped back. He watched her, his green eyes moving along her as she reached the top and stopped beside them. He never looked at her like those men that watched her had. They all had a strange look on their face when she would get out of the tank and her skin returned. The way he was looking at her, was not like that at all. His glance was respectful and something else, she wasn't sure of the word, but it made her feel special.

When he turned and went over to stand with the other man, she put the vest on and then her clothes, moving fast. As much as she liked being out here and free, the pit of her stomach reminded her that she wasn't safe yet. Konner nodded to something the Tripp man said. He would keep her safe, she felt that when he said it.

Pulling the shoes back over her feet, she cringed at the way they pinched her toes together. How did they wear them all the time? It was uncomfortable, made her feet feel heavy, and her balance off. She looked down at them as she straightened up. Maybe once they were at Konner's Sanctuary, she wouldn't have to wear shoes again. She would be very happy with that.

Konner came over and held out the backpack. "Tripp will lead, we'll follow him."

Putting her arms through the straps, she nodded. "Okay." She looked over at the other man, "I am walking with you," motioning with her head to Tripp, "he smells strange."

Konner's mouth curved into a smile. "He's some sort of cat, I believe."

A shiver moved along her back. "There is something about the smell that sends," She moved her hand up and down her arm, "a strange feeling along my skin."

He didn't question her, she liked that about him. "It's likely that you're sensing how dangerous he is." Leaning closer, he zipped her coat up for her, "he's part of the team that goes in when no other team will."

She frowned and looked over at him. "It is your team that found me." She nodded, giving him a hard look. "I am staying with you."

Konner looked down at her, the expression in his eyes changed, "yes you are." He motioned for her to go. "We're going to have to go into a town where he left his ride, so stay close."

Terah nodded, her stomach tightening. The idea of being around people bothered her. "Can I wait, and you come and get me?"

Shaking his head as he swung the large bag to his back, he turned to look at her. "No. We stick together."

Chapter Seventeen

For the whole ride in Tripp's vehicle, Terah had been nervous. She sat in the back watching out the windows, afraid at any moment that someone would come after her again. That fear was the only reason she got on the helicopter with Konner. She was trusting him to keep the large thing in the air. In front of her were so many switches and things all lit up, she didn't know how he knew what each of them was for.

He gave her something called a headset to put on and currently it was trying to squish her head, but it was better than the loud noise the machine-made. Terah didn't know where to look, by her feet was glass, beside her as well, her stomach did funny things when she looked down to see how far in the air they were. She could feel the vibration of the machine in her chest, it felt like it was humming through her entire body. Terah couldn't wait to feel the ground beneath her feet again.

"How are you doing?"

She turned and looked at him, he sounded like he was inside her ears with this thing on her head. "I don't think our kind were meant to fly."

He smirked at her, "you get used to the feeling." Motioning to the window beside her, he pointed, "I'm going to circle around, so you can see all of the Sanctuary."

"We are there now?" She gripped the side of her seat, trying not to show how scared she was.

"We're coming up on it in a minute." His gaze moved over her face for a second, before he looked back in front of them. She didn't know what he watched, there was nothing there but air. It seemed to her they were even too high for the snow to fall up here, which was silly, it came from the sky.

Turning, she looked out the window, careful not to put her body too close to the glass. Below them, as far as she could see were trees. She liked trees; she had been surprised to find each kind tasted different. Rayne had explained it when she found her licking the bark of the many kinds at their campground, it had taken Terah a while to understand. Like there were different types of people, and shifters, each had their own scent, as the trees did.

"You'll see one of the rivers that run onto the land shortly."

She listened to his voice in her ears and sat straighter, looking for the river. Swimming in the river had been fun. "There is more than one?"

"There are two larger ones that run through. We use that water for our in-ground pools, to keep the water fresh."

Turning, she looked over at him, to see he was watching the air in front of them still. "In-ground pools?"

He glanced at her and then looked down at the things in front of him. "We have a few that are in the houses and a bigger one for the young ones."

Excitement filled her; she couldn't wait to meet the others that were like her. She had spent so many years thinking she was the last female of her kind. To know there were more after all this time, made her want to laugh and cry at the same time, which made no sense.

"When we clear this ridge, you'll see the lake."

Leaning closer to the window, she looked down. The motion of the trees beneath her didn't bother as much this time. She suspected it was because of seeing the lake she would swim in.

"The whole Sanctuary is fenced in from the point." He turned the helicopter, making it hard for her to see this fence. "No one gets on the property without us knowing."

She didn't take her eyes off the land below. As the lake started to appear beneath them, her heart sped up. It was much bigger than the one at the campground. They flew over something that looked like a big swimming pool.

"That's the fishery." He cleared his throat, "and no you can't swim in there."

She grinned, even though he wouldn't see it because she was now leaning, her face almost pressing against the cool glass. When he turned to follow the lake, she noticed several buildings below. They were close together with one large one in the middle. "How do you make all the buildings? I see no roads."

"There are a few narrow roads in, you can't see them because of the trees from here."

Terah turned to see he was focusing on what he was doing and not looking at her or the area beneath them.

"My clan owns a construction company, so the building is not an issue."

"I don't have any money." She hadn't meant to say it out loud, but it was true, she had nothing that was her own. Her stomach felt like it was rolling inside her as he took the helicopter closer to the ground.

"Once we find out which clan you're from, you may have a lot more than you think."

He turned it as it went down. She gripped the seat tight, afraid to talk and disturb him as he did this. There were so many trees around them, that she didn't want to distract him from getting them back onto the ground.

When the machine met the concrete, Terah released the breath she'd been holding. She watched him pushing buttons and doing things on the panel in front of him. The whirling slowed.

When he sat back and turned to look at her, she knew they were safely on the ground. "What do you mean I might have more than I think?"

Konner pointed to the headset he wore, then took it off.

She took hers off quickly and was glad the pressure was off her head.

"When clans started vanishing, I traveled to all of their locations and gathered up all of their paperwork and records."

She frowned; she didn't understand what this meant.

His mouth moved to form a small smile. "I'll be able to look up what clan you're from and the portion of their investments that helped build everything will become yours." He motioned to the door beside her as he opened his own. "I took all of the money and properties and," he smirked, "part of this," he moved his hand toward the area around them, "and all of our companies are yours."

Terah got out of the machine. Her legs felt funny when her feet were both on the hard surface that covered the earth. Before she could recover from that, he stood in front of her. She really didn't understand what he'd said, except for one part. "You can find out about my family?"

Konner nodded his head slowly, then turned to get the bags out of the helicopter. Terah had no family—that she'd ever known. Only her mother. To her family were the names she said each night before sleep and any time she was scared. The sound of a vehicle had her spin around to see a black truck come out of the trees. She stepped back and hissed.

"Easy. He's here to pick us up and take us back to the complex."

"Okay." She nodded, but inside, her heart felt like it was going to beat out of her chest. A tall man got out of the truck and smiled at Konner. He was almost as big as him but had short black hair and his eyes were a darker green.

"Malachi." she turned and looked at Konner as he spoke, "this is Terah."

Her head snapped back to see the man coming closer. He

was smiling at her.

"I was expecting weak and frail," his smile got bigger, "you are not either of those." She watched his eyes move as he looked her over. It made her feel uncomfortable. When he was closer, he held out his hand to her.

She looked at it and realized she was meant to clasp it with her own and shake it. She didn't know what the significance of this was or why people did it. With a quick look at Konner, she decided she would do this strange custom and try to abide by the rules she didn't understand.

His hand was cool when she placed hers in it and closed her fingers around it. She didn't know why, but she had to check his scent and store it in her memory—instinct told her to do it and she never ignored that.

Gripping his hand harder, she jerked her arm and pulled him closer. Reaching up, with her other hand, she took a hold of his short hair and yanked his head down closer to her. With her face close to his neck, she inhaled. There was a scar there, a different scent inside it. She released his hand and hair at the same time and stepped back. "You have a female." She looked at his neck where the mark was. Turning, she looked at Konner, who had his hand over his mouth. His eyes looked like they were smiling.

"I have a mate, yes." The man, Malachi, said as he rubbed the side of his head.

"I can smell her from your scar." Terah didn't know what the female had done to him to put her scent inside him. She frowned, did the scar on her back smell like the man that had done it?

"It's a mate's mark." Konner was watching her with that look in his eyes, the watchful one.

Had she done something wrong? "A mate's mark?" she looked at his neck, she didn't remember seeing one when he had his shirt off. "It was done on purpose?"

Konner grinned at that. "Yes. Raelyn, his mate, has one as well."

Terah had been in her tank for the human mating rituals. In those, they gave each other a ring. She didn't understand that at all, what good was body adornment that you could lose? A mark made sense to her. She turned back to Malachi again. "Are you good to your mate?" She knew nothing about mates and what it involved but had seen enough mistreated females during her life. She was not going to stand for it happening ever again.

Malachi's mouth quirked, "she'd beat me to a pulp if I wasn't." He sobered, "I adore her, I need her more than my next breath. My children and she are the most important thing in the world."

Terah gasped, "you have children?" Her heart sped up again.

"We do. Our daughter Lillee is thirteen and the baby is due very soon."

New life. Terah had experienced that when the women kept with her had babies. They'd always be afraid or sad until their little one was born. New life changed everything. "I want to see the children." She looked at Konner. "I tried to have babies, but it never happened."

Konner exchanged a look with Malachi, his jaw was tight. "You can meet everyone, just," he glanced over at the other man, "don't grab people," his gaze met hers again, "like that."

Terah sighed. "I don't know about the clan," she waved her hand around, "things." She hated not knowing and never understanding. "I don't know what is good to do and what is bad."

"We'll all help you." Malachi took the one bag from Konner. "Just ask if you don't understand.

"Thank you. I will." She took the other bag out of Konner's hand and walked toward the truck. Her stomach was dancing inside her. She couldn't be sure if it was nervousness or excitement, but it wasn't fear and any feeling that wasn't fear she could handle having.

Chapter Eighteen

Konner opened the door and held it so Terah would go inside. "This is my house. It's big because most of the clan end up here."

He watched her walk in slowly and tried to see it the way she would be for the first time. Pointing to the left, "the common house is through there."

"Common house?" She stood there; her hands clasped in front of her. Her expression was apprehensive.

"It's where clan meetings and gatherings are held." He set the bags down and moved out of the hallway, hoping she would follow. "At the other end of it is where our Alpha lives."

She took small tentative steps out into the open area. "The Alpha is the leader?"

Konner nodded, "yes, and also is my great aunt, Alviva."

Terah looked down at the dirty shoes on her feet and then reached down and took them off her feet. She didn't set them by the door, just held them in one hand. She closed her eyes for a moment and then looked down at the floor. "The floor is stone."

"You won't find wood or carpet flooring in our homes."

He grinned, "we're more inclined to love the cool dampness beneath our feet." He swept his hand out encouraging her to move out into the main area of his home.

When she did, she stopped, then looked at him with wide eyes. "You have a pool in the middle of your home."

Konner turned to look at the round stone inground pool that was in the center of the house. "For those days I don't have time to go for a swim." He went over and knelt and put his hand in, "it's fed by the river water, so it's always fresh."

Terah came over and sat down beside it and put her hand in it. When she lifted it to her mouth to taste the water, Konner was reminded again that something as simple as freshwater had been withheld from her for most of her life. She leaned down and investigated the water, "how did you get the river in here?" Lifting her head, she glanced back at him, "I see it moving, how does it do that?"

"The lines were run under the house." He stood up and offered his hand to her. "The tubs in the house have fresh-fed water as well," he shrugged, "Or heated water for actual bathing."

Terah placed her hand in his and allowed him to help her to her feet. She pulled her hand away immediately and looked around. Moving around the pool, she walked over toward the big open kitchen area.

Konner had opted to have a long island in the open area instead of a table and chairs. Often some of the clan would end up here throughout the day and evening, so this allowed for many to sit around the island instead of having to have a dozen chairs taking up the space. Most of his kind preferred open concept homes to small rooms. He knew he felt better without walls too close to him. You couldn't swim in the freedom of the lakes and feel okay within the confines of a house.

"It is so big here." She stopped at the island and then turned around and looked at him.

"I like open space." He pointed to the door down the hall to the right. "Offices are through there." Turning he looked back to her, "the door on the other side of the kitchen goes to the medical wing."

"Medical wing?"

He shrugged, "we've mostly used it for research up until now. The vest you're wearing, the mix you add in your water."

"You are a very smart man." she smiled at him.

Konner shrugged, "I'd love to take all the credit, but it's taken many minds and companies to come up with these things."

"You are still smart." She turned in a circle and looked down the hall.

"The boys' rooms are down there." He paused to wonder where they were, "they were sharing a bigger room, but I had them clear out so you can use it."

"I have a room?"

He wasn't sure if it was excitement or fear he saw on her face. "And your own bathroom, with a large tub."

"A tub with fresh water?"

He grinned, "yes."

"I might never get out of the tub." She came back around the island. "At the houses, I stayed at the others would let me lay in the tub for hours," she sighed, "it was a good thing most of them had more than one bathroom."

"Well, here you don't have to share a room or a tub."

He pointed to the door beside the exit to the common house, "that's the entertainment room." He could tell by the look on her face she didn't know what that was. "It has a tv, gaming console. It's good for relaxing."

"Does it have a pool too?"

Konner grinned, "no, water and electronics don't mix well."

She nodded her head slowly, her facial expression saying she didn't understand that.

"Would you like to see your room?"

Her face lit up. "Yes, please." She rushed around the pool, and back to the entrance to grab the backpack with the clothes Rayne had given her.

He walked slowly, allowing her time to run her hand along the fine stone wall. "That's my room," he pointed to the door on the other side of the hall, "and this is yours." He stopped beside the door and opened it. Standing on the outside, he allowed her to go in first.

When he went in behind her, he was taken back that the room had been not only cleaned but decorated in deep turquoise colors. How had the clan had time to do this in two days' time?

"This is just for me?" She gave him a quick look over her shoulder, "it's huge." She went over and touched the bed, then jumped back as it moved beneath her hand.

"It's a waterbed." He went over quickly and pushed on it, so it rocked.

Terah leaned down and lifted the cover, "the water is inside it?"

Konner nodded, "most of us have adapted to sleeping on a normal mattress, but," he grinned, "it's nice sleeping with the weightless feeling and motion the waterbed offers." He stepped back, "go ahead, try it."

With hesitant moves, she sat down on the very edge of the bed. "It feels," she lifted her weight and bounced on it, then giggled as the wave from her movement rocked her. Laying back, she closed her eyes and let her body sway with the motion. "I like this." She opened her eyes and looked at him, "It's like sleeping in the water, but I'm still dry." Sitting up, she stood up and looked down at the bed again. "The water stays *in* the bed?"

Konner nodded slowly, "yes, or we'll have a huge mess." He remembered when Lucus and Paxton thought using theirs as a trampoline would be a good idea. Rubbing the back of his neck, he looked out the window, wondering where the terrible duo was and who they were annoying. He watched her go over and open the door to the closet, then she just stopped and stood there looking at everything hanging in it. "I wasn't sure of your size but asked the women to round up some clothes for you."

She spun around, "these are for me?" He nodded. Turning back, she ran her hand over the material of a few items. "I will have to thank them for this gift." She set the backpack down in the bottom of the closet. "Are there rules here to staying dressed, like at the camp?"

Konner bit the inside of his cheek for a second, trying to figure out how to say it. "We do have young ones here." Those were really his concern, "and a few teenage boys, so keeping somewhat dressed is a good idea."

Terah nodded, "Yes. Okay, I will stay dressed unless I am swimming." She made a face, "the suit Rayne gave me feels strange after I have changed in the water."

Konner understood that he'd gotten into the habit of swimming with shorts on when the young ones were around. Mostly to avoid questions he didn't want to answer about anatomy and various other topics in the area. The males of his kind bodies underwent more of a change than the women and explaining how his body changed to reflect that he didn't relish.

Terah went over and opened the bathroom door. She gasped and went in.

Konner leaned against the open door.

"This tub is so big." She stepped inside it and turned to look at him. "All of me will fit."

"That's the idea."

She put her hand over her mouth, her eyes swimming in unfallen tears. "All of this is," she waved her hand around. "I don't..." She was visibly shaking now.

Konner moved over quickly and pulled her to the edge of the tub, so he could wrap his arms around her. "I know this is a lot to take in." She was trembling. "It's going to take some time for you to adjust, to having freedom and settle into life here." She rested her face against his chest, her hands gripping his jacket.

Moving back, she looked up at him. "I never thought I'd be free," she whispered.

Konner brushed the silky hair back from her face in an absent movement as he looked into the depths of her ocean blue eyes, he saw so much pain there it made his chest hurt.

"Whoa, guess that answers that question."

They jolted apart to see Lucus and Paxton standing in the bathroom doorway, big grins on their face. Their timing, as always, was bad. The clan called them day and night, for good reason. Lucas had pale blond hair and Paxton's was jet black. "What question was that?" He stepped back from Terah, taking her hand so she could get out of the tub.

"If she was old or," Paxton grinned and looked at her, "not."

"Sorry, Uncle Konner." Lucus blushed, "Malachi told us to stay out of sight for a bit so she could settle—"

Paxton nodded, "but no one said how long a bit was."

"Oh," Lucus lurched forward and held out the handful of flowers to Terah, "all girls like flowers, right?"

Konner looked at the fresh flowers and knew immediately the boys had been where they were not supposed to go.

Terah took them, a stunned look on her face. "T-thank you." She said softly and raised them to her face to smell them.

Lucus shrugged and jammed his hands into the pocket of his hoodie. "Yeah."

"Terah, this is Lucus," he motioned to the fourteen-year-old and was entertained to see his cheeks go a dark red, "and Paxton." Paxton didn't blush, he just grinned at Terah with that look in his eyes that sixteen years old got when looking at any woman they deemed hot.

Terah smiled a shy smile at both. Clasping the flowers in one hand, she went over to Lucus and touched his cheek. He was a few inches taller than her, but Konner knew he'd grow to be much taller in the next year or so. "You are a boy, but so close to a man soon, I think." She told him quietly.

Turning she looked up at Paxton and made no move to go near him. "Uncle Konner?" She looked back at him.

Konner shrugged, "not by blood, but I've been looking

after them since they were babies." He knew by the look in her eyes, that he didn't need to explain that their parents had gone missing. He looked the boys over, "so, what's this about painting Nolyn's door pink?"

Lucus dropped his head forward and looked at the floor.

"It was meant to be a joke," Paxton sighed, "you know, pink is the new black." He shook his head, "she didn't see it that way."

As hard as he tried not to, Konner smirked. "Has she forgiven you yet?"

"Not hardly." Paxton looked at Lucus, "we have two essays due now that we didn't have a week ago."

"You can read?"

He turned to see Terah looking at Paxton. She was chewing something. With shock he couldn't hide, he watched her pull a petal off one of the flowers and pop it into her mouth.

Paxton, with his eyebrows almost in his hairline now nodded. "Yeah." He glanced to Lucus, whose expression was similar.

"You can teach me," she said and put another petal in her mouth.

"You're not like one of those vegans, are you?" Paxton asked her.

"I don't know what a vegan is." She chewed the petal and swallowed it.

"They don't eat the meat of animals or products." Lucus supplied for her.

Terah smiled, "I am not a vegan then."

Konner cleared his throat and leaned down to talk to Terah, "the flowers were to be put in a vase and looked at."

She frowned and held the flowers out from her. "But when I smelled them, I knew I could eat them." She flicked her eyes from them to look up at him, "what good is just looking at them?"

Konner opened his mouth to explain, then decided she made sense. Straightening, he looked at the boys, "you were in the greenhouse."

Lucus' eyes went wide, and he turned to look at Paxton.

Paxton shrugged, "wildflowers are dead now, and," he shrugged, "we thought it would be okay because it was a gift to welcome a new member." He grinned wide, "it's a bonus she's hot and not old."

"I don't feel hot."

Konner squeezed the bridge of his nose and shut his eyes for a second. When he opened them, he noted the boys were both looking at Terah, confusion plain on their faces. "Terah doesn't understand a lot of things we do and say," he watched both of them turn to look back at him, "so we're going to have to help her and explain things when she has trouble understanding them."

"You really can't read?" Lucus asked after a long moment of silence.

"No, I can't." She shrugged and pulled another petal off, "my only purpose was to swim in a tank and look vicious when I was told to." She put the petal in her mouth.

Konner watched the look of horror, that he felt, reflected in the boy's expression. They were born free and despite wanting to strangle them more than not, Konner had insured they always have their freedom.

"We'll, uh, teach you how to read." Paxton glanced to Lucus, who nodded.

"Yeah. We can help you, for sure." Lucus looked up at Konner, his eyes were glossed with emotion.

"You two go get your chores done," he didn't need to ask if they were, because they never were until the third or fourth reminder, "I have to take Terah to meet Auntie Al."

Chapter Nineteen

Konner waited until Terah had taken in the size of the large common room. To most, it would look more like a cafeteria with long bench tables and many seats around it. There were only thirteen, he glanced to Terah, fourteen members of the clan, but when the room had been built, he'd made sure it was large enough to hold three times that number if needed. Someday, he reminded himself, he would see that all the chairs in this area were filled with his own kind.

Terah went over and opened one of the double fridges, then gave him a happy look. "So much food."

"We eat together at least once a day." He shrugged, "discuss businesses and things."

"I don't know how to cook." She stated with a look of shame on her face.

"That's fine, a few of us don't do very well either, but there are other things that can be done to share the workload." He turned when the door to his aunt's living quarters opened. Aunt Alviva Flores moved down the hallway, her cane tapping the floor with each step she took. She didn't need a cane to walk but decided at her age she could use any accessories she liked. Personally, he thought she used it because liked to threaten the boys with it when they stepped out of line. They didn't know that she would never strike them, regardless of what they did. Alviva valued life too much to ever threaten it. Especially young members of their kind that she hoped would slowly rebuild their numbers.

The entire clan knew this was their mission now, but no one, except for his aunt spoke of it. Repopulating a clan was heartbreaking, to say the least. The expectations with each new member they found meant silent prayers that they were someone's mate and in turn, would have a chance of bringing new life to the clan.

He watched his aunt assess Terah as she approached her. Turning, he watched Terah look over at him and give him a hesitant look. He held out his hand to her and was pleased she came over and put her hand in his. He knew that she didn't know the protocol, as he was sure his aunt did, but he still meant to show her a proper greeting for an alpha.

"Auntie." He bowed his head down and left it there for a few moments. "It is my pleasure to introduce Terah Matthews to you." He looked at Terah and couldn't help feeling a moment of pride when she bowed her head politely to her new Alpha.

"Everyone calls me Aunt Al or Alvie, child." Alviva smiled at her, her green eyes sparkling with a look that Konner hadn't seen in nine years, not since he'd brought Reeves home.

"Auntie Al." Terah's voice shook with a nervous vibration. "I love your braid."

His aunt smiled wide at that and lifted the long braid that was greyer than brown now. It hung past her waist. "I get one of the girls to help me with it now." She smiled, "lest my arms go to sleep trying to work all this hair into it."

"It's lovely." Terah smiled down at her. "I can help you with it if you like sometimes."

"I would love that, child." She inhaled a deep breath, her eyes moving down the length of Terah. "It does my heart good to see you well and free."

Terah nodded, "I thought I was the only female of my kind left." she admitted.

"You have seen men of our clan?"

Terah nodded, "not for some time, but yes a few."

His aunt moved just her eyes to look up at him. She didn't need to speak the words; he knew exactly what she wanted from him. "I'll find them." He said in a quiet tone.

"I know you will, nephew." Nodding, she turned back to Terah, "while everyone is here meeting you, I'm going to go sneak in a quiet swim." She smiled. "I will see you at dinner, child, I look forward to getting to know you."

"Thank you for letting me come here," Terah said quickly.

His aunt stopped and nodded, "this is your home, and will be the home for all our people when we've found them." With that, she turned and walked back toward the door.

Terah watched her go and didn't speak until she'd gone in and closed the door. "Is she all right?" She glanced at him quickly, "I don't see that her legs aren't working well."

Konner smirked, "she can probably still outswim all of us, but walking on land does bother her joints now."

"She is in charge? And is a female." There was a spark of something in her eyes.

"With the water clan, our Alpha's are always female, Terah. Always." He smirked when he saw the surprise on her face. Some other time, he'd explain the reasons why, but for now, he'd let her feel empowered knowing that females were not caged and used for amusement in the real world

"Are other clans like that?"

He shook his head, "no, at least I don't think there are clans that are specifically male or female leaders."

"Our kind is special." She said quietly and then turned and looked at the door when it opened.

Konner went over and caught up Kole as he raced across the floor. He was six and had endless energy. Kole giggled put his hands-on Konner's head and messed up his hair.

"You're back."

Konner grinned, "yes I am, and I think you gained ten pounds while I was gone."

"Mom says I eat too much."

Konner leaned down and set him on the floor, holding the child still by his shoulders, so his back was against his legs. "I want you to meet Terah."

Kole looked up at her. "Hi."

Terah dropped down to her knees in front of him. "What's your name?"

"Kole."

She smiled at him, "hi, Kole. Let me guess how old you are," Konner was surprised to see the stress melt right from her expression as she made an exaggerated face and tapped her finger against her jaw. "Seven."

Kole shook his head. "Six."

"Six? Are you sure? You're really big for being six."

Kole grinned and nodded. "Do you have kids?"

Terah shook her head, "no. There were some boys where I was staying though. You're as big as one of them, Indy and he was eight." She gave him a wide-eyed look.

"I'm going to be big like my daddy," Kole told her.

"Yeah? How big is your daddy?" She turned when Kole pointed to Auburn. Terah smiled at the boy, "that's really big. I think I'll meet him now, okay?"

Kole nodded and then took her hand as she stood up and tugged on it to go over to where Auburn and Olanna stood.

"This is Terah." He told them like he had known her all his life.

Terah offered a brief smile to both. "Hello."

Olanna gave her one of those brilliant smiles, "I'm Olanna, and this," she motioned to her mate standing tall beside her, "is Auburn." Auburn inclined his head, a watchful look in his eyes. "And our daughter Nakisa."

Terah turned to look at Kole's sister, and the smile was genuine and real this time, "hello, Nakisa." Reaching toward her, she touched the tips of Kisa's long wavy hair, "I think you are close to changing into what we really are." She removed her hand away from her, "I would like to do your hair with the flowing flowers and songs of the sea, as my mother did for me on that day—" she gave Olanna a hesitant look, "if you want."

Konner straightened, his gaze meeting Auburn's briefly, both were old enough to remember the rituals that their clans used to perform, but it hadn't happened in years. Terah was from an old clan deeply rooted in their traditions. Konner glanced toward the door, hoping Reeves got here soon, so he could ask about the records.

Nakisa nodded and looked to her mother, "I'd like that," Olanna nodded, "please." She smiled at Terah.

Terah's smile brightened again, "we will plan that." Putting her hand to her mouth, she turned and gave Konner a quick look and he saw the emotion in her eyes. He didn't know if they were happy tears forming or something more, so he went over to her quickly, so he was close in case she needed him.

Terah sniffled quietly, then smiled at Kisa, "I'm sorry, I'm just so happy." She looked over at Kole, then back to her, "I thought I was the only one left."

Nakisa launched herself into Terah's arms and hugged her. "I'm glad you're here."

Auburn looked at him again, the look said to intercede before they had more than one emotional female on their hands. Konner grinned; Auburn would go to any lengths to not see a woman's tears.

The sound of boots clicking on the floor echoed in the silence of the moment. Konner turned to see Nolyn coming into the room. Her hair was even shorter than when he'd left, as it now stood straight on end only a few inches long. She was one of the few women that wore makeup, and the black of it made her blue eyes the focal point of her face.

"Terah," he touched her shoulder, as Nakisa released her, "this is Nolyn, she teaches all the children." A job Konner was thankful he didn't have to do.

Terah turned and took in the black clothes she wore and then paused on the boots on Nolyn's feet. "I like your boots." She smiled at her, "you must help me to know how to wear shoes." She made a point of looking down at her bare feet. "I never had shoes until I met Rayne." She gave her a helpless look, "and I have trouble moving in them." She glanced over her shoulder at him, "Konner had to help me a lot when we were running through the trees to get away from the men who broke the van."

Terah's bare feet were forgotten as all eyes in the room zeroed in on him. Konner hadn't planned to tell anyone of their adventure getting here. He shrugged it off, "they tried to run us off the road."

"Where?" Auburn moved to stand in front of his family.

"When we left the campground." He held up his hand, "priority was to get the prince and princess out of there, so we went into the bush until the teams were called in."

"That's why you were late?"

He turned to see Reeves standing behind Nolyn now, his grey eyes giving him a hard look, "I thought you were sightseeing or showing her the outside world."

"He did." Terah's posture stiffened. "Beautiful lakes and rivers." She elaborated in his defense. Her gaze narrowed in on Reeves, and Konner recognized the cold look in them, it was the same one she'd had on her face when she'd held Tripp's head in her hands.

"We were perfectly safe the whole time." Konner put his hand on Terah's shoulder, so he'd hopefully be able to stop her if she went for Reeves. "In fact, Terah got the jump on one of the Special ops guys when he came to pick us up."

Reeves's annoyed look changed to a wide-eyed one.

"I did not know if he was a friend or not." Terah looked up at Konner, "I am not going back."

Reeves smiled at her, "that is a story I want to hear sometime," he jammed his hands in the pocket of his jeans, "how you got the jump on him."

Terah's expression changed to confusion, "I did not jump at all." she shook her head, "I was behind him."

Reeves laughed, "that's still pretty amazing."

Konner watched to see the cold look was gone in her eyes. Reeves had undug the deep hole he'd started. "Terah this is Reeves."

Terah went over to him and held her hand out to him. He could see by her face that she didn't understand why she was doing it, had seen the confused look on her face when Tripp had done it to her, but now she was copying it.

Reeves took her hand in his and shook it.

Konner held his breath waiting to see if she did the same thing to him as she had Malachi.

Terah didn't release his hand, and from the look on Reeves's face, she was gripping it hard. "You do not have a female." Terah let go of his hand and motioned to his neck, "you have no scar."

Reeves sent Konner a quick shocked look, then looked down at her, "uh, I'm not mated."

Konner had to put his hand over his mouth so no one would see the grin. On the phone, Reeves had been so excited about another woman in the clan, he'd thought it had been for a chance to find a mate, then why did he now look like he wanted to throw up and the thought of having one? Konner was certain Reeves would avoid swimming with Terah at all costs.

Reeves backed up a step and jammed his hands into his pockets again, "when you get a second, boss, I have the plans for the Elden clan for you to check over before I send them."

Konner nodded, "I'll come to look later."

Terah turned her back to Reeves and went back over toward Kole.

With long strides, Konner went over to him, "have you checked the records for those names?"

Reeves shook his head, "every time I start it, the phone rings." He raised his eyebrows, "we have a lot of jobs to get

145

done before the snow is ass deep."

Konner rubbed the back of his neck and then turned to look at Terah, he wasn't about to leave her here and go look right now. "Tread carefully around her." He said in a hushed voice, hoping whatever Nolyn was saying to her she wouldn't hear him. "She was ready to snap the ops guy's neck before I got involved."

Reeves's expression sunk to one of shock. "Okay, I'll make sure everyone treads carefully around her for now."

Konner nodded, "no one swims with her for now either."

Malachi walked in holding Lillee's hand. Each time Konner saw her, he was shocked by how much she was changing. He knew children grew, but she was only thirteen and was looking more like she was twenty now. Her raven black hair was now down past her waist, and she had dark green eyes and he hoped they continued to hold that innocent look. He didn't blame Malachi for being protective of her, if she were Konner's daughter, he'd forbid her from ever leaving the house. He also admitted that would never work with Lillee, she had her own opinion on how things were going to be. He watched her tug her hand out of her father's and go over to Terah, an animated look on her face.

"I was so worried you were going to be old," she glanced over her shoulder at her father, "and all about rules and stuff, but you're so young and pretty."

Terah smiled immediately, her gaze assessing the young woman in front of her. "Thank you." She reached and touched Lillee's hair, "your hair would look good braided, with flowers in it."

Lillee's eyes lit up with excitement. "Yes."

Malachi came over and stood beside Konner and Reeves. Auburn stayed over behind the women, ever watchful.

"Raelyn will be here shortly."

"Is everything all right?" Konner worried about her pregnancy more than he admitted. There had been a lot of miscarriages and complications over the years. He wondered now that he'd met Shaelan if speaking to her would yield anything useful. She seemed eager to learn and thorough in her research.

"Yeah, she just doesn't like any of her clothes right now," he smirked, "or her shoes, or the weather," he grinned at Konner, "all of which is a good sign that the baby is coming soon."

Konner nodded. It should have been a joyous time and it would be, once the child was here and well. He watched Olanna laugh at something Nolyn said. "They're going to have to help her a lot." He said more to himself than the men.

"And be careful." Malachi rubbed his hand over the side of his head. "When she grabbed me earlier, my heart stopped."

Reeves looked from him to Konner, "she grabbed you?"

"Your mate is here," Konner jerked his chin toward the door. He'd known Raelyn since she was born and knew every expression she had. Right now, her expression said she was excited to meet a new water clan member, but also that she was exhausted and could have an emotional eruption at any moment.

When he turned to check on Terah, he saw she had already noticed another person coming in. She walked, with slow steps toward Rae, a look of wonder on her face. It was good she liked children, he thought, especially considering the entire clan would eventually look to her to bring more into it.

Raelyn held her swollen abdomen with one hand as she accepted her mate's other hand. Malachi leaned down and kissed her on the cheek and said something quietly to her.

When Terah stopped and looked across the room at him, Konner moved to go stand with her. He wasn't sure what the look on her face meant and that worried him, that she wasn't easy to read, and very unpredictable.

"Terah, this is my mate, Raelyn." Malachi smiled down at her.

Raelyn smiled, then wiped at her cheek. "Ignore me, I'm emotional about everything lately."

"It's hard work creating life." Terah told her in a soft voice, then she smiled and motioned to her belly, "can I touch?" Her face lit up with joy, "I love little ones."

Rae nodded and swatted another tear off her cheek.

Terah reached over and lightly touched the rounded stomach. Then she dropped to her knees in front of her and leaned her face closer. Konner was a step from taking her elbow and helping her back to her feet when she started to hum, her mouth close to Raelyn's stomach. It was almost the same as the song she'd used on the hurt girl at the campground, but a few notes were altered.

Konner looked around to see all in the room could hear the song and the gobsmacked looks on their faces said it all. They affirmed the wonder he'd felt himself when she'd first done it. There was something about her, something from her mother, or clan, he wasn't sure, but he had to know.

Terah stopped and smiled up at Raelyn as she leaned in and put her ear against her stomach and did it again.

Konner checked to see Rae had no problem with what Terah was doing. She smiled up at Malachi and looked happier than he'd seen in months.

When Terah stopped, she leaned back on her heels, "they are very happy in their mother's loving body." She dropped her hand away and stood up. "Thank you for letting me do that." She shrugged, "some of the women I was with said that always helped them feel better when their little ones were close."

Raelyn nodded; her eyes filled with tears again.

"I'm sorry, did you say *they* were happy, as in more than one?" Nolyn came over and looked from Terah to Raelyn's belly.

"Yes. There's two of them." Terah clasped her hands in front of her throat and smiled at Raelyn, "you are so lucky."

Raelyn flipped her long red hair back from her face and looked up at Malachi. "Two?"

Malachi dropped to his knees in front of her and placed his

ear against her belly. Everyone watched him.

"You need to sing to them," Terah said softly.

Malachi's brow creased as he looked at her.

"Like this." Terah leaned over so her mouth was closer to the pregnant belly again. She hummed a few of the notes, then motioned to Malachi, who placed his ear against his mate's protruding womb once more.

Konner watched his eyes widen and knew that whatever Terah was doing, the babies inside were responding.

"Oh my god." Malachi dropped back onto his heels and looked up at his mate. "I can hear them. Two very distinctive vibrations."

Raelyn put both hands on her stomach now. "I don't know if I can do two." She gave Konner a panicked look. "One is hard enough to get here alive."

"I don't understand." Terah straightened and looked at Raelyn.

Malachi got to his feet and hugged his upset mate against his chest. "It's rare to carry the baby to term and often things don't go well during the birth."

Terah spun around and looked at Konner, a terrified look on her face. "You need to call Shaelan, she will help."

Konner looked from Terah to Malachi, his expression was just saying to do something. Raelyn was clinging to him. Losing one child was hard, if she lost two, she would never survive it. Nodding, he pulled out his phone. "I'll see what Calum has to say." He realized he didn't have his number, He glanced around at everyone, "we'd have to bring Calum and his mate here," he gave Rae a quick look, "she can't travel."

"She's very good." Terah nodded and smiled at Raelyn, "I don't think I would have lived if it weren't for her."

"I say we forego voting and ceremony and just do it, call her," Olanna said looking around at the adults. "

Konner glanced around to see all of them nodding. He turned to Reeves, "go let Auntie know what is happening." He motioned with his hand around the room, "we'll meet back here for dinner, I'm sure Terah would like to clean up and rest." He held his phone up, "I'll get in touch with Calum."

"Calum Dante?" Reeves clarified.

"Yes."

Reeves nodded, "I hear he's like some kind of superman in the Alliance."

Konner smirked, "he's the man you always want on your side, and his mate," he turned to Malachi, "is a brilliant healer that we could use right now."

Malachi looked down at Raelyn.

"Please get her here." She whispered.

Malachi scooped her up into his arms like she weighed nothing. "We'll be back for dinner." He kissed Raelyn's forehead, "you need to go float in the pool and take some of that weight off your spine."

Lillee ran over and all but leaped into Terah's arms. "Thank you. If it weren't for you, we would never know." She leaned back and wiped her hands over her eyes, "you need to teach me how to sing like that."

Terah had a shocked look on her face. "Of course, all of our kind should sing."

"I have to go see if mom needs anything, I'll see you at dinner." She released her and bolted out the door.

Chapter Twenty

"So, I'm just supposed to stand in your house like a statue and watch her?" Reeves looked at the open door again.

Konner smirked, "you could sit. I just don't want her to come out of her room and not know where I am." He took off his jacket and tossed it on the chair behind his desk. He hadn't even paused long enough to change his clothes yet. "I don't need her wandering out in the bush and getting lost on the first day she's here."

Reeves grimaced, "okay, I see your point. I'll go hang out and try to look like I have a purpose there."

Konner waited until he left the room to go over and set his phone on his desk. He brought up Illias' number. He'd know how to reach Calum. He hit send and then put the phone on speaker. Going over to the table, he looked at the records that Reeves had carefully set on the hard surface. Some of the pages were fragile with age, so he'd done well not letting the sides of them touch the others sitting there.

"Do I want to know how you still have your own phone, Konner?"

Konner smirked and opened the first book, "ask your

151

teammate, Fallan about it sometime."

"Ah, okay. So at least it's secure. I momentarily seized when your name came up on the screen."

"Sorry to alarm you. I'm told it's very secure and safe to use." He leaned on the table and looked at the list of names. They were faded. He really needed to get these records transcribed onto a hard drive or something less fragile.

"Oh, it is, I tried to track it—you know, just 'cuz I can. What can I do for you?"

Konner straightened up and went over and grabbed a notepad and pen. "I need to reach Calum Dante."

"Everyone wants Calum Dante when they call me, how come no one calls to ask how I'm doing?"

Konner grinned, "I'm sorry, how are you doing, Illias?"

"I'm fantastic, thanks for asking. I'll get his number and text it to your spy-proof phone."

"I appreciate it. Any more ops soon?" He looked at the books on the table.

"Everyone is scrambling and going through that information they found, if it pans out, we could be busy for a long time, so enjoy your downtime."

"I plan to." It was a lie, if Fallan turned up anything, he would be going there without pause or without asking permission.

"I gotta go, we're getting close to finding some—details." The line went quiet.

Raising an eyebrow, he looked down at the phone, hoping he remembered to send him that number. Tapping the screen, he brought up the recording of Terah saying the names. He'd remembered the first three or four, but not all of them.

He wrote quickly, trying not to be distracted by the tone of her voice as she spoke to them. If he could find even one or two of the mated couples that were in her family tree, he'd know where her mother came from. When he wrote down the last one, his phone buzzed with the message from Illias.

Exhaling, he hit the number to dial it and then went around

the desk again. He hoped the records went back that far or had been updated. Scratching his head, he wondered if he should start as far back as possible or to more recent years.

"Hello?"

"Calum, it's Konner Flores." Setting the list down, he glanced at the last four names and started scanning the information for them.

"Everything is all right?"

"Yeah." He turned the page. "We're back at the Sanctuary now."

"I heard about your adventure."

It shouldn't have surprised him that Calum would. "It wasn't the trip I had hoped for, but we managed."

"I always wondered if Aiden's goons he sent after Rayne had told him where the campground was, I guess they knew better than to share the exact location."

He looked over at the phone. Some time when there wasn't so much going on, he needed to find out more about the princess's connection to Aiden Tomas.

"I'm guessing you're not calling just to chat."

Konner smirked and turned back to the books, "no, I'm calling because I need your mate's help."

"With? Is Terah all right?"

"She's fine." Konner turned the page, "stronger than I thought." He smirked, "she got the jump on Tripp when he came to retrieve us."

"I doubt that. No one gets the jump on Tripp Carson unless he wants them to. He comes across as all laid back and relaxed but make no mistake, he's lethal."

"Noted." He checked the list he'd written again and decided he needed to look for all of them, regardless of how far back the records were, there was no way of knowing if Terah had the order correct. "One of my clan's women is pregnant, near the end actually."

"Hang on, I'll go put this call on speaker for Shae."

Konner nodded but said nothing as he hovered his finger

just shy from touching the fragile page. Turning the page, he noticed some spots were so faded, that he was going to have to work on getting them copied sooner than later.

"Okay, Konner."

"Hello, Konner."

"Shaelan, hi." He straightened from the table and looked at his phone. "I was wondering if you have any experience with pregnancies and delivery."

"What's going on?" Her tone changed to something less cordial.

"One of my clan is due soon and Terah," he shook his head, "I don't know how, but she sang one of our songs to Raelyn's belly and heard two babies inside."

"That's fascinating."

He grinned; she wasn't wrong. "That's not the issue, although once everyone calms down, I need to ask Terah how she did that." He frowned and looked at the floor, "our kind haven't been able to use their vocals out of the water for generations," he shook his head, "okay skipping all of that, the survival rate of our children is low and now with two..."

"Can she be transported?"

Shaking his head, he went over to his desk and leaned on it looking down at the phone, "no, she's due any time now." He cleared his throat, trying not to let the emotion through, "listen, we have our own medical wing here, complete with ultrasound and just about any other gadget you could want." He stood up and crossed his arms over his chest, "but we have no one that knows how to use them."

"I have a little experience with ultrasound, I mean, I'm not a qualified technician or anything like that..."

"I'd like to bring you here, even if you can assure Raelyn that all seems well, it will go a long way in calming her down..."

"That's a long trip," Calum mused.

Konner shrugged, "not if I fly you in." He went over to the map on the wall beside the window, "I just have to land close to somewhere to refuel the chopper."

"You have your own helicopter? That simplifies things."

"It does." He grinned. "Where are you now?"

"We're at Blair's now," Calum said in a quiet voice.

"Which reminds me, I have the plans for his projects somewhere on this desk. Tell him I'll get them to him in the next few days." He glanced at the books, then back to the map. "While I have you, the children found when Terah was, they're all fine?"

"They're actually here, Konner, and very well adjusting to life here."

He nodded his head slowly, "I'll let Terah know."

"I need to make some calls." Shaelan sounded anxious now, "are there women from your clan that has had successful deliveries?"

"Yes, not in six years, but there are a few." He focused on the phone.

"Okay, good I'll need to speak with them." She said something he couldn't hear. "I'll let you men discuss travel arrangements. I'll see you soon, Konner, and tell the mom-to-be that I will do everything I possibly can to get her little ones here."

There were muffled voices for a moment. "She'll know everything about childbirth before we get there." Calum's tone was filled with amusement.

"Sorry if I blindsided you, Calum, I know you were probably looking forward to some downtime."

Calum laughed, "until every shifter within the Alliance's reach is healthy and thriving, Shaelan is not going to allow for downtime."

"I don't recall any times of hearing you were on holiday either."

"Guilty." He chuckled. "You can land at Ed's; we'll make sure there's fuel for you and whatever else you may need."

Konner found the location on the map and tapped his finger on it. "Is tomorrow good?"

"Doesn't sound like we should delay it too long if the birth is soon."

"I'll message you with my ETA later on." He looked at the books, "I haven't even had a chance to shower and change since getting back."

"We'll be ready."

"Thanks." Konner hit the hang-up button. He had a lot to do in the next twenty-four hours. Picking up the phone, he text a quick message to Malachi telling him that the doctor would be here by tomorrow night.

Tossing his phone on the desk, he went back over to the list. If he had to spend the rest of today looking up those names, he would. Terah could do things that his people hadn't in decades, he wondered for a moment if they'd just forgotten how to do them or if it was some other reason. Grabbing the chair from in front of the desk, he dragged it over to the table and sat down. If he could just find one...

Closing the second book, he heaved a deep sigh. Eight more to go.

"I just went to see Raelyn."

Konner twisted in the chair to look at his aunt standing at his door. She could be very silent when she wanted to be, confirming once again that she really didn't need the cane she always had with her. "How is she?"

"She calmed when Malachi said the healer would be here tomorrow." She held his look, with that expression that said he should have discussed it with her before doing it.

Turning completely in the chair, he held her look. "The healer is the mate of Calum Dante, and the entire Alliance trusts him, so we can safely bring them into the Sanctuary."

"I've heard that name before." She came in and went over to his desk and leaned against it. Konner knew better than to offer her a chair. If she wanted to sit, she would.

"He's the one that finds people and does a lot of things specifically for the king." He didn't even know how to explain

Calum.

"And his mate, the healer?"

"Terah wouldn't have survived if it weren't for her fast action when she was found." Getting up, he went over to his bag and opened it. Reaching in, he pulled out the crumpled folders. They hadn't been his priority. He tossed the folder with the information found on his desk and held the other one to her.

With a focused look she took it and opened it. He didn't need to offer any explanations; he could tell by the expression on her face when she saw the photos of Terah that she was feeling the horror their clan member had gone through.

Her eyes were glossed with unshed tears when she looked at him. "We owe the prince a lot of fish for his lake."

"A small price to pay." She closed the folder and set it on the desk with great care. "Has she seen others of our kind?"

Konner nodded, "some. Most died off when she was young," he clenched his jaw for a moment, "saltwater." He knew those two words would cover all the details she'd need. "They tried to breed her with males," her eyebrows shot up, "out of the water." Relief filled her face. "Also, there are more out there, they were working on acquiring some the last she heard."

His Aunt pushed away from the desk. "Do we know where?"

"Not yet, the Alliance is working on finding them." He motioned to the other desk, "journals and ledgers were found, but it's in some sort of code."

She nodded, looking from the folder to the books on the table. "Is that why you're going through those?"

"No, actually." He went back over and picked up the list. "Terah's mother taught her to memorize her family tree." He held it out, "she rhymes it off like a mantra when she's frightened," he shrugged, "if we can find the names in the records we'll know where she's from."

"She sings the songs of our people. Raelyn said the babies

responded to it."

Konner held the piece of paper out to her, "I know, and that's why I need to find out which clan she came from," he motioned to the map on the wall, "so I can go there and test the water, plant life..."

She held up her hand to silence him, "I can't say for most of these names, but I do recall Xavier and Willow," she glanced at him briefly, "they're not common names." She motioned to the books, "you will find those in Raelyn's family tree."

Konner looked at the books, he hadn't thought to start in their own clan books. "So, part of her line was from ours?"

"A long time ago, before the splits, I believe." She stared at the floor, her expression hard, "I could be wrong, but I think Raelyn's mother's sister mated a Matthews."

Konner grabbed his clan's book and set it carefully so it wouldn't touch the others, he flipped through the pages as fast as he could manage without causing the paper stress to find Raelyn's family. The names were there. Beside them were notations of other clans the line came from. "Holy shit." Hovering his hand over the volumes, until he found the one, he was looking for, he carefully shifted it free of brushing against the others and opened it. Without an ounce of respect, he reached over and plucked the note from her hand, and glanced at the names. Opening the volume, he skimmed the page, then flipped back to the next one. He wanted to shout when he found the names, Gregory, and Blythe. "She's from two alpha lines," he waved the piece of paper around, "that were joined to strengthen the clans." He felt like someone had just smacked him in the head.

Turning around he looked at his aunt. "I'll write out the details later, but not only is she Rae's distant cousin, but she's also from strong alpha lines."

"I don't think it's her breeding that allows her to sing, Konner."

He blinked, bringing her back into focus, "how do you mean?"

"I think it's because she doesn't know any better." He frowned at her. "She didn't know her people, or if there were others of her kind, her mother had to have taught her and it's what allowed her to stay strong all these years. Over the years, our kind repressed our natural instincts and abilities to survive, to blend in—Terah hasn't done that." She pointed to the books on the table, "once you calm down, find her mother and if there's any information about her mating or pregnancy, so we can at least tell her how old she is." She nodded her head, and turned toward the door, "and I'll allow the healer here because those babies are the most important thing right now."

She walked out of the room, suddenly needing to click her cane on the ground again. Konner blew out a long breath and looked back at the books. He wanted to go check on Terah, but he admitted his aunt was right. Terah deserved to know how old she was. He sucked in a breath and wondered how emotional Rae was going to get when she found out that she had a living blood relative. He chuckled, everything, even a cup of juice made her emotional right now. He shrugged and went back over to the books.

There was something deep inside him, that he was going to have to take a serious look at soon. He felt protective of all his people, but Terah—she was different. Was it because of how she had lived, not knowing her own kind? He wasn't sure. It could be because there was something more about her than the others he'd found over the years. She knew so much of their people, yet had never been outside a day in her life. He tapped the pen on the table and looked at the books. Not now, but soon he had to search a bit inside himself and figure out the whys.

Chapter Twenty-One

Konner glanced at Malachi, he was watching his mate and his expression said he wasn't sure what she was thinking either.

"We're family?" Terah sat forward on the chair and looked from Raelyn back to him.

"Distant cousins, but yes you are."

Terah turned to Raelyn, "I don't know what that is. Cousins."

The shocked look on Rae's face faded and was replaced with a smile, "the details don't really matter." She took a deep breath and then blew it out and changed positions so breathing would be easier in her condition, "any family is important right now." She looked at Konner and nodded as if asking him for clarification.

"That's true." There were so few blood connections in their clan. "From the other side of Terah's family tree, her great, great grandparents on her father's side we from two different Alpha lines."

Malachi's head jerked around to look at him. "I read something in one of the journals that they were discussing doing that to strengthen the lines, hoping to hold onto more of our natural traits." He looked at Terah, his eyebrows raised, "I guess that worked." He smirked, "your song," he shook his head slowly, "some of us have never heard it out of the water."

Confusion filled Terah's expression; Konner could see her trying to puzzle out what everyone was saying. She looked away from Malachi and back to him, "I don't know what that means." Her brows puckered, "to be from two Alpha lines." She said slowly, tasting the words as she spoke to them.

Konner leaned back in the chair, now that Rae's reaction had settled, he didn't feel the need he may have to spring into action. "Well, at this point, it means you hold stock in the assets that have been held in reserve for those two clans." He gave Malachi a quick look, "as there are no others here from them."

"Assets?" Terah was gripping her own hands tightly as if she was wringing them dry.

Konner nodded, "I took all of the clan's properties and sold them, then put the money from the sale into trusts and," he shrugged, "invested most of it in companies that we've started. You have a lot of money."

"I don't know what I would need money for."

His heart was breaking, watching the lost look on her face. She had no knowledge of money or any dealings that were normal outside of captivity. He gave her a brief understanding smile, "you don't need to worry about it right now. Later, we'll get into it, and I can explain."

Her gaze locked on his face for a moment and then she nodded. "When I can read." She glanced to Raelyn, then Malachi, "Lucus and Paxton are going to teach me." She looked quite pleased with her announcement.

"That's wonderful." Raelyn smiled, "it will also give them something to do." She looked up at her mate that sat on the arm of the chair, watching her, "maybe talk to Nolyn," she turned back to Terah, "she'll have good books to start with."

"Okay. I will."

Konner cleared his throat, "I haven't read all the journals

yet," he rubbed his eyes, which felt gritty, he'd barely managed a quick shower before bringing Terah to Malachi and Rae's house, "but I have a general idea of how old you are as well, Terah."

She looked at him so quickly, he had to wonder if it hurt her neck doing it. "We would have birthday parties for the children." She smiled, "sometimes the men that kept us would sneak in cakes and treats for them."

Konner grinned, "well, I'm sure we can come up with a cake if you want." He paused and watched her face; she was trying to sit there patiently and not look too excited. "You're twenty-five."

She held his look for a second, no more, then lowered her gaze to the floor. She sighed audibly, "I understand ten." She lifted her gaze back to him, "is that old? Twenty-five?"

Konner couldn't help the laugh that almost choked him, "no." He looked at Malachi, then back to her, "in fact it makes me feel like an old man."

Raelyn's sob had them all turn to look at her, she was struggling to get to the edge of the chair, Malachi stood up took her hand, and helped her to her feet. Tears were running down her face now. Konner's back stiffened, he didn't know what was wrong.

She shook off her mate's hand and went over to the couch and awkwardly dropped down onto it beside Terah. Knowing she was carrying two babies made sense now, how big she had gotten. he remembered when she was pregnant with Lillee, and she'd still been running around at the end of it.

"I can't believe you were there that long," she sobbed again, "your whole life," she reached out and touch Terah's face, "it's not right."

Terah leaned over and wrapped her arms around Rae's shoulders, "I'm here now and I'm not going back." She said in a soothing tone.

"We'll have a birthday party for you," Rae swatted at the tears on her face, "with cake and presents and anything you want." The tears started flowing again.

"Shh," Terah shifted so Rae's head could rest on her shoulder, "you're going to upset the babies." She began to hum. The sound echoed from her to fill the room around them.

"You have to teach me how to do that," Raelyn said in a rasping voice.

Terah only nodded closed her eyes and continued to sing.

A shiver went down Konner's spine as the notes hit him. He watched Terah as she held Raelyn, encouraging her to lay back and relax. Her song was light, and it felt like it gripped his heart in its hand as she continued. A motion beside him forced him to look away from her. Malachi stood there pointing to the door.

With a jerk of his chin, Konner got up and walked out of the room. Once out the door, he turned to see a stressed-out man behind him. He was shaking his head as he walked out.

"When are you going to get the healer," he waved a hand at the room they'd just left, "the emotional outbursts are getting bad," he rubbed his hand over his head in a jerky motion, "the babies are coming soon."

"I'm going first thing in the morning. Make sure the chopper is fueled and ready."

Malachi nodded, "I won't survive it if something..."

Konner put his hand on his shoulder and gripped it hard, "it's going to be fine."

He could see the pain in Malachi's eyes and knew he was remembering the baby they'd lost five years ago. "With Terah here and Shaelan coming, it's going to be fine."

Nodding, Malachi turned and looked back into the room. "I don't care what lines she's from, Konner, but if there are more like her out there," he snapped his head back to look at them, "we have to find them."

Konner crossed his arms over his chest and stared in the door to see Raelyn was laying down now and Terah was standing beside the couch and pulling a blanket down over her.

"They recovered records and I have someone tracking sales of the tanks they used, so we should have some directions to go in soon."

"Good." Malachi sucked in a breath and blew it out slowly, "is the Alliance going to help?"

Konner smiled at Terah as she started walking toward them. "The prince himself has assured me they will."

"The prince?"

Konner nodded slowly, "that's where Terah was taken after she was found, to his campground." He smirked, "the princess is very invested in finding and freeing all of those from our world."

"I can't," he shrugged, "knowing there are more, it's just—" He looked at Terah who stopped and stood just outside the door. "You've brought us hope," he said softly, "when we had none left."

Terah moved just her eyes to look at Konner before speaking, "hope never runs out," she smiled at Malachi, "you just have to look for it sometimes."

Malachi nodded his head in almost slow motion. Konner could see the emotion in his eyes. "Thank you for helping her."

Terah looked over her shoulder to where his mate lay sleeping, "new life renews hope, always."

Malachi released a shaking breath, "I'm going to get some tea brewed and make Rae a snack for when she wakes up." He glanced at Konner, "I'll go get the chopper ready when Olanna comes over to sit with Rae."

"We'll go back over to my place; I have to get the plans to take to Blair when I pick up Shaelan and Calum."

"We'll build them a damn mansion if they want it," Malachi said with a tone of conviction as he stomped toward the kitchen.

They walked without talking until the house was in view again. Overall, the complex had all of the homes far enough apart that everyone had their privacy but getting from one to the other was no more than a five-minute walk. He glanced back to Malachi's home and wondered if they would need to add to it to make more room for three children. He smirked and looked down at the ground, if they had to expand it ten times, they would. Although with how harrowing it was to bring a child into the world, he hoped they didn't go for that many. Their kind lived longer and had children at a later age than most did, but that didn't mean it was without risks. The few women in the clan felt it was their responsibility to repopulate the clan's number. Konner agreed, within reason. He glanced at Nolyn's door as they went by, it was black again, thankfully. He still couldn't believe she had considered getting pregnant to bring another life to the clan. Of course, when the options for available father came down to himself or Reeves, she'd changed her mind. For the longest time, Konner thought the two had a clandestine romance happening, but other than the odd look between them, there was no proof.

"You are leaving?" Terah stopped and stood where she could see the lake, "Malachi said he would have the helicopter ready."

He stopped and crossed his arms over his chest, watching the ripples in the water. "I'm going to go get Shaelan so she can check on the babies."

"She can do that?"

He looked down to see she was watching him now and not the water, "with a machine, yes she can actually see the babies. It's called an ultrasound."

"Can I see the babies?"

Konner shrugged, "I don't see why not."

He was rewarded with a brilliant smile, which cued his own whether he'd felt like smiling or not. She had some sort of contagious chemistry. "I will leave in the morning and be back before dinner time."

"Your helicopter goes fast." She didn't sound amused.

"I think it's more that I don't have to follow roads to get where I'm going." He cleared his throat and looked back to the water. "Listen, I know you're probably wanting to go swimming, but for the next while, I need you to avoid swimming with the others."

She gave him a distraught look. "You do not swim together?"

He stepped back and motioned to the path, "we do. I'll explain it while we're on the way to the fishery." He grinned down at her, "I thought you might like to see it."

"I would like to see the fish." Her tone was much lighter now.

"We don't eat from the fishery." He gave her a quick look.

"I understand, I will behave."

"We can go see the greenhouses too if you like." He kept the pace slow, appreciating that this was the first time he'd been able to walk along at an easy pace, without looking over his shoulder.

"What is a greenhouse?" Terah bent down and pulled off her shoes, "the path is smooth." She clarified her action.

"It's where the flowers and plants grow that we use for health research," he noted she looked relieved to have the shoes off, "that stuff we mix to drink came from many years of researching the right plants."

"The taste is different, but not bad."

He shrugged, "it's come a long way."

"Yes. I would like to see the greenhouse." She turned her head and looked into the trees that surrounded the complex.

He wanted to explain to her as much as he could about their kind before he had to leave. It was for everyone's safety. "The reason I want you to wait before you swim with others is for a few reasons," he glanced to see she was giving him her complete attention, "first, you've never swum free with others, it could trigger underlying aggressiveness." He looked down to see if she was trying to understand. "Our kind, in the past," he thought of trying to get close to Olanna and Reeves when he'd found them, "were very territorial, protective of their area." When she nodded, he continued, "because you haven't been in the water with others, I wouldn't want anyone to get hurt accidentally."

"I understand." She nodded her head quickly, "it is so new, swimming like that." She grinned, "I was exhausted after the first time, but I feel stronger each time."

Konner smiled, if that was her weak state in the river with the rushing water, he didn't know if he wanted to see her full strength. "There's another reason and I don't expect you to know about it, because you've been isolated from your own kind for too many years."

She stopped and put her hand on his arm. "Are you okay?" She searched his face, compassion bleeding from her eyes, "your tone is tense as you speak of this."

Konner hadn't even realized that he was expressing that outwardly. "I'm okay, I just have a lot," he shrugged it off, "on my mind."

"I understand. You are a very important man to your people and others."

"Our people" He corrected.

Her eyes rounded, as the corners of her mouth turned to smile. "Our people."

He motioned to keep walking, "anyway, the other reason I'd like you to wait, is for another reason entirely."

Terah watched him closely, he had to focus on keeping his legs moving and not stopping to watch her watch him. He needed sleep soon. "One of the males here could end up being your mate—" He rubbed his jaw, trying to figure out how to explain it. "We don't know until we're in the water with them and," he looked away and into the trees, trying to gather his thoughts, he looked down at her, "it can become quite," he waved his hand around, "aggressive." He searched her face to see if she understood. She was puzzling it out, but he kept going, not wanting her to think he was calling her weak or unworthy, "you feel good now, but after years of neglect, I'd like you to be much stronger, internally," he motioned in a circle in front of his stomach, "inside your body."

She nodded in a slow, jerky motion, "you do not want me to get hurt?" She said the words slowly.

"No, I don't." He rubbed his hand against the side of his neck, trying to figure out if he should keep going, or just leave her with that to ponder. "If it's one of the younger males, instinct will help control you," he gave her a brief smile, "as much as your maternal instinct is with the little ones, I have no worries with that."

"One of the young could be my mate?" Her brows were creased.

Konner nodded, "if they've changed the first time, then yes, you could be one of theirs." He stared at the ground, not wanting her to see the internal thoughts he was having about one of the guys being her mate. Again, he was sure it was because of wanting to protect her after the atrocity that had been her life so far.

"So, Lucus or Paxton could be?" She tilted her head and looked at him, "Or Reeves, and you?"

Konner cleared his throat, "any of us could be."

"What if no one is?" Terah touched his arm, but didn't stop him this time, "can I still have babies with no mate?"

As uncomfortable went, Konner was at a high ten on the scale right now. "Yes. You can. Unlike some of the other clans, we do not need a mate to have children."

"That is good." She dropped her hand and smiled up at her, her eyes sparkling. "I want ten babies."

Konner choked on the air he was trying to take into his lungs. "Ten?" He stopped walking this time. She nodded. He knew she understood how many ten was, but still found himself holding up both hands with his fingers extended, "that many?"

Her smile was beaming, and he wouldn't have done anything to dim it. She was breathtaking.

"I guess you'll need a big house." He finally settled on saying.

"Yes, with a big pool like yours." She nodded. "I was born

in a pool, my mother told me." She walked alongside him now, "she said it was the best moment of her life when I arrived—except it had tap water and she wasn't happy with that."

Konner frowned. Childbirth was hard on both mother and child, tragedy was the result often. "Okay, with a big pool." He would have to get one of the women to talk to her about this because he couldn't bring himself to do it.

They reached the fishery ponds and Konner raised both eyebrows to see Auburn and Reeves tossing feed into the water.

"Malachi didn't want Raelyn to try to walk here," Auburn said over his shoulder.

"I came looking for you." Reeves shrugged and tossed more in.

Terah went over quickly and leaned down to look in the water. "There are so many."

"They're not fully grown yet," Konner pointed to the waterway they'd designed, "as they grow, we release them into the lake."

"Is the lake full too?" She straightened up.

Konner smirked, "there are enough."

Terah nodded and went over to Auburn and held out her hand, "I can do that?"

Auburn looked at the pail in his hand and then held it out to her, "just walk around them and toss it in."

Terah smiled, "I will." She lifted the pail and inhaled, "more good food for them means bigger fish." She grinned and walked toward the other pond.

Reeves set the pail down and came over to stand with Auburn and him. "I know you have to get ready for tomorrow, but I need you to return some calls before you." He shrugged, "supplier issues."

Konner blew out a breath and nodded, "I'll do them when we go back."

Auburn watched Terah walking slowly around the pond. "How's she doing?"

He watched her for a moment, "we should get her to help here until Rae is ready, Malachi already has enough on his plate." Both men nodded. "I just explained why she shouldn't swim with anyone for a while."

"How did she take it?" Reeves jammed his hands in his pockets and looked at him.

"She understands, mostly, I think." Konner cleared her throat, "she wants ten children, with or without a mate."

Auburn's eyebrows went so high that they almost blended into his hair. "Ten?" his voice cracked.

Konner nodded, then turned to see Reeves giving Terah a thorough assessment. He blinked and looked at him then at Auburn, "sorry, just," he shook his head, "does she know how dangerous that is?"

Konner shook his head. "I'm going to get the girls to talk to her."

"Ten." Reeves whispered, "hopefully she'll change her mind once she finds out."

"I don't know, Reeves," Auburn gave Konner a quick sideways glance, "she lights up as bright as the sun when she saw the kids."

Konner smirked, realizing Auburn wasn't going to pass on a chance to harass the younger man. "It's true, I wouldn't be surprised if she wants a dozen at least." Reeves was the most awkward adult around children, their size and intellect didn't compute in that man's statistical brain.

"Who knows, those could be your dozen children," Auburn said, trying to keep a straight face.

Reeves looked at Terah, then back to them, his brows knitted. "I need to get back to the office," he backed up a step and shook his head, "you guys are," he took another step and then slipped off the edge of the wooden platform. A splash followed.

Auburn laughed so hard, that he started choking.

Konner couldn't help but laugh even as he went over and extended a hand down to an unimpressed Reeves looking up at him. The tie holding his long hair back off his face had come off and half his face was covered in it now.

"I didn't think we could swim here," Terah called over to him from the other platform.

Konner chuckled, "we don't." He gripped Reeves's hand and lifted him high enough he could get his hands on the wooden walkway.

Auburn was bent over, still laughing.

"Bastards," Reeves muttered and walked the other way. The squishing sound from his shoes only made Auburn laugh harder still.

"He's going to pout for hours now." Konner looked to the man behind him. "Is Olanna over at the greenhouses?"

Auburn nodded, as he took deep breaths, trying to settle himself down.

Konner looked over a Terah, "want to take Terah over? I told her I'd show her the greenhouse, but if we're having supplier issues, I need to get on it, so it's sorted out."

Auburn blew out a long deep breath, "I'll take her over after we finish here."

Chapter Twenty- Two

Terah watched the helicopter disappear in the sky. Snowflakes fell on her face as she did, leaving cool spots behind. She smiled and lifted her chin higher, loving the feeling of it on her skin. Last night at dinner, Reeves had said it was pretty until you had to shovel it. Terah had never shoveled snow or walked in it, and despite how unhappy he sounded about it, she looked forward to it.

Sitting at the large table with all the others had been so different that she had barely managed to eat. There was so much going on at once, talking, laughing and the children being silly—she'd never experienced that. Lowering her chin, she looked out over the lake. She'd never experienced anything, really.

When it was time to sleep, she had lain there in the floating bed and tried to remember if she had ever had something like sitting around a table with others. She couldn't recall it. For a short while, she thought maybe there had been a time around a pool with her mother and the old one, possibly the boys that had been there in the beginning, but the images were so faded, she decided it was made up and not a real event that had taken place.

She looked over her shoulder at the house and wondered who she would have to talk to about going for a swim. She hadn't been to the lake yet. Turning she looked out over it and grinned like it was calling her name.

"No one is swimming right now if you'd like to."

Startled she turned around to see the elder of the clan standing on the walkway from the other end of the house. "I would like to, yes." She smiled at her. "I feel like it is calling to me."

The older woman smiled slowly, "one shouldn't ignore things like that then, should they?"

Terah bit her lip, she wanted to strip down right here and run into the cool water, but she had told Konner she would not do that. "I will go get my suit."

Alviva shrugged, an entertained look on her face. "Don't worry about the suit." She looked over at the line of houses. "No one else swims at this time of day."

"Are you sure? Konner told me I had to wear clothes at all times."

Laughing a low sound, she waved her hand toward the water. "If the Alpha can't break a few rules, what fun would it be? Go, child, I'll stand guard in case anyone comes out."

"Thank you." The excitement bubbled up inside her. The big tub was fine, even the pool in the center of the house, she was sure would be nice, but a lake—there was nothing like that.

She moved through the water with as much speed as she could manage. Her mind felt heavy with so many things she had been told or heard since Konner had landed his helicopter in his Sanctuary. She didn't know what to do with half of it.

Aside from the children here, and the joy she felt seeing them, the fact that she had a cousin was not weighing on her mind at all. She still wasn't exactly sure what a cousin was, but Raelyn was a family no matter the definition. It filled some of those empty places inside her just knowing that she was also related to Lillee and the babies that Raelyn would soon have.

When she was younger, Terah would dream about having a family of her own but had long ago given up on that when none of the others that were made to live with her were her kind.

Flipping to her back, she twirled in the water, always keeping what was around her in mind. The lake was deeper than it had looked from above in the machine and she was glad for it. Twisting, she rose toward the surface and felt elation as she broke the surface and the air brushed over her. Bending, she dove back down into the water, and moved with powerful strokes, taking her to the bottom. She stopped and slowed her arms to hold herself just above the floor of the lake. Stilling herself, she controlled her breathing, so she could just float here and observe what was around her.

A group of fish swam by and didn't even notice her presence, which pleased her more than she thought it would, to blend in and be part of this. Of course, she thought, if they knew that she loved the taste of them, they probably wouldn't be so relaxed with her in the water.

Moving her arms wide in an arc out from her body, she felt carefree. Hovering on the spot, she looked down at her legs and wondered about the story that Konner had told her, the one about what her kind used to be like. What would it be like to always be in the water? She wasn't sure she would like it all the time. She liked the smells and sounds of things out of the water. She watched as she moved her legs at the same time, had her mother taught her that, or was it just something her kind was born knowing? If they had once had a long tail and no legs, it made sense that they swam the way they did. Opening her legs, she moved them like she was walking, it worked, although she wouldn't be able to go as fast. She grinned and looked toward the surface, and she liked going fast.

When she decided she should go back to the land, in case anyone else wanted to swim, she caught the taste of something that wasn't fish. A tingle went down her spine. What was it?

Moving with long strokes, she went in that direction as quickly as possible. She was careful to stay low enough in the water that there was no sound, so whatever it was it wouldn't be alerted to her being there.

As she got closer to the shore, she saw something moving down in the water that looked like it was fuzzy. She frowned, fuzzy didn't belong in the water. At least she didn't think it did. Should she go find one of the others and tell them there was an intruder in the water? She floated closer to the surface, not sure if she should leave here. What if they came back and it was gone? How would they find where it went? The water only held scent for so long, she'd discovered at Rayne's lake.

Moving to the bottom, she went across the floor of the lake, disturbing nothing as she went by it. Beneath the creature, she stilled her limbs and watched as it circled around a small indent in the bank beneath the surface of the water. A small fish darted out from it and the fuzzy beast tried to grab for it. Terah moved up further, she didn't know what it was, but it was trying to eat Konner's fish that he grew in his Sanctuary. She couldn't allow that.

It took her more time than she had anticipated to catch it, when she did, she was feeling drained instead of invigorated. She paused to catch one of the larger fish for herself and then swam, dragging the body of the thief along with her.

Closer to the shore, she went to the surface and looked around to see if anyone was there. She didn't want to bring the dead creature to the surface and upset the younger children. The elder stood there, with Lucus beside her. Terah stopped as the water grew shallow, she didn't want to do something to upset Konner and not be without clothes in front of Lucus.

Alpha Alviva said something to him, and he turned around, so his back was toward her. Moving quickly, Terah walked to the shore and dropped the carcass as she bent down to grab her dress. Slipping it over her head, she looked to see the elder was looking at what she'd brought out of the water. "It was stealing the fish from the lake."

Lucus turned around and looked to where it lay beside her feet. "It's a…"

"Thief." Terah nodded.

"Lucus why don't you go and deal with the" the Alpha looked at her, a small smile on her face, "thief before one of the young ones come out."

"Yes, Alvie." He picked it up and held it in the air, then looked at Terah, "you caught it?"

Terah nodded, "I couldn't let it steal the fish from the lake."

He grinned, "I guess not."

She watched him walk away and then turned to the elder, "thank you for letting me swim without the suit." She looked down at the damp dress, "it is uncomfortable."

"They didn't clothe you when you swam where you were?"

Terah bent down and picked up her shoes. "No."

"I see." She leaned on her cane and looked to the left of the path where the houses were, "if you go that way, and walk to the end of the trail, there's a good spot to get into the lake without clothes on."

Terah looked at it, "is that allowed? I'm trying to follow all the rules."

Alviva smiled at her, "I don't know if it's allowed, but that's what I do." She studied her for a moment, "now if you'll excuse me, I'm going to go for my swim." She looked up in the sky, "more snow is coming this afternoon and the water will be murky with the creatures all scurrying around in there to find shelter until they adjust to the water change."

Terah nodded, "enjoy your swim. The lake is wonderful." She watched her walk along the path, then turned to look at Konner's house. She had so much to think about still. What did she know about money and investments? She didn't even know what an investment was. Who would be the best to talk to about things like that? She bit her lip and looked at the homes Konner had pointed out. Reeves, she needed to talk to him, he seemed to be a very smart man, however clumsy he was. She still couldn't believe he fell into the fishponds.

Chapter Twenty-Three

Konner had been having feelings of anxiousness all day. That was the only label he could place on them. Normally he loved to fly, but the moment he'd gotten in the chopper to fly up to Ed's he'd wanted to be back at the Sanctuary. Terah. She was the reason for them, he didn't have to dig too deep to figure that out. He'd left her with several adults to watch over her, she would be fine.

Checking the gauges, for the tenth time in the past minute, he looked behind him to see Shaelan and Calum looking out the window as they approached the property. "The tree line is the start of the land." He said into the mouthpiece like some tour guide. "The river is one of two that feeds the fresh water and lake."

"It's beautiful, Konner." Shaelan's soft voice filled the headset.

"You fenced in the whole thing?"

Konner nodded as he navigated a gentle turn to head for the helipad, "except across the rivers." He'd considered it, "I wanted the creatures that live in the area to be able to come and go.

"I've been trying to talk Devin into fencing the campground."

"Arcadia," Shaelan interjected.

Konner grinned, having been there for that discussion. "Ah yes, Arcadia." He smirked, "I believe that's my fault because I call my home Sanctuary." He maneuvered the helicopter so it just skimmed the top of the tree canopy, "but it actually is registered as an animal sanctuary." He shrugged, keeping his eyes focused on where he was going, "I just didn't say what type of animal." It had taken five years and a lot of generous 'donations' to make it happen.

"Oh, you have somewhere to land." Shaelan sounded relieved, "I half thought you'd land on the lake."

"I'd need pontoons on the chopper to do that and I wouldn't risk having someone swimming where I land." He concentrated on taking it down as smoothly as possible.

"I didn't think of that."

As soon as he felt the vehicle touch the cement, he started the shutdown. He didn't like the look of the one gauge, so he'd had to get Malachi to give it once over and make sure everything was good with it. If he could get Malachi to leave Raelyn's side long enough. "Welcome to the Sanctuary." He said and then plucked the headset off his head and hung it on the small hook near his head. On second thought, he could fly over to the site that looked after the planes in the area that was for the Alliance. Until Rae had those babies, Malachi was going to be too distracted.

He got out and opened the side door for them to get out. Shaelan had insisted on bringing several cases with her. He'd assured her that they were well stocked with medical supplies, but she'd insisted. As he lifted two of them out, he supposed she had to travel with anything she'd need if she was called elsewhere. The Alliance needed more of their kind trained in medicine.

When the truck came out of the trees, Konner knew Malachi wasn't driving. Never would he approach the chopper at that speed. His chest tightened, fearing something was wrong with Raelyn.

Auburn hopped out of the truck and started for him. Konner met him halfway. "Is everything all right?"

Auburn looked surprised, "everything is fine. Malachi is at the fishery, so I said I pop over to get you."

Konner blew out a breath. "How's Rae?"

Auburn started for the chopper, "cranky, happy, angry," he shrugged, "you name an emotion and she's felt it in the past hour."

Konner smirked. Raelyn had always been highly emotional. He turned around to get the cases.

Calum was nodding to whatever instructions Shaelan was giving him about the two bags they were carrying.

"Just let Auburn know what goes to the house you'll be staying in," Konner told him when they reached them. "Auburn, this is Calum Dante and his mate Shaelan."

Auburn nodded to both. "Do you want to settle in or..."

"I'd like to see," she glanced at Konner, "Raelyn?" He nodded, "first, please."

Calum didn't look surprised at all that she wasn't concerned with where they were staying.

"I'm just going to check in at the house, then I'll meet you at Malachi's." He didn't want to say he needed to affirm with his own eyes that Terah was doing fine.

Auburn smirked, "might want to ask Lucus what he had to bury this morning."

"Bury?" His heart jerked in his chest.

Auburn nodded, "Terah caught it stealing *your* fish from the lake when she went for a swim."

Calum was grinning now too.

"I'll ah," Konner brushed the hair back from his eyes, "talk to Terah about that."

"Might be a thought." Auburn picked up the two cases Konner had abandoned and walked toward the truck.

Calum tilted his head and followed, leaving Konner

standing there wondering how in the hell she'd caught something in the water. Blowing out a breath, he snapped out of it grabbed the last bag, and went to the truck.

He checked the entertainment room and found she wasn't there either. Coming out of it, he stood there. Maybe she was over with Rae?

Lucus' door opened, and he stepped out of it. "You're back." He smiled at him.

Konner nodded, "is Terah over with Rae?"

Lucus smirked and shook his head slowly, "no." He pointed to the doors that lead to the common house, "she's in there with Lillee and Kisa, they're baking cookies to thank Shaelan for helping her when she was found."

Konner looked at the door. "Who's helping?"

Lucus jammed his hands in his pockets. "Pax is manning the fire extinguisher in case the smoke alarm goes off again." He closed the door to his room, "I had to get changed. I was covered in batter." He grinned, "using the beaters is more complicated..."

Konner darted for the door and ran down the short hall to the dining area. He stopped so suddenly, that he swayed for a second. The entire island and floor, and possibly the wall too were covered in flour. It looked like someone had set off a bomb inside the flour canister. Nakisa sat on the counter, holding the cooking timer, and staring at it. Lillee was waving a towel in the direction of the oven. Terah, who looked like she'd been rolled in the flour stood holding a tray and frowning at it. Her hair was pulled up into an unsuccessful bun on the top of her head, hair sprung out of it all over her head giving her a mad scientist look. He looked over to see Paxton sprawled in one of the chairs, the fire extinguisher·sitting on the table in front of him. He gave him a hard look, to which the teen shrugged as if to say 'what else could I do?'.

"You're back." Nakisa hopped off the counter and came

running over to him. She hugged him, with flour-covered clothes and all. Pulling back, she smiled up at him, "we're making cookies." She grinned, "it's a lot harder than it looks."

"So I see." He stepped carefully on the flour-dusted floor and went over to stand on the other side of the island.

Terah had her head down and was scraping charred cookies off the tray, her forehead was covered in flour, along with her cheek and most of her top. She gave him a quick look, "we're making thank you cookies for Shaelan," her forehead creased, "it's not going well."

Konner cleared his throat and didn't know how to approach the situation. An armed enemy, he could handle, with the expectant faces of the three females that had destroyed the kitchen, he had no idea what to do.

"I found the recipe online." Lillee held up a tablet, that he noted was also covered in baking products.

Terah heaved out a breath and turned to her. "We should watch that," she waved her hand around in the air, "video thing again." She frowned, "maybe we didn't *fold* the flour in right."

Konner's eyebrows shot up; they'd been trying to bake by watching a video.

"My mom always measures the butter, maybe we should have measured the butter." Nakisa nodded and looked down at the timer in her hand, "one minute."

Terah nodded, a serious expression on her face as she went over to the oven and stood like a linebacker would waiting for a hit. "I think maybe too much fell in."

Konner turned around to see Lucus standing behind him now.

He lifted both hands, "I offered to look up an actual recipe, but was outvoted."

He spun to look at Paxton, he shrugged. "You know I can't cook."

The timer buzzed, making Konner's head snap around to see Terah opening the oven. Lillee was there waving the towel beside it to clear the smoke that came billowing out.

"I don't think these worked either." Terah turned, holding a tray of very crisp-looking cookies.

Konner put his hand over his mouth, trying to stall before he took a chunk out of the two teen boys that had let this happen. "Maybe next time, you should, uh," he glanced at Lillee to see her trying to brush the flour off her shirt, "ask one of the women for some pointers?"

Terah set the tray on the counter beside the pile of charred cookies and exhaled a loud breath, "they were busy, and we wanted to surprise everyone."

"I'm very surprised." It came out of his mouth before he could stop it, "that, uh, you want to learn how to—bake." He glanced to see Lucus smirking at the way he bumbled his way through that. "But uh," he leaned over and looked down at the counter, "perhaps the video you watched wasn't a legitimate one."

"It's true," Lucus stepped over and stood beside him, "people do that all the time, put gag videos online."

Terah frowned and pushed back the hair that had fallen on her face, "that's not right."

Konner glanced at Lucus, conveying a silent thank you to him for stopping him from digging the hole any deeper. "With dinner time so close, maybe we can postpone cookie making to another time." He turned and looked at Paxton, "we need the dining hall cleaned for that."

Paxton's mouth dropped open, "I didn't..."

Konner glared at him, "that's right you didn't *do* anything." He grasped Lucus' shoulder firmly, "Lucus will help you clean up the kitchen while the girls go home and get changed."

Terah blew out a breath again, disappointment on her face.

"Shaelan is checking on Raelyn now, so if you want to be there for the ultrasound," he motioned to her, "perhaps you should have a quick shower?" He felt like he was standing on paper-thin ice right now and the slightest wrong move was going to plunge him into unknown depths.

"Yes. I want to see that." she nodded her head slowly, then

turned to look at Lillee and Nakisa. "We will do it right next time."

Nakisa nodded, a smile on her face.

Lillee blew out a breath, "I'll get one of mom's recipes next time." She picked a piece of batter from her hair.

"Yes. No more videos." Terah smiled at her. "Thank you for helping me. When I can read it will be better."

"I will practice with you. I have a lot of books." Lillee came over and hugged her.

"I would like that." Terah leaned down and kissed the top of her powder-covered hair. "Now go, get clean." She looked down at the front of herself and swatted at flour on her top. "I will go shower." She nodded and walked quickly to the door.

Konner waited until the door closed then turned back to the three teenagers.

"I thought if I helped it would go better," Lillee said quietly.

"I'm sure you tried." Konner motioned to the door. "You better get back; we don't need your mother worrying about you right now."

She nodded hugged the tablet to her chest and went out the side door.

"I'm sorry, Konner." Lucus looked around the kitchen, "I tried to jump in and help when I walked in, but it was out of control by then."

Konner put his hands on his hips and looked around the area. "That's an understatement."

"It's not as bad as when we tried to make the volcano in your kitchen." Paxton walked over through the flour trail and opened the fridge to look inside it.

"Don't even remind me of that." He looked from one to the other, "you just better get this cleaned up," he looked down at the black cookies on the counter, "before Olanna and Nolyn come to get dinner ready."

Both boys' eyes rounded.

"Crap." Lucus spun around and went over to the garbage

can.

"I just wanted cookies," Paxton mumbled as he opened the cupboard where the broom was kept.

Konner glanced around at the mess once more and then backed away from it. Turning he saw the white footprint trail leading to his house. "Might want to do the floors when you're finished." He didn't bother to look at their faces, he knew they'd have that 'my life is so harsh' expression on them.

Shaking his head, he went back into his house. That was not what he'd expected to come home to. Blowing out a breath he went to the kitchen and grabbed the kettle. There were times he wished his kind could consume alcohol, and right now was one of those times.

Chapter Twenty-Four

Konner watched Shaelan as she leafed through the manual for the ultrasound machine. He'd purchased it a few years ago, but until now he wasn't sure it had even been turned on. Auburn teased him saying that if he was holding out for one of the children to get a medical degree, he had a long wait ahead of him. Yet the whole clan had agreed a fully stocked medical wing was a good idea. All of them, himself included held onto the hope that one day they would thrive again, and then it would justify every purchase they had made.

"Okay," Shaelan said softly as she sat down in front of the machine, "it's not the same model as the one I used at the Alliances med, but I can figure it out."

Calum leaned against the wall, watching his mate. Konner could tell without asking that he had every confidence in her ability.

"Where did you receive your training?" His nerves were starting to get the better of him, so he needed the distraction. Everything *had* to be okay with the babies.

Shaelan looked over her shoulder at him, "I was trained to be the healer for my clan, but I've taken other courses as well."

Calum scoffed, "and read an entire medical library."

She smiled at her mate, "reading is good for the soul." She nodded, "Nona says that."

Calum shrugged, "I just think you should start teaching some of this," he pointed to his head, "that you have up there."

"It's not a bad idea." Konner looked at the door again, wondering if he should go get Terah or if she would find her way here. "I have hopes that one of the young ones here will aspire to work in the medical field." He smiled at her, "so you're not running here too often."

Shaelan turned back to the machine, "I like it here. Cal is actually relaxed, not worrying someone is going to come out of the bush after us."

Konner eyed Calum, while he leaned against the wall, he was still aware of everything around them. He doubted that man ever totally relaxed.

The door opened and Malachi walked in with his arm around Raelyn. Right behind them was Terah. She stopped and smiled at Shaelan as she got up off the stool.

"You've made a remarkable recovery." Shaelan went over and stood in front of her.

"Yes." Terah glanced at Konner briefly, "the prince had very good fish in his lake."

Calum chuckled and moved out of the way, so Malachi could help his mate on the bed.

Shaelan hurried back and helped adjust the pillows, so Rae was comfortable. "You'll have to be patient with me as I get this setup." She picked up a towel and lay it across Rae's belly. "Have you ever seen one of these?"

Raelyn shook her head.

"Okay, well, you're going to hear your own heartbeat and the babies, and any movement they make is going to be amplified, so don't panic, it's all normal." She moved Rae's shirt up out of the way.

Raelyn nodded excitedly. "I just want to see with my own eyes that they are well." She blew out a nervous breath.

"Let's take a look." Shaelan turned around and picked up the gel. "This might be a little cold."

Konner watched Terah as she stood at the end of the bed, looking at the screen in front of Shaelan.

"I can't really do measurements, I haven't been trained to do that, but we should be able to get a good look at the babies." She gave Raelyn a smile.

Konner moved over closer to the bed, admitting that he was just as intrigued with the idea of seeing the infants that would soon be part of the clan.

"That's your heartbeat." Shaelan reached over and turned the volume down. "Mom's pulse is doing great." She smiled and then moved the wand lower.

Konner watched her spine straighten when she looked from it to the screen again.

"Is something wrong?" Raelyn's voice shook with panic.

"Baby number one's heart rate is a bit higher, but it could just be because you're nervous." Shaelan's voice reflected no worry, but her posture did. Konner had to hand it to her that her professional etiquette was good.

"And the other one?" Malachi held Rae's hand, his eyes looking at the screen.

"I'm having," Shaelan moved the wand around some more, "trouble picking it up, they're behind their sibling."

"Sing to them," Terah said and nodded, "calm them."

Raelyn looked at her, tears shining in her eyes, "I don't know how to out of the water."

Terah smiled and went over to the little sink on the other side of the room. She opened a cupboard and looked in it, then another, "I had trouble at first too," she turned and saw the small fridge and went over to it, bending down, she opened it and took out a bottle of water. "I found out if my," she motioned her hand up and down her throat, "was too dry it was difficult." Nodding, she opened the bottle as she went back over to the bed. "Take some drinks and we'll sing to your babies."

Raelyn took the bottle; her hand was shaking. Malachi lifted her head so she could sip it.

"Do you want me to start?"

Raelyn nodded, a nervous look on her face.

Konner found he was holding his breath, if Rae tried and failed, she would take this as her first failure for the little ones inside her.

Terah sat on the bed beside her, careful not to crowd her mate that wasn't going to move for anyone. She put her hand on the side of Rae's stomach, far from where Shaelan continued to move the wand. As she started to hum, even Calum turned to look at her.

Terah looked at Rae and nodded, encouraging her to try.

Rae took another sip and then held the bottle out to Malachi. Leaning her head down on the pillow, she closed her eyes and blew out a breath. If she'd been in the water, she wouldn't have had to think about it, it would have just been there. The first few shaky notes that came from her throat made Terah start the song again, later, he'd ponder how he knew that she had. This wasn't a song he'd heard from his people since he was a child.

Terah smiled at Raelyn when she opened her eyes and continued to hum softly. She didn't have the volume that Terah had, but her children would feel the vibrations through her body.

"That's helping," Shaelan said softly and moved the wand to the side.

Konner looked at the screen and watched the image of the second child, he assumed, as it came on the screen. Shaelan reached up and did something and then he saw the blip on the screen. he didn't know the first thing about fetal images, but he could only assume it was the heartbeat.

"Both pulses are strong and regular." Shaelan said softly, "can you keep doing that so I can try to look around with them behaving?"

Terah continued, even when Raelyn had to pause because

her emotions were getting the better of her. Malachi leaned down and kissed her and then offered her another sip of water. The tears were running down her cheeks as she took a small drink. Nodding she leaned back and started to hum quietly with Terah.

Konner's chest was tight with emotion, he stepped back and then turned to see his aunt standing in the doorway. Tears were running down her cheeks as she looked at Terah. Placing her hand over her heart, she nodded her head slowly and closed her eyes, letting the melody move over her. Turning, he noticed that even the seasoned warrior, Calum was not unmoved by the song either.

"Okay," Shaelan turned to look at Terah and nodded, letting her know that the song wasn't needed now. As she hummed the last notes, Raelyn quietened as well. "Both babies sound and look healthy, I can't get any pictures of the little one hiding behind the big brother, but..."

"A boy?" Malachi leaned and looked closer at the monitor.

Shaelan smiled, "yes the one hogging all the limelight is definitely a boy." She moved the wand over to the other side and then looked at the screen. "They're both about the same size, but I honestly can't get a peek at the second baby."

"As long as they're both healthy that's all that matters." His aunt said from the door. She nodded, "it will help with the birth."

"Was that a worry?" Shaelan wiped off the wand and hung it back in the machine.

"Our kind has a hard time with childbirth and," Raelyn glanced at Malachi, "the babies surviving."

"I wasn't told this." Shaelan stood up and wiped off Rae's belly. "What is the issue? Is it your anatomy or—"

"It all seems to be well and normal at the start," Konner glanced to his aunt, knowing how upset she got talking about it, "then the bleeding seems to accelerate and..."

"I'll need to look into the cause." Shaelan went over to the cupboards and started opening them, "is there any data at the

Alliance that would be helpful?"

"I doubt it." Konner wanted to help her in any way she could, he went over and gave her a questioning look.

"I want to do some blood tests, on Raelyn and maybe one of the other women, to establish a baseline," she pulled the drawer open, "do you have lab equipment here?" Finding a syringe, she took it out and set it on the counter, "it could be a simple protein or imbalance..."

Konner turned to look over at his aunt, sharing any information about their kind was something they went to great lengths to protect.

Her face held concern, but she nodded, "if she can sort it out, we will have to take that risk."

"Risk?" Shaelan spun around and looked at her, then she immediately bowed her head in a respectful way. "I can assure you anything I find out will be purely for medical purposes and it will be well guarded."

Terah got off the bed and looked around, "my mother said it was easy to have me, the water helped as it should."

"The water?" Raelyn accepted Malachi's assistance in getting up. "You were born in the water?"

Terah nodded, "of course. I have watched others give birth," she scrunched up her nose, "it's very messy. Having the baby in the water is much cleaner, easier—more natural?" She glanced to Shaelan.

Konner turned back to look at his aunt. "Did our women give birth in the water? When did they stop?" If anyone knew this, it would be her. He honestly hadn't cared to note such things until he was well into his forties and even then, childbirth hadn't been a man's task.

"I don't remember." She looked at the floor, leaning on her cane. "I remember as a girl, the women would circle the mother to be in the shallow's and sing to her as she brought the new life into the world." She looked from Rae back to him, "it became hard to be safe in the water during it when we were being hunted." She gave him a look, "we didn't have the security of the Sanctuary."

Konner, his hands on his hips looked from her to Raelyn, could it be something as simple as the water? He turned around and gave his aunt a questioning look, "I'll go get Olanna and Nolyn, so you can take some samples from them." His aunt normally didn't go for anything related to modern medicine, but she understood how necessary this was to repopulate their clan.

"I'm going to take Terah and have some tea with her."

He noted the surprised look on Terah's face but knew he couldn't shelter her from everything, and at least if she was with their Alpha, she wouldn't be trying to cook again.

Chapter Twenty-Five

Konner stopped and stood by the window; Terah was outside standing on the shore of the lake. Snow was falling around her, and she just stood there with her face raised to the sky. She wore no jacket or shoes, he noticed. The cooler temperatures wouldn't bother her, at least if she were at full health they wouldn't. He frowned and debated on going to explain that to her. His kind didn't get cold and sick normally, but she'd been deprived of basic health needs her whole life.

She opened her arms out and lifted her face to the sky again and he was struck by the image of the snow in contrast to her jet-black hair hanging down her back. In many ways, she was as pure as the first snowfall before it touched the ground.

"The cold doesn't bother her?"

Konner jumped and turned to see Calum standing beside him. He'd been so caught up in watching her, that he hadn't heard him come into the office. "We like cold." He felt like he should explain why he stood here when he was supposed to be doing other things. "She's never been in the snow."

"There's a lot she's never done." Calum smirked, "like bake."

Konner grinned, "yeah that was something to walk in on." He looked toward the door, "Shaelan with Rae?"

Calum shook his head, "no, she's mumbling over the manuals for some of your medical equipment."

Looking out at Terah once more, he forced his feet to turn and go back to his desk. "I feel like she's our best chance to both those babies surviving."

"She'll move mountains to make it so."

Konner couldn't help noticing the expression of pride on the man's face when Calum spoke of his mate. "We'll all help." He motioned to the chair and then went around the desk and sat down. "I didn't realize until my aunt told us that birth used to be in the water." He leaned back in the chair and exhaled, "which makes sense really, that they were."

"Shae was eyeing up your pool in the middle of your house, so don't be surprised if the birth happens in it."

Konner shrugged, "whatever it takes."

"She was on the phone with one of our midwives for an hour, discussing water births." Calum rubbed his hand over his jaw, "most of our kind wouldn't be comfortable with delivering in the water, so this will be new ground for many."

"It makes total sense, now, birth in water." Konner had berated himself in the last few hours over his own stupidity. "We can't find our mate unless we're in the water, same with conception, so the baby being born in water—" He shook his head.

Calum didn't add anything, just looked at the open folder on his desk. "Have you gotten anywhere with that?"

Konner looked down at the creased papers in front of him. "No," he picked up the top page and looked at it again, "puzzles aren't my sort of thing." He jerked his chin to the door, "Reeves is going over it though and if there's a key to figuring it out, he'll find it."

Calum grinned, "he didn't even notice I walked by, he was mumbling to himself."

"He's better with something to keep his brain busy."

Konner smirked, "life is awkward for him, but thinking," he nodded his head slowly, "that's his happy place."

Calum reached into his pocket and pulled out his phone. "Devin wants me to call him, Rayne is demanding an update about the babies." He smirked as he looked at his phone.

Konner leaned on the desk, "we can call him now. I've been wondering if he's heard from Fallan as well."

Calum nodded and tapped his phone a few times and then set it on the desk. It was answered before the end of the first ring.

"That's a record, you are calling back this fast."

Calum smirked at the prince's tone. "I'm here with Konner, he needed to call you as well."

"Right. I spoke to Fallan," he stopped, there were voices in the background, "which I'll get to in a moment. Rayne's right here, I'll put you on speaker."

"Calum?" Rayne sounded like she was yelling into the phone, "are you with Konner? Are the babies okay?"

Konner didn't know how Rayne knew, but with the urgency in her tone, he wasn't going to question that. "I'm here with Calum. The babies are fine, Shaelan did an ultrasound, and everything appears to be fine with their health."

"Oh good." She must have been holding the phone because it sounded like she exhaled into it, "if you need anything, *anything* at all you call us."

"Thank you, I think we have it well in hand now that Shaelan is here."

"Yes. She is amazing." She said something away from the phone, "how long do we have to be here Calum? I don't like being tossed into a helicopter and *tucked away* safe."

Konner gave Calum a questioning look.

"I thought you'd like visiting with Shae's clan now that things have settled down."

"Of course, I'm happy to see them, but don't you think you should share evacuation plans with us before we're whisked away?"

Konner had no idea why the plans were up to Calum; he'd be asking if the opportunity prevailed.

"It was only a backup plan, Rayne..."

"Which I do not approve of. I should be at Arcadia, not roaming these mountains." Devin said something quietly in the background, "we need to be with our people, helping, not sitting on a mountain top like some sort of shifter Buddha statue for all to look at," from the look on Calum's face, this outburst wasn't normal for the princess, "I want off here, I want to meet those babies when they're born and you are going to make that happen or I'm going to borrow Mari's fork."

There were muffled voices for a moment. "I'm sorry about that." It was Devin now. "She went to go see Billie."

"How are Billie and Dale doing?"

Devin cleared his throat, "your guy is losing his mind, mostly, impending fatherhood I think."

Calum nodded, then leaned closer to the phone, a look of concern on his face. "Is Rayne all right?"

Devin snorted, "no, far from it." He cleared his throat, "She's uh," he blew out a breath, "her, um," another loud breath, "I'm going to need a week or so off from official duties soon." His voice was clipped.

Calum smirked and nodded his head slowly. He looked like he wanted to laugh, "you're welcome to use the cabin if you need."

"Yeah, uh, that might be a good idea."

Konner raised one eyebrow at Calum, who in turn held up one finger telling him to wait for an explanation.

"Okay," Devin sighed, "I spoke to Fallan, she's confirmed, two locations where the tanks were not used for fish enthusiasts and we're waiting on two others, the rest have all been vetted and are for normal people that like a lot of fish."

Konner sat straighter in the chair, "where are these locations?"

"Four locations, four different states, so it's going to be a clusterfuck figuring that out because we don't want to alert the others if we hit one."

Konner stood up and leaned over the desk. "We'll need four teams." He looked up to see Calum's amusement was gone and in its place was a hard-calculating look. "Have you brought the teams in on it?"

"Not yet. I just found out a few hours ago, I told her to keep it to herself because Raymond and the Alliance headquarters are up to their ass dealing with the windfall of Tomas' crew we're dropping on them lately."

Konner spun around and looked at the maps on the wall. "If you send me the details of where," he glanced at Calum, "Calum and I can start coming up with plans."

"All right, I'll deal with the teams once we know more." He sounded calmer when talking about this than he had about his mate. "There's more, Cal, you'll be interested in this too,"

Calum tilted his head and looked at the phone, "Fallan's contacts found two members of Deacon's clan—or new clan," he paused for a second, "I didn't ask details, Konner, I can't officially be part of that, but we may need a few to go retrieve them, they can't get out on their own."

Konner nodded and looked at Calum, "Deacon's a good operator, he'll be best to take to do that."

"I'll leave those details up to you two, I'm currently being strangled by red tape and protocol to keep the teams in place for when we figure out the encrypted records."

Konner looked at the office door, the longer Reeves had his head working on that, the better their chances were to figure it out. "I have one of mine working on it as well."

"There's a lot of brains trying, so someone will figure it out."

"Are we going to have enough teams and people to run multiple ops?" Calum continued to sit, Konner didn't know how, his nerves wouldn't allow it.

"I don't think so, which is also one of the reasons I wanted you to call me, Cal, you have more pull with my father than I do on this sort of thing," he snorted, "and you know every shifter on the planet, so I need you to sit down and come up with a list of twenty or so good fighters you've met along the way, we're going to need them."

"What are you thinking? Add a few to the teams, so we can have more teams?"

"I don't even know. You are better to figure that out than I am," he heard a door slam, "shit, I have to go, Rayne is raging. Think about it and run it past Dad, okay?"

Calum nodded, "go deal with your mate, we've got this."

"Thank you." Devin swore softly, "I'll talk to you later." The line went quiet.

Konner looked at Calum and then the phone.

"Her first, uh," he waved his hand at the phone, "cycle I believe."

Konner opened his mouth and then snapped it shut again, there were no words to say to that.

"I think I have something," Reeves burst into the office waving a page, "fuck, wait," he looked back down at the paper, mumbling under his breath then started nodding his head quickly, "yes, yes." He looked at Konner, his eyes were huge, "there are common variables in this, took forever to see them, but they're right in front of my eyes." he looked from him to Calum, then back to him again, "I need help," he waved the page around, "it would take me weeks to break it down with pen and paper."

Konner knew when Reeves got like this he wouldn't sleep or let it go until he worked it out. "What about with a computer?"

Reeve's excited look faded, "I'm not that good with a computer."

Konner held up his hand, "I may have someone who is." He picked up his phone and brought up Fallan's number. He hit send and then put it on speaker.

"Fishman, hold on." That was how she answered the phone. Whatever she was doing, she didn't bother to mute the call. There were loud voices in the background, they could hear her clicking on the keys, "grab that one, Dane, yeah, okay, I got it," more clicking, "another second..." Shouts and cheers erupted. Konner looked to see Calum and Reeves were both fixated on the phone. "Holy shit, Konner, we did it. We tracked them and *now* they will forever be blocked from accessing anything of ours."

Konner put his hands on his hips and looked down at the phone, "the breach? You've figured out how they did it?"

"Yeah. Damn, they were good too, like epic greatness, it's no wonder it's taken us this long to find them." She laughed, "Woo, I might sleep for a week after this." She chuckled some more, "or more than two hours."

Calum was grinning now, "do you know where they are?"

There was a pause, "Calum?"

Konner grinned at the phone, "Sorry, yes I'm here with Calum and one of my clan, Reeves."

"Uh, yeah, Nate is informing the leader of the special ops right now, they'll go round up their asses and hand out some *justice*, or whatever it is they do." There was still a commotion in the background, "so are you calling about the tanks?"

"No, actually, the prince just told me about that."

"Oh, right. He's cool to talk to, nothing like I'd imagined. So, what's up then?"

Konner sat down, relief filling him to know that they had figured out how the Alliance databases were breached. A thought hit him. "First, do you know how they got in?"

She snorted, "it came from the inside, not in this building, but someone with a password and access, so yeah, we're still hunting them down."

Konner nodded and looked at Reeves, who looked shell-shocked, he'd never bothered to bring him in on any of that. "Reeves has been going over the records found, the ledger one."

"It's all mumble jumbo to me, I took a quick peek, if it's on paper it just doesn't grab my attention."

Konner rubbed his hand over his forehead, "do you know

anyone that excels at that sort of thing?" He looked to see an expectant expression on Reeves's face, "Reeves believes he's found common variables..."

"No shit. That's awesome, uh, Andi, you need him to talk to Andi. She's like a puzzle master or something. My brain does ones and zeros', Andi can do those anagram things and puzzle stuff so fast you can't even blink before she's solved it."

Reeves looked excited and leaned over the phone.

"Is Andi part of your team?"

"Yeah, she's due back here in about an hour."

"Is there any way Reeves could talk to her about his discovery?" Reeves was nodding.

"I'll get in touch with him, she just started working on it, so if he has figured something out, that's good for us, we'll have that deciphered in no time."

Konner grinned, "I'll text you his number."

"Sounds good." She paused for a second, "did the prince tell you about the maned wolves our contacts found?"

"Briefly. Send me more details, so I can see what's involved."

"Will do." She laughed, "now if you'll excuse me, we're going to go do a victory lap and then buckle down on finding out who left the door open in our system."

"Thanks, Fallan."

"You scratch my back and all that, my friend." She hung up.

"There was a breach at the Alliance?"

Calum stood up and turned to Reeves, "yes, very few knew."

Reeves looked at Konner, "you knew?"

Konner nodded, "yes, but as we're not on the record in their system, it was no threat to us."

"Just all the rest of the clans in the Alliance."

Calum patted his shoulder, "it was handled fast, and everyone is safe."

"Jesus, I'm so glad I just sit in my office." He put his hand over his heart, "I'm not cut out for the action stuff."

Calum smiled, "no, but your brain is very much appreciated."

Konner picked up his phone, he wanted to send Fallan the number so as soon as possible that coded ledger was unraveled. Hope filled him for the first time in decades. Hope that more of his kind would be found. He looked at the window, thinking of Terah. Sending the number, he put his phone in his pocket, "I'm going to go check on Terah and then work on that," he glanced from Reeves to Calum, "those plans for Devin."

Calum nodded, "I'll go track down Shae and see how things are and then meet you back here." He grinned, "you can help me when I call Deacon, he's going to need some reassuring on that front."

Konner wasn't sure what that meant exactly, but he turned to Reeves, "are the plans for the Parrish build ready?"

Reeves nodded, "I didn't know if it was one house or two, so it's flexible, but the plumbing part is all ready to go."

"Good. I'll let him know they'll be there for that soon." He was anxious, worrying about Terah, but he needed to settle down and focus on coming up with plans. The sooner they came up with more teams and plans to hit four states at once, the better the chances were that more of his clan and others were brought home.

Chapter Twenty-Six

He found Terah in the kitchen of his house, sitting on top of the island counter, not one of the chairs surrounding it. She was sitting crossed-legged and leaning over a tablet in her lap. Grasped tight in one hand was a stylus.

"If you're planning on stabbing the tablet, I'm afraid that won't do much damage."

Her head popped up and she looked over at him. Lifting her hand, she looked down at the stylus. "I was trying to remember what Lucus told me."

Curiosity made him decide against mentioning what chairs were for. "Maybe I can help." He went over and stood beside the island. With her sitting on top of it, they were the same height.

"This," she pointed to the screen with the object held in her hand, "I am supposed to drag it to move the pieces." She lifted just her gaze to look at him, "but I don't know if I'm doing it right." She sighed, "it looked easy when Lucus did it."

Leaning his elbow on the counter, he tilted his head so he could see the screen. It was a picture-word game. It reminded him that she had a lot of catching up to do, in life, education included.

"See," she put the tip of the stylus on the screen and moved it, "it does not work."

"May I?" He held his hand out for it, nodding, she handed it to him. Shifting so he was leaning over the counter more, he studied the screen, it seemed simple enough to do, match the pictures with words spoken. He tapped the screen with the tip so it would say the next word, but nothing happened. "Maybe it needs to be restarted?" He tried hitting the exit button and nothing happened again. Frowning, he set the pen on the counter and used his fingertip. "I think it might be frozen."

"It is not cold in my hands." She held his look, confusion in her eyes.

"Not temperature, uh," he inhaled, trying to figure out how to explain it, "with programs and computers sometimes they lock up, stop working," he looked from the screen back to see she was listening to every syllable he spoke, "it freezes on one screen and won't do anything else."

"I see." She still looked bewildered, "how do I thaw it?"

Konner couldn't help the smirk on his face, "you restart it, not thaw it."

With a serious look on her face, she nodded, "restart. Okay." She glanced at the tablet, "how do I do that?"

Reaching, he pointed to the button at the top. "Hold that down for a few seconds."

He watched her do it, "now let it go."

"Oh." The screen went dark.

"Now push and hold it again and it will restart."

She focused as she did it, a smile on her face when it started rebooting. "Thank you." Lifting her lashes, she glanced at him, "Nolyn said this is better than using too much paper." Her eyes widened, "trees die to make paper, did you know that?"

Konner nodded. "I did." He decided not to tell her he preferred paper to electronics because it was more secure.

"I don't want to be the reason trees die."

To anyone else, he would have laughed, but she meant every word she was saying. It was an odd thing, that she'd kill an otter because it was stealing the fish, but she didn't want to be the cause of some trees being cut down.

"I think it was a good idea to use stone for your house," she nodded, watching his face as she spoke, "rocks are not alive."

"Stone holds the moisture, so it made sense to use it."

"Yes. You are smart. I feel good here in the stone, not like the houses with carpet and wood everywhere." She searched his face, several thoughts moving through her eyes, "Lucus was explaining numbers to me," a small smile appeared on her lips, "I know how old I am now."

Konner could only smile in return.

"He says you are old," her brows creased, "you don't look old," he was distracted watching her eyes shift as she looked over his face, "just a few lines, not like the old ones I've known."

He raised an eyebrow, "a few lines?" He smirked.

She nodded, a soft look in her eyes, she knew he was teasing her, "yes, tiny, tiny ones," she touched beside his eye, "here," she lowered her lashes, blocking his view of her eyes, "and here," she trailed her fingertip down to beside his mouth. "Face hair is prickly."

Konner remembered he hadn't shaved for a few days. "Whiskers, yeah, I need to shave."

She moved her hand along his jaw, "I like them, your whiskers." Terah looked from her hand to his eyes, "they look good on your face." She smiled. "Even with your serious eyes. When you are looking at something you get these lines here," she moved her fingertip along his forehead, just above his eyebrows, "and your eyes darken and go very serious." She gave him a hard look as if she was trying to mimic it.

"I have a lot to think about most days." He knew he should straighten away from her; he couldn't afford to form any personal attachments to her, but being close to her, even just like this settled something inside him he wasn't ready to address.

"I know. You look after so many." She trailed her finger

down his face again and then took it off, "you free those trapped." The look in her eyes lightened, "you are very special, Konner."

He wasn't sure if special was the word she wanted to use, but he didn't want to correct her. "Thank you." He allowed his gaze to wander over her face for a second, her skin was perfection, and the only hint of the lack of care she'd had was in the haunted look deep in her eyes. He would do anything to take that look away and replace it with the one she had when she sang the songs of their people. "You," he smiled, "are quite special as well." She kept looking at his mouth, and it took all the restraint he had to not kiss her. "What you did for Raelyn," he took a quick breath and held it, "thank you," he whispered on his breath as he released it.

"I didn't do anything." Her gaze met his again, "I sang to her babies, that is all."

"You calmed them, and their mother," the panic in Rae's voice still resonated through him, "if it weren't for you, we wouldn't have known there were two."

She smiled, excitement in her eyes, "I can't wait to see two babies." Her smile brightened.

He nodded his head slowly, "I'm sure Rae will welcome the help." he couldn't bring himself to say he hoped they both survived. Terah had a fragile grip on things in her new world, and he didn't want to crush that glow inside her.

Without warning, she leaned over and kissed his cheek. "Thank you for bringing me here, Konner." When she leaned back, she put her hand over her lips. "Your whiskers tickled my mouth."

Konner sucked in a breath and slowly released it. He needed to get away from her. Looking back at the tablet she held, he saw it had rebooted several minutes ago. "Your program should work now."

"Oh." She lifted it and looked. With great focus, she tapped the icon on the screen to open it. "Yes, it does." She smiled and glanced at him. "Thank you for fixing it."

With regret, he stood up straight. "I'll be in the office if you have problems. The door by your room will take you there."

She nodded. "Thank you."

He stepped back, forcing his feet to move. When she has focused on the tablet again, he turned and walked with long strides to the door. Blowing out a breath, he scowled at the floor, he needed to get his head together, there was a lot to do. Lifting his hand, he ran it lightly along his cheek he could still feel her touch on his skin.

Closing the door, he walked to the window in the hall and stared out at the lake. He couldn't do this again. Get attached to another female, only to watch her walk away because she was mated to someone else. Grinding his teeth, he crossed his arms over his chest. It had been like that with Olanna. She had been living on her own for so long it took him time to gain her trust to bring her back to the Sanctuary. Of course, at that time, he got a little too close to her and they had both enjoyed their time together. Somewhere deep inside he'd known she could be mated to one of the males at home, but the years of loneliness had superseded any reasonable thinking.

It had been bittersweet when they found out one of the men he'd known his whole life was her mate. Auburn was a good man, and Konner couldn't begrudge him his happiness for a summer romance. It had taken a few years for him to look at her and not see her in that way.

"Everything all right?"

Konner looked over his shoulder to see Calum standing there. "Yeah, just lost in thought." he turned away from the window.

"Looked like some deep thoughts."

Konner sighed, "yeah," he waved his hand around, "lack of sleep probably."

Calum pointed to the office door, "do you want to do this tomorrow then?"

Shaking his head, Konner started walking, "no, we'll sketch out some ideas tonight then sleep on them."

"Sounds good to me." Calum smirked, "I decided to let Deacon get a good night's sleep before I tell him his clan is expanding." Calum turned toward the office, glancing back at him, "I think he only agreed to the Alpha position because he didn't think any more like him were out there."

Konner followed as he went into the room, "there's always a chance of more of ours out there."

Calum set his cup on the table and looked over at the map behind the desk. "I was part of the Alliance before I knew what it was all about." He shrugged, "as one of the prince's seconds, I didn't have a choice."

"That explains how it was you that set up the evacuation plan."

He nodded his head crossed his arms over his chest and looked at the floor. "Devin and I grew up together, along with Gage, his other choice for a second," he shook his head, "a wolf, a tiger, and a jaguar," he grinned, "it was quite eventful, but our clans were all working together to get the Alliance heading in a different direction," he looked over at him and Konner watched something change in his eyes, "then the Tomas organization happened, or became apparent that they were out there." He ran his hand down over his jaw, "every one of our clans has lost members because of them, yours probably the most."

"Is that why you do it?" Konner leaned back against the desk, "because you've lost too?"

Calum looked at him without seeing him for a moment, "my mother." His expression lightened for a moment, "I don't hold any fantasies that she's still out there," he smirked, "she was a fighter, so I doubt they kept her alive this long." He sucked in a breath, "but that doesn't mean I can't do everything in my power to find as many as I can and make Tomas' vast empire crumble."

Konner put his hand over his mouth and stood that way looking at him for a moment. Dropping his hand, he gave him a quick shrug, "regardless of reasons, I'm glad you're with us and not against us."

Calum smirked. "So, where do you want to begin this long night of plans, backup plans, and contingency plans?"

Konner chuckled, "I thought we'd start by opening my email from Fallan and seeing where the locations are."

"Think we'll be lucky enough they're four states all lined up in a row?"

Konner leaned over his desk and opened the email, he scanned it quickly, just looking for names, and then lifted his gaze to look at him. "No such luck."

"Good side to that is a delay in sharing information. If they were neighboring, news travels fast." Calum went over to the map crossed his arms and looked at it. "Personally, I don't care where they are, we'll find them all eventually."

Konner turned to the map and nodded, "I still have six thousand, four hundred and six lakes, small bodies of water, and deep rivers to check in North America, so the more I travel the better."

"That many?"

Konner didn't look at him, just nodded, "which considering there are over thirty thousand," he lifted one shoulder and let it drop, "I'd say I'm doing good."

"You said North America, did your clans split worldwide?"

Konner put his hands on top of his head and held them there while he blew out a breath. "I don't know. Nothing for sure at least."

"Okay, well, that puts our current task into perspective and now it doesn't seem so daunting."

Konner dropped his hand and looked at him, "glad I could be of help."

"I feel like I should be out there helping you by swimming in lakes." Calum went around and picked up the cup.

"Unfortunately, unless you use high-tech sonar, you can't just jump in a lake and find one of my kind."

"I didn't think it was that easy." He paused before taking a sip, "but I'm still willing to help."

"I might take you up on that sometime, just the traveling constantly wears on me." He turned the laptop around so Calum could read the locations, "having someone to talk to while I do it would be great."

Calum, grinned, "I travel all the time too, now I have Shae, so it's not as bad."

Konner nodded, turning his back to the desk so he could look at the distance between the locations. Even if he found a mate someday, he doubted he'd risk letting her ever leave the Sanctuary. The only two of his clan that had left it since the fence was complete were Auburn and himself. Auburn only if he had to go to a building site, otherwise he did most things remotely. Konner was the one that took all the risks so his clan could be safe, and he didn't see that changing in the future.

Chapter Twenty-Seven

Terah walked along the path, there were many footprints, so she knew it was okay to walk here. She had put on the jacket and shoes at Konner's request, even though the snow didn't bother her at all, but he would know best with things like this, so she did it.

The path was leading her to a building she hadn't been to, and she was curious why so many were going there. If the size of the footprints were right, it was mostly the children. When she reached it, she stopped and looked at it. It was made of stone, as most of the buildings here seemed to be, there were no windows, so it wasn't a greenhouse. She smirked, the greenhouse turned out to be glass and not green at all, but who was she to question the name of it.

Opening the door, she put just her head in and listened. She could hear laughing and splashing. Driven by curiosity, she stepped in and closed the door quietly. Going up the short ramp, she stopped and looked to see a large pool. Lillee, Nakisa and Kole were swimming in it. Nolyn sat at the end of the pool, reading a book.

"Terah," Nakisa shouted and started swimming toward her.

"Have you come for a swim with us?"

Terah smiled at her, then glanced to see Nolyn smiling at her. "I will talk with Nolyn right now."

"Okay." Nakisa dove under the water and swam back to the middle of the pool.

Taking off her coat, and kicking off the shoes, she left them sitting with the others on a bench beside the ramp. The air was warm, but not dry. The floor was cool on her feet though, so she knew Konner had helped to make this place, he knew how stone worked and must have found a way to make the air warm here.

She went over and sat on the chair beside Nolyn. She closed her book and just held it in her hand.

"This was built for the kids, so they can swim all year round."

"They do not swim in the lake?" She watched Kole dive under and smile as he did it with ease.

"In the warmer months, they do." Nolyn smiled when Kole poked Lillee then swam fast the other way. "Until the change, their skin is more susceptible to the cold though, so," she waved her hand at the pool, "Konner and Reeves figured out a way to use freshwater but heat it so they don't get a chill."

"It is a very smart idea." She smiled at Nolyn, "the children are lucky to be able to swim when they want."

"Oh, it's not really a want." Nolyn set the book down behind her in the chair, "they can swim when they're born," she shrugged, "even one-form babies are able to, but to build strength and knowledge of how to move in the water, they swim every day."

Terah looked at them, the way they moved in the water. "I would yearn for water and swimming every day."

"I can't imagine being without water."

She looked to see a soft expression on Nolyn's face. "There is water everywhere here," she smiled at her, "I can be in it any time I want." She leaned closer, "I woke up last night and swam in Konner's pool in his house." She shrugged, "I would have preferred the lake, but I don't know the rules and when I can."

"There are no rules with the lake." Nolyn's brow creased, "you can swim anytime you want." She smirked, "it's kind of who we are."

Terah nodded, not wanting to disagree with her. "Konner said I should not swim with others until I am stronger and more adjusted." She frowned, not sure if that was the word he had used. "Or settled, or," she lifted a hand, "something like that."

"Oh." Nolyn watched the children for a moment. "You are pretty aggressive in the water," she turned back to her, "with good reason. If I'd been denied water my whole life, I probably wouldn't get out of it or want to share it either." She got up and pulled her shirt over her head. Terah noted, that she wore one of those suit tops. "Come on." She motioned to the pool, "this is a safe indoor swim, no fish or plants to bring it on," she pulled her pants off and those sock things Terah still couldn't bring herself to wear, "and I know you wouldn't feel aggression toward the children in or out of the lake."

"I would never hurt the children." Her chest felt tight at the very thought.

"I know, come on, it's warm, but still feels great."

Terah stood up and then looked down at what she was wearing. "I do not have a suit on."

Nolyn shrugged, and then pointed to the door on the other side, "there's plenty in there, go grab one and hop in."

Terah smiled, excitement filling her. She wanted to swim with the children, as her mother had her. "Yes." she went toward the door with fast steps.

"My turn. My turn again." Kole yelled when Terah broke the surface of the water. He swam toward her quickly.

Lillee laughed and pushed away from Terah, "I can't believe how high you get." She pushed the hair back from her face.

Terah smiled; her heart felt like it was going to burst with joy from playing with them in the water. "I am used to small pools, so it is easy."

Nolyn rested against the edge of the pool, grinning at her. "I can't even do it, which is crazy, I've been swimming my whole life." She tilted her head to the side, "I can't wait to see how fast you can go in the lake," she glanced at Nakisa, "bet she's faster than your dad."

"Or Konner," Lillee nodded, "he the fastest one."

Kole tread water beside her without issue, but she didn't want to leave him there too long, he was quite small still. She moved over so he could get on her back and placed his arms where she had instructed him to the last time. "Konner swims much looking for others like us."

Nolyn nodded, "Auburn used to look too, but not since," she glanced at Nakisa, "Konner found Olanna, now he won't risk leaving his family."

"That is wise." Terah agreed. "Did he find you?"

Nolyn shook her head, "No, well, not that way." She looked at her webbed fingers beneath the surface, "when I got separated from my clan," she glanced at the children quickly, "or whatever, you know?" She nodded, "I knew there was another clan close to us, so I made my way to them."

"How old were you?" Lillee asked her, a sad expression on her face.

"Not much older than you, Lil."

"You are very brave." Terah felt the need to put her at ease.

"So yeah, other than me, Konner has found, Malachi, Olanna, Reeves, and now you." Nolyn smiled at her.

"He is going to find more." Terah nodded, "they know where to look now." She smiled, hoping that settled the darker mood.

"Is that what he said?" Nolyn pushed from the edge of the pool and glided toward her.

"Yes. He was talking to Calum, and they have locations," she nodded, "that is what they said."

Nolyn's smile was slow, her eyes looked glossier, "that's great." She sucked in a breath and then turned to Lillee and splashed water in her face, "back up to the edges so Kole gets his chance to fly."

Terah grinned and patted Kole's hand, "hang on tight."

"I'm ready." his grip tightened.

Terah started for the far end, not moving too fast. "Use your legs, I'm going under." She made sure to use a playful tone as she turned and faced the other end. Diving down, she felt the bottom brush along her front with a whisper of a touch. It wasn't as easy as she had told them it was, but if she were to get strong enough to swim with the others, it was worth the effort. As the far end grew closer, she pushed off from the bottom and parted the water, using all the strength her legs had to launch her body into the air above the pool. Twisting, she spun herself around, once, twice, and then they plunged back down into the water. As Kole let go, she turned to make sure he wasn't disoriented and made it to the top.

He spit out water and laughed as he treaded above the surface. "I want to do that in the lake when the snow is done." He grinned at her.

Terah turned to see Nolyn wasn't watching them but was looking behind her. Letting her body turn, she saw that Konner was standing at the side of the pool.

"Konner." Kole shouted and swam toward him, "did you see that? Did you see how high Terah can go?"

Konner squatted down beside the pool he held out his hand to the child. He lifted him right out of the water. "I did. You were flying."

Kole gripped his neck and nodded, "it was so much fun." He looked at him, eyes wide, "can you do that?"

Konner made a face like he was thinking hard, "I don't know, but I will have to try it sometime." He set him down. "Go get dressed, we're having lunch in the common house." He glanced at Nolyn, "a meeting afterward."

Nolyn nodded and swam to the end of the pool.

Lillee got out and wrapped a towel around herself. "She can even do it with me, and I'm a lot heavier." She walked by him, "so I know you can do it."

Konner grinned at her, "I guess we'll find out once you can go in the lake again."

"Yes." she giggled and ran over to the door.

Nakisa didn't speak to him, but she was giving him a big smile as she followed Lillee.

Nolyn picked up her clothes and book and went over to him, she glanced from him to Terah, "it was my idea." She waved a hand around, "safe indoor location."

Konner nodded his head but was still looking at Terah.

Terah trod the water and watched the door close. Not sure why the mood was suddenly heavier. "It was fun to swim with children." She moved over toward him, "I would never hurt them."

Konner squatted down and looked at her as she got nearer. "I didn't think you would." He motioned to the water, "as fun as it was, I can see you're exhausted now and that's what I want to avoid."

"I am okay." She smiled up at him.

He blew out a breath, those lines appearing above his eyes, "I guess we checked one male off the list."

"The list?" Terah put her hand on the edge of the pool, so she could look up at him.

"Of possible mates." His tone was very low.

Terah looked at the door everyone had gone in. "Kole? He's a little boy." She frowned, "I would know before his change?"

Konner nodded, "you would know." His eyes had darkened, and it bothered her to know that something she had done put that look on his face.

"I did not know. I am sorry."

His eyes moved around like he was memorizing her face. "I know. Nothing would have happened, at his age, but it was still risky, Terah."

Terah rested her forehead against the cool stone and looked at the water moving against it. "I am sorry, Konner." she lifted her chin and looked up at him. "I wanted to swim and play with the children."

He didn't speak, but after a few breaths time, he nodded and held his hand out to her. When he stood up, he pulled her from the water without trouble. Still holding her hand, he looked at how she was dressed.

Terah looked down at the suit with the flowers on it. "Less suit was more comfortable."

Konner licked his lips and released her hand, "I'm sure it would be." He cleared his throat and motioned to the door. "I'll wait here while you get changed." He put his hands in his pockets, a somber expression on his face. "You may not be steady on your feet after the energy you just burned."

Terah looked down to see her feet had changed back, "My feet feel fine."

His mouth twitched, "I'll still wait and walk back with you."

"Okay. I will go put my clothes back on."

He nodded and then turned to look at the pool.

Chapter Twenty-Eight

Konner hung up the phone and tossed it onto his desk. Usually, things came together quickly, except the one time he needed them to.

"Having trouble?"

Konner looked to see Calum leaning in the doorway. "Hitting a lot of walls right now."

"With?"

Konner motioned to the folders stacked on his desk. "We have eight building sites, including Deacon and Blair's, and the contractors are whining about the weather."

"Maybe you should recruit some of Lois White's clan or one of the others that like the snow and cooler temperatures."

Konner looked at the folders, then back to him, "they don't need to specialize, just able to build." He waved a hand around, "all of the supervisors will work through any weather." he picked up his cup, "normally this is when things slow down, so the crew makes plans with mates and families—" the cup was empty. He didn't remember drinking it.

"Okay, well there are several at Blairs that will jump in and help, I know that, so send a small crew there." He grinned, "they have any equipment needed right down the road."

Konner set the empty cup down and picked up the book with the list of men in it. "Blair won't mind if we enlist their help?"

Calum sat down, "he'll probably thank you for giving everyone something to do."

Konner glanced at him to see the amused look on his face.

"His clan went from ten to twenty-seven in a matter of a few weeks, the sooner they're all busy and have their own place to stay, the happier all will be."

He envied that Blair had found many members of the clan. Although the sudden chaos would drive anyone crazy, he imagined. "Okay, I'll talk to Auburn and see how many he thinks we'll need at Deacon's," he looked at the empty cup again, really wanting more tea, "instead of separate units, we're going to do a one-level duplex type of build for the time being."

Calum nodded, "how many can it house?"

"Comfortably? Probably six to ten," he shrugged, "I guess it depends on whether there are children or adults."

"Did you get any more details about those two needing to get out?"

Konner shook his head, "I'm waiting for a call about the finer details."

"Who helps you on the other end? Are they part of the Alliance?"

Shaking his head, he crossed his arms over his chest. How much did he trust this man? Calum Dante was reputed for doing whatever was required, but he wasn't sure if any of that was outside of what the Alliance would or wouldn't allow. "They're not part of any faction."

"But they're shifters?"

He nodded again.

"So why not bring them into the Alliance?" Calum sat down and looked up at him. "I assume they can take care of themselves."

"They can, they've helped me numerous times, but not out of honor, if you know what I mean."

"So they're mercenaries." Calum shrugged, "most often than not, they're only taking money for help so they can look after their own." He shrugged, "you should talk to them, feel around a little and see, they might want to trade money for security."

"I'll do that." In all the years he'd been working with them, he'd never thought they may want something different. "They're pretty rough around the edges."

Calum chuckled, "that just gives them character."

Konner went over to the window and then stopped, Olanna, Nolyn, and Shaelan were going down to the lake. All three of them were wrapped in blankets. "Calum?"

"Yeah?"

"Why is your mate going for a swim while it's snowing? We have an indoor pool house."

Calum got up and came and stood beside him, "she's testing a theory."

"What theory?"

Calum sighed, "she wants to see if the women's levels change when they're in the water."

"Levels?"

Calum shrugged, "blood tests, I don't remember what she went on about, but if they change then the water birth will definitely be the route to go."

Konner watched Olanna and Nolyn drop their blankets and run into the lake. They probably only brought blankets to make Shaelan feel better. "She can test something like that?"

Calum leaned on the window and kept his gaze locked on his mate as she slowly walked out into the water. The way she stepped; he knew it was too cold for her. "Apparently." He sighed, "if you'll excuse me, I'm going to make sure my mate jumps into a hot shower as soon as she's done this."

Konner watched Olanna go out to the deeper part and then turn to come back. "She could have sat on the dock over by the fishery."

"Could have, but that would be half measure and my woman doesn't do half measure." Calum shook his head and turned to the door.

Konner watched Shaelan go out waist deep, he could see she was shivering from here. Women were tenacious creatures. Nolyn swam up to Shaelan floated on her back and held her arm up out of the water. Shaking his head, he turned around and grabbed his cup, he needed a cup of tea—and should probably check on Terah while he was there.

He checked her room, the entertainment room, and as a last resort the common house, praying the whole time she wasn't trying to bake again. When he exhausted all possible rooms, he went to the front of the house to look out the window, thinking maybe she was down at the lake where Shaelan was doing her tests. The younger children would be doing their studies right now and the two boys should be over at the fishery doing chores, so he wasn't sure where else to look.

He was just about to turn around and go get his shoes when he saw her coming out of the trees that ran to the side docks around the lake. She was wrapped in a towel. He checked the shore again and saw that Olanna and Nolyn weren't there now. Relief filled him; he'd been concerned she'd been in the lake when they were. Swimming in a pool with children was nothing like being in the lake with others. Breathing another sigh of relief, he was just about to turn to go back to the kitchen when Lucus and Paxton came out of the trees, towels wrapped around them. They were laughing and called out something to Terah. She stopped and smiled at them, pointing to the lake, Pax shook his head at whatever she'd said.

She'd been in the lake with two males. His mind started flying with all the ways that could have gone very wrong. He squeezed them shut, he knew she'd understood when he'd explained it. His gaze narrowed in on the boys wondering if Paxton had coerced her into going for a swim with them.

Grinding his teeth, he spun on his heel and went back to the kitchen. Putting the kettle on to boil, he stood there leaning on the island tapping his hands on it. Paxton wasn't that naïve, to ignore the warning that he knew Malachi had given all of them.

They came in the door, one after the other, still laughing and talking. Konner stood there, motionless, waiting for them to notice him. Lucus spotted him first and stopped so suddenly that Paxton, who was looking at Terah at that moment, walked right into him. His eyes went wide when he saw why Lucus had stopped. Paxton on auto defend mode, opened his arms, raising his hands. "She joined us; we didn't know."

Lucus bobbed his head quickly. "She startled Pax so bad, I thought he might die on me."

Konner stood there, not even able to find the words to speak to them.

"I saw them leave and followed them," Terah said, walking around the pool, toward the kitchen. "Do not be mad at them."

Konner dragged his gaze from her to the two boys, still standing where they'd stopped. "Go get dressed." He tried to keep the bark out of his words but failed.

Both teens jolted and made fast work of getting down the hall to their rooms.

Terah stood on the other side of the island now. "They were safe. I would not hurt them." Her hair was dripping onto the towel, soaking it.

"You couldn't know…"

Terah shook her head, a hard expression on her face, "I am strong, Konner, not weak as you think." She practically spat the words at him. "I know they are boys; I would not hurt them."

He gripped the counter tight and inhaled slowly, buying time to try to find the words to explain it to her.

"I am fine. They are fine." Her words were clipped, "you can take two more off *the list*." She turned and walked quickly toward her room.

Dropping his head, he closed his eyes. That was a big failure on his part.

"You shouldn't be mad at her."

Turning, he looked to see Lucus standing there, wearing a navy bathrobe.

"She was careful. She stalked us halfway across the lake, checking for herself how she felt about being in the water with another water clan." Jamming his hands in his pockets. "We didn't even know she was there until she popped up out of the water and did this epic twirl," he waved his hands in a circle above his head, "like some kind of freaking mermaid or something." He gave Konner a serious look, "she," he opened his hand and made a face, "practically glows when she's in the water, Konner, I've never seen that." He sobered, "why does she do that?"

Konner wiped his hand over his face, feeling like a slug for reacting the way he had, "I'm not sure, but there's a lot of things about her that are different."

"But she's like us, right?"

Konner nodded, "her line was the combination of Alpha lines from other clans, they hoped to strengthen the clan."

Lucus snorted, "well they succeeded, she's crazy fast, like swam circles around us and that, that twirl thing, I don't even know how she does it." He scowled, "I can get like four feet if I really build up the momentum," he snorted again, "it's like she grows wings and soars."

Konner smirked at his dramatic expressions, but he couldn't argue with them. "I saw her do in the pool house, with Kole on her back."

"For real? She can do that carrying someone?" He frowned, "Kole isn't that big, but still." He blew out a breath, "just don't be mad at her. She even warned us if she did anything funny to get out of the water." He shook his head, "not that it would have mattered with how fast she is." He shrugged, "I'm going to grab a shower." He backed up two steps and then turned and walked back down the hall.

The kettle whistling caught his attention. Going over, he

took it off the burner and then set it down. Two more off the list. That left Reeves and himself. Closing his eyes, he took a deep breath and then blew it out. He had no idea how he felt about things if Reeves turned out to be her mate. None at all. Shaking his head, he turned and started for the office. His want of a relaxing cup of tea was gone. He needed to get his head into work and keep it there.

Chapter Twenty-Nine

Konner checked the boys were buckled down doing their assignments. He grinned as he closed Paxton's door, maybe they'd learned not to make the teacher angry.

He needed to get back to the office, Reeves would be waiting to go over the rest of the contracts. Normally things would be winding down for the winter months, but with the Alliance clans on alert—there were clans joining, adding on, or like with Deacon, just starting out. They had enough jobs that they'd have to try to finish some during the winter.

He remembered when they'd built the homes here at the Sanctuary, Auntie had thought he'd constructed too many. Now that several had tenants, there was hushed talk of which direction to take the complex when the last four were filled.

Konner supposed at some point Terah would be moving into one. He frowned, it was too soon for that, at least until she learned more about living, instead of just barely existing.

Stopping near the pool, he listened, where was that music coming from? Konner heaved a loud sigh, he'd fallen for it a few times, but not this time. The boys would appear to be complying with the rules of homework but would leave their game paused so they could sneak back out to play when he was busy.

Turning on his heel, he went back down the short corridor to the tv room. The door was half-open, so he stopped to glance in and confirm his suspicions before laying into those two again. It was not a game on pause, it was a movie playing.

Pushing the door open further, he looked in to see Terah sitting on the corner of the sofa with her legs pulled up hugging them. Her face glistened with tears.

When he stepped into the room, she rushed and grabbed the remote, and paused it.

"Lucus showed me how to work this." She held up the remote toward the screen.

"It's fine." He went over and crouched down beside her. "Are you all right?"

She swiped at her damp cheek and nodded her head in a jerky motion. "Yes." She looked at the TV. "That is love." A soft look filled her eyes.

Konner turned to see a man and woman embracing. Actors in a movie. "They are actors." He looked back at her. "It's a movie, not real. It's for entertainment."

She looked back to the screen, "but I see it when they kiss, that they love each other."

He leaned against the arm of the sofa, "they are very good actors, but it's not real, you understand?" He watched her look at them again, a strange expression on her face.

"I have never been kissed," she glanced at him quickly, then back to the screen, "not even when we tried to make a baby." She sighed softly and turned the TV off.

He stood when she got up from the sofa. She looked down at her hands, her dark eyelashes shadowed her eyes from him. Konner hadn't meant to ruin her watching it. "You can stay and watch it."

"No. I have seen enough." Lifting her chin, she looked up at him. Beneath her eyes still shone from the wet tears.

Konner would regret this a thousand times later, but right

now he had to wipe that forlorn pain from her face. Touching her chin with the tip of his finger, he leaned down and kissed her lips softly. Watching her reaction was his undoing as her lashes fluttered and her cerulean eyes locked on his.

Like a fool with no restraint, he cupped the side of her face and kissed her again, longer this time, gently with care until her mouth moved beneath his. He felt her grip his shirt in his hand and stretch up onto her toes to return his kiss.

It was heartbreaking that no one had ever shown affection for her, but he was glad they hadn't at the same time. When the tenderness inside him began to turn into arousal, he ended the contact and lifted his head.

She didn't object, just stood there giving him a sexy clouded look. "Was that acting?" She whispered, still close enough to him that her breath caressed his lips.

"No." He was barely able to find his voice, "that was real." Lifting his head, he caught movement out of the corner of his eye and saw Reeves standing in the corridor.

Reeves cleared his throat and point to the door leading into the common house. "I was coming to find you."

Konner stepped back and put some space between himself and Terah, "I'm coming now."

Reeves gave him a stiff nod and walked quickly back up the hall.

He looked down at Terah and could see she was still processing what had just happened. "I have some work to get done."

She blinked and looked at him. "You work a lot."

Smirking, he backed up more, "yes, there's always a lot to do."

She nodded as if she understood, but she doubted she did. "I wanted to swim in your pool." She gave him a hopeful look.

Stepping to the side, he motioned out the door, "feel free." He was glad for it. If she swam in the pool, in the house, he wouldn't have to worry about her outside alone.

"I am free." A small smile lightened the lost expression on

her face as she walked by him and up the corridor.

Konner followed, wanting to get to the office and get the work done so he could get some semblance of sleep. He had too much to do in the next few weeks to allow himself to get run down. As he turned to go around the pool, he almost lost his footing when Terah stopped and dropped her robe to the floor.

His legs stopped completely as he watched her go down the steps and the water embrace her as she immersed herself. Her skin, even before the water kissed it, shone with a slight iridescent glow. She was absolutely beautiful. He recalled the folklore he'd read of the radiant women of the sea that captured men's hearts and for the first time in his long life, he believed that could have been true at some point.

She broke the surface and smiled up at him. "I love this pool; the water makes me feel good."

He couldn't find his voice to answer her. Going over to the wall, he dimmed the area's lights, leaving her to appear she was swimming in the moonlight.

She gave him a quick look; amazement was on her face. "It's like magic."

Konner nodded, it was magical, and it had nothing to do with the light switches. "I'll see you in the morning." As he forced his feet to move toward the exit, the entire foyer was filled with her soul-wrenching, skin-tingling, lilting notes of her song.

Reeves stood by the desk when he walked in. "Sorry," he motioned to the door, then dropped his hands.

Konner shook his head, "it's fine." He looked at the door, "it was just a moment of weakness."

"Is that what you're calling it?" He smirked. "I want to say we're only human, but that doesn't fit, so I'll lead with we have needs too." He shrugged, "And Terah is beautiful," he grimaced, "if not a little intimidating." Reeves moved over to the desk and started arranging things with nervous energy.

Konner watched him for a moment, he didn't know why he hadn't seen it before, but Reeves was way too relaxed with that comment. "You and Nolyn?"

Reeves stopped, his head jerking up to look at him. Dropping the folders, he straightened. "It's not like we have a lot of choices without leaving the Sanctuary—which neither of us wants to do."

Konner understood, loneliness was the hardest. "It's not wrong, but—"

Reeves shook his head. "It's not without affection," he blinked a few times, "we made a pact, we're both in our twenties, so still young." He frowned, "if we hit forty and still have no mate, we're going to have some kids and co-parent."

Konner wasn't sure what that entailed, he'd also thought Nolyn had given up the idea of having children without a mate. He cleared his throat, "and if one of you find a mate?" He thought of Terah, then focused hard not to have his mind go there. Reeves could be her mate and honestly, he didn't know how he would cope with that if it happened.

"Then we walk away," Reeves shrugged, "as you and Olanna did—so I've been told, that was before I was here."

Konner looked at the floor for a moment. "Things were different with that," he'd spent a year convincing himself of that, "Auburn was away for courses, so we could get construction permits, it never occurred to us—"

"Yeah, well, I hope I'm not Terah's mate."

He looked back at him—there was no male that would honestly think that when it came to the water spirit swimming and singing in his pool.

"Not because she's not beautiful or-or kind but," Reeves moved his hand up and down Konner, "I've never seen you like that," he smirked, "relaxed, intrigued by someone," his smirk changed to a blank expression, "I was beginning to think you were cold, broken…"

Konner held up his hand, so he'd stop, "I get the point." He straightened his shoulders, "it doesn't change the fact that

227

Terah may—"

"Find someone that will give her ten children," Reeves shook his head, "fate wouldn't do that to me."

Konner smiled. "You just said you were willing to co-parent with Nolyn."

Reeves picked up a stack of folders, "yeah, in fourteen years, not in nine months," he shrugged, "or however long it is." He frowned, "it doesn't equate. I heard Shaelan say gestation is forty weeks, like one-forms, that's ten months but why do they say nine months?"

Konner had honestly, never in his life given it any thought at all. The calculation involved in conception had never been at the forefront of his mind. "I know nothing about it."

Reeves snorted and started walking into Konner's office, "might want to look into that, because Terah seems adamant about having children. She has told *all* the females. And unless we light up like light bulbs or whatever if we ever swim together, that's all on you, boss."

Konner stood there staring at his back. He hadn't even considered the children she wanted being a definite part of her plans. Yes, she's said it, but he'd assumed she meant later. He scowled at the floor, it explained why she was checking the males off the list.

"Konner?"

He blinked to see Reeves standing in his office looking out at him.

"I'd like to sleep before dawn."

Shooting him a hard look, he went into the room. "You're going to have to swim with Terah before I go away."

Reeves froze, then moved just his eyes to look at him.

Konner tried to shrug it off, "so we know soon than later."

"I thought you said—"

"It wasn't right for me to deny her swimming with her own kind after a lifetime alone." If he hadn't been waging an internal war, he would have laughed at Reeves shell shocked look. "She swam with the boys earlier, Lucus was in awe of her."

"In awe how?"

Konner tugged the folder Reeves had a death grip on, "her speed, how powerful she is."

Reeves's jaw snapped shut. "So basically, she's going to make me look like a tortoise crawling along the sand."

Konner grinned. He'd swam with Reeves; he wasn't slow or lacking in the water. "I guess we'll find out." He knew it was mean and slightly juvenile but knowing that Reeves would now avoid swimming with her as long as possible, took some of the sting out of old wounds Konner thought long healed. Konner opened the file and look at the materials list, without really seeing it. Since when did he play on others' weaknesses? He needed to go for a long swim when they were done and clear his mind—he couldn't afford to be distracted from work and the upcoming ops.

Operations that would bring them more clan members and closer to fulfilling all their hopes and wishes.

Chapter Thirty

He hadn't slept, despite swimming almost to the point of exhaustion. Konner stared at the cup in his hand, the herb mix was doing nothing to shake the fog from his head.

"Temperatures are really dropping."

He turned to see Calum coming toward him, he held a steaming cup and Konner could smell the coffee. Did they bring their own, he wondered because it wasn't anything they stocked?

"A few more degrees and the snow might stay." Calum stopped beside him, "does the lake freeze over?"

"For the most part."

"Do you swim under the ice?"

Konner nodded slowly, "some of us do, we break a trail along the other side, the rest are content with the pool house."

"Shaelan's tests have told her water birth is the best route."

Konner looked at him, "I've been wondering." He cleared his throat, "Is Shaelan staying for it?"

Calum chuckled, "I'd have to tie her up and carry her away from here before those babies arrive."

"Sorry about taking so much of her time, but I can't say

things would be as calm if she weren't here."

"It's fine. It's peaceful here and it feels like we've been watching over our shoulder since we met."

Konner nodded and watched the ripples in the water after a fish jumped. "I know this is an odd question," one he hadn't even known he was going to ask, "but does your or any of the other clans have children between un-mated couples?"

Calum sipped his coffee, watching him over the cup. He lowered it and then blew out a forced breath, "before Shaelan—I would have said no, for the most part, children aren't possible without the mate connection—but some have found a way to trick the mind and body in that area," he took another drink, "I gather from the talk at dinner last night that it isn't that way for your kind?"

Konner shook his head, "no, we can breed with any of our kind, as long as it's in the water during the right cycle."

"I read the report, doesn't sound like Tomas' group has figured that out."

Konner sighed, "either part of it. From what Terah described, I'm not sure she's even aware of it either."

Calum grinned and lifted the cup. "Pretty sure she's going to figure it out soon enough." He toasted him, "I'll catch up to you in your office, I'm going to coax my work-a-holic mate to go for a run."

Konner watched him walk back up to the path leading to the house they were using. He supposed he should allow for guests in the future building plans. Having Calum and Shaelan here had brought new energy to the clan.

"Serious thoughts so early?"

He smiled at his aunt's tone. "Always." Turning, he smiled at her. He hadn't seen her as lighthearted as she'd been lately in a long time. They were going to have to have a clan meeting and discuss changing things.

"It's a different place here now." Her tone was very contemplative.

"I noticed."

"Notice anything else?" She looked like she wanted to grin but didn't.

Konner glanced around, "like what?" He looked down to see her watching the lake. Turning he saw there were two wakes splitting the surface, like when someone moved close to the surface. Terah popped above the surface and turned to wait for someone to catch up. He couldn't have looked away now if he had to.

A good ten seconds later, Reeves surfaced and shook his head at her.

Terah laughed at something he said.

"I thought you asked everyone to wait to swim with her."

Konner frowned, "I did." He continued to watch as they came toward the shore.

Alviva chuckled. "I don't think she's big on your rules, nephew."

He gave her a brief side glance.

"You should go swim with her."

He wanted to more than anything. "It's more complicated…"

"Why because you're attracted to her?"

He knew she was watching him now and refused to look down at her.

"It won't be like you and Olanna."

Snapping his head, he looked at her.

"I'm old, not blind."

"I just—I don't know if I'm strong enough to swim with her," he blew out a breath, "if she's mine—I want her to experience life before…"

"Talk to her."

"If she's not," he rubbed his hand over his face, "then at some point, I'll have to let her go if *I* find her mate."

"So you're going to avoid the problem? It's not your way— you conquer problems as if they've never been there."

Reeves walked through the shallows as Terah did a flip and went back out. "Maybe I'm just getting old."

His aunt chortled.

He didn't think she understood. "With or without a mate, she wants children—*a lot* of children."

"How is that bad, Konner? She's young, incredibly strong, and has qualities we thought long gone…"

"I don't want her to be used as a breeding mare." That would make them no different than Tomas.

"Talk to her…"

"She doesn't understand…"

"She may not know words, but she knows feelings, talk to her."

"I can't right now, I have to…"

"Fly off into the sunset and save the world?" She smirked.

"No," he scowled, "I have to go meet someone that's saving another almost extinct clan."

"You are noble to a fault, my nephew, but I do wonder," she looked out at the water.

"Wonder what?"

"Who's going to save you when your heart gets to the point it can't face another false lead and empty lake." She tapped her cane on the stone and motioned with her chin, "you might want to calm your man down, he looks like he's going to jump right out of his skin." Still chuckling, she walked away. "I'm going to go swimming with Terah." Her tone was daring him to object.

Konner watched her walk away before turning to see Reeves standing in front of him. The baggy shorts, that he didn't know how he swam in, were dripping onto the stones in front of him.

"She joined me." Reeves held his look, "I didn't think anyone else was up when I went in."

Konner looked at his neck, despite already knowing they weren't mates. "I guess you're stuck with your fourteen-year plan then."

Reeves looked like he was going to drop, the relief was that visible. "We are not mates." He blew out a loud breath and turned toward the lake. "She is so fast I don't know how she gets up to speed so quickly."

Konner dragged his gaze from the water and looked at him.

"Pretty sure even you are going to have to work to keep up with her."

Konner raised an eyebrow at him.

"I'm not joking, Konner, apparently the genes from more than one Alpha line give you insane strength and speed." He smirked, "if you two have kids, a boy, we'll have the equivalent of the man of steel."

Konner laughed, "you watch too much TV."

"Or you don't watch enough and have forgotten how to dream." Reeves held his look for a moment and then turned and walked away.

Konner scowled at his back. Forgotten how to dream? What did that even mean? Shaking his head, he looked back to the lake to see his aunt swimming alongside Terah.

Sucking in a breath, he turned on his heel and walked quickly, before he stripped down and jumped into the lake with them.

Chapter Thirty-One

Terah watched Olanna and Auburn disappear under the water together. She felt like sitting here in the trees and watching them together was wrong, but still did it. It was so strange to see others like her but in a good way. She had been in the water with people of her own kind. She swatted the tear off her cheek, she'd never thought that would happen.

Before they found her, sometimes when the pains weren't too bad, she would close her eyes and try to remember being in the pool with her mother and the old one, the pictures of that in her head were fading though and it was harder to see them now.

Lifting her head, she took a deep breath. She wasn't alone now. Would never have to swim alone again. She grinned to herself, she liked swimming alone, going fast and exploring, but it didn't compare with watching the others in the water with her though.

She had been on her way to the dock that Alviva had told her about when she spotted the couple walking toward the water holding hands. It felt wrong to join them. If she had a male that was hers, she wouldn't want to share him with others in the water. So now she sat there trying to decide what to do next.

All night she had woken to feel different, and then her stomach started with this weird feeling, she thought a swim would settle what was wrong but taking time from Olanna with her man, wasn't fair.

Getting up, she turned to look behind her, she could go for a walk and explore. It was dawn now and there was more light in the trees, so that was sticking within the rules that Konner had laid out for her before he left. Use the pool at night. Only go in the bush when there's enough light to see and do not cook without one of the other women present. She smirked thinking of the last one. The look on his face when he'd said that one was so serious.

Twisting her hair back, she tucked it into the back of her jacket, so it wouldn't get snagged on the branches. Her stomach was tensing again, and she wondered if she had overdone it as Konner feared she might in the last few days. It was true she had never been able to swim as she had since been found, but the rest of her felt strong from it. Biting her lip, she navigated around a large tree, maybe she should ask Shaelan about it when she saw her. She didn't want to bother her too much though; she was staying close to Raelyn and the babies were far more important than aching muscles.

Konner had been gone for two days now and it was an unsettling feeling with him gone. She hadn't been here long, of course, but seeing him several times a day was normal. Maybe her stomach was like this because he was missing? Was that possible? It had never been the same people every day of her life. She was moved around, and the people that were also held where she was changed from one day to the next. She was feeling anxious about him being gone, worried something could happen. Terah had witnessed firsthand how things were in his world and they weren't safe at all.

A small creature, a squirrel she thought Lucus had told her, darted out of the trees and paused to look at her. Its tail twitched back and forth a few times and then it turned and abruptly ran back into them. She smiled as she watched it go up a tree so fast. How were they able to do that? Run on land so fast but climb things without pause. Touching the tree beside her, she tipped her head back and looked up to the top of it. There would be no climbing for her, she did not like being in the air at all. She would have to tell Nolyn she let it go and didn't catch it for being on the land. Now that she understood how nature worked, she felt bad about all the animals she had killed at Rayne's campground and the otter in the lake. Nolyn explained to her how each creature was part of the ecosystem and all of them contributed to its healthy state of it. At the time Terah hadn't completely understood, but the app thing on the tablet had explained it to her. She felt a small joy each time she said a word to the tablet, and it explained to her what it was. She didn't yet understand how the tablet could talk, but she was glad it did.

All the machines were a marvel to her. Paxton and Lucus had shown her how to take a picture and videos, which made watching movies clearer to her. When she had first seen it, she couldn't understand how the people were inside the screen. Her tablet was very smart, it knew everything. She didn't spend as much time on it as she would like, Alviva told her too much staring at it would give her a headache, and while she didn't know how it could do that, she listened and made certain to do other things.

Pausing, she undid the jacket, it was a lot warmer than she first thought. Little beads of water were covering her forehead now. When the cool air reached her, she nodded, much better. Looking down, she studied a plant beside the tree. It looked like it was sleeping. In fact, all of them did. The trees too had shed their leaves and now they lay on the ground in a blanket of color. She couldn't wait to see the plants and trees after the winter. Terah loved being in the greenhouses with Olanna, the flowers and leaves were so pretty. She told her that in the spring when the forest was coming back to life it was amazing.

Never having felt a lot of 'amazing' things in her life, she looked forward to feeling that.

The wind was cold today, but there was no snow yet. The jacket was doing its job, even undone it was keeping her warm. She didn't care about the weather; she would have been out here. She's had too many moments of looking out a window wishing she were outside and that there was no weather or temperature that was going to keep her indoors now. The boots on her feet felt heavy and made her steps harder to place, but she would go slow and carefully on her walk today. She wanted to take them off and feel the ground on her bare feet. Would it be warm with the blanket of leaves or cold and wet? Curiosity had her crouching down so she could touch it. It was odd, they were wet and cool to the touch, but beneath them, there was a warmth. She looked up at the naked branches of the trees and realized Nolyn's words were true. In the summer the leaves gave shelter from the sun, in the winter they protected the earth from the snow.

Getting up, she started walking again. Konner had told her the two rivers crossed on the land and she decided that was her target for this walk. To find them. she had seen them from his helicopter but had no idea which direction they were in. Maybe once she found them, she could swim there. The fast-moving water had been exciting.

Distracted by a scent, she tripped over a rock and stumbled, landing on her bottom. She huffed out a breath and looked at the rock. Stretching she put her hand on it and felt the cold of it. She didn't understand about rocks, but she was going to ask her tablet when she got back. How did they grow in the middle of the forest?

Getting up, she looked down to see the leaves clinging to her pants. She brushed them off, "I do not need you like a blanket, you have to stay here and cover the ground." At one of the houses, she had been kept at, the window of her room had let her look out over all the other houses, she recalled watching a man gather up the leaves and stuff them in a bag.

She didn't understand why he saved them. Why didn't he just let them stay on the ground and keep the earth protected? The ecosystem in the areas where she had been kept was broken, that much she knew now. They didn't like the earth and ground much at all, there were only small parts of it visible, the rest they covered in hard surfaces, that used to hurt her bare feet when they would put her in the van to take her to the tank. Nolyn should think about going and explaining to them the importance of keeping the balance in their ecosystem. She paused and touched one of the trees, they should keep the trees too and let them be trees. Instead of letting them grow and stretch to the sky, they would use loud angry-sounding machines on them that chewed them up and stopped their growth. Patting the tree, she silently vowed to let it grow to reach the sky. Who was she to control nature?

Reeves needed to listen to one of Nolyn's lessons too, she thought, he had told Konner that money didn't grow on trees when he'd suggested Reeves take a break the other day. She was sure Konner knew that the trees grew leaves, but again she didn't understand what the work was that Reeves had to do to grow money.

Stopping, she watched large birds fly over her, there were so many of them and they were talking to each other as they flew. How did they fly and stay in the shape of an arrow? She hoped they paid attention, if there were any helicopters up there, they would have to be sure to avoid them.

Leaning down, she touched a single flower that didn't seem to know it was not supposed to be growing now. She smirked, maybe it didn't like rules either. "Good for you little one, you do what feels right for you."

Inhaling, she tried to pick out the scent of water from all the others. There were so many smells in here. She was still trying to master that, smelling things out of the water. The taste on her tongue was dirt and leaves if she wasn't mistaken. She looked down at her feet and decided she was not going to taste them to find out. She'd made that mistake with a log on her last walk. The taste took hours to get rid of.

Frowning, her mind went back to Reeves and his money. She had money, according to him, a lot of it. She hadn't seen it yet but needed to decide what she wanted to do with it when she did. Konner, Reeves explained used a lot of money to help clans in the Alliance, so perhaps she should do that too.

Lucus had told her about the Alliance, that it was all the shifters—she smirked, she was a water shifter, she shook her head, trying to keep her focus on her thoughts. According to Lucus, there were many kinds of shifters, and the Alliance protected them all. Konner and his team were part of the Alliance as well and helped the clans and those that needed it. Terah had heard Calum and Konner talking about the teams and how they were going to free many more of their kind. She didn't know if they had meant water shifters or Calum's kind of shifter, because she had seen him in his other form, and he was not the same as her. Lillee told her that Shaelan and Calum were part of the jaguar clan. Terah had looked that up on her tablet and it was true, Calum had turned into the very pretty cats that it had shown her. What would it be like to be a cat? To run that fast on land. She didn't know but had to assume it was as exciting as swimming fast.

Pausing, she listened to a sound that made her smile. She could hear the water from the river rushing fast. Wiping the moisture off her face, she started moving with bigger steps. She was so hot right now; the cool water was going to feel so good. Maybe after her swim, Konner would be back. Auburn and Calum had said he would be today. She hoped he was, his house seemed large and empty without him there.

Chapter Thirty-Two

Konner dropped his bag on the floor and went into his bathroom. Turning on the shower, he started stripping his clothes off. He felt like he had been crawling through sludge and grim the past two days, metaphorically for the most part, but he needed to physically wash it off. Opening the panel beside the shower, he flipped the valve over so it would be raining freshwater down on him and not processed water from the tanks. He wanted to go for a swim, but he didn't have time for that right now, so this would have to tide him over.

Stepping under the spray, he closed his eyes and let the water run down him. The whole time he'd been away his mind had driven him to absolute distraction thinking about Terah. Wondering if she was doing all right, picturing her in his pool singing, he could hear her song still playing on a loop inside his head. Sighing, he opened his eyes to see his skin was changing like it would if he was swimming and not showering.

Gritting his teeth, he focused to force it to go back. *Complete fucking distraction.* He hadn't had that problem since he was a teen, it was ridiculous, that he couldn't control his body. That's just what he needed, to be standing in the rain with the team and his normal-looking epidermis changing to the thick, porous scales of his kind. He doubted any of the team would suddenly grow fur or whatever if they were distracted.

Looking down, he ran his hand over his chest to feel it was normal enough skin now. Around hour twenty-two of no sleep, he decided he was moving Terah into one of the empty houses. Three hours after that, he overrode his own decision, she was staying right here in his house. He needed sleep, that's what he needed right now. The refreshing three-hour nap he'd struggled to force his body to have while he waited for his contact to reach him, had long ago expired.

He'd practically run from the truck to get here without seeing anyone. He didn't know why it had been left there for him but was glad, he wasn't ready for conversation and questions just yet. Reeves and Auburn had both assured him anytime he'd checked in that Terah was fine, Raelyn and the babies were fine, and he needn't worry. Well, worrying was a new skill he had recently acquired, and he hoped once he saw them with his own eyes, he'd be able to think rationally once again and get things done.

He had to talk to Calum and Deacon about what he found out, and after that to Devin. By all accounts, it wasn't good, and it was a game-changer. The problem was going to be how to explain it to the King and Alliance council when the time came. His contacts weren't exactly legal Alliance allies, he shook the water from his face. Apparently, the legal allies weren't all allies either. He stopped and went over his own thought. Sleep, he needed sleep.

The plan was, to pop into the office, check on business, go see Raelyn and stare at Terah for a moment and then issue a do not disturb order for a few precious hours of rest. The probability of that happening—he turned and let the water pound on his back, sixty percent, seventy if he growled while he did it.

Wrapping the towel around his waist, he stood in the middle

of his room dripping water on the floor. He should talk to Calum, he was an Alliance man, but he seemed like he was willing to bend rules when needed to get things done. Konner looked at the bed, wanting nothing more than to drop down on it and close his eyes. Calum had resources and contacts everywhere, which would be helpful too.

A knock on the door had him jerk his head around and glare at it. "Come in." He growled, hoping this wasn't some emergency that would prevent him from sleeping. The door opened and Terah peeked around it.

"Olanna said knocking on the door before going in was the right way." She gave him a hopeful look.

He was struck speechless seeing her again. It had only been two days, but it was like he was seeing her for the first time again.

"Is it okay I knocked on your door?" She stood there, those alluring eyes moving over him slowly, causing an adolescent reaction with his body.

"It's fine." He winced at the bark in his tone. Clearing his throat, he forced his mouth to smile. "What is it?"

"I missed seeing you."

Her voice was soft, and he felt like a jerk for acting the way he did. The exhaustion was forgotten for now. A real smile moved his lips. "I've been thinking about you too."

"You have?" She stepped closer, her gaze moving up his chest to his face again. "I followed all your rules."

Konner smirked, "I'm just trying to keep you safe."

She nodded, "I was very safe."

She rubbed her hand over her stomach, bringing his attention to the outfit she was wearing. The pants she wore were low on her hips, hugging them emphasizing how trim and curved she was. The top she had on stopped midway down her rib cage, leaving her midriff bare and in his opinion, it was a tantalizing outfit that he wasn't sure she should wear around the boys. "What, uh, have you been doing?"

"I went for walks." she looked at him, an odd expression

on her face. He was too tired to try to figure out what it could mean. "I found the river and went for a swim."

He nodded, even though he wasn't really hearing what she was saying. It just wouldn't register in his head. He needed sleep if he was meant to control the wandering thoughts inside his head. Right now, they were wandering all over that bare skin of her waist.

"I think——," her brows creased, and she huffed out a breath, "there's something," she shook her head, "I am having troubles and I don't know if it is right, what I want to do."

Konner's mind prodded him to focus harder. She looked down at the floor and didn't look back up at him. Stepping closer, he touched her chin briefly, so she'd look up at him. He'd prefer to be dressed for conversation, but if something was bothering her, he wanted to help. "What is it you want to do?" The last thing he needed was another near-disaster like in the kitchen, or worse, something worse could happen with her limited knowledge of things.

"I keep thinking about it," she glanced at him from beneath her lashes, "it doesn't go away when I close my eyes either," she lifted her chin, and he was struck by the full power of those deep blue eyes of hers. He couldn't have looked anywhere else. The look changed to confusion, and she shook her head, "I will think about it more." She nodded and backed up a few steps.

He would never sleep knowing something was bothering her, and his chest felt tight seeing her struggle with it. Gripping the towel so it would stay put, he went over and tilted his head down to look at her. Touching his shoulder, he paused, she was quite warm. "Are you feeling all right?"

"It was very hot on my walk; my jacket works too well I think."

He searched her face; her complexion wasn't paled and there were no signs of drying anywhere. If she'd just been in the river that wasn't the problem. Wearing heavy clothes was problematic for their kind. "Maybe leave it off if you're taking brisk walks and doing physical things?"

She nodded and looked up at him. Her gaze moved over his face and stopped on his mouth. She licked her lips.

Konner's mind was chiming like some sort of alarm. *Back away from the female.* The internal war was short, and he was just about to step away from her when she grabbed the back of his head with strength that shocked him and assaulted his mouth. Was it considered assault when he was willing? He didn't know. He didn't care. Gripping the back of hers with his free hand, he took over the kiss and was rewarded with a fevered passion he'd never experienced before.

Her warm hand moved up his chest to wrap around behind his head, locking together with her other one. Maybe it was the cold water from his shower, but it felt like she was burning his flesh. His body responded and he was all in until some deeply recessed part of his brain intruded and reminded him who he was crushing against him and everything that she'd been through. With control he didn't know he had in him, he slowed the kiss and tore his mouth from hers.

Her eyes flew open, and she looked up at him, as she fought to catch her breath. "That was real," she whispered.

Any more real and he'd have flames licking over his skin, he thought. "Yeah." He gasped and tried to find the will to step away from her. He caught up the towel that started to slip. "I need to go speak with Calum." he frowned at his own words, not the most tactful thing to say to break this up.

"I understand." She said the words, but her hazed eyes were locked on his mouth as she spoke them.

Did she? He doubted it. He didn't even understand what the hell he was doing right now. "Maybe we could go for a walk together later."

Her eyes flicked to his and he saw this pleased her. "Yes." She smiled, "I let the animals live now, so the ecosystem stays in balance."

His eyebrows shot up; he hadn't seen that one coming. "That's good." Not that he cared one damn about the ecosystem at this moment.

Moving her hand across her chest, she watched it for a moment. "I will go lay in my pool until you want to go for a walk." She stepped back. Raising her hand to her mouth, she dragged it over her lips lightly, "I like kissing you, Konner." she gave him a shy smile and then turned and went out the door before his brain could offer a response.

When the door shut, Konner dropped his chin almost to his chest and exhaled a long deep breath. His body was aroused and throbbing, not caring if the female that caused it had just left. Raising his head, he looked at his bed again. Sleep was not going to happen now. If he lay on that bed, his mind was going to be overrun with erotic thoughts of the female that had just blindsided him with desires he'd clamped down on for years.

Ripping the towel off, he tossed it at a chair and stomped over to his dresser. He could turn this frustration into a few more hours of very focused work. His jerky movements ceased, at least until he was out in the bush, alone with her for the walk he'd offered. Maybe if he was lucky some emergency would pop up and distract them both from it. Stabbing his legs into his pants, he yanked them on. He should have gone to bed, ignored the knock on the door. He was already having trouble keeping her out of his thoughts and now, he licked his lips, now he could taste her. Closing his eyes, he drew in a slow breath, her taste was tinged with passion and all the things he could ever want. Blowing it out, he opened his eyes and looked down at the front of his pants. Cursing his body, he went over to the closet and flipped the hangers along the bar trying to find a shirt that was going to hide his obvious desire from the rest of the clan.

He didn't know if it was ego or some stupid male part of him, but the fact that she had literally attacked his face made him smile. He touched his mouth much like she had and smirked beneath his fingertips. She'd damn near branded his lips with her hot... His mouth dropped open, and his gut tightened. *Shit. Damn.* Growling at his own stupidity, he did up his shirt and then went over and grabbed his phone. He should have known right away but hadn't because his brain and body were so obsessed with her, he'd ignored all the signs.

Jerking the door open, he took two steps toward her door on the other side of the hall and then stopped and stood there frozen in place. He needed one of the women. He couldn't go in there and, he shook his head as the images of her naked in her tub filled it. Nodding, he twisted his body, hoping his feet caught up, and headed for the front door. He needed one of the women with him to explain to her what was happening. She was starting her cycle, he frowned remembering how hot she was, or was already in it. He knew this was her first or she'd know what was bothering her. If it wasn't, not having even been around her own kind, she wouldn't know what was going on.

He stopped outside and turned to go get Olanna, then changed his mind and went the other way toward Nolyn's. She would help explain it and hopefully he didn't have to try to help. Clenching his jaw, he walked faster. Getting her to understand what was happening was going to be hard, especially considering her to-do list included ten children. Until her cycle was gone, he hoped it was the normal two days, no man, woman, or child could swim with her. For everyone's safety. When one of their females was caught in the thrall of their breeding cycle, they were aggressive, even violent toward others. Terah would never hurt one of the children, he knew this, but during this, he didn't know if she'd be able to control her baser instincts.

Nolyn was just coming out her door when he reached it. "Konner?"

"I need you to come to talk to Terah with me." Inside he was panicking, and he wasn't sure why. He was going to have to forbid the boys and Reeves from being anywhere near her during this. He frowned, not because of her hurting them, but because he would hurt anyone that went near her. He scowled at the ground. *Shit was getting out of control.*

Nolyn stood there looking at him, the expression on her face was the one she gave the children when she was waiting for them to answer.

"It's her cycle and I think it's her first."

Nolyn's mouth formed an o and then she nodded. "Okay, where is she?"

"Her room I believe." He walked beside her. "I don't think she knows what's happening."

Nolyn looked up at him, "relax, we'll help her."

Konner nodded. "I'm worried..."

Nolyn gave him her stop talking look, "it will be fine." She frowned, "we just have to keep the unmated males away from her."

He wondered if she was thinking about Reeves in particular.

Chapter Thirty-Three

Terah watched Konner walk away, he looked back at her three times. She couldn't be sure, but he seemed like he didn't want to leave her.

"Terah."

She turned back to Olanna and Nolyn.

"He just worries," Olanna said with an understanding smile.

"I think worrying is his unofficial position around here." Nolyn grinned.

"I don't understand." Terah put her hand over her stomach, the tight feelings were back.

"Not only does he oversee everything with the businesses, but he's put it on himself to search for more of us," Olanna said as she started walking, she paused, and Terah realized she wanted her to follow. "But he worries about all of us here too, keeping us safe, healthy, our happiness—"

Nolyn nodded, "they say money can't buy happiness, but he spends whatever it takes to make sure we have what we need."

"He is a good man." Terah looked from one to the other. "His team saves everyone."

"That's part of the problem," Olanna said softly.

"That is a problem?" She was having trouble focusing on what they were saying, she was too hot again. She stopped and touched her brow.

"Come on, the pond will help." Olanna touched her arm and motioned to the path again.

"The tub did not help." Terah wasn't sure what was happening to her. "I have never felt like this before."

"Shaelan says it's probably because your health was so poor when you were," Olanna looked at Nolyn quickly, "there."

"So, it is good I feel this? My health is good now?"

"It is a good sign." Nolyn's smile was warm and friendly, "and it only sucks for a few days."

"That feels endless," Olanna added.

"When this happens, I can have babies?" Terah looked over her shoulder, wondering if Konner was all right. He looked very tired and those lines on his forehead were very deep today. She smirked, thinking of their talk about his tiny lines.

"Yes, but I wouldn't advise trying for babies for a while." Olanna gave her a quick look. "It's very hard at first, our bodies adapting to pregnancy."

There was something in her tone that made Terah want to comfort her. "You have lost children?"

Olanna nodded, "Raelyn and I both have." She motioned up and down her body, "things have to be optimal inside and out to keep the baby."

"What makes them *optimal*?" She said the word slowly, wishing for her tablet to explain what the word meant.

"We're still trying to figure that out." Nolyn admitted, "Shaelan says she's on it and I believe she'll get to the bottom of the problem."

Terah nodded and walked along behind them. She needed to do whatever they told her she had to so her body was good enough to have babies. She put her hand over her stomach and wondered what it would feel like to have life inside her.

"Rule number one," Nolyn said in a firm tone. "No one goes in the pond with you." She looked over her shoulder to make sure Terah was listening. "They can come and talk to you, and visit, but only you are to go in the pond."

"Yes. Okay. I swim alone." Terah decided that wasn't a bad rule, she was at least allowed to be in the water. Anything that allowed her to be in freshwater was something she could live with.

"*And,*" Olanna paused for a moment, "sometimes it's best if you stay in the pond when they're visiting," she made a strange face, "emotions can be harder to control right now and we wouldn't want you to..."

"Grab anyone and shake some sense into them." Nolyn shrugged, a trace of a smirk on her face.

"That," Olanna gave her a wide-eyed look, "and you will just feel better in it."

"This pond is special?" Terah was sweating now and wanted nothing more than to strip off her clothes and walk naked the rest of the way.

"We have placed certain plants in the water and along with it." She nodded, "it's high in minerals and other properties that are helpful."

"Okay, good." Terah stopped and put her hands on her knees. "This is," she blew out a breath, "a very hot walk."

"Oh, you poor thing." Olanna came over to her, "first let's lose the jacket, you definitely don't need it right now."

"Shoes off." Nolyn knelt beside her, "I can't stand anything on my feet during it."

They started helping her strip the confining items from her body.

Nolyn stood up and looked behind them, "no one will bother us for a bit, you can take off the shirt too."

As soon as the air hit her skin, she breathed a sigh of relief. "That is better. Thank you."

"We know what it's like." Olanna took her shirt and hugged it to her body with Terah's jacket.

"Yeah, it's like you're standing in a pit of lava." Nolyn's tone made Terah look at her.

"You do not want your body to be ready for babies?" She nodded that she felt well enough to walk again.

"I do," she shrugged, "just think it's extremely unfair that the guys go through nothing but the fun part in having one."

"The fun part." Terah nodded, even though she wasn't sure what that part was. "I don't think I have felt the fun part." She kept her feet moving, wanting more than anything to be at this pond that would make her feel better. "I tried to have babies three times and it didn't work."

Nolyn caught up to her, "wait, they tried to breed you?"

Terah kept her eyes on the ground in front of her, the hot feeling was coming back. "Yes. It's what they are doing." She blew out a breath, her stomach was not happy with this heat. "Konner talked on his phone when we were in the vehicle before they chased us," she would never forget how scared she was when she heard the metal crunching when they hit the other one, "he said that they want to make more of us to sell."

Olanna gasped and hugged Terah's clothes tighter. "I didn't know."

"All of the clans or just ours?" Nolyn was right beside her now, bending her head low to look right at her face.

"Yes. There are papers they found that tell them that."

"Holy shit," Nolyn whispered. "It makes sense now." Terah lifted her chin to look at Olanna, who looked very frightened. "Why he's so motivated to go back out with the team so often."

"His team have found many." Terah wanted to make them feel better now. "At the campground with Rayne, there are many that are free, like I am."

Nolyn stopped and put both of her hands on her head, she stood that way, looking into the trees. Terah turned to see what she was looking at but could not find anything there. "I had no idea it was that bad." She dropped her hands and looked at Olanna, "he needs to level with us adults and let us know what's really going on outside of our," she waved her hand to the trees, "safe haven."

Olanna moved her head quickly to agree with her, "yes he does, but right now, let's get Terah settled at the pond."

Nolyn jolted and turned to look at her. "I am so glad you survived and are here now."

The smile on her face was so real that Terah felt it inside her. "I am too." she smiled at her, "I like it here. I like swimming in the lake and not in a glass tank."

Olanna gasped loudly again. "Come on, let's get you in that pond."

Terah looked in the direction she moved her hand to see a large pond. Beside it was a small house that she thought looked cute sitting beside the pond. It was like her own private pond to swim in and a little home. She'd never really known what having a home was like.

"Go on, strip down and jump in. We'll put your things in the cabin." Nolyn held out her hand and it took a moment for Terah to realize she wanted the pants that she wore.

Taking them off quickly, she smiled at Nolyn and then turned and ran to the pond. Using her strength, she pushed off from the bank and dove into it. Immediate relief hit her as the water moved over her. She didn't know what plants they used or what minerals were, but she hoped they had plenty of them.

Breaking the surface, she looked over to see the women standing beside the little house smiling at her.

"Is that better?" Olanna asked her.

Terah trod the water and moved toward the little dock beside them. "Yes. Thank you for bringing me here."

"Inside there is a jug to mix the Biotrien in, drink plenty of it." Olanna grimaced, "the hunger is never-ending, and it helps."

"Biotrien?" Terah put one hand on the dock, so she could pay attention to what they were telling her.

"The green stuff we drink." Nolyn smiled.

"Oh, yes, I will."

"There are fish," Olanna motioned to the pond, "and we'll bring fresh stock a few times a day." She looked amused, "you are going to be hungry like you never have been before."

"Makes sense though," Nolyn glanced at her, "your body wanting to stock up for impending conception."

"I know. I always feel like I've gained twenty pounds before the cycle is over." Olanna laughed, "then I sleep for two days afterward from gorging."

Terah didn't know what that was, but after the night of no rest she'd had, she looked forward to it.

Nolyn sat on the dock and looked down at her, "you really are gorgeous in the water." she motioned to her arm, "I know I don't shine the way you do."

Terah looked at her arm, it shone now that it was wet, the many colors reflecting in the light. "It wasn't like this in the tank."

"Good." Olanna was on her knees now next to Nolyn, "they didn't deserve to see how you really are."

Terah looked up at her, "I still can't believe I'm free." She looked at the pond over her shoulder, "my mother told me what it was like to swim free, but I didn't think I ever would."

Olanna put her hand over hers, "you are, and you can be sure that if there are more of ours being held, Konner will find them."

"Yes." Terah smiled, "and if there are boys, then I can check them off the list too."

"The list?" Nolyn smirked at her.

"Yes, to see if they are my mate." Terah pushed away from the dock and used her legs to keep her head above the water, so she could talk to them. She enjoyed talking to others that were like her.

"Oh." Nolyn gave Olanna a quick look. "That's why you've been swimming with everyone when Konner forbade it?"

Terah really wished for her tablet, so she could ask it was that word meant. "Yes."

"You swam with Reeves?"

She studied her eyes when she said his name and wondered why there was worry in them. "Yes. He is not."

"Okay then." Nolyn turned to Olanna again before looking back to her, "do you want us to stay and keep you company?"

Terah liked they were here, but knew they had other things they should be doing. "I am fine. I know you need to teach the children." She smiled at Olanna "and look after your greenhouse."

Olanna stood up, "okay, we'll pop by later, is there anything you want us to bring?"

Terah nodded, "can you bring my tablet?" She glanced to the house, "when I am not in the water, I want to ask it words, so I understand."

"Of course." Olanna looked at Nolyn and nodded, "we'll bring it when we stock more fish."

Terah grinned. The idea of more fish was very welcome. She spun in the water and looked back in the direction they had come. "I hope Raelyn's babies wait until I can leave the pond."

Nolyn laughed, "I just hope they wait until Shaelan figures things out."

"Yes." Terah wasn't sure what Shaelan was figuring out, but she was happy she was here.

"Something tells me she'll be visiting you too." Olanna nodded, "Shaelan, she's testing out blood in all circumstances, and your cycle would be good data for her."

Terah moved her arms and kept her body turning slowly, the water moving over her was soothing. "I would like to help her with her data." She didn't quite know what it was but knew that what Shaelan was figuring out had to do with babies.

"I'll let her know." Olanna smiled at her. "Enjoy your quiet time."

"I'll be back when the kids take a break this afternoon."

"Yes. Thank you." Terah watched them turn back to the path and then dove down to the bottom of the water. When she reached the floor of the pond, she stretched out her whole body and floated there looking up at the surface. She could see the light above the water and thought it was the most peaceful thing she had ever seen. The movement distracted her, and she jerked her head to see a few fish swimming fast away from her. Smiling, she righted her body again and started after them.

Chapter Thirty-Four

Konner took the last turn on the path and then stopped and looked at the pond. Dusk cast highlights on the water and there was no mistaking Terah in the water with the way her skin reflected it. She looked radiant and he couldn't help thinking of the water spirit folklore again. He didn't know why he was here. The only males that visited the pond were the mates of women using it. For some reason, this was the direction his feet had taken him when he'd left the office.

Sleep had been hard to find, even exhausted, but he had managed some before going into the office and starting on the long list of things he had to do. Blair's housing situation was well in hand and despite the impending arrival of winter, he would have his builds underway this week. Gia would be singing in her custom-made shower with indoor plumbing by the end of the week. It had taken some work to get all the pieces in motion on both, but in the end, money bought the willingness of the shippers to get the supplies to the remote areas.

He'd checked in with Shaelan to find her processing blood samples herself, which had surprised him until Calum told him that one of the Alliance's med techs had been on the phone with her for hours walking her through the steps. She explained everything she'd been doing and her findings, and he'd understood about a quarter of what she told him, but the result, combined with her enthusiasm lead him to believe Rae's babies and subsequent pregnancies in the clan wouldn't be as difficult.

When he had convinced himself that everything was working out, Olanna and Nolyn had cornered him in the hallway and in no delicate way had torn a strip off him a foot wide. Conversations with Terah had clued them into how bad things were with the Tomas organization and they were less than impressed that he'd hidden what was really going on. So now he had to look forward to an adult-only meeting of the clan members to fill everyone in. He looked forward to that about as much as he would rolling in a bin of salt. He'd only done it to save worries, but now his biggest one was the others would want to leave the Sanctuary and go help look for more of their kind, or worse join one of the teams rescuing any being held. That conversation was what lead him to call it a night in the office and go for a brisk walk to clear his head before a swim.

This is where the walk had led him and his brain was telling him to turn around and go to the lake, his body refused that suggestion, and he was now walking around to the small dock beside the cabin.

When he reached it, he looked down to see Terah's tablet sitting on it, the screen still lit up. He squatted down and looked to see what was open. It was a book. He looked at the water to see she was nowhere near the surface. Frowning, he read a few sentences and his eyebrows went up, she was reading a romance story? There was no way she was reading this yet, to his knowledge she still couldn't read the primary books Nolyn had given her. When he noticed the play icon, he understood the book was being read out loud by a program.

Water splashing beside the dock had him jolt like someone caught where they shouldn't be.

"Konner."

He looked down to see her smiling up at him. "I thought I'd check in and see how you were doing."

She smiled, "I know it is your unofficial position to worry, but I am doing much better now."

He smirked; the women had been chatting up a storm today. "I'm glad to hear that." He motioned to the tablet.

She gave him an excited look, "the tablet can read books to me." her smile was wide, "I try to look at the words, but then forget because of the story."

There was no way he was discussing a romance novel; he didn't know the first thing about them. "At least you're enjoying it."

"Yes. I had to ask about words though and then listen again."

"Ask about words?" He sat on the dock, deciding she seemed to be in good spirits, and it wouldn't be wrong to visit for a short while.

Putting a hand on the dock, she held herself in place, letting the rest of her body float. "Yes. Lucus showed me how to ask the tablet what words mean, and it tells me."

"That's clever."

She watched him for a moment, "the tablet is very smart."

He smiled, there was no way to explain to her that it wasn't the tablet, but a program, so he just nodded in agreement. "You look much better than you did earlier today."

"So do you," she touched her forehead, "your lines are gone."

"Ah, yes I got some sleep."

"I am not tired, I thought I would be after swimming so much, but I'm not."

Konner knew enough from the other women to have a moderate understanding of what happening to Terah, and with any other woman, he would have just smiled and nodded his head, but this was her first time and he felt like he should offer her something. "It is my understanding that rest is hard to do until the cycle is over."

"Yes, then I will sleep for two days." She smiled. "It is good though. My cycle." She nodded, "it means I am healthy, and my body is stronger." He watched the emotions change on her face from a serious look to one of delight. "When things are *optimal,* I can have babies." Her brow furrowed, "I don't understand what the data is important for, but Shaelan is figuring it out."

Tilting his head, he glanced at the tablet. "Did the tablet tell you that?" He waved his hand around, "when things are optimal you could have babies?"

She frowned, "no, the tablet does not answer about our kind. I have tried. Olanna told me."

He wondered how long the women had stayed with her, there had been a lot of information passed back and forth. "Don't take this the wrong way, but why do you want a baby so much?" He shrugged, "you just got your freedom for the first time..." He stopped not sure if he should say what he was really thinking.

"I will never be alone again." she smiled, "with a child of my own."

It felt like someone had stabbed him in the chest to hear the sad tone in her voice. "You're not alone now. You have the rest of the clan." He couldn't even imagine what it would be like to think you were the only one of your kind left. "There's no rush, you could live for a hundred years..."

"Is that how many you have lived for?"

Konner sputtered, trying not to laugh at her serious question. "Not quite."

"I know how many numbers I am," she nodded, "my age."

"Well," he watched the tablet screen go dark, "I'm three times that, roughly."

She was quiet for a moment, looking down and not at him. "You don't look old." That was what she settled for after some careful thought. "Auntie doesn't look as old as the old one that was with Mother and me."

Auntie? No one called her that except him. Even the

children called her Alvie when things were unofficial. He'd have to speak with his aunt and find out why she'd told Terah to call her that. "Staying near freshwater makes a difference." He couldn't go into why the elder she'd been with had been aged from saltwater. Women during their cycle could get very emotional and he didn't want to upset her when she seemed to be handling it so well.

"I am glad you came to see me, Konner." She pushed off from the dock and tread the water beside it, "I have decided what I am doing with my money." Her voice changed to a quiet serious tone.

"And what is that?"

"I want to use it to help others." She came closer again, so she could hold his look, "even if they are not our kind."

"Our clan funds already go towards helping all those under the Alliance..."

"You do not understand me." She put her hand on the dock and pulled herself up, so she could rest her arms across the wood and keep the rest of her body in the water. *"Everyone."* She said, enunciating it slowly, "even those that do not change into something else." She held his look, "there are children out there, they need help." She nodded.

"Ah." How did he explain to her that they had enough issues helping shifters?

"Nolyn was talking to me about things like that." She nodded, "Olanna and Nolyn talked to me a lot today..."

"I'm aware." He cleared his throat, "they chewed my ear off over a lot of it."

She frowned, "your ear is still there."

Konner smiled, "it's a saying, they didn't really." He blew out a quick breath, trying to find a way to explain it. "It means they were not happy with some things I didn't tell them, so they told me," This was harder than he'd thought, "they were a bit angry with me."

"It is not your fault people are taken, why would they get angry with you?" She inched up higher and watched him

261

carefully.

"They weren't angry for that, they were upset that I hadn't told them how bad it is, how many were taken."

"Oh." She let herself drop back into the water, without making a splash. "I don't understand why sometimes things are said when that isn't what they mean." She watched her hands move through the water, "Nolyn told me to stay in the water if anyone came to visit me so I wouldn't grab anyone and shake some sense into them. I asked the tablet, and it doesn't seem like a good thing to do to someone."

Konner wiped his hand over his face until he could get the big grin under control. "It's hard to explain, but in Nolyn's case, she is very aggressive." He frowned, "uh, she says what she means, and it can be pretty blunt," that wasn't a good word to have her looking up, "very straightforward and honest."

Terah was quiet for a moment. "Yes. I want to be very straightforward and honest too."

"It's not a bad thing, really, if more were honest there would be fewer issues in the world." he didn't want to explain that sometimes honesty caused problems, that was a talk for later when she knew a little more about life.

"Yes." She came back over and looked up at him, even in the lower light her eyes seemed bright to him, the silver with the hint of that blue in there. "I want to kiss you again."

Whatever he had planned on saying evaporated in his mind. He looked at her, and of course looked right at her lips, recalling the kiss in his room. Clearing his throat, he leaned back so he wouldn't be tempted to lean down and kiss her. "It's best to wait until your cycle is gone—it could only be because of that," he motioned in the air, trying to word it, "you know, how you're feeling..."

"How will I know this?"

He should have just checked on her and then left, he decided. Too late now. "Uh, I suppose, see if you still feel that way after your cycle has passed." His traitorous eyes were tracing her lips as she moved them and thought about what he'd said.

"Okay," she nodded, "I will."

Blowing out a breath, he leaned back and looked at the darkening sky. "The stars will be out soon." He kept his gaze on the sky above, not tempting himself by looking at her.

"Out from where?"

He smirked, "it means they will be visible when it's darker."

"Oh. There are so many of them up there." He heard her put her wet hand on the dock again, "I didn't know how many until I was at the campground."

He nodded, glancing out of the corner of his eye to see her looking up. "There are too many lights in the city, to see them clearly." He pointed, "when they're out, the big dipper will be there."

"The big dipper?"

"Mmhmm, a group of stars that look like a scoop." It was the easiest way to explain it, "most of them have names, but I don't know them all."

"How do you know they have names?"

"Astronomers studied them and name them."

"*Astronomers*," she said like she was tasting the word on her tongue, "Is that a real word?"

Konner grinned and looked at her, "Yes."

She gave him a wary look, "Paxton uses words that my tablet doesn't know."

Konner hid his smirk, "probably best not to say those ones then." He'd had to have a chat with the boys about their language around her.

"I don't use them if I don't know what they mean."

He searched her face for a moment, seeing that she was healthy and somewhat content, he decided he needed to make his exit, otherwise, it would be dawn and he'd still be sitting here on the dock talking to her. "I should get back." The light in her expression faded in a not-so-subtle way and his chest felt heavy. He looked at the tablet, "would you like me to hit play on your book and you can just listen for now? While you swim?"

She smiled. "I did not think to do that." She nodded, "yes, I can listen again later and look up the words."

He nodded and got to one knee. "Did the girls bring you the cord for it?" He turned on the screen and looked at the battery, "you'll have to charge it later to keep using it."

"Yes. They brought the power cord and my robe earlier today."

"Okay." He waged a silent war inside his mind, as he moved back further so he wouldn't lean down and kiss her and bid her good night. "I'll see you tomorrow."

"Yes." she smiled up at him as he moved away from her.

Tapping the screen, he started the book again and then stood up and back away from the end of the dock. "Have a good night, Terah."

She pushed away from the dock and kept her focus on him. "You get more sleep, Konner, so those lines do not come back." She smiled. To her, he supposed, she had just bid him a good night as well.

"I will." He spun on his heel and took long strides to move around the pond and get out of here.

He was berating himself inside his head, cursing every few feet as well, he shouldn't have come here tonight. What possessed him to break an unwritten rule and do it, he didn't know.

Chapter Thirty-Five

He was walking so fast, lost in his thoughts, that he almost walked into his aunt where the paths connected.

"Jogging in the dark?" She smirked at him.

Konner blinked and looked down at her. "Uh," he motioned in the direction he'd come from.

"How is Terah doing?"

"She's uh," he rubbed his hand over his forehead, "doing good." He nodded, "seems to be coping with it well."

"She has a private pond to swim in, I'm sure she's very pleased with that."

"We're you going to see her?"

His aunt nodded her head slowly, and that's when he noticed her long hair wasn't braided. He couldn't remember the last time he saw it down. The brown was streaked with greyer than he recalled.

"Yes. As the alpha, I thought it was my job to check in on new clan members." She smiled up at him, "and as a female, I understand what she's going through, although I haven't missed it these last fifty years."

He watched her carefully, wondering if she still regretted that she never had children of her own when she was still able.

"You're all mine." She told him quietly as if she'd been able to read his thoughts. "Since when do you visit women at the pond?" She raised one accusing eyebrow at him.

Konner jammed his hands in his pockets, trying to focus past the way that Terah looked while floating beside the dock. "I, um, just thought I'd see if she needed anything."

Alviva chuckled quietly, "and did she?"

He shook his head as a caught child would. "No. So we talked a bit." He frowned, "did you know she uses the tablet to find out what words mean?"

"Yes." She nodded, "you know I'm not much for all the technology gadgets, but it seems to be helping her." She leaned on her cane and looked up at him for a moment, "she's very intelligent, I have no worries that she won't be up to speed in a short time."

"Yeah, she's picking up on everything really fast."

"What's worrying you now?"

He blew out a breath, "she wants to use her profits to help others, even one-forms, abducted children..."

"I can see her wanting that, she's very giving."

Konner couldn't deny that. "The logistics of it is just," he blew out a breath, "I mean I understand why she wants to, but with the way things are right now in our world..."

"Give her some time, to understand fully, then talk to her about it again."

"Yeah."

"There was a time we did co-exist without issues." Her tone told him she was remembering simpler times, as she did often.

"I know, but times have changed." He glanced back along the path for probably the tenth time in the last minute. "It's dangerous now."

"She's just trying to find her place, Konner." She motioned around them, "in this new life she's been given, in the clan."

"I didn't think of that."

She smirked at him, "did you expect her to just spend her days swimming around?" She gave him a nonchalant shrug, "sure that's fine until she's adjusted, but she needs a purpose, everyone does."

"I don't," he blew out a breath, "I don't know what she could do." He rubbed his forehead again and wished for a swim instead of talk. "Maybe once she understands more..."

"Don't underestimate her or try to fit her in a box."

He gave her a blank look, "I wasn't. I'm just..."

"Your head is so full of her you can't even think straight."

He scowled down at her, she wasn't wrong, but he wasn't ready to admit it out loud to anyone.

"I see the way you look at her and how she sees you."

"What does that mean?"

"You're already half in love with her..."

He shook his head, "I thought she'd died, when they found her," he didn't even know her, how could he be in love with her, "when they told me she was alive, I-I..."

"I know you feel you have to watch out for her, you feel that for all of us, but that's not what I'm seeing now."

He frowned as he looked down at her, "she could have a mate out there somewhere," he clamped his mouth shut, not wanting to say it. "I'm not making the same mistake again..."

"You weren't in love with Olanna, you were lonely and randy, and she was a female."

"Randy? I don't think that's a word anyone uses anymore, Auntie." He thought to distract her from this conversation.

"When you live as long as I have you can use any words you want, even if they're not cool anymore." She looked up at him, thoughts going through her gaze so fast he couldn't figure them out. "You need to swim with her, nephew."

Eyebrows high, he motioned in the direction of the pond.

"I didn't mean right now, during her cycle, I mean after it's gone."

"I just want her to..."

"Adjust, adapt, settle in," she nodded her head slowly, "it's going to take some time and you know that." Reaching up, she patted him in the center of his chest, "I know you put it off, every time, I don't know why you do, but this time I think you should sooner than later."

Looking over her head, he wished he could see the lake from here. The moonlight would be reflecting off it now and casting its spell of peace and serenity throughout the Sanctuary.

"I know you're too noble to have a child without your mate, but she's having one regardless." She shook her head, "never met a female more determined than she is to bring new life into the world," she grasped the front of his shirt, drawing his attention back to her, "how are you going to feel if she does this with someone else?" She quirked one eyebrow at him, "have you thought of that?"

He scowled down at her, not really seeing her. "A bit." He admitted.

"How did that bit make you feel?"

"Not good."

"So maybe you should do something about it before it happens."

He now understood how Lucus and Paxton felt when he was dragging answers out of them. "What if..."

Alviva grinned, "What ifs tend to take care of themselves when you stop procrastinating." She patted his chest and stepped around him, "go swim off your overthinking, Konner, then get some rest, your angst is wearing me out."

Konner watched her walk along the path leading to the pond. His angst? When she went into the trees and he could only hear the click of her cane on the stones, he spun around and walked, no, basically stomped toward the lake. The level of his stress was higher now after that conversation. He knew Terah wanted children; everyone knew that. Reeves wouldn't agree to it, that he was certain of, he was pretty sure she scared the hell out of him. He stripped his shirt over his head and carried it clenched in his fist. What Reeves had shared about Nolyn still shocked him, they were going to have a child if no mates were found. He tossed the shirt to the ground and bent down to take off his boots. What if a mate for one of them was found before this? They'd just walk away and not look back? He of all people knew how hard that was. One boot hit the sand after the other. No, he hadn't loved Olanna, but he cared about her, still did. Straightening he frowned at the water, he cared about all the others here. Taking his jeans off he dropped them like they were trash, not caring about the phone in the pocket. Terah having children with someone else, there was no one if not Reeves. Well, there was Paxton, but he was too young. He walked out into the cool lake, normally it would settle him, just the water touching him, but that wasn't the result this time. Paxton would be more than willing to try in a few years. He blinked and rushed further into the water, diving in with hopes the lake would wash that thought right out of his head.

There was no peace, no serenity as he moved with swiftness to the deepest part of the lake. He'd been caught in the draw of Terah's magic when he'd left her, in the memory of her lips under his and now after his chat with his aunt, it felt like there was a storm moving through him.

He stopped swimming and let his body drift through the water. Why hadn't he seen it? He did love her. How was that possible? It had been right there this whole time, while he'd been thinking it was her beauty, the ethereal way about her that drew him to her, it had been his heart all along. Turning, he looked around, like the water held some answer he just couldn't see. What the hell was he going to do now? What if the next trip out, he brought back a male and he was hers? Then what?

Konner rushed to the surface, like he couldn't breathe, which was insane, he could breathe under the water better than he could air. Gasping as the air hit his face, he wiped his hand over it and looked up at the stars. Snapping his head around, he looked back to the shore, had she known her little talk was going to push him to the brink of insanity? He glared at the empty space along the water's edge, knowing his aunt, she'd be smiling to herself because she'd planted the seeds of suggestion in his head.

He rubbed his hand over the smooth ridges of the skin covering his chest as if it would comfort him. This is what he didn't need, his mind distracted, his head filled with Terah. He had a lot of pieces moving right now and if things fit together the right way, he'd soon know where to find members of the water clan that needed his help. Not to mention the babies were coming and that was going to stir up everyone here. A new life tended to do that, making everyone look around and find a new purpose.

Closing his eyes, he let his weight pull him back beneath the surface, focusing on the water as it moved over him. When he opened his eyes, he saw a few fish swimming away from him. Normally, he'd be after them without thought, right now he couldn't even find the motivation to do it.

It was crazy. Pure insanity, was the next thought that surfaced in the muck of confusion inside his mind. Terah would be through her cycle within the next day, likely. He could swim with her then and put it all to rest, the not knowing. Twisting to move along the water on his back, he looked up to the surface and was able to see the moon's beams of light hitting it. Swimming with Terah was not going to change how he felt about her. Flipping backward, he moved toward the bottom of the lake, which meant he had to decide now, before any of it if he was willing to have children with her mates or not. Images of her carrying a child flashed through his mind like they were slides on a screen, she'd be breathtaking with the glow of motherhood.

He stopped like he'd hit an invisible wall. He couldn't be thinking about her being pregnant, her health was improving, but it was far too early to take that risk of losing a baby and possibly her.

Several fish went past him, coming close to hitting him, and it shook him out of the muck of thoughts in his head. He looked in the direction they were fleeing and smiled, there was something in the lake that was a predator. He grinned, normally he'd look the other way, but right now, he needed a task to take his mind off things. Dipping down until he was almost touching the lakebed, he watched and waited. A good chase and execution would suffice to get his thinking back on track.

Chapter Thirty-Six

Konner looked up from the phone to see Calum standing at the door grinning. He motioned to the phone as if to say, you try.

Calum came over and stood in front of his desk. "Deacon."

"Cal?" Deacon made a strange noise, "I'm not even surprised you're there."

Calum's grin widened. "I hear you have two clan members en route."

"Uh, yeah, Konner just told me." His tone was completely flat, Konner wondered if he was in shock or just not showing the emotion.

"Boys? Girls? Adults or children?" Gia, Deacon's mate sounded excited enough for the two of them.

"Mother and daughter, eleven." Konner inhaled and gave Calum a quick look, "and there's two more, but getting them out of there is more complicated."

"Out of where?" Now Deacon's tone held emotion and it wasn't a friendly one.

"The other side of the ocean, my friend," Konner didn't want to go into too many details over the phone and especially

272

because it was bending a whole lot of rules to the point of breaking.

"We could…"

"No, we can't." Konner finished before he got too many ideas. "We can't break Alliance treaties and go there and pull others out."

"Shit." There was mumbling as he explained to his mate. "When are they due to move?"

"In the next few weeks, I don't have a date because things have to stay flexible." A polite way of saying if shit went sideways, they had to adjust plans on the move.

"There's a trailer on the way to your place now, Beckett is taking care of it for me," Calum added.

"That solves that panic." Deacon sounded relieved. "Think we'll put it up by the cabin until the house is ready. Leaving them down there alone doesn't feel right."

"We still need to get supplies, and clothes," Gia sounded like she was holding the phone to her mouth and yelling in it now. "Your foreman said the new units wouldn't be done for a month."

"We'll figure it out." Deacon told her, his tone changing again.

"Maybe if we can rush through one and put them all together for a bit?" Gia mused, "well, unless they're men, then that's not right to put them with them."

"I don't have details right now." Konner straightened and crossed his arms. "I'll let you know when I do."

"Are there a lot over there?"

Konner looked at Calum, they both knew his young teammate was now realizing what he signed up for might be quite different than he'd planned. "I'm not sure. It's hard to track them down without setting off any alarms."

"There has to be something we can do about that."

If he wasn't mistaken, Konner thought he saw pride on Calum's face. "We're going to be taking it to the king later and filling him in."

"Yeah, good. Being held in a country you don't want to be in isn't much different than the then shit they we're dealing with here with Tomas." Deacon's growl was back in his voice.

Konner nodded. Finding his mate had changed him in a few ways that Konner hadn't imagined possible. Deacon was usually good with a few words and no conversation, never mind him displaying actual emotions more than once during the call. "We'll get them out one way or another."

"Did you find any of yours, Konner?" Gia was near the phone again.

Konner sucked in a deep breath and blew it out quietly, "not so far, but there are several leads."

"I hope you find them."

He nodded, not wanting to comment and voice it, or get his hopes up again. "I'll call you when I have more details."

"Thanks, Konner." Deacon scoffed, "I have to go slow Gia down or we'll have to have a transport deliver the list she's making."

Konner grinned, "I'll send details when I have them." He hung up the phone and looked at Calum, "he handled it better than I thought he would."

"Oh, he'll be freaking out shortly," he sat down, "Deacon processes in a different way and then it all catches up to him at once." He shrugged one shoulder, "he'll get through it, Gia is very grounded."

Konner sat down, he was running out of momentum finally, the last two days he'd burned through a month worth of tasks he'd been putting off because he didn't have the time. "We're you looking for me?"

Calum held up his phone, "I just got off the phone with Devin, his father agreed a conference call with the team leaders was warranted with the information you brought back."

"Which team leaders?" He sat back and rolled his head from side to side, trying to relieve some of the tension in the muscles.

"The eight relevant ones."

He couldn't hide the surprise in his reaction. "That's a good thing, though, to get them involved. Maybe they can figure out a way to get around this and correct it."

"You'll be part of it," Calum smirked at Konner's rubber neck response when he jerked his head around to look back at him. "It should happen shortly, Nate from the tech team is working on a secure conference call right now, while your pal Fallan gets in touch with all the leaders."

Konner sat forward, leaning on his desk. "All right," he nodded, "I don't know the teams like you do, so give me a bit of background." What he wasn't in the mood for was flack from anyone right now and the last thing his exhaustion would tolerate was some team leader harping about how he'd bypassed all and any protocol and been poking around in countries that were off-limits to the North American branch of the Alliance.

Calum sat back, looking relaxed, although Konner now suspected he never truly was as chill as he let on he was. "Some of them you know,' he smirked, "your own team leader, of course, Devin, Jesse, and Raymond." He looked down at the floor, like he was trying to recall the others, "Nate from tech, nothing we do now will be without the tech team keeping us off the airwaves," he glanced up, "or whatever it is." Calum glanced down at his phone, "Kenzo from the special ops team, he's pretty easy going," he shrugged, "at least off mission."

Konner had encountered a few of the ops team, like Tripp, they all seemed like they didn't have a care in the world, he assumed that flipped like a switch when things were heavy, because some of the stories of what they'd done, there was no way easy-going, quiet mannered personalities could pull that off.

"You may have met Kaid Rivera along the way, he's in charge of the clean-up team."

Konner smirked, "they are in and out so fast, I don't know how they do it."

Calum grinned, "but they're good at it." He nodded his

head slowly, "the last one is Uri from the surveillance team, I don't know him that well, but it's said he can be standing right beside you and you wouldn't even know he was there."

Konner's eyebrows went up.

"Most of his team is the same."

"Are they all flyers?" Konner leaned back, "I always wondered how they managed to keep eyes in so many places at once."

"I'm not sure. I know Uri is, but the rest of his team I'm not familiar with." He grinned, "I guess that's why they're the unseen and do their job so well."

Konner rubbed his forehead, this call needed to happen soon, he was starting to fade now that he'd stopped. Pushing back from the desk, he went over and picked up the water jug, "all I know is without them, most of the other teams would have walked into some pretty intense situations without their help." Grabbing a glass, he poured some of the river water and took a big drink of it.

Calum's phone rang at the same moment Reeves leaned his head around the door and looked at him.

"Yeah?" Calum nodded at Konner, "hold on, I'll put it on speaker."

Konner looked at Reeves, "is it imperative? I need to be on this call."

Reeves opened his mouth and then shook his head, "no it can wait."

Konner nodded his head once as Reeves closed the door.

Calum set his phone down, "okay, we're both here."

"Dad will be on it just a minute," he recognized Devin's voice without issue.

Setting the glass and water jug on his desk, he sat down, it was going to be hard to follow a conversation with voices he didn't know.

"I hear we have you to thank for this new information, Konner."

Konner knew that voice as well, "I suppose you do,

Raymond." He hoped his friend wasn't put off that Konner had been going behind the Alliance security protocol to get things done.

"Konner kept me in the loop," Devin said, surprising Konner that he was sticking up for him when it had only been the past week they'd been communicating.

"Mister Flores and I have been in full communication with his dealings over the years." Shepard Addison had joined the call. "There was no way for him to operate under the radar if we brought all of the community in on it."

"Understandable, sir," Raymond said in his clipped no-bullshit tone.

"My concern is if anything has leaked out there to anyone we don't want knowing it."

Konner looked at the phone.

"I can assure you, Nate, that any of Konner's dealings are more secure than anything." The King responded, "I believe one of your team has ensured that."

"I'm guessing Fallan was involved." He sounded exhausted the way he said it.

"She is very helpful anytime I talk to her." Devin validated her involvement with that answer.

"I don't mean to be a pain, but I had to stop on the side of the road for this call and I don't like standing here cooling my jets when I need to be somewhere else."

Konner smirked over at Calum when Wynter spoke in the politest way he'd ever heard her talk.

"We'll keep it brief, Wynter." Shepard's tone was light. "Konner has been dealing with some associates in South America for quite some time, in locating members of his clan, and a few others whose numbers have dwindled, he has a network set up to get them over here, without causing too many waves."

"Waves? More like a tsunami if they're caught."

"That's exactly why it's been kept to a few, Kenzo." The king cleared his throat, "on his most recent check-in with his contacts, some information has come to light that we, collectively, need to deal with."

"Information?"

"Yes, Uri, it has come to light that the ambassadors and their representatives that are part of our allied network are not working for our combined worldwide plan." Shepard sighed loud enough everyone on the call picked it up, "I've been worried about this happening for some time, not just over there, but elsewhere as well. Feeling it and proving it are two entirely different things."

"Does this tie into our current situation here, because things have been getting hotter by the minute?"

"It does, Kaid, which is the reason for this call now, we need to start reaching out to friends and contacts that we know are aligned with us and come up with a way to put a stop to it."

"Are you telling me that these *ambassadors* or whatever are working with the Tomas organization?" Raymond cut off the King without thought.

Konner leaned on the desk, and blew out a quick breath, "I'm not even sure if it's that way, Raymond, or if the Tomas organization is working for them."

"There's been chatter for as long as I remember about how bad it is in other countries, that what Tomas has been doing is nothing new—" he recognized Nate's voice this time, "this is way too big for us to handle from here." He sounded overwhelmed.

"Your task hasn't changed at this point, Nate, we need your team to find out who left the door open for that breach."

"Yeah," Nate made a sound of annoyance, "we're still on it. It's like looking through a pile of thread on the floor, for one particular piece, without moving any of the other threads."

"We understand how difficult it is, but I have faith in your team's abilities."

"Oh, don't worry, sir, we will find it."

"Are we tackling the South America problem first, because worldwide seems like we're biting off more than we can chew?" Wynter sounded frazzled now and Konner knew there was nothing more dangerous than an upset Wynter Carr.

"For now," Shepard's tone was harder, "we reach out to any we know and *trust* implicitly to see if we can find a direction to deal with this." He cleared his throat, "I don't want to endanger any of our kind anywhere in the world and if we start stirring things up, that's what will happen."

"So, we reach out to one area at a time, bring them in, do some planning before we execute anything," Uri said in a contemplative way.

"I agree," Kenzo added, "do a little recon in all the directions and see what we're up against."

"Many of the clans have origins across the globe." Konner recognized Jesse's voice. "Might be an easier route than jumping right to teams and associates of the other ambassadors."

"Until we vet them and see who can be trusted," Raymond added briefly.

"I agree, that is a route we should explore." Shepard seemed content to let the leaders come up with that plan. Konner couldn't imagine what it was like for him, to sit there and know there were these problems, but his hands were tied because of red tape. "I know I don't need to say it, but I feel obligated to do so," he paused, "we can't let the ambassadors know are we are reaching into their domain and poking around."

"That's going to be hard to pull off."

"I understand that, Kaid, which is the reason for this call. All of you will need to work together with your combined strengths—I know we can succeed."

"I'll be the coordinator for this." Devin piped up, "keeping you as far out of it as possible, Dad."

"I'll work with Devin on this." Calum's voice startled Konner, he'd been silent up to this point.

"Thank you, Calum, I knew I could rely on you." The king sounded amused.

"I know this isn't the topic of this party, but Konner's clan member was right on the money with deciphering that journal we confiscated, and now more pieces are fitting together."

"Journal? The one with the transactions in it?" Wynter wasn't big on paperwork, Konner knew that from personal experience, she was more for guns and not pens.

"That's the one." Nate confirmed, "it makes sense now if there are other organizations like Tomas' across the globe..."

"You think our missing clan members have been shipped to other countries?" Jesse's tone was more focused now.

"I think it's a possibility." Nate sounded distracted. If he was anything like Fallan, Konner suspected he was doing ten things at the same time as being on this call.

"Well shit. That tosses a fucking wrench into it, doesn't it?"

Calum and Konner both smirked, Wynter's polite King-worthy speech was now gone.

"I understand it's a lot to take on, Wynter, but our priority has not changed, we shut down all locations here in North America before we branch out."

"Understood, sir, just point me in the direction, I will send my team and hand them their asses." She cleared her throat, "that's to say, my team is ready—sir."

Calum covered his mouth, but there was no hiding the big grin behind his hand.

"I'm right there with Wynter, sir, if you need my team to jump in with the incursion and retrieval team, we have no problems mixing it up."

"I'm glad you volunteered, Kenzo, you were my next call," Devin spoke up, "we have a lot of locations that need to be breached in a short time of one another," he paused, "just as soon as Uri gives me the details."

"My team are on them now, Devin, we should have enough information to act on in the next few days," Uri informed him.

"To save ten more calls today, how are those four locations I called you about for Konner?" Calum looked across the desk at Konner.

"We're on those too, three of them will be a walk in the

park, low security, like they think they're gods or something and untouchable. The fourth one is going to be more of a challenge, but" he stopped for a second, "I'm assuming I can speak clearly on this call?"

"You can." The king interjected, "all the teams here will be brought on it."

"Okay, we've confirmed two of your kind are at the fourth location, Konner."

Konner stood up and looked down at the phone, "how have you confirmed this? I've had many false leads over the years."

Uri cleared his throat, "well, unless one-forms have learned how to breathe underwater for hours at a time, I'd say it's a pretty good indication."

Konner put his hand over his mouth, so he wouldn't blurt something out to rush an operation.

"That saves another call," Devin said before he could speak, "planning is already underway, Konner."

Konner dropped his hand and nodded, "are they safe until a team can get there?"

"As *safe* as they've been this long." He sighed, "they're treated fairly from what we can tell, so that buys us the time to figure out how to get in there."

"Electronic security?" Nate asked.

"And a few other obstacles." Uri sounded annoyed.

"You hash this out with any of the leaders here you need, Uri, collectively there is nothing these teams can not do." The king told him.

"I'll do that, sir, I'll set up a call when I have more intel to go on."

Konner paced away from the desk and stood by the window, two more of his. His mind was going so fast, he didn't know how to process it.

"Shaelan has a list of what will be required to get them home safely without endangering their health." From Calum's voice, he knew he was now standing too.

Konner was just about to turn and tell them about Deacon's clan members when Terah walked into his line of sight. She wasn't at the pond now? Her cycle must have ended.

"Konner."

He jolted and turned to see Calum giving him a pointed look. "The information about Deacon's clan members."

Konner nodded and came back to the desk, "sorry, just processing that there are two more of mine out there." He blew out an abrupt breath, "Two of Deacon's will be here in a few days, but there's two more that we're having trouble getting to and getting out."

"Kaid, you may be of assistance for that, I believe some of your distant relatives are in the same area," Shepard informed him.

"I have a few wily cousins that will likely be happy to help." Kaid sounded amused.

Konner nodded, "I will get in touch with you later with some details." He needed to reach out to his contacts, and process that there were two more coming home to his people soon. He glanced at the window, and he needed to see Terah, he'd worked himself to the point of exhaustion to avoid her the past few days.

"Sounds good."

"This has been a very productive call, everyone. Thanks to Konner's information, I feel like we're turning a corner that's been in the far distance for a long time." Shepard Addison acknowledging everything Konner had been doing would have normally been a huge ego boost, but right now he couldn't even focus enough to remember what day of the week it was.

"I know you all have tasks to be doing, so we'll end this call for now and schedule one when we have more information."

Konner looked back at the phone.

"I'll make space at the center for as many new guests as you bring me." Raymond's boots echoed in the hall he was walking in.

"Enjoy your brief downtime," Devin told everyone. "We

have several ops in the works for the next few weeks."

Calum crossed his arms over his chest and nodded. "Shaelan and I are with Konner until we're called for setup."

Konner barely heard the rest of the goodbyes; he'd gone back over to the window and was watching Terah talk to Kole. He didn't know what it was about, but the boy looked up at her with a huge grin and excitement on his face.

"You all right?"

He turned to see Calum standing beside him now, his phone in his hand.

"Yeah," he said in a quiet way, "just processing."

"I'll be there when they go in and get yours out."

Konner looked back out the window, "appreciate it." He watched Terah kneel in front of Kole and the child sit on her legs as they looked out over the lake. "Maybe bring your friend, the one that took down his brother."

"Blair. Yeah, I have a feeling we'll have no problems getting Blair to leave the mayhem at home from now on." Calum chuckled. "You should deal with distractions, my friend." He gave him a light smack on the shoulder.

Konner turned to see Calum motion out the window with his chin. He nodded reluctantly and then blew out a breath. "I should."

Chapter Thirty-Seven

Konner stepped into his house and closed the door; he didn't even remember the walk from his office. His mind was moving faster than he could in water. More had been found, alive. He'd been so stunned he hadn't even asked gender or approximate age. How could he tell the others with no details? None. Not even when they could be rescued.

The sound of laughter dragged his mind back to the here and now. Turning, he saw Terah's bedroom door open, the sounds were coming from there. Going over, he looked into the room. Nakisa, Kole and Terah sat on the floor leaning over papers scattered in front of them.

"Konner," Kole jumped up, "Terah wrote her name." His smile was filled with so much excitement.

Terah and Kisa looked over at him. Terah held up a piece of paper and her name was there in purple crayon.

"We came to color and then helped her write her name." Nakisa looked so pleased.

The expression on Terah's face was pure pride.

Leaning against the doorframe, he smiled down at them. "I didn't know you were back from the pond."

She nodded, "I came to tell you, but Reeves said you were very busy with important phone calls."

Nakisa got up, "we better go help with dinner, Kole." She held out her hand.

He leaned over and hugged Terah. "You should put your name on the fridge, that's what mom does with my work."

Terah looked at the paper her name was on. "I will do that."

Konner watched them race down the hall toward the community room, when he turned back Terah was putting crayons back in the box and picking up the scattered papers off the floor. "Most of the women sleep after they leave the pond."

Getting up, she went over and set the papers on the dresser. "I am a little tired, but not too much." She stood there, looking at him like she was memorizing his face. "You didn't come back to see me."

Guilt struck him. "I had a lot to do."

"Yes. You do important work."

"Two more of our kind have been found." He blurted out like a kid that needed to distract someone from the topic.

Her eyes rounded, "you are going to get them?"

"Soon, it's more complicated, so we have to come up with a plan to get them out." He rubbed the back of his neck. He'd like to have already been on the way to get them.

"You will do it." She nodded, "you and your team." She smiled at him, one filled with confidence.

"We will." He could only stand there and look at her like he hadn't seen her in months, she was doing much the same to him. The silence grew awkward.

"I thought about what you said." She nodded.

Pushing away from the door, he stepped into the room. "About?" He honestly couldn't remember what he'd said that would require thought. When it came to her, he seemed to overthink everything or not be able to think with clarity at all.

"To see if I still wanted to kiss you after my cycle was gone." She moved toward him slowly. "I still want to." Placing her hand over her stomach, she gave him an anxious look, "When I think about it, I get this feeling inside me, it is strange but not bad."

Konner forced air into his body, he searched for something to say, but couldn't think of anything to say.

"Dinner in five."

Konner jolted and spun to see Paxton standing behind him grinning.

"Oh good. I am hungry again." Terah smiled up at Konner as she stopped in front of him. Placing her hand on his chest, she held his eyes with her own, "I want to finish talking to you after we eat."

He watched her walk down the hall while holding his hand over where she had touched. There was so much to do in the next few weeks, and he had little time to decide what he was doing about her. Part of him wanted to take her out to the lake and dive in with her, get that out of the way. he forced his feet to move. What was he going to do when it became evident that they weren't mates? More of theirs had been found, one of them could be her mate. It was going to be a very distracting two weeks.

He ate without tasting a single bite of the food the women had prepared. He couldn't have made himself not look at Terah if it had been life and death. Everything she did intrigued him, beguiled him. The way she smiled at everyone, the way she ate, gracefully, if not a little awkward with the fork, the way she spoke...

"Konner, is that true?"

Someone kicked his leg under the table. He turned to see Auburn giving him a pointed look. He blinked, having no idea what had been said.

"Terah said there have been two more of ours found."

Konner glanced to Terah; he'd forgotten to tell her not to tell anyone just yet. "Yes. I don't have details yet, only that they're in decent health and treated *fairly*."

"Where are they? How soon can you get them out?" Reeves leaned on the table and looked down it at him.

"I don't have specifics right now, one of the Alliance teams is monitoring the location." He glanced to Malachi, "it's hard to get into."

"But you'll get them out." Raelyn stared at him.

Konner nodded, "we will." He looked over at Calum. The big man returned his look and then slowly turned his head to look at Terah, silently telling him to get it together and deal with her. He turned his head and saw that his aunt was smirking at him from the head of the table.

"We'll have to prepare more of the homes." Olanna turned to Nolyn, "just in case they'd prefer privacy."

Nolyn nodded, "I was thinking," she waved her fork around, "that we should set up some kind of intercom system or something for the new ones," she glanced at Terah and then down the table at him, "so they can reach out when they are in their houses."

Reeves jerked his head from her to Konner, then back again, "or just give them a phone."

She scrunched up her nose and then turned back to Konner, "then they'd have to call around to reach whoever isn't busy, an intercom could be a general thing, so whoever is closest can answer."

"Walkie-talkies." Paxton blurted out, "like you make us carry when we go for hikes." He shrugged, "signal is always good." he turned to Lucus briefly, "or you could just give us phones."

Konner held up his hand to slow the conversation, "we'll assess what's required once we know more." He lifted his glass and then paused before taking a drink, "I don't have gender, age, or any details right now."

"When will you have them?"

"I'll text Devin and see if he knows." Calum offered.

Konner sent him a grateful look when the others nodded.

Calum turned to Shaelan, who smirked. "Go ahead." She

said in a soft tone.

He winked at Lillee, "it's rude to use a phone during dinner." Pulling it out, his fingers moved quickly to send the message.

All eyes around the table were on him, Konner couldn't look away either. When Calum's phone buzzed the room was silenced.

"He's going to contact Uri and let me know." Calum set the phone, face down beside his plate.

Konner looked down at his plate to see it was almost empty. He didn't recall half of what he'd eaten. The conversation and motion around the table started again when everyone realized Devin wasn't going to answer immediately. Looking up, his gaze connected with Terah's, how long had she been watching him? She searched his face like she was going to be able to see what he was thinking about and then her expression changed to one of understanding. She gave him a brief smile before turning to see what Nakisa was saying to her.

Leaning back, he looked down the table, then to empty tables set up on the other side of the room. Some day, he'd see those chairs filled.

Chapter Thirty-Eight

Devin had given them an answer before everyone had finished cleaning up. Two females were being held, ages unknown, but appeared to be young adults. While everyone was buzzing with excitement, Konner was worrying about how 'young' they were and if the lunatics that thought his kind were zoo attractions had figured out how to breed.

Nolyn and Olanna cut off his path before he could take two steps inside his house.

"We were thinking we'd get one of the houses ready, the one between our homes," Nolyn looked at Olanna who nodded, "they might adjust better if they're in the same house together and not suddenly on their own."

Konner rubbed the back of his neck. "That's a good idea." He looked from one to the other, "and it's close to the lake." If they were anything like Terah, they would spend a lot of their time in it for the first week. Freedom was an unknown thing to them, and he wanted them to know that they were. "We'll just have to..."

"We know, keep an eye on everyone around them." Olanna gave him a blank look, "they'll also have Terah, who will relate the most to their situation."

Terah. Konner glanced in the door he was holding open. "I'm sure she'll help them."

"Okay," Nolyn nodded enthusiastically, "let's go take stock of what needs to be added," she grinned at Olanna. "We may have a shopping list."

Konner smirked, "wrangle Reeves attention away from whatever his brain is stuck on to get it ordered." He looked inside again, "I'll pick it up when it comes in."

"Perfect." Nolyn inhaled a deep breath and nodded some more. Her expression said she wasn't as thrilled as she was letting on. He wondered if she worried that one of those females would be the mate to her lover.

"Go get some rest." Olanna used her mother's tone on him. "you're like talking to an empty shell tonight."

Konner flashed her a brief grin. "Yes, 'mam."

Rolling her eyes, she ushered Nolyn back into the community house, "I just want to check in on Rae before we start, see how she's feeling."

Konner didn't wait to see if they thought of anything else, he stepped into the hall to his home and closed the door quickly. He could hear the boys in the entertainment room and started for it to ask them if they had homework, then stopped and decided he'd let them have some game time tonight. He just wasn't in the right frame of mind to wrangle teenagers right this minute.

He had even intention of going to his room and getting some real sleep. Maybe it would help some clarity come back to him. When his feet stopped moving, he found himself standing in front of Terah's door. She had wanted to talk to him, so he was going to pretend he meant to be here. The door was open a few inches. Holding it with one hand, he knocked on it.

"Thank you for knocking," she called out, "come in now."

Opening it, he went in. She wasn't in the main part of her room. "Terah?"

"I am in here."

He turned to the bathroom; the door was also open. "You said you wanted to," going over, he went in. She was in there. In the large tub, filled with water and completely naked. "Talk." He couldn't remind her of the rules, as it was her own bathroom. They were going to have to discuss when to close doors though.

"Yes." She smiled up at him.

Konner glanced at her, then to the floor, trying not to look right at her.

"Did you want to sit in here with me? It's big enough." She moved over to the side and leaned, her arms hanging over it.

He opened his mouth to reply and then couldn't remember what he was going to say. Clearing his throat, he went over leaned back against the counter. He could still see in the tub from here, but the distance between them would help him focus. "I'm good now, thanks." It was a complete lie, there was nothing good about him right now, not with the thoughts in his head.

She moved from the edge, giving him a quick flash of a smile. "I wanted to swim in the lake at night, but I don't want to break any rules."

He was trying to keep his eyes on her face, and it was hard, the slightest movement from her flashed a bit of skin here and there. "Once you're," he waved a hand around, while he tried to prompt his brain to help out, "adjusted to life here, you can swim at night." He frowned, "the couples tend to later in the night though, so checking," his mind popped to why those couples preferred then, he frowned, "for others is a good idea." He finished as the breath rushed from his body. He felt like a teenage boy that had never seen a naked female before right now.

"I will. Thank you." She leaned on the edge, and smiled at him, her eyes sparkling, bluer than silver right now.

With an abrupt nod, he straightened away from the counter to leave.

"Konner?"

He stopped and looked back at her.

"I still want to talk about what we stopped to go to dinner."

His brows creased as he looked at her. "Right." He nodded, then motioned to the tub, "I can wait out there until you're finished soaking," he pointed to the door.

"Oh."

He forced himself to look at her face.

"Is it another rule I don't know? Talking when in the tub?" A look of defeat came over her face. "I keep doing things wrong."

"It's not, uh, wrong." He scowled at the floor for a second, "it's just that *most* don't have conversations while they're in the bath," he gave his head a quick shake, "couples do, sure, but normally you close the door or doors for privacy." As explanations went that one had been as clear as mud.

"Oh." She looked around the room. "I have never had that," her eyes flicked to him, then to the water she was in, "closing of doors and that."

He hadn't wanted her to feel bad, that's the last thing he'd want.

"I will get out." She nodded her head, "we can talk then."

As he started to turn to leave, she stood up and stepped out of the tub. Water cascaded off her partially changed skin. He knew it was wrong, but he could only stand there and look at her. She practically sparkled, as the water glistened off her. He swallowed as his gaze moved slowly down her, she was perfection in his eyes, nothing like the almost skeletal woman that had been rescued.

Her skin slowly changed back to regular skin but was still radiant, he knew if he reached out and touched her it would be silky smooth. He wanted to reach out and touch her and despite knowing how much he needed to back his ass out of this room his feet remained stationary.

"We can talk now?"

He jerked his head up and looked at her face. "Talk?" His

voice was barely audible.

"Yes." She moved closer, making no indication that she intended to put on a robe or towel. "Before dinner, I was telling you that I still think about kissing you."

Konner licked his lips at the mention of kissing.

"I feel this strangeness in my stomach when I think about it." She moved her hand to place it over the smooth skin of her abdomen.

Konner tried to swallow to create salvia so he could speak, without success. Females of his kind were without body hair, as it wasn't their true form and below her hand was bare for him to see.

"And lower," she moved her hand down to cover her sex, "in my vagina, that's what it's called, I asked the tablet. My vagina gets wet when I think about it." She was right in front of him now, "Is that wrong?"

What? Konner blinked. He tried again to speak, the images in his head from her words now rendering him mute. His body was hard as he struggled to answer her.

She stood there looking up at him, waiting. Lifting her arms, she undid her hair and let it fall to drape her upper body like a picture frame.

Konner went from no clear thought to what seemed like every synapse in his brain firing at once. With something between a moan and a growl, he reached over and grasped the back of her head, pulling her closer. He crushed her soft mouth beneath his, forgetting she was essentially innocent. He needed to taste her, to feel her against him. Wrapping his free hand around her back, he bent his knees and then stood up, lifting her with him.

When she wrapped her arms around his neck and tried to keep up with his kiss, it dawned on him that he needed to slow down, for her sake. Angling his head, he reduced the pressure of his lips on hers so she could return his kiss. His knees almost buckled when she put her tongue in his mouth. It was not the reaction he anticipated from someone who knew little about kissing.

He started to move and then remembered he'd left the bedroom door wide open. Breaking the kiss, he gasped to speak. "I need to close the door."

"So we can kiss more?" Her voice rasped.

Konner nodded and stepped backward toward the bathroom door. It took every ounce of control he had to not turn around and run and slam it closed so he could get back to her.

Closing it with as much grace as he could manage, he turned to see Terah had followed him into the bedroom. She stood there, her body flushed with passion and her eyes were locked on him, devouring him. He should turn and walk away. Stop this before it went too far, but instead, he pulled his shirt over his head and dropped it on the floor beside him. It wasn't the years he'd convinced himself that alone was okay. It wasn't that he'd been denied physical contact for too long. It was her. Just being near her, changed everything. "Come here."

She came to him, without comment, stopping right in front of him. Her hands touched his chest and then moved slowly over it like she was memorizing its shape. Konner sucked in a breath when they strayed closer to his belt. He grasped her hand before she could continue her exploration. His control was already wavering.

Leaning down, he pulled her closer and kissed the side of her neck. She gasped and tipped her head back further to give him access to do it again. Tasting her skin again, he closed his eyes as he brought her flavor into his body. Of course, it was everything he'd imagined it would be. Purity, seduction, sin, and perfection all at once.

Growling, he lifted his head and kissed her mouth. It took a lot of restraint, but he managed to keep the kiss slow and gentle this time. Turning, he walked her backward toward the bed. Should he be doing this? No, but he was going to. He knew it was going to change everything and for the first time in his life, he didn't care what anyone, but the woman in his arms thought.

Lowering her to the bed, he followed her to it and let the motion of the water inside it rock her to him. Turning to his side, he pulled her close and continued to kiss her. She clung to his head, returning his kiss with fervor.

When he lifted his mouth from hers, she clutched his head, not wanting him to stop. Reaching, he untangled her one hand from his hair and held it in his as he leaned down her body, to take one sensitive nipple into his mouth. She gasped and arched her back. The hitch in her breath told him that she'd never felt that before.

Letting go of her hand, he shifted so he could hold one breast in his hand when he moved his mouth to the other. She cried out when he swirled his tongue around her other tight nipple. Both of her hands gripped his hair so tight it stung, but he didn't care. This was for her right now, not him. She'd been forced to have sex to breed and had been denied how good it should feel. He meant to correct that for her.

Terah sucked in another breath and then moaned. "I didn't know they could be kissed." She gasped.

Lifting his head, he grinned, his mouth against her ribcage, "all of you is for kissing."

To that, she opened her eyes and looked at him, the confusion plain in her eyes.

"Let me show you." He stretched up and kissed her mouth softly. "Let me make you feel good."

"I do feel good," she sounded breathless, "but there is something…"

He kissed her again, "shh." He placed a feather-soft kiss along her jaw, then moved his mouth down to her throat. With each placement of his lips against her, he was rewarded with a breathless gasp.

He wanted to tell her that it was more intense in the water, with their real skin, but now was not the time for words. Their skin may appear like scales, but not in the way that a fish would be. There was a thermal layer against the cold waters but was so soft it felt like it was covered in fine hairs.

Opening her legs, he moved down to taste her. He loved that in this form, a female's body was easily accessible, not hidden as it would be for protection in the water. With her taste taunting him, his tongue inside her, he decided that no other male would ever taste her. Ever.

As she moaned and called his name in a rasping breathless way, he decided no male of their kind would ever swim with her. She was the one thing in his long life that he wasn't going to be able to let go of.

Arms shaking, he raised over her and was about to ask her if she was all right when her eyes popped open and silver eyes looked up at him. She grabbed his face and pulled him down for a kiss. Not a satisfied, easy kiss, but one filled with so much passion he thought he would explode from how hard it made him.

Her skin literally glowed, and he knew if he looked at his own, it would be close to it as well if he could focus to look. It was what happened when their kind was consumed with passion, it was also why they couldn't ever be with anyone that wasn't their kind or didn't know what they were. With Terah, it made her even sexier than she already was.

He flipped onto his back and brought her to sit on top of him. He needed her to be in control, for this to be on her terms. He wasn't sure if he would be able to control himself if she needed slow or gentle. After what she'd been made to do when she was being held by those lunatics, he wanted her to experience what this should be like between two consenting adults.

She looked down at him, an unsure look on her face. Grasping her hips lightly, he lifted her and aligned their bodies. He guided her to lower onto him slowly, watching her face the entire time. The expression on her face showed her every response, it was the most erotic thing he'd ever seen.

When he filled her, she stopped and sat there, looking down at him. He really wanted her to set the pace and had intentions to do just that, but his restraint was at its end, gripping her hips tight, he lifted her up and thrust as he lowered her again.

One gasp left her mouth and then she began to move on her own. Konner forgot all his plans to allow her to set the pace, his needs took over, and nothing registered outside their bodies connecting, the way her muscles squeezed him with each movement of her body. He watched her, fighting to keep his eyes open when all he wasn't to do was close them and let the feelings take over him.

A few minutes later, he couldn't separate who was moving or controlling this, they were both frantic and reaching for completion. He heard a loud groan and couldn't tell if it came from his throat or hers, then they both crashed over the edge together.

Trying to breathe burned as he fought to bring air into his body. The silence in the room was filled with gasping, as both struggled to catch their breath.

She smiled down at him and then collapsed on top of him. He didn't have the energy or desire to move from this position. Wrapping his arm around her, he pulled the long hair away from her face. She looked happy and content and it was suddenly the most rewarding feeling in his life to know that he'd done that for her. He ran his hand down her back, they were both covered in a sheen of sweat now. He paused, reality crashing through the euphoria. Sweating was bad for someone so young and still recovering.

He patted her hip lightly. "We have to get you in some water."

"I don't want water right now." She sighed contently.

"I know, but you need it, you are sweating."

She lifted her head and smiled at him, "it is a good sweat."

Konner grinned, "yes, the reason is good, but with your age and health, it's not."

Her expression sobered. "Oh, I can go back to the tub."

Konner shifted and lifted her into his lap, "no, the lake is better." Setting her on the bed, he stood up and looked for his pants. "Just grab your robe." She sat there for a moment, he hoped it was just the drugged feeling after sex that had her foggy.

Pulling his pants on, he rushed into the bathroom and found her robe laying on the counter. Grabbing it, he went back out. She was standing now, that was a good sign. Leaning down, he looked to see her skin wasn't looking translucent yet. He held the robe so she could put her arms through it. Before she could tie it together, he scooped her up into his arms and headed for the door. Hopefully, none of the other adults were in the lake, that was the last thing he needed was to be seen carrying her out of the house.

Chapter Thirty-Nine

Terah stumbled a few steps going into the water. Konner jolted and stripped off his pants and rushed after her.

She stopped and looked up at him, "you're going to swim with me?" He nodded, "good we can check you off the list then."

He felt annoyed at the thought of that for some reason. "The list can wait; I just want to make sure you're okay."

"I feel good," the pallor of her skin pinked as she smiled.

Putting his arm around her, he urged her gently to keep going into the water. "Don't try to swim full speed for a few minutes, let your body replenish the lost fluids first."

She nodded but made no comment. "How come you're not weak too?"

He decided quickly that saying it wasn't the first time he'd had real sex was wrong on all fronts. "I'm older, my body has built up more resistance."

She made a quiet noise, and he wasn't sure if it was acknowledgment or annoyance.

The water was at their waist now. He moved back, giving her space to glide out into it. He watched her, practically holding his breath as she moved away from him. She listened and did it gently and didn't dive into it and try to power stroke her way out to the deeper water. When she stopped and just floated, he took a few more steps, his heart pounding like some sort of tribal drum. Cursing in his head, he dove into the cooling water and reached her in a few powerful strokes. Reaching her side, he put his hand under her back, "are you all right."

"Yes. I am letting the water renew me. It feels nice."

Relief filled him. He pushed back from her, putting some space between them. The moonlight was bright enough that it reflected off the luminous scales that now covered her. Just looking at her made his heart skip a few beats before it settled into a heavy rhythm that he felt throughout his whole body.

When he put his arms out in front of his body to tread the water and move back away from her, he paused and stared at his arm. The changed tone of his skin was usually almost unnoticeable, it had been that way for years and was the only reason he could get away with swimming in lakes all over the continent to look for others. Right now, he looked like he'd been rolling in the glitter that Nakisa adored with great zeal. He blinked and looked at his other arm. It was the same.

"Konner."

He jerked his chin up to look at her.

"My chest," she put her hand against her breastbone. "It is thudding."

He looked at his arms again, then at her, shaking his head in disbelief. His own heart felt like it was trying to break free of the bones that protected it.

They were mates. He looked from her to his arm one more time. It was the only explanation. Konner opened his mouth to speak, and no words formed. For half his life he waited for this day to come and had long ago given up on the idea that it would ever happen.

"Konner, your skin," Terah's voice jerked him out of the stupor he was lost in, "it's beautiful."

He looked to see she was beside him now, no longer relaxing on her back. "Men are not beautiful." He winced, that was not the first words he should have spoken to her right now.

Terah gave him a surprised look, "As long as I am looking with my own eyes, I can say it is."

He smiled then, unable to argue with her about something so trivial. "Terah, your heart, my skin, it only means one thing."

"We should have more sex?"

His entire body responded to that idea. Shaking his head, he removed it from his mind, in normal cases of mates finding one another he would have agreed that should happen, but once had already taken too much of her energy and he wasn't going to risk it so soon again. "We will, not right this moment though."

"You do not want me right now?"

"Yes." He answered quickly before thinking it through. "Always." He added after in a hushed tone. "We're mates." He moved closer and let his body sink lower in the water, so their faces were level. "Our hearts are trying to synch with each other."

Her eyes rounded, "it feels like a dance party inside me. How do we fix it?"

Later, he'd inquire as to where she got the dance party from, but right now, he needed to claim her and put his mark on her so no other male would ever go near her again. "We mark each other, once our body's scents blend, our hearts will beat in time and settle down."

She nodded, a nervous look on her face. "So, no more list."

His smile was slow, almost predatory, "no more list, no more males, no more searching." He took her hand, "we need to get to the deeper water."

He swam fast, pulling her along with him with ease, suddenly spurred with an urgency that he needed to know his soul was bound to hers. Once they were in the deeper water, he spun back toward her and wrapped his arms around her, taking her under the water without warning. He'd watched her swim; knew her body could go from air to water in a heartbeat and have no problems.

Once below the surface, he grasped her hips and kissed her, long and gently. No frenzied passion this time, just emotion that came from some deep place inside him, letting her know that she was his everything. His tongue scraped over her sharper teeth and a shiver went through him.

Breaking the kiss, he looked at her and his heart hiccupped inside him. Her hair floated out around her and her skin, even this deep was illuminated in the darkness. As if it weren't enough her eyes were the brightest silver shade he'd ever seen on one of his own.

Reaching, he brushed the hair back from her face and wrapped his other arm around her waist, and pulled her closer to him. Touching her, here in their natural state, was like running his hand over satin, another shiver went through him. He was going to have to work hard to not ravish her and risk draining her further.

Tilting his head, he exposed his neck to her and watched her face. She looked at his neck, then to his eyes, without words asking him if he wanted her to mark him. When he placed his hand behind her head to pull her closer to him, she gripped the back of his head almost painfully. His heartbeat was so strong now, it took a lot of focus to think around the distraction. He was just about to coax her closer, to put him out of this anxious feeling that was setting in when she jerked his head by a handful of hair and then bit into the muscle at the base of his neck.

She wrapped her legs around his waist and locked her heels behind him, sending erotic images to his brain. He couldn't stand it another second, he grasped her hair and pulled her head back, and bit into her flesh. Using his legs, he sent them drifting through the water as if they were one body and not two.

Releasing his bite, he pulled her face to his and kissed her, claiming her mouth as his and no other. His whole body quaked for a moment and then a feeling he'd never felt in all his years filled him. Peace, a serenity he'd never known could exist filled every molecule of his being.

Tearing his mouth from hers, he looked at her to see she was feeling it also. The hidden pain, guarded torment that was usually lurking behind her eyes was gone, replaced with something that made him feel like he was the luckiest male alive.

Using his throat muscles, he hummed to her, although beneath the water it wouldn't be a melody as it would be when it hit the air. She smiled slowly and responded with a song, a real smile of genuine happiness on her face.

Konner stopped singing and hugged her to him, feeling the vibrations of her melody inside his body as he took them spiraling through the water, with no thought inside his head but her. He ran his hand down the length of her silky hair and smiled to himself.

Taking them to the surface, he decided he wanted all to be blessed with her melody, a sharing of the joy he felt inside.

Closing his eyes, he floated along, holding her close. He could feel his heart beating in time to hers and couldn't help the smile on his face. Never in his long life had he ever imagined he'd feel this. It was peaceful but exhilarating at the same time. He had never thought to ask if they stayed in sync all the time, or if it was just when they were close. If hers changed when he did, that could be a problem when he was out on ops with the team. He couldn't think like that, not right now. This was a time to thank the stars for bringing him Terah, not pondering missions.

Opening his eyes, he looked up at the night sky, it was so clear tonight like even the heavens knew they had found each other and didn't want to mar the moment with storm clouds.

"Konner?"

"Mmm?" he turned them so they would float back toward the middle of the lake.

"Do you think I will ever be able to run fast without it feeling strange on my feet?"

It was an odd question, but tonight he didn't care what she asked, he'd give whatever she needed to make her happy. "With practice, I'm sure you'll be able to."

"Is that how you do it? Practice?"

He looked at her, to see his own image reflecting against the silver in her eyes. "I honestly don't remember. Why do you ask?"

"I wondered if that was what Reeves is doing, practicing."

Frowning he leaned back, putting a little space between them. "You saw Reeves running?" He smirked, "I don't think he does that."

"He is right now." She turned and looked toward the shore, "going back and forth on the shore."

Konner released her and turned to see Reeves running along the shore waving his arms. "That's not practicing, something is wrong." He grabbed her hand, "come on."

They dove down together and moved fast through the water. Later when he wasn't plagued with worry, he'd think about how they were able to swim at the speed they were while still holding hands.

Breaking the surface, he pulled her up with him. "Reeves?" He called out.

Reeves jerked his head to look in their direction. "The babies." He ran into the water a few feet, "the babies are coming." He looked over his shoulder, then back to them, "Shaelan wants Terah there to sing." He nodded his head so quickly he looked like his neck was a spring.

"We'll be there shortly."

"I need to go to the greenhouse," Terah said with excitement. "The plants will help Raelyn if we put them in the water." She released his hand and moved to the shallow water.

"Did Shaelan tell you that?" He had no problem catching up to her, walking before shifting back was something he'd been doing a lot longer than her.

"No." She glanced at him, "I just know it will."

Konner wasn't about to argue with her. Whether she knew it or not, she retained parts of their heritage that the rest had long forgotten. "Grab your robe, I'll come to help you get them." She wobbled in the ankle-deep water but kept going. Pulling his pants on with quick moves, he glanced up at the stars again, silently praying the babies and Raelyn made it through this.

"Don't think bad thoughts." She chastised, "it is beautiful, to bring new life here and I won't have bad thoughts for Raelyn while she does that." She gave him a warning look and he had to work hard to not smirk at her. Even when being stern she was absolutely gorgeous.

He held out his hand, "we'll have to hurry. I told Malachi to bring her to the house and to use the pool as soon as it started."

She seemed to be having no problem keeping up with him, likely because she wasn't thinking about walking. "Yes. Good, the water will help." Her blue eyes connected with his, "my mother told me this. The water makes it easy."

Konner doubted any part of delivering children was 'easy', but again he wasn't about to argue with her. She started tugging on his hand, making him go faster and it was then that he realized she was going to be his greatest strength—and his biggest weakness for the rest of their lives.

Chapter Forty

The lights were low over the pool, creating a relaxed atmosphere. With the flowers Terah had selected floating in the water it completed the picture of a tranquil scene. Then the men standing around the pool, looking tense completely ruined the whole picture. Konner glanced to see Reeves would have rather been anywhere but here.

The women were in the water, along the border, and not one of them looked tense, his aunt in fact looked happier than he'd seen her in years. They all wore some sort of robe that floated out around them, the white of them making them appear like clouds. Shaelan was beside the ladder, he assumed standing on it because she couldn't float in as the others could. She had offered to wear a mask and go beneath the surface, but a strong contraction had ended that amusing conversation.

Malachi was in the water, supporting his mate as she relaxed between contractions. Seeing that set something inside Konner off that he didn't think he had in him—until right now in this moment. He did want this part of life to be his own. Family, children, all of it.

Terah was hovering on the surface near Raelyn's belly, her

hand on it like she was feeling the children inside. She began to hum softly, then nodded at Raelyn, a soft look on her face. Olanna and Nolyn moved a little closer and while they didn't have the control that Terah did, they too began to hum in the way of their people.

Konner watched as his Auntie smiled and moved closer to the woman in the center. He had never heard her sing, in or out of the water, but she did now like all she'd been waiting for all these years was someone like Terah. Blinking, he glanced at the other males of his kind to see they were as affected by the melody as he was. Sitting down, he put his feet in the water and focused on Terah, his mate. Somewhere from deep inside him a melody he'd never heard started to come from his throat. In all his years he'd never thought to use his vocals out above the surface of the water in the way he was right now. He didn't pause to think about it or was afraid he wouldn't be able to continue.

Even Calum sat down at the edge of the pool and put his feet in. He may not be able to sing like the water clan, but he was right there with them and the vibes they were sending out.

Shaelan slipped and dipped into the water, without stopping her song, Terah moved over and put her arm around her to keep her above the water. She nodded, "just a bit more Raelyn and then you can push."

Konner had no idea how she knew this when most of Rae's body was immersed in the water, but he wasn't about to start asking questions and break the hold the song was embracing the entire group with. Reeves sang as well, but had his eyes closed through it, he noted. Somethings were better left to his imagination Konner figured.

When Nolyn and Olanna moved over to help support Raelyn, Konner's spine stiffened. There was a collective gasp among the women and then his aunt moved over and cradled a tiny babe in her arms. She nodded at Raelyn and moved to her side so the mother could see her child. Having assured herself that the infant was well, Rae closed her eyes and sucked in a breath.

Terah's song grew louder than all the others and not one of them was going to complain, it moved over his skin, leaving a trail of bumps in its wake. His heart rhythm changed, and he knew his's mate song affected him more than all the others.

"Deep breath and then bring this baby out," Shaelan said softly.

As the child moved into the water, Nolyn replaced Terah holding Shaelan above the surface and the brand-new member of their clan was placed in Terah's arms. Her song immediately changed to one that Konner could only label a soothing lullaby. He could see the tears on her cheeks but knew they were ones of happiness as she smiled down at the baby. His heart pounded in his chest and his throat seized, bringing an abrupt end to his attempt at the song.

Malachi turned his mate to hold her in his arms as Shaelan did doctor things below the surface, for which Konner was sure Reeves was very thankful. Auntie and Terah placed the infants into Rae's arms and moved back out of Shaelan's way.

"A boy and a girl," Malachi said with emotion thickening his voice. He leaned down and kissed Rae's forehead.

Terah came over to where Konner was and looked up at him, her eyes glistened with happiness. He reached out for her hand and then held it as they looked over to the new members of their clan.

"Traditionally the clan names the babies. We didn't pick any this time because we'd like to go back to some of the traditions of our people." Raelyn said in a tired voice. She turned to Shaelan, "you name one," she looked over at Terah, "and you the other please."

Shaelan stopped and looked at her. "Oh." She smiled slowly, "what an honor." She gave Calum a quick look and then looked at the babies in their mother's arms. "The little girl, Danu." She looked at Raelyn quickly and then looked relieved when she smiled.

"Danu is a lovely name." She glanced to her mate, who

nodded. "And for my son?" Raelyn looked at Terah.

Her hand squeezed Konner's and he wasn't sure if she was nervous or what the cause was. "Kai." Terah said softly, "if that's all right." Her grip was still tight on his hand.

"Danu and Kai." Raelyn looked down at the babies. "I think that's perfect."

Malachi turned to look at Reeves, "can you go get Lillee so she can meet the babies."

Reeves nodded and got up so fast, Konner was sure he'd end up falling in.

"Let's get these babies swaddled and mom cleaned up." Shaelan was back in healer mode.

Calum was smiling as he watched her, then he turned and pulled his phone out of his pocket. Konner watched a serious look remove the smile from his face. He looked over at him. Konner didn't need to ask. From the expression on his face, the ops were going to happen soon. He nodded at him and then slipped into the pool to pull his mate into his arms.

"I still want ten." She whispered, her silver eyes holding his.

"Five, then we'll discuss it." He kissed her mouth softly.

"Okay. Five, but soon." She smiled at him.

Konner looked at her mouth and then back to her eyes, "three cycles until you're strong enough."

She frowned in thought, "how often do they happen?"

"Every month or so, it varies." If she kept looking at him with that soft look in her eyes, he wasn't sure he was going to be able to hold out that long.

"Okay. Three and then I get babies."

Konner grinned, "I prefer one at a time if it's possible."

Terah looked over to see Malachi and a few of the others helping Raelyn to sit beside the pool. "Yes. Okay. One at a time works for me." She turned back to him and gave him a slow smile. "I think we should go to the pond and little house for the night."

He frowned, not sure if there was something wrong.

"The house seems very full right now." She kissed his chin,

"and I want to know more about sex." She reached under the water and rubbed the front of his pants.

Konner sucked in a breath and then nodded at her. "I think we can probably slip away without being noticed."

"Calum and you will be leaving soon, won't you?" She continued to rub her hand over him, he could barely think.

"Yes." His heart kicked up a few beats, thinking about leaving her to go with the team. He didn't know if he could do it.

Terah traced his lips lightly with her fingertip. "You will go and free all the people, Konner, I know you can." She smiled at him and at that moment, he would have battled the masses to free any being held anywhere.

A splash broke them apart. Kole swam between them. "There are two babies." He sounded very excited.

Terah wrapped her arms around him and swam to the middle of the pool.

Konner looked up to see Calum coming over.

"Two days." He said in a low voice.

Konner nodded and hopped up to sit beside the pool. "Does it say where?" He didn't want to ask about the locations with his kind being held, he didn't want to spoil the moment of the births.

"Where we left off." He squatted down beside him, "four places have been confirmed." He smiled over at Shaelan when she gave him a look because she knew he was talking about more than just the birth. "Uri's team are on them now."

Konner smirked when Shaelan gave him the same warning look from the other side of the pool. "Okay, keep me up-to-date if anything changes," he motioned to Terah, "I'm going to go find somewhere to hide for the next day."

Calum nodded, then smiled at him, "looks good on you."

Konner frowned, then saw he was looking at his neck. He put his hand over the bite, "never thought I'd have one."

Calum chuckled, "fate has a way of changing the rules mid-play."

Konner stood up and held out his hand to Terah as she came to the edge. Now all he had to do was figure out how he was leaving her behind when he left with the team.

KEEP READING FOR AN EXCERPT OF

Fury

Animal Senses Series Book 8

By Jacqueline Paige

Chapter One

She turned and looked at the small window, it was night again. How long did that make it? A month, longer? She'd lost count. The only thing she was thankful for was no one else was down here with her. That was good for the other women. Did they ever have more than one locked up at the same time? She couldn't be sure.

Emersyn sat up and tugged on the collar around her throat. She should be used to it by now, but it still felt like it was choking her, even though it wasn't. After wearing it for years, you would think it would feel like it belonged there. She closed her eyes and shook her head slowly, how could anyone get used to that?

The reason it was there was enough to constantly remind her that her life was not her own. It had not been hers since she was a child. Over the years the images and memories of freedom had faded. She remembered the boat trip and the excitement of being in a new country. Her parents, she remembered them dancing to be there. She knew she used to run outside and play, knew that somewhere out there she had a mother, father, and two older brothers, but she could no longer see them inside her head. There was just an emptiness where those memories with family should have been. She'd held onto her mother's smile the longest, but now with it was gone, there was only a void left behind.

Getting up, she lifted the chain that weighed down her ankle and moved slowly toward the window. It was the only thing she had to focus on. The lights were off, and the basement was dark through the night, the only thing she could do was look out the small window, level with the ground, and hope to see something. Anything.

The pains shot up her leg from the swelling caused by the cold metal rubbing against her ankle bone. The throbbing was endless. She didn't know why they kept it on her, where was she going to go? The door was bolted shut, the window, even if she could reach it was too small to get out. Of course, if she hadn't attacked her captors on more than one occasion, they would probably allow her more freedom. There was some part of her that made her fight back, even though she knew the consequences of doing it.

There was snow falling tonight. She inhaled a shaky breath. Another year had passed. Winter was on its way. Aspyn's fifth birthday would be soon. Putting her hand over her chest, she clutched the fabric covering her heart while she silently asked the universe to watch over her baby. If she closed her eyes, she could see her pale blue eyes and a cheeky little smile. She *had* to be okay. It was the only thing that got Emersyn through each day. Her baby was the *only* reason she had to keep breathing. Born into a life with no freedoms, yet when she smiled all the terrors faded away.

She was okay, she decided. There was no other possible outcome in her mind. Her little girl was a fighter with an attitude much bigger than her little body. A tear rolled down her cheek as she remembered when Aspyn had punched that man, her father, in the face for upsetting her Mommy. She would survive the cruelties of their world; of that she was certain. Aspyn didn't know it yet, but she was guided by the spirit of her animal. Emersyn's mother used to say that and now she had no choice to believe it was true.

Opening her eyes, she blinked, had someone just gone past the window? She started to move closer only to stop when the chain reached its end too soon. She looked around, there was nothing in the room to throw at it to draw their attention. She considered yelling, but that would only alert her guards upstairs and she didn't need that.

How long had it been since he'd come and shown her pictures of her only reason to live? She couldn't be certain but thought it might have been longer than his normal taunting visit. She bit her lip, not even sure if it was a good or bad thing, but she desperately wanted to see the pictures proving that their daughter, she scowled—no, *her* daughter was well.

Without blinking, she stared at the window, hoping to see someone outside it again. Anyone that could get her out of here. Away from this world, she'd been stuck in for far too long. Other than the first few years of endless houses, she'd always been here. Many women had come and gone from this house in that time, but Emersyn was still here. She didn't know where they went or what happened to them, this was the only place she could loosely call home. She cut off any further thoughts when she saw more feet moving by the window.

"You be brave, Aspyn, Mommy's going to find you one day, and no one will separate us again." She whispered in a soft breath.

The sound of footsteps upstairs had her turn and look at the door. Was he here? Did he bring her daughter back? Each time she heard movement up there, she thought the same thing. Maybe he realized that holding their daughter hostage and trying to force her cycle to come back was impossible. If a woman had that power the world would be a *much* different place.

The sounds grew louder, there was something wrong. No one in this house was ever that loud. Grasping the chain, she rushed to the back corner of the cold-tiled room and crouched down beside the cot. In the darkness, she focused on where she knew the stairs ended, waiting. Were they moving the women? It wasn't unusual to do it at night. Would the others get to keep their children? The sound of the lock opening on the door at the top of the stairs echoed like a hammer on metal in the silence.

She closed her eyes and dug deeper for the courage to stay quiet as heavy boots hit the stairs. If she could just pretend to be compliant, just once—maybe they'd let her keep her daughter with her.

Opening her eyes, she watched in the dark as the outline of a large man appeared before her. A light hit her face and then moved around the room. She was momentarily blinded by it and unable to see who it was.

"One in the basement," his tone was low, and frightening in the dark space, "chained to the fucking wall. Do we have bolt cutters?"

Her heart started pounding in her chest. Bolt cutters? What was going on?

"Send him down here."

She listened as he moved around the room, afraid to speak.

"Watch your eyes. I'm turning the light on."

Chapter Two

Noah bolted upright and freed his legs from the blanket. He was covered in sweat and his heart was racing so fast he couldn't breathe. Wiping his hand over his face, he blew out a breath. *Just a nightmare. I'm not there anymore.*

Swinging his feet to the floor, he breathed slower and rested his face in his hands. He was glad this op had allowed him to have his own room. Rubbing his jaw to ease the tense muscles, he looked around the tiny space. Okay, so his room had been a closet at one time, but it was just him and he didn't have to worry about waking others as he fought the demons in his sleep and woke up ready to run—or fight

Grabbing his shirt, he yanked it over his head and jammed his arms into it. There would be no going back to sleep now. There never was. Once they started, they didn't ease up and allow any sort of rest. The only thing he could do was take his body to the point of exhaustion and hope for a few hours of dead sleep before they returned. Thrusting his legs into his jeans, he stood up and zipped them. Coffee and fresh air and he'd be ready for the day.

He moved down the stairs silently, making sure not to wake anyone else in the house. Being part of this team had given him purpose, one he was proud to have. They also ripped off all the scabs on old wounds and made him relive it all again, over and over.

Glancing at the door, he made sure it was closed and he wouldn't wake Illias—if in fact the man ever slept because it didn't seem like he did. He used his phone to light the way into the kitchen and found a coffee pot already on and almost full. Someone else was anxious for the op to start too. They were supposed to go in last night, but the other teams weren't all in place. Four hits at the same time spread out all over the map, was a logistical nightmare, or so they'd been told. He left all the planning to those with minds for it. His mind was filled with fury, hate, and violence—all hidden beneath the torment.

Taking the cup, he went out the back door and looked into the woods. He was more comfortable with this location than the last few. Fenced-in yards brought back too many memories of closed-in spaces. It was also nowhere near where they were going, but the planners had decided it was safer to stay further away, so here they were.

As he was raising the cup to his mouth, he heard something coming from the bush at the side of the property. He held his breath until Blair and Kobie stepped out of the trees. At least he knew who else was up. He moved away from the back of the house, not caring if he was barefoot in the light snow on the ground.

Blair motioned to the cup, "you didn't drink all our coffee, did you?" He grinned.

Noah shook his head, "just starting now."

"He'll drink the pot before you can get your cup out of the cupboard," Blair informed his mate.

Kobie swatted Blair's arm, "you don't exactly share it with anyone either."

Blair faked a hurt look, "hey with all the bodies in the house now, I'm lucky if I get half a cup."

Noah grinned, he didn't envy Blair, having all those people around him all the time. He did feel a few pangs of jealousy, however, at the thought of *having* that many of your own around you. Taking a sip, he relished the burn on his tongue. He couldn't think about his own family right now, not when he needed to stay alert and functional.

"I'll sneak in and get you a cup." Kobie kissed his cheek and then walked away.

Blair looked down at Noah's feet and raised an eyebrow. "Nightmares again?"

Noah nodded. The problem with sharing a bunkhouse with the men at Ed's meant there had been no way to hide it from them. "Just being back here—" he shrugged one shoulder, "there's no way to escape them."

Blair nodded, even though his expression said he could never fully understand. "The delay has me antsy."

"Yeah. Better to follow the entire plan than a piece of it I guess." He took a sip and watched the snowfall from the branches of one of the trees. "Good area to run?"

"It's not home, but it's all right."

They both turned when the door opened, and Konner Flores came out. He carried a cup in one hand and a water bottle in the other. When he was closer, he held the cup out to Blair, "Kobie was on the phone and asked if I'd bring this to you."

"Thanks." Blair took it and glanced at the house. "I wonder who is having what crisis now?"

Noah noticed Konner smirk, then take a drink so it wasn't obvious he did. "At least you're not there trying to delegate tasks with the building."

"I'm thankful for that." Blair smiled, "so many women overseers."

Konner pulled out his phone and looked at it. "Speaking of crisis," he held up the phone, "if you'll excuse me."

Blair pointed to the trees, "nice deep section of river that way if you need it."

Konner followed where he pointed, "good to know."

They watched him walk back toward the front of the house,

the phone against his head. "I can't believe he left his mate at home."

Noah turned to look at him, "bringing her back here wouldn't end well."

"That's true." Blair looked at the house again, "you going to be all right?" He jerked his chin in the direction of the house, "I should go see what drama is happening now."

"I'm good." He smirked, "have fun with your drama."

Blair rolled his eyes in a playful manner, "it's not drama that scares me now. Quiet is apparently bad with that many females and kids."

Noah chuckled, "I'm sure Daisie will wrangle those boys and keep them in line."

Blair started walking backward away from him, "that's what scares me." He laughed and turned toward the house.

The amusement on his face faded as soon as his friend went into the house. He turned back to the trees. Even the thought of shifting here, in this area, and going for a run had his muscles tense and his mind screaming not to. He had to wonder if that inner voice was ever going to go away. If he was ever going to feel safe shifting into what he was meant to be.

"Noah."

He turned around to see Calum standing at the door. "We're going to make breakfast, most of the house is moving now."

Turning around, Noah started back. The sooner they went over the plans meant they could get back on the road and get to where they needed to be. Tonight, couldn't get here fast enough for him. He looked forward to breaching another holding house that belonged to Aiden Tomas. Somewhere inside he knew it wasn't his fault, the things he'd been forced to do, but he felt dirty, like he had a lot of sins to atone for. That conflict alone was what made him decide he would be part of this team until they ended Tomas. After that, he didn't know, he couldn't see past it to think in the terms of the future or living.

About Jacqueline Paige

I am a multi-published author of 'all things paranormal'. My book list proves this is my niche with my stories of witches, ghosts, psychics, shifters, and more now on the shelves. My current genres are paranormal romance, paranormal fantasy, and paranormal romantic suspense.
My books are available in many formats around the globe, including book/reading apps. Since adding them during the pandemic, my books have had over a million reads and my 'to be written' list is growing longer each day. I can't write fast enough.

I began my writing career in 2006 (as a joke) and my first book was published in 2009. I haven't stopped since then. I am an avid reader and will read 'anything with words', whether it's a novel, article, or even every sign I pass.

I live in Ontario, Canada in a small town that's part of the popular Georgian Triangle area. Even though I can see the mountains, I do not ski.

When I'm not in one of my writing worlds, I spend time with my grand-monsters. I have nine of them (so far) and I look forward to corrupting them in the years to come.
Jacqueline also writes under the pseudonym of J. Risk

Jacqueline loves to hear from her readers, you can find her at

http://jacquelinepaige.com/

Author note:

Did you enjoy reading one of my books?

If so, PLEASE help spread the word on social media. You can help by sharing on Facebook, tweet about it, post something on Instagram, Pinterest. Posting a review on your favorite book sites go a long way to help authors. With your help in keeping my books "out there", I can continue writing to keep those stories coming.

Writing and promoting can be very time consuming. I love talking to readers, but the hours spent on keeping so many social media outlets current can become overwhelming and time for writing pays the price. If you can take a few minutes to help, that would be awesome. Thank you!

www.ingramcontent.com/pod-product-compliance
Lightning Source LLC
Chambersburg PA
CBHW032147050726
47591CB00001B/121